Rainbow Hill

'One day we'll be rich!' Alex Grant assures his young wife Mhairi Diack when they first come to Rainbow Cottage with its two scrubbed rooms and its kale-yard. 'One day granite from our quarry will be as famous as stone from Silvercairns.' But 'one day' is far away, and meanwhile the meal-tub is nearly empty, there is a baby on the way – and, worst of all, Mungo Adam, choleric owner of the rich Silvercairns quarry, has vowed revenge on his ex-employees who have set up as rivals in the new quarry on Rainbow Hill.

Mhairi shivers when she thinks of old man Adam – a tyrant who does not forgive or forget. When she remembers his son Fergus, though, her heart softens. On her marriage to Alex, Fergus gave her a fine linen tablecloth – 'in friendship'. Mhairi has it hidden away in her kist so that Alex shall not see it – for what friendship can there be between the powerful Adam family and the impoverished Grants and Diacks who are determined to beat them at their own game? How, to begin with, could they ever bridge the social gulf that separates them?

That divide is a problem which troubles someone else as well: pretty and protected Fanny Wyness, daughter of the man who owns the new quarry, who has set her timid heart on Mhairi's handsome brother Tom . . .

Agnes Short has made the world of nineteenth-century Aberdeen her own. This delightful new novel evokes its diverse social scene and its flourishing commercial life: stonemasons, seamstresses, market stallholders, canals and railways. Against this bustling, detailed background she continues the engrossing saga begun in *Silvercairns*: a story of struggle and divided loyalties, of sorrow and enduring love.

Agnes Short

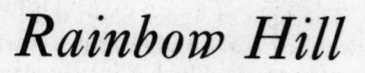

Rainbow Hill

Constable · London

First published in Great Britain 1991
by Constable and Company Limited
3 The Lanchesters, 162 Fulham Palace Road
London W6 9ER
Copyright © 1991 Agnes Short
The right of Agnes Short to be
identified as the author of this work
has been asserted by her in accordance
with the Copyright, Designs and Patents Act 1988
ISBN 0 09 470730 8
Set in Monophoto Ehrhardt
by Servis Filmsetting Limited, Manchester
Printed in Great Britain
by Redwood Press Limited
Melksham, Wiltshire

A CIP catalogue record for this book
is available from the British Library

Part 1

'I will see him,' she said aloud. 'No one shall stop me.'

Frances Wyness, only surviving child of George 'Head-stane' Wyness of Wyness Granite Yard, and known to family, friends and the generality of Aberdeen as Fanny, a name spoken with, at one end of the scale, benign tolerance and at the other dismissive contempt, attempted to tie her bonnet strings with fingers that fumbled and bungled the task until, in her trembling excitement, she spoke aloud a rare and daring 'Botheration!' and immediately looked over her shoulder in case any of the household might have heard.

But her father was safely in his granite yard, her mother had retired to her boudoir to minister to a hovering headache and Fanny was still mercifully alone. Reassured, she frowned again into the looking-glass and concentrated on the crimson bow which at last was tied to her satisfaction. There. She was ready.

Under the brim of her twist-edged straw bonnet, brown ringlets hung in bouncing symmetry on either side of her guileless, clear-complexioned face and only her anxious expression marred what was otherwise an unremarkable, but not unattractive appearance. Her walking dress was last year's model, but it was of best merino wool and in a shade of dark red which suited her. Besides, it was the gown she had been wearing when she first met Tom Diack. She wondered if he would notice and remember? As she reached for the bell-pull fear quickened her heartbeat and set her ringlets trembling: fear that her father would be angry, that her mother would scold, that Tom might not be there or, if he was, would ignore her – fear that she herself would lose her nerve and turn back.

But when Ina the maid answered her summons she managed to say, with passable authority, 'Tell Cook to send up a large pat of butter and a jar of plum preserve, or honey if the preserve is finished. And should there be a pickled tongue, that too. All to be suitably wrapped in a clean napkin, for a lady of my acquaintance who is unwell. And tell Mackie to bring the phaeton to the front door. I intend to drive into the country to deliver them myself.'

Ina looked at her in astonishment. 'Nae alone, Miss Fanny, surely? Them horses can be awful frisky.'

Fanny paled. 'Of course not alone. Mackie will drive me.'

'I don't know as how Cook will like that, miss, what with wanting him to chop wood and fetch water and I don't know what else, seeing as how her back is playing up something terrible today. It's the damp, she says, and that blessed stove smoking fit to kipper the lot of us. She tellt Mackie as how he'd best chop her a wee bit dry tinder, smartish, afore we're all smoked to Finnan Haddies. Nae, Miss Fanny,' she finished, shaking her head. 'Cook'll nae like you taking Mackie, not one wee bittie.'

Fanny wavered, all her natural timidity returning at the housemaid's solemn words. Ina had been with the Wyness household as long as Fanny could remember: a small, wiry woman with a plain face and an outspoken tongue, she regarded herself as one of the family, with family rights and obligations. One of these was to keep young Miss Fanny in order: not that the child had ever needed much chastisement, her being a timid, docile sort of a quine, but on the rare occasions when she did, then Ina had stepped in, usually with dire warnings of the effect Fanny's unruly behaviour would have on her dear parents. 'And you don't want to upset your Papa, do you?' she would invariably finish. 'Or your dear Mamma.'

Dear Mamma Fanny could cope with, but not Papa. She knew he loved her, cherished and indulged her without thought to his purse and would do so ten times over were she to ask him, yet he only had to look at her from under those bristling brows of his and say, 'Well Fanny? And what have you been doing today?' for her heart to start pounding with agitation and for fear to choke the words in her throat. Anything she thought of saying seemed too trivial and she would discard it in search of something better while her father frowned in impatience and Fanny grew increasingly tongue-tied, wishing as she wished every day of her life that she had a sister or, better, a brother to share the obligation and deflect some of that paralysing attention away from herself. If he smiled that patient, encouraging smile of his and said, 'Well, Fanny?' it was worse: she became as mute as poor Donal Grant until her inevitable tears released them both from the ordeal.

Now fear of her father and a lifetime's docility urged Fanny to obey the woman and withdraw her request. But if she did so, she might never find the courage again. And if she did not contrive to see Tom Diack soon, just for the smallest minute, she knew she would die of longing. Remembering her resolution, Fanny lifted her chin a tremulous inch, clenched her hands tight – behind her back so that the maid should not see – and said in what she vainly hoped was a firm and unwavering voice, 'Mackie can finish the wood when he returns. We will not be long.'

'Oh miss, I'm thinking you'll be sorry afore the day's out, that I am. Knowing as how the master sets such store by his food and Cook not liking to be thwarted. She'll maybe burn the master's mutton, accidentally on purpose like. Or hand in her notice.'

'My business is not with Cook,' said Fanny, blocking her ears against these insidious threats. For courage she conjured up the picture of Tom Diack in her mind, Tom who was strong and kind and handsome and who had talked to her about weasels when she first came across him, building a wall in her friend Lettice Adam's garden. Tom did not like Lettice, she could tell, and Fanny was not sure she liked Lettice either, not all the time. Lettice was rich and clever and malicious and very beautiful. Suppose Lettice set her cap at Tom? Out of devilment? She was perfectly capable of doing so if the mood took her. The thought set her heart thumping hard with new resolution.

'My business is with Mackie,' she said. 'I require him to drive the phaeton for me without delay. Otherwise I shall have no course but to drive myself and, when my father asks why, as he is sure to do, to tell him that his servants refused to obey his daughter. That, I am sure, will concern him more than burnt mutton.'

'Yes, miss,' said the maid, her eyes widening in astonishment. Miss Fanny had not spoken with such spirit in all the years Ina had been in the Wynesses' service, and that was many.

'Tell Cook so, and do not forget the butter!'

When the maid had gone, shaking her head and clucking to herself in a mixture of wonder and disapproval, Fanny bit her lip in apprehension at what she had done: Cook was a fearsome woman who must not, under any circumstances, be gainsaid, but timid Fanny Wyness had got the bit between her small, neat teeth at last and nothing was going to stop her now. It was seven weeks and two days since she had set eyes on Tom Diack, except in her dreams, let alone spoken words to him. The last occasion had been when she and her mother had called in to the granite yard with a message for her father and Tom Diack had happened to be there, reporting on the progress of the quarry which her father had newly leased so that when he wanted good granite slabs he did not have to go begging to his arch rival Mungo Adam for them, as he had been forced to do in the past. Tom had smiled at her, asked how she did, and said it was a rare day for winter sunshine and maybe the promised snow would hold off for another day or two. Fanny had gone home radiant, treasuring every simple word to take out and sigh over in the weeks that followed, in the privacy of her bedroom, or in the quiet afternoons when her mother had no committee meetings, but dozed over her sewing before the fire while Fanny sat obediently on the sofa, waiting for Mamma to wake up and order tea.

But, since that precious day, Fanny had had no reason to call on her father in his place of work and certainly Tom Diack had no reason to call on her. He was a simple quarry worker, a qualified mason to be sure and a good one who had signed some sort of special arrangement with her father, but still one of her father's tradesmen. What reason would he have to call on his employer's daughter? Or she to call on him? Then Fanny had remembered that Tom's married sister Mhairi, with whom he lived in a small cottage by the quarry, was expecting her first child and she had hit on the brilliant idea of visiting her with fortifying foods to sustain her in childbed.

'Mamma,' she had suggested, 'do you not think it would be a kindness for us to visit Mhairi Grant, the wife of Papa's new workman at the quarry, now that her time is close? You know

[10]

Papa said that she will be missing the company of the town now that she lives so far from Aberdeen.'

But Mrs Wyness, usually so willing to undertake such missions of charity, had brushed her daughter aside with, 'Not now, Fanny. Some other time. I am sure I feel a headache coming on and I must be fresh for the Soup Kitchen Committee tomorrow. You know how busy we are with the present grievous scarcity, or had you forgotten the day of Fast and Humiliation only last Wednesday to pray for its relief? With the Temperance Committee and the Bibles for Africa, not to mention Mrs Macdonald's tea-party, I declare my head will be in a sorry whirl if I do not rest it today. I shall lie down for an hour or two in my room, with the shutters closed.'

'Very well, Mamma.' But Fanny's docile acquiescence had flared into rebellion the moment her mother left the room and thence into uncharacteristic resolution. She would go herself. After all she was a grown woman, almost nineteen. Lettice Adam, who was no older than Fanny herself, did whatever she wanted without a thought. Admittedly Lettice had no mother, but then Lettice's father was every bit as strict as Fanny's father, if not more so.

'I will go,' Fanny had decided. 'If I do not see him soon, I know I will die . . .'

But now, standing in the silent hall of their elegant and commodious house in Skene Square, with the grandfather clock ticking admonishment from the shadows and every panelled creak and murmur reminding her of her father's intimidating presence, Fanny felt her courage ebbing away. If Mackie did not arrive soon with the phaeton she knew she would lose her nerve and retreat ignominiously to the safety of her bedroom. Then came the sound of wheels from outside and the slow clop of hoofs. She opened the heavy front door to see her father's smart double-seater with hood and German shutters and her father's manservant Mackie at the near horse's head.

'Cook says you wants a run into the country, Miss Fanny. I told her as how she must have got it wrong, you never going anywhere like, leastways not without the mistress, but she would have it you was wanting the carriage. Proper angry she was too, but I told her it was likely a mistake and not to split her corsets for no reason.'

'It was not a mistake,' said Fanny with dignity, though at the thought of Cook's fury her knees momentarily weakened and her mouth went dry. But she had got this far and would not be thwarted now. 'I wish you to drive me to Woodside, to my father's quarry. Unless,' she finished with asperity, 'you would prefer me to drive myself? And explain to my father why?' The sensation of anger was a new and not unpleasant one. All her life Fanny Wyness had submitted to one or other figure of authority until it had become a way of life. Now she had glimpsed the alternative and the sight was sweet.

'You, miss? Drive this, miss? That's a skilled job that is, not a game for a young lass like you to try her hand at on a sunny afternoon. If you're set on going, then I'm the man to take you. I like a good run in the country. Better than breaking my back chopping wood for someone we could mention, so give me your hand, miss, and I'll help you up.'

Her father's conveyance was seldom used by Headstane Wyness, being called into service most often to transport Mrs Wyness to one or other of her numerous committees, or on morning calls, or to tea at the houses of her respectable acquaintances. There Mackie would disappear into the kitchen regions to pass the time with the domestics of the house and reappear at the bell's summons to transport his female cargo home again. A trip to the Wyness quarry at Donside was something new.

'Are you sure as how the roads is suitable for a vehicle like this one?' he said now, as he handed Fanny into the polished and leather-padded interior and tucked the rug around her knees. 'I wouldna be wanting to break an axle.'

'I have no knowledge of the roads,' said Fanny with admirable hauteur. 'That is your province, Mackie. I assume you are capable of judging for yourself.'

'Yes, miss,' said Mackie in some surprise. 'Just so long as you don't mind walking if the going gets a bittie rough.'

'Fair took my breath away,' he reported afterwards to the Wyness kitchen. 'That little Miss Fanny, who never so much as opened her mouth before, told me my job with as much face as the mistress herself. You could have knocked me down with a feather, I was that taken aback. But if you ask me, it was time

[12]

she upped and spoke for herself, poor lass, after the way she's been kept down all these years. I wonder what set her off?'

'Boredom, like as not,' said the scullery maid, eyeing the pile of dirty dishes with a malignant eye. 'I wonder she hasna broken out afore now. I would, if I had half her chances.'

'Well you havena and the only breaking you'll do is them plates if you slam them around like that,' snapped Cook. 'Then it'll be your backside as does the breaking – of my broom handle!'

'Daft old besom,' mouthed the scullery maid behind Cook's back, but she bent over her scrubbing with conspicuous attention.

'Maybe it's love?' said Ina, taking up the flat-iron from the stove and testing it a careful inch from her cheek. 'She's the age for it, after all.'

'Love? Her? If a man so much as looked at her she'd hide her face in her mother's skirts.' Cook thumped the dough she was kneading as if it was Fanny herself.

'Don't you be so sure o' that, Mrs Beattie,' said Mackie, with a wise look. 'I've seen things and I've heard things,' but to all their eager questioning he would say only, 'Folk is strange creatures and not always what they seem.' Deep in his pocket he turned over the coin Miss Fanny had given him, 'to keep the events of today a secret between us'. It was a handsome coin, worth a month's wages, and certainly worth holding his tongue for: especially as, if he did, there might be another where that one came from.

She had promised her mother, and she would find the money somehow, but as Mhairi waved goodbye to her little sister Annys that morning she could not quite fight back the dread. Annys was seven and a bright child: she deserved at least another three years of schooling, but with her three brothers, her husband and her husband's brother to feed, and all too soon her own baby too, how was Mhairi to manage? To be sure the boys were all earning, even young Lorn and Willy, though Lorn's pay as a yard boy at the Wyness granite yard was negligible and Willy, as a raw apprentice mason at the quarry, fared little better. Both started work early, both were healthy, growing lads with healthy, growing appetites, and limbs that outgrew their sleeves and trouser legs as soon as Mhairi let out the hems. Both could cheerfully have put away twice the amount of food that Mhairi managed to provide. Her brother Tom and husband Alex brought home a mason's wages each week, little enough to feed a family of seven, but once the quarry prospered they had Headstane Wyness's word for it that as working partners they would receive a share of the profits. As for Alex's brother Donal, deaf from birth but by no means stupid, he was in charge of the quarry horses, but only until the place was running smoothly. Then he was to be promoted to the granite yard in Aberdeen, to work with the pattern book and design new styles.

'One day we'll be rich, Mhairi!' Alex had assured her when they first came to the cottage. They had been strolling in the tiny garden after rain, the new sun glistening on grass-head and leaf. 'One day we'll build ourselves a fine granite house in the best part of town and you will sit in the drawing-room and hem fine linen for our own family instead of for yon Ladies' Working or that skinflint Roberts women wi' her fancy Union Street shop. One day we will hire a maid to keep the fires burning and a cook, maybe, to bake fancy scones and suchlike while you drive about in a carriage like the Adam woman does.'

'Dreams,' she had teased. 'As far away as the gold at the end of that rainbow.'

Together they had watched the brilliant arc span cottage and quarry in splendour and when Alex spoke again, he had said, 'But it is our rainbow, lass, and our pot of gold.' There and then they had renamed the cottage and quarry both, as a promise for the future, while Alex wove dreams.

'One day,' he would say, as they sat round the fireside in the crowded cottage in the evening, 'when we have blasted the next seam and the next one after that, our quarry will be as famous as Silvercairns and twice as rich. Our granite is as fine a colour and though the "posts" may not be as large, they polish up as bright as any Silvercairns stone. Besides, we have the canal practically at our doorstep to carry our granite into town, and when the railway comes, we'll have that too, as well as the contract for the building work north of Aberdeen. We'll

[14]

beat Old Man Adam at his own game one day. You'll see.'

But 'one day' was far away and on this particular morning at the end of March, with the meal tub almost empty, the kale yard long denuded of its vegetables and the hens not laying, the future was as bleak as it had been when they lived in that malodorous and overcrowded tenement off the Guestrow in Aberdeen. Besides, had not Old Man Adam vowed revenge on Headstane Wyness for snatching that railway contract from under his very nose? And on all who worked with him? Old Man Adam was a powerful man who did not forget or forgive.

A gust of wind swirled suddenly round the corner of the cottage and rattled the gate under her hand. Mhairi shivered, with apprehension as much as cold, and gathered up the folds of her plaid tighter about her. Her thick hair was twisted up into a coil on her neck and shone like polished jet, for her mother had told her long ago that ladies brushed their hair a hundred strokes a day. Mhairi had long ago abandoned her childhood dreams of a prince who would whisk her away into a fairy castle, but she brushed her hair nevertheless and saw that Annys did the same. You never knew who might come calling at the cottage, asking directions to the quarry perhaps, or looking for the quarry manager, and she would not like to be found looking less than her best. Out of nowhere came the memory of Fergus Adam, Old Man Adam's son and manager of Silvercairns: he had given her a linen tablecloth at her wedding, 'in friendship', and she had hidden it away in the kist so that Alex should not see. She would have liked Fergus to call, but of course it was impossible. After what had happened, there could be nothing but undying enmity between Silvercairns and Rainbow Hill. She thrust away the thought of Fergus Adam and thought instead of her dear husband Alex, the father of her unborn child. He was a good man and she loved him.

Pregnancy had made her skin porcelain clear and her eyes were blue as harebells as they followed her sister's diminutive figure along the winding path from Rainbow Cottage. The path was rutted and in places glistening with puddles from last night's rain. It wound between drystone dykes, smothered later in the year in yellow broom, or the deeper yellow of gorse, but at this dead season as colourless as the brittle winter

[15]

grasses underfoot and the ploughed winter fields on either side. This was the path the quarry men used, and the quarry horses dragging their heavy granite loads, but the quarry was further up the hill behind the cottage and the men had trudged to their work long ago. Unless the wind was in the wrong direction the granite dust did not penetrate this far and there was no tell-tale greying of the hedgerows, or of the crocuses in Mhairi's tiny garden, which were every shade of violet from a mauve so pale it was almost white to a deep and throbbing purple. Soon, when the weather softened, she would plant pot-herbs and kale and maybe Alex would dig a trench for potatoes, but in the mean time the crocuses, planted by some unknown crofter's wife, were promise enough. She bent to gather one or two for the house, but changed her mind. Her back ached this morning. She must have strained it, lifting the wash-tub perhaps or carrying water from the pump in the yard. At the thought of that pump, of the endless water to be boiled and the endless clothes to be washed if her family was to be kept spruce and clean, her spirits momentarily failed: and failed again when she remembered the day's kale-pot still waiting to be filled. Suddenly, piercingly, she missed her long-dead mother and her tenement home in Aberdeen. There, behind the Guestrow, there were always neighbours to call upon for help, to ask for advice, to talk to, whereas here . . . She shivered again. The wind was decidedly chill.

But Annys had reached the point where the path dipped beyond the tussocky outline of the hill and, as always, turned and waved. At the same moment a flight of geese appeared high overhead in a straggling 'V' from which the sound of busy chattering came faint on the wind. With a lifting of the heart, Mhairi raised her hand in farewell, and remained where she was at the little wooden gate, long after her sister's small shape had disappeared into the valley, listening to the birdsong and the stillness, the faint sounds from the quarry a half-mile further up the track, and the soft bubbling of a nearby burn. It was a mile walk to the school, but Annys would be safe enough. The Macrae children would join her when she passed the farm, and the Bain girls from the blacksmith's cottage. She had a pair of stout boots to her feet and a newly baked potato to warm her hands on the way, and on the way home Mrs Macrae at the farm would likely give the child a jammy piece, or an oatcake hot from the griddle. She was a motherly body and a good neighbour.

Remembering, Mhairi wondered at her own stupidity. How could she have compared their poverty here to those dreary years in the Aberdeen tenement? Here they had a whole cottage to themselves and though it had only two rooms and a loft, it had a bread oven which many similar did not, and a patch of ground. The air was pure and clean, the neighbours a blessed space away, but kindly. Two weeks back, when the new tenant arrived at the Braes of Sclattie and was behindhand, all the ploughs of the neighbourhood – thirty-four of them – had turned out to plough his land for him and afterwards everyone had retired to the farmhouse to drink success to the plough and to the stranger who had come among them.

Mhairi and her family had found equal kindness and she knew she had only to ask and Mrs Macrae would give her milk fresh from the cow, but until she herself had something of equal value to offer in return Mhairi's pride forbade it. Once, when it had been spread on the hedge to dry and got caught on a thorn bush, she had mended a tear in Mrs Macrae's best tablecloth with stitches so fine they were practically invisible and at the end of February she had gladly lent the strength of her arms and her skill in the kitchen when the annual ploughing match had been held at the farm. Twenty-six ploughs had taken part and at the end of the day judges, competitors, farmers and friends had all sat down to dinner together in the huge farm kitchen. Mhairi had joined the other womenfolk to help Mrs Macrae and, at the end of an exhausting day, had triumphantly carried home a hen, half a cheese and a dozen eggs as thanks for her help.

But that had been a month back, the unaccustomed riches long eaten and Mhairi too cumbersome and too easily tired now to attempt the walk to the farm. It was a rough path and exposed to the bitter winds: Alex did not want her to risk a fall, or a chill, with her time so near.

At the thought of that time, Mhairi could not suppress a tremor of fear. It was too far for anyone from the Aberdeen tenements to come, had she wanted them to, but Mrs Macrae would help her, and the other women. There was a midwife in Woodside, and a doctor should she need him, though the thought of the bill made her shudder. Everyone told Mhairi she was young and strong and need not worry. But she could not help remembering her mother, bleeding on her deathbed after the premature birth of what would have been her ninth child, remembering her anguished words, 'Don't ever marry, lass, it isna worth it!', remembering the deathbed promises she had given to bring up her brothers and sister as her mother wanted and to keep them all from the workhouse. Her brother Tom remembered too, and shared her fear. She saw it in his eyes when he said goodbye each morning, heard it in his anxious 'Are you sure you'll be all right?' And her husband Alex, catching Tom's fear, felt his own quiet confidence falter.

For their sakes Mhairi brushed aside anxiety, smiled reassurance, promised to send word if she needed help, and the moment she was alone in the cottage, felt all her fears come crowding back again. Then she polished and swept and baked and sewed; washed clothes, scrubbed floors, aired bedlinen and blankets; if one of the boys had brought home a rabbit, which they tried to do whenever they could, she would make rabbit stew or nourishing broth. When she could find no more to do inside the house, she would go outside, search the hedgerows, the peat stack and behind the privy for some hidden nesting place where one or other of her puny hens might have laid a precious egg. Then, finally exhausted, she would subside into her chair and take up her sewing. But sewing did not keep the thoughts at bay, however hard she tried. How would they manage when the baby arrived? In the summer months, when there was no school, Annys could help, but for the rest of the year? Would Miss Roberts, with her fashionable Union Street shop, still give her sewing if she knew there was a baby in the house? And if she did, how would Mhairi fetch and deliver it? Finally would come the blackest thought of all: how would the family manage without her if . . . But at this point in her thoughts Mhairi would pull herself firmly together. She was young and strong and healthy. Why should anything go wrong?

By the afternoon of this particular day, the last day of

[18]

March, her back ached with a dragging persistence. Tom and Alex had both looked in at midday to see how she did. Young Will had called in two hours later on the pretext of fetching a hammer Alex had forgotten and barely an hour after that, Donal had stopped the horses at the door, to beg a mug of water and inquire in sign language if there was anything she needed. Yet her spirits remained low.

It was perhaps half an hour after Donal had gone again, leading the team of dray horses with their wagon-load of granite blocks at a slow and careful pace down the rutted track towards the canal where one of the Wyness barges would be waiting to take them to the yard, when Mhairi caught the sound of different, lighter wheels and the sharp clop of brisker hoofs. Her heart quickened with curiosity and she moved to the door and opened it, the better to see. Coming over the brow of the little hillock, at the point where Annys had waved goodbye, was some sort of gentleman's carriage pulled by a pair of fine greys. Whoever could it be? Surely not Fergus Adam? Her heart thudded fast at the thought and she raised an unconscious hand to her hair, to smooth it into place.

But Fergus would not drive a carriage. He would come, if he came at all, on horseback: remembering how handsome he looked on horseback Mhairi was ashamed. She had no business to think of Fergus Adam, let alone with pleasure, when his father was their sworn enemy, Silvercairns their deadliest rival, and her husband working his heart out for her less than half a mile away on Rainbow Hill.

As the carriage drew closer she saw that it contained a man and a woman, a young woman in a red dress, with a white fur muff in her lap and red ribbons to her bonnet. She had a knee rug tucked around her and the man held a whip in one hand and the gathered reins in the other. There was a small wicker basket at the girl's feet. Then Mhairi remembered where she had seen the girl before and at the same instant realized that she must be coming to visit *her*.

Swiftly she drew back into the tiny hall of the house, closed the door to the bedroom on her right, and to the stairs which led up to the loft overhead where her brothers and Donal slept. Then she cast anxious eyes over the spotless kitchen, the remaining room of the two-roomed but-and-ben, checked

[19]

that there was water enough in the kettle, pushed it further over the peat fire to which she added a handful of fir-cones from the sack which Annys had filled for her, to make it burn bright. In her mind she ran over the small store of provisions suitable to offer such a guest: there was the last of the shortbread which Mrs Macrae had sent home with Annys only yesterday, and the fruit bun Mhairi had been saving for Sunday. If she cut the slices thinly, perhaps there would be enough? She had baked bread for the evening, but no scones, and she could not offer Miss Wyness plain bread.

But the carriage was drawing up at the gate. Mhairi opened the door and stood waiting. The man climbed down, held out his hand to assist the young lady, then handed her the little wicker basket. With a timid smile Fanny Wyness came up the path towards her and it was as Mhairi reached out a hand in welcome that she felt the first warning twinge. But it was quickly gone and Miss Wyness was speaking.

"Hello, Mhairi,' She pronounced the 'Mh' correctly, Gaelic fashion, as a soft 'V'. 'I hope I may call you Mhairi, may I? Mrs Grant sounds so very formal.'

'Of course,' said Mhairi, ignoring her pain in the interests of courtesy. Besides, it was probably only the backache which had plagued her all day. 'Please come in, Miss Wyness. I was just about to make tea.'

'Please call me Fanny. Otherwise I shall feel so very old and unfriendly, and it was as a friend that I ventured to call on you. I hope you don't mind?' she finished, suddenly anxious. It had occurred to her that this girl who was no older than she was herself, but so obviously pregnant, might not welcome the intrusion of a comparative stranger at such a time.

'I am always glad to see visitors,' said Mhairi, 'but what about your . . .' She hesitated to say 'servant' and temporized with 'driver'.

'Mackie? Oh, he will wait outside with the horses. They are not safe to be left alone,' she explained. 'At least, Mackie likes to think they are not. Really it is an excuse for him to smoke that dreadful tobacco which Mamma has forbidden him to bring into the house, even into the back scullery. I brought you something,' she finished shyly, holding out the basket. 'It is only butter and a little honey, for your health. I wanted to bring you a pickled tongue, too, but Cook did not . . . I mean to say, the tongue was not quite squeezed. I think she said "squeezed",' Fanny finished uncertainly.

'Pressed,' corrected Mhairi, smiling, and then in case she had embarrassed her guest, added, 'But either will do. And it is very kind of you to bring me anything at all. But please sit down, Miss Wyness . . . Fanny . . . and I will make tea for us directly.'

Fanny almost urged her not to trouble herself, especially when she saw how Mhairi paused and caught her breath when she reached for the china cups and saucers from the shelf, but prudently she refrained, for the longer she spent in this charming little cottage, the more chance there would be of seeing Tom. Instead, she offered to help, taking the plates from Mhairi's hands and setting the embroidered cloth on the scrubbed deal table. When Mhairi lifted the heavy kettle to make the tea for them, Fanny held the teapot for her, and pulled up the chairs to the table. With its dainty china plates and hand-stitched cloth it looked utterly charming, as did the triangles of sugared shortbread and the thin slices of loaf with fresh butter.

'I am so glad I came,' said Fanny, helping herself from the plate Mhairi offered. 'Papa was worried that you might be feeling lonely, so far from Aberdeen and all the friends you used to know. Especially . . .' She lowered her eyes in sudden embarrassment, not knowing whether it was quite polite to refer so openly to Mhairi's condition. 'Mamma would have come too, but she is a little unwell this afternoon. She said I was to be sure to say she was asking for you. She sends you her good wishes,' elaborated Fanny, 'and hopes you are keeping in the best of health.'

'Thank you. You are very kind.'

There was silence as they both drank, Fanny's eyes over the rim of her cup taking in every detail of the neat, whitewashed room: the meal tub and wooden salt box, the shelves of crockery and the pans which hung from nails on the wall, the black-leaded grate with the bread oven beside it and the iron sway from which the kettle and the kale-pot swung on little iron chains. There was a rag rug in front of the fire and an oil lamp on the pine wood dresser. It was warm and cheerful, with the fire burning bright and those pretty curtains at the little window, but hardly bigger than a scullery and not half the size of the Wyness dining-room. Fanny wondered what happened when all the family came home at once, for she knew that Tom was not the only brother and was there not a little sister, too? And where did they sleep? The thought brought a blush to her cheek and she looked down at her plate where the thin triangle of fruit bun lay reproachfully untouched. Carefully, she picked it up between finger and thumb and bit.

Mhairi, watching her visitor from under lowered lashes, noted the white hands and soft, unroughened skin with envy and regret for dreams lost. There had been a time when she had dreamt of having such hands herself, when she had rubbed hers secretly at night with lemon or cucumber or even mutton fat, though that had smelt too pungent for a lady's boudoir. Fanny Wyness would not use mutton fat: she would have rose-scented lotions instead. Except that Fanny's hands did not have to scrub and clean all day and would be white and soft if she used no creams at all. But she was a kindly, unassuming girl and Mhairi did not grudge her her idleness. Some were born rich, others poor. Some had large families, others none at all. It was the way things were, that was all. But the thought of families brought the old worries crowding back and as she thought of her unborn child, she realized with a thud of fear that the pain which had been with her all day had shifted and changed. Oh God, please not yet.

'Is anything the matter, Mhairi? You look a little anxious?' said Fanny with concern. When Mhairi did not immediately answer, but instead gripped the table edge with white-knuckled hands, all Fanny's new-found confidence left her and she said in a small voice, 'Would you rather I went home?'

'No. It is nothing. Just that I expect Annys home from school very soon and I always grow a little anxious, waiting for her. She will play with the Macrae girls from the farm though she knows that I . . .' But Mhairi could not keep up the pretence. She looked at Fanny with eyes large with fear and said suddenly, 'I think the pains have begun.'

Fanny's eyes were as frightened as Mhairi's. For a long moment they looked at each other in silence, then Mhairi said in a voice of quavering entreaty, 'You will help me, won't you?'

It was the most terrifying moment of Fanny's life. She had heard of childbirth of course, but when her mother's friends spoke of it it was always in hushed voices, one eye on Fanny lest she hear what she should not. But she knew that childbirth was women's work, the doctor only summoned in the most difficult of cases. And Fanny was the only other woman here.

'We must summon help,' she managed. 'Mackie shall go to the farm you mentioned. Was it the one we passed on the road?' Mhairi nodded. 'Mrs Macrae will come?' Again Mhairi nodded. 'Then I will send Mackie at once, and,' she added with inspiration, 'I will ask for your little sister to be kept at the farm till she is sent for. Then I will boil water.' Water was always boiled for childbirth: she knew that much, at least.

'And will you tie a cloth to the rowan tree at the corner?' managed Mhairi. 'It is the signal, you see. That blue striped cloth beside the door.'

After that, things happened so swiftly that afterwards Fanny could not remember the order, though her mother pressed her over and over for the details. Mackie was sent to fetch Mrs Macrae, she knew that, and came back not only with the farmer's wife, but with the blacksmith's wife too. These two capable women took over, removed Mhairi to the room on the other side of the tiny entrance hall and closed the door, leaving Fanny with instructions to 'Clear away they fancy tea things, miss, afore the menfolk come home. Mhairi doesna want her best china broke, do you, lass, and men are aye clumsy with yon flimsy bits and pieces.' When Fanny asked whether there was not something else she could do to help, Mrs Macrae cast a practised eye over Fanny's ensemble and said with brisk kindness, 'Nay, miss, there's no call for you to be rolling up your sleeves. You'd best sit yourself down till yon fancy cartie's ready to take you home, but while you're waiting, you can see the fire doesna burn away, and if it's needing peat, rap at the door and Jessie'll see to it. We're needing plenty boiling water and the menfolk'll be wanting their tea, likely, whether there's a new bairn on the way or no.'

Humbled by her dismissal, Fanny, who had never washed a dish in her life, looked around for a water-pipe and, finding none, was standing helplessly in the middle of the room with a teacup in one hand and a plate in the other when the outside door opened on a rush of cold air and Tom Diack burst in. 'I saw your signal, Mhairi, and I sent word straight to Alex. He'll be here direc . . . tly.' He drew to an embarrassed stop as he saw Fanny Wyness and blushed in confusion.

'I am sorry, Miss Wyness, I did not realize Mhairi had a visitor.' But the bedroom door had opened enough for Jessie Bain, the blacksmith's wife, to slip through and close it behind her.

'Oh, it's you, Tom Diack. And me thinking it was Alex.'

'He'll not be long. I sent word the moment I saw the signal, but he's working on the new blasting, and . . .'

'Aye well, there's nae need to panic. The bairn will be a whilie yet. My Aunt Mary's husband's cousin's wife over Persley way, the one wi' the brother who took ship to Port Phillip the Michaelmas afore last and no word of him since, well, she was two full days labouring and then one, two, three. Triplets. Small as kittens, mind, and two of the wee mites dead, but the third little runt grew to be a fine strapping lad.'

Tom exchanged a glance with Fanny and all awkwardness was forgotten in shared horror.

'Died five years later of the measles,' continued the woman with no change of expression, 'but a fine strong lad while he was spared. Is there plenty whisky in the house?' When Tom nodded, she turned back towards the bedroom, then stopped, her hand on the doorknob, and said in a stage whisper which would have penetrated the thickest wall, 'Whisky's fine if you've nought else, but some of yon new ether-stuff would come in real handy. There's a doctor down Stonehaven way, seemingly, cut a man open a month back on his own kitchen table, took out whatever it was he was looking for and stitched him up again and the man not feeling a thing on account of him having breathed the fumes of ether which stole away his senses *for a full twenty minutes.* "Doctor," he says, waking up, "I'm ready for yon operation, but if ye dinna hurry I'll lose my nerve." "Look at your stomach," says the doctor, solemn-like, "and if you tell me yon fancy cross-stitch was there twenty minutes since, I'll not believe you." That's the magic of ether. Yon doctor-laddie fixed a lassie's squint with the stuff not long after and her not feeling a thing. But we've nae ether here, more's the pity. The lass will have to make do with the bedposts to pull on, a rag in her mouth if she needs it, and whisky.' With that comforting thought, the voice of doom disappeared behind the bedroom door, to their mutual relief.

'Oh dear,' said Fanny, her lips dry, then as Tom said nothing she added, 'I was going to wash these pretty plates and cups, but I am afraid I could not find the water-pipe.'

'That's because there is none,' said Tom. 'There's a pump behind the house and buckets in the scullery.' He indicated a door Fanny had not noticed before which opened into a narrow, stone-flagged room with a small window and an outside door to the yard. 'But there's no call for you to wet your hands wi' Mhairi's tea things. Annys will do them when she comes home.'

'She is to stay at the farm,' said Fanny, wondering for the first time if she had done the wrong thing. Perhaps Annys was needed here, young though she was? 'If you show me where to find water, I will do them myself.'

'And what would Mhairi say if she heard I'd let a visitor of hers wash dishes? Besides, that's not the sort of work for you to be doing, Miss Wyness.'

'But I want to,' she said, with vehemence. She saw Tom look at her dress, as Mrs Macrae had done, at her hands, the white fur edge to the revers on her bodice, and knew he thought her unsuitably clad for housework of any kind. Suddenly she wanted to show him that she was not an idle gentlewoman like Lettice Adam, but could work as hard as Mhairi if she had to; that just because her hands were white and her dress of soft merino it did not mean she thought herself above such things. She turned back the cuffs of her sleeves and said, 'Show me where to find a bucket, and the pump.'

But when she could not lift the bucket, Tom lifted it for her, and when she spilt water from the steaming spout of the kettle, trying to pour hot water into the cold, so that it sizzled and spat on the glowing peats, Tom did that for her too and the intimacy of those simple shared tasks warmed her heart and brought a happy glow to her cheeks. She was standing at the sink in the back scullery, drying the last of the plates, when Mackie appeared at the scullery door.

[25]

'Unless you've apprenticed yoursel' as scullery maid till Michaelmas, Miss Fanny, it's time we was leaving. It'll be dark afore we know it and the road uncommon stony and yon horses not awful fond of the dark at the best o' times. I wouldna want them to fall, or break an axle and toss us into a ditch. The mistress sets great store by yon carriage and she'll not want it delivered home in pieces and her needing it the morn.'

Before Fanny could reply the front door opened and Alex, with young Will at his heels, came bursting in. 'How is she? I came the moment I heard, but the fuses had been newly lit and we daren't move till the powder fired, then I had to find Mackinnon to take over and . . . Is Mhairi all right?'

At a nod from Tom in the direction of the downstairs bedroom, Alex disappeared inside, only to emerge a minute or two later looking at the same time relieved, shamefaced, and anxious. He hardly noticed Fanny and when he did, merely nodded an abstracted greeting. Then Donal arrived and young Lorn, both weary after a long day's work. Suddenly the little house seemed full of menfolk, awkward in the presence of a stranger, politely trying to conceal their tiredness and hunger, and their helpless anxiety for the woman who was the centre of their world. Perhaps Fanny should try to produce a meal? Mhairi had prepared something in a great black pot with a lid which hung by a chain over the fire, but Fanny had no idea what she should do with it, whether it was ready to eat or waiting for some vital final process, and if she asked, it would show Tom and all of them the abysmal depths of her ignorance. She felt unwanted, excluded by her useless gentility and completely out of place. Quickly she dried her hands on her skirt, found her muff where she had laid it down on the dresser, retrieved her little basket and said to Mackie, 'Bring the horses to the gate. We will leave now, just as soon as I have said my farewells.'

Tom went with her to the gate.

'Promise you will send me word,' she said, 'as soon as the baby is born. And do not worry about what that woman said,' she added shyly. 'Hundreds of babies are born quite safely, every day.'

'I know,' said Tom, managing a grin. 'But thank you for

reminding me. And thank you for coming to call.'

He handed her up into the phaeton himself and she felt the warmth of his hand in hers long after Mackie had driven them down the long, stony track in the gathering darkness and out on to the Woodside road. It was then that she gave Mackie the coin and bought his discretion: she had too many precious memories to risk exposing them to the brazen questioning of the Wyness household. She had called, offered her gifts, exchanged a polite word, and left again when she was sure that Mhairi was in safe hands. That was all. The thought reminded her of her own hands and how ignorantly they had been employed at Mhairi's scullery sink. She blushed to think of her incompetence, but at least she had made a start. She would speak to Mamma, tell her that needlework, dancing and a little French were not enough. It was time that she, Fanny, learnt the practicalities of housekeeping: not just how to tell the servants what to do, but how to do the tasks herself. If her Mamma asked why, when she had money enough to employ what servants she chose, she would say merely, 'So that I will know, Mamma, whether they are carrying out their tasks correctly.' Whether she was rich enough to employ servants or not, Tom Diack would not want a wife who was useless, and she meant one day to be Tom Diack's wife. Smiling blissfully to herself, Fanny settled back in her seat to relive every moment of Tom's company on the long road home.

Of what her father would say when she reached the house in Skene Square for once she gave no thought.

In the drawing-room of the Adam town house tempers were less than tranquil. Aunt Blackwell, who since Mrs Adam's death had taken over the nominal running of the house, had pleaded tiredness and retired early to her room, leaving Old Man Adam and his two children together. Fortified by a tolerable dinner and two glasses of her father's claret, Lettice Adam had dared to raise the question of the Adam country residence, to which the household had been in the habit of removing every April, and which she had driven out that very afternoon to inspect. Dust covers removed, the furniture had proved to have suffered little from a winter's damp and cold,

[27]

but the structure of the house itself was another matter. Bravely, Lettice had told her father so, with tempestuous results.

'Rebuild the south wall? Do you think I am made of money?' glared Mungo Adam from under fiercely bristling brows. He was a big man, who looked even bigger in rage. Now he lifted his coat tails to the smouldering fire and frowned reproof on the world in general and on his daughter in particular. She was a good-looking girl, no one could deny that, and in that pale blue thing she had on tonight, with ribbons in her yellow hair, she looked as handsome a lass as you'd find in the whole of Scotland. But she was a mite too headstrong and fond of her own way. For all her good looks she had not snared a husband, or consented to take one of her father's snaring, and the sooner she did, the better for all concerned. No fly-by-night, jumped-up tradesman with ideas above his station either, but a rich, respectable husband who could do them good, and he knew just the man. The only trouble would be persuading his daughter to agree. But persuade her he would, by force if necessary, and before she had drained his purse of every hard-won penny.

Something of his grasping antagonism penetrated Lettice's defences and sent a shiver of apprehension down her spine, but on this occasion she knew she was right. Fergus must know it too and, relying on his support, she stood her ground.

'But Papa, you know the quarry is prospering, you said so yourself only yesterday.' Lettice directed her most beguiling smile at her father, but at the word 'quarry' his attention swung to his son and her smile was wasted. She bit her lip in annoyance and the smallest twinge of fear. Aspects of her past life had brought his disapproval thundering around her ears and though for the most part she was able to smooth away his irritation, in her heart she knew that only a sensible marriage of his choosing would completely heal the rift. Knowing on whom his choice would fall, she had set her chin resolutely against all matrimony, though she had had the wit not to say as much aloud. Now, surreptitiously studying her father's glowering face and her brother's carefully expressionless one, she hesitated, then remembering Fergus's particular anxiety, continued bravely, 'It is a false economy to neglect repairs

[28]

which, if neglected, multiply. The house at Silvercairns is such a case. Since last autumn that dangerous crack has appeared in the south wall, one of the chimneys is definitely awry and will no doubt fly off and kill someone before the year is out, and there is damp in the . . .'

'Enough!' thundered Old Man Adam. 'You find too many ways to spend my money already without adding a list of imagined disasters. That last dress bill of yours was outrageous.'

'Yes, Papa,' said Lettice meekly and looked across at Fergus in mute appeal. For once, he responded.

'Lettice is right, Father,' he said, laying aside the newspaper. 'That last blasting operation at the quarry cracked more than a garden wall. We will have serious subsidence at Silvercairns if we do not revise our thinking about the whole blasting programme.'

'Revise? What sort of word is that for a quarry manager to use? I do not pay you to *revise*, but to think properly in the first place.'

'If you recall, Papa, I warned you six months ago of what would happen. I suggested we refrain from further blasting on the house side of the quarry and instead lease extra land, or a second quarry, on Donside. You disagreed.'

That was an unfortunate reminder and had Fergus not drunk a bottle of good claret at dinner and half as much again of even better port, he would have held his tongue: the quarry Fergus had suggested they lease had instead been leased by Old Man Adam's enemy George Headstane Wyness who, rumour had it, was already making an enviable profit from the venture.

'And I still disagree!' roared Adam. 'I told you then and I tell you now, there's enough rock in that quarry of ours to build Aberdeen twice over without throwing away good money on extra this and extra that and if you can't see it then you can get out! Join your brother in Jamaica. Or if it's Donside quarries you want, go and work for that shark Wyness, and God rot the pair of you.'

There was a small silence as each of the three retreated into private thought. The drawing-room of the Adam town house was low-ceilinged, dark-panelled, the shutters closed securely against the night. Lamplight glinted on darkened oil-paintings in gilded frames and the polished floorboards gleamed black around crimson and gold patterned turkey rugs. Solid, two-hundred-year-old walls of enduring strength ought to have wrapped the occupants in warm security and ease, but though the room was hot enough, at least when Old Man Adam moved away from the fire and unblocked the heat, there was little sense of security and certainly no ease.

Lettice, for all her bravery, feared her father for the power he held over her fate. Her brother Fergus, manager of the quarry and his father's heir, felt the same fear and for much the same reasons, though in his case it was not a forced marriage that he dreaded, but a forced dismissal. Silvercairns was his life: for that very reason he was driven to speak out when he knew his words would bring only anger, for whereas his father saw Silvercairns Quarry as a mere hole in the ground from which could be hewn precious, and endless, riches, Fergus saw it as a living creature of sensitivity and brooding strength, a creature content to co-operate with man as long as the deal was fair, but capable of terrible retribution were man to overstep the mark. Fergus feared his father would overstep, might already have done so, for the crack Lettice talked of in the wall of Silvercairns House was not the first, as it would not be the last – until the last crack of all when the whole proud edifice came crashing down around their feet to sweep them, with the crumbling rubble, into the bottomless pit of the quarry. Suddenly, with appalling clarity, Fergus saw the cracking walls, the blocks of dressed granite separating, arching up, then out and down in a slow shower of smaller stones, window frames, roof slates, rubble, and afterwards the silence of settling dust . . . But unlike the silence after a quarry blasting, there would not be the sudden flurry of busy activity, checking the quality of the new rock, comparing its colour with the old, measuring 'posts' and marking out particularly fine specimens for this contract or that. After the fall of Silvercairns House there would be nothing . . . only endless silence and a sea of dust and in the misty distance a girl with black hair and blue eyes, forever out of reach. In spite of himself Fergus shivered and reached for the brandy.

'That's right,' growled Old Man Adam, 'drink me out of

house and home. You're as bad as your sister, always finding new ways to spend my money. You should find yourself a rich wife and spend hers instead. Why you let that Burnett girl escape I'll never understand. She looked at you with doe's eyes for years. All you had to do was ask her, but no, you let that minister fellow snap her up under your very nose. Well, you'll not lose the Macdonald girl the same way or you will have me to answer to.'

'The Macdonald girl?' said Fergus and immediately wished he had held his tongue.

'Amelia, you dolt. Or did you think I meant her mother? Though if your fancy lies that way the mother will serve as well. With that villain Wyness setting up against us, we need a good granite yard on our side and Macdonald's is the best. Amelia may be only a cousin, but she's a Macdonald nonetheless, and a rich one, with influence where it counts.'

When Fergus made no answer, sympathy and an uncontrollable urge for mischief prompted Lettice to say with solemn innocence, 'Why do you not marry Mrs Macdonald yourself, Papa? You know how much she admires and respects you and she is a handsome woman for her years.'

'Handsome she may be,' grunted Adam, 'but I've no time for matrimony. One wife was enough for me.' But Lettice could see that he was flattered by her suggestion and when he spoke again, his temper had mellowed. 'When we move to Silvercairns, we must give a dinner or two, ask a few suitable young people. We don't want to make things too obvious. Then, maybe in the summer . . .' and here he fixed Fergus with an implacable eye, 'you and Amelia can announce the engagement prior to an autumn wedding. It's time I had a grandchild, for the inheritance, provided you and your sister have not spent the lot of it before the first banns are read. As to you, miss,' he said, taking Lettice unawares, 'you will be told my plans for you in due course.'

Ignoring the awful implications of this last threat, Lettice seized on an earlier part of her father's speech. 'I was trying to tell you, Papa. The ceiling in the dining-room at Silvercairns is badly marked where the rain came in above the windows and will continue to come in unless something is done to repair the south wall. We cannot ask our guests to sit under a leaking ceiling. Suppose it were to rain, or the plaster give way?'

Her father did not immediately answer, pride obviously struggling with avarice. Pride won. 'Fergus, take a look at this so-called crack next time you are passing. Have it repaired if necessary, but cheaply, mind. Send a man from the quarry in company time. As to the ceiling, what's whitewash for? One man with a ladder can do the job in five minutes. See to it.'

'Yes, Father,' sighed Fergus and, before Old Man Adam could change his mind, changed the subject. 'I see the prospectus of the Dundee and Northern Junction Railway is out. To connect Dundee with the Edinburgh and Northern, and eventually with the Aberdeen line.' He retrieved the newspaper, found the place and read out, 'A capital of £250,000 in 12,500 shares of £20 each.'

'Very grand. But does it say when shareholders can expect a dividend? This year? Next year? Or in ten years' time, always supposing the railway is actually built by then?' But in spite of the old man's ritual grumbling, Fergus knew his father was interested.

'It will be built, Father, no question of that. Look how well the Aberdeen line is progressing. They took on fifty more men to work on the line at Arbroath only last week.'

'Aye, Orkney fishermen! I knew some fellow had invented fishplates to join the tracks together but I didn't realize it needed actual fishermen to lay them. They'll drink their pay within an hour of getting it, terrorize the neighbourhood, and lay the rails awry into the bargain.'

'The work will be done,' persisted Fergus patiently. 'And when the Great North of Scotland track is completed it will be possible to travel by train all the way from Inverness to London. Profits on the Aberdeen–Inverness line alone are expected to be in excess of £116,000, equal to a dividend of at least ten per cent.'

'They have to build the line first,' grumbled Old Man Adam. 'And find the passengers to use it. As to profits, you have only to look at the North British. Promised dividends of eight per cent and what do they pay? Two, if you are lucky.' At the height of railway mania Mungo Adam had invested heavily in the North British Railway Company and the fate of his incautious investment had given him more than one

[32]

sleepless night. 'What sort of an investment is that?'

'A long term one, Father. With a project like the railways you cannot hope for quick profits. But one day, when each line is connected up to the next, in a grid which covers the length and breadth of the country, the railways will take over the country's transport, of people as well as goods. It will mean the decline of the stage-coach, of course, and the toll roads will inevitably suffer, the canals too, but I am convinced the railway is the way of the future.'

'Maybe, maybe,' grumbled Adam. 'But that does not mean every fool in Scotland should fight for the privilege of handing over his money on the mere strength of a prospectus.'

But Fergus had reminded him of an old annoyance. That crook Wyness had a yard which most usefully abutted the canal, and a quarry with access to the same waterway; to crown all, the projected railway would pass that way too. As if that was not insult enough, the man had had the effrontery to snatch the contract for building work on the line north of Aberdeen from under Adam's very nose. It would serve the villain right if he lost by the transaction instead of gained. Adam smiled a mirthless smile at the thought. It might be possible. Naturally, like everybody else, Adam had bought into the venture when it was launched: now he was prepared to lay out whatever extra was required to buy himself a seat on the Board. That done, he would be in the ideal position to plot the man's ultimate downfall. He found the thought remarkably cheering. Reaching for the brandy decanter he poured himself a hefty measure, raised his glass to Fergus and said, 'To the railways – and the profits of the future.'

'The future,' breathed Alex Grant in awe, looking down at the sleeping face of his new-born son where he lay cocooned in swaddling linen in the wooden crib beside the bed. 'Our future, Mhairi,' he added, taking her exhausted hand in his. 'From now on, every hole I bore, every fuse I plant, every block of granite I hew and dress will be for this little fellow, and for you.'

Tears sprang to Mhairi's eyes and she could find no words. She was at the same time utterly drained, and filled with overflowing love, for her precious new-born son and for his father, who looked down at her with an expression of such protective tenderness. She noted the lines of tiredness in his face, and those other lines which she knew were of worry and strain.

'You must not work too hard, Alex,' she said now, gently pleading. 'What would little Hamish and I do if you were to fall ill? Besides, you have Tom and the others to help you. The burden of the quarry is not yours alone.'

'Perhaps not, but I feel it is so. George Wyness has placed great trust in me. I know old Mackinnon is nominally in charge, but experienced though he is and more than most men, he is old and not as strong as he was. He's aye been kind to me and Donal since we were wee orphan laddies in the same tenement, and I'll not stand by and see him kill himself with work a younger man should do. For advice you could not go to a better, but to carry out that advice, with strength on the hammer and shoulder to the rock, it must be myself, and Tom.'

'And the work-force,' prompted Mhairi gently. 'You have upwards of fifty men working for you . . .'

'Who would think nothing of a man who expected them to carry out work he couldna do himself. Besides, we'll need to hew out all the rock we can, and as fast as we can, if we are to make a profit at the end of the year. We are to have a share of that profit, remember. Sixty per cent goes to Mr Wyness, twenty per cent to Mackinnon and ten per cent each to Tom and me. I mean that ten per cent to be as large as I can make it, Mhairi. For Mr Wyness's sake, to show my gratitude for taking on Tom and me as working partners when we had no capital to invest, but most of all, for you.'

'And will you always get only ten per cent, however hard you work?' she asked, suddenly anxious for the needs of their growing family. Last winter, she had heard dreadful tales of poverty in the Highlands, starvation on the islands of Coll and Tiree through no fault of the people, who were as hard-working as Alex was, but through dearth and the hand of fate.

'That is the arrangement,' said Alex. 'Besides that, I will have my mason's pay, to be increased in time, as the quarry prospers.' But his mason's pay was little enough. He was

[34]

silent, suddenly beset with doubt. Since the birth of his son, so short a time ago, his whole outlook on life had changed, the perspective shifted. He could no longer take each day as it came, content to think only of himself and Mhairi and a time no further away than tomorrow. Now he looked with sober clarity down an endless vista of years in which he aged and tired, as Mhairi's father had done, and his children grew until the day when they had children of their own and he was no more than a memory, as Cassie Diack was now. But when I die, he thought with new intensity, I will leave my son more than a bag of tools and a memory. More than a toe-hold on the bottom rung of the ladder from which it was all too easy to fall. *I will leave him the solid worth of Rainbow Hill.* Then he remembered Mhairi's warning words. Suppose he were to fall ill?

'Do not look so worried, Alex my love,' said Mhairi, lifting his hand and holding it against her cheek. 'We will manage fine. You have a son who is strong and healthy and a wife who is the same. You should be celebrating with the others, drinking your baby's health and good fortune, not brooding about disasters that may never come.'

'Aye, lass. You're right,' said Alex with an effort. He grinned, bent over the bed and kissed her forehead. 'Donal will be here soon, with Annys, and no doubt half the neighbours too. Wee Hamish will be holding his first ceilidh afore we know it.'

As predicted, the neighbours came. In the family kitchen, Alex poured whisky for the menfolk and many of the womenfolk too, while in the bedroom Annys, after the first delighted cuddle of her new-born nephew, did her best with the teapot and the cheeses, bakery and cold meats which arrived with the neighbours in a steady stream. There was congratulation, gossip and laughter; much praise of the new-born child who was pronounced a fine, healthy lad and 'fair set to be a terror with the lassies, wi' yon black curly hair and blue eyes', but in spite of the air of celebration and jollity Alex could not rid himself of that niggling doubt. When Tom mentioned that they ought to send a note to Miss Wyness in the morning, with young Lorn, 'for I promised her I would let her know when the baby was born,' Alex's brow cleared for the first time since Mhairi's innocent question.

'Aye, we must, Tom lad. And to her father. But I'm thinking I'll ride in with the granite tomorrow and take the note myself. There's something I want to discuss with Mr Wyness, afore it slips my mind.'

The Wyness granite yard was flourishing. After twenty years in the same premises, George Wyness had bought a strip of adjacent land with a view to expanding the business and already it was hard to see where old gave way to new. He had taken on half as many men again, added an extra polishing shed to the existing two, where rough stone was passed to and fro on bogies under cast-iron rings until sand and water had scoured the surface to a satisfactory gleam, and every inch of open ground was utilized for one or other of the many stages involved in converting a lump of raw granite into a smoothly polished, elegantly ornamented headstone, mantelpiece, balustrade or Grecian pillar. Occasionally, they made the plinth for a statue to be sent to Glasgow, Manchester or London and it was Wyness's dearest dream that one day his yard should produce the statue itself. A solid granite statue, taken from the plaster model and polished to the gleam of marble, but with twice its enduring qualities. Donal Grant was the man to undertake the business, but Donal was still in charge of the quarry horses and the whole business of transport from the new operation on Rainbow Hill. Another six months, perhaps, when everything was running smoothly, would be the time to bring him into the yard and set him to work on the company pattern book. The lad had an eye for shape and form and knew instinctively which design would work and which would not. One day, Donal Grant would do the statue: a royal statue, that would stand for ever as an enduring tribute to the success of the Wyness yard.

But what was he thinking of? Wyness shook his head impatiently to clear it of such idle day-dreams. There would be time enough for statues when every inch of his yard was producing double its capacity and more. When his profits had trebled. When he could sit back and let the next generation take over.

Except that there would be no next generation until Fanny married and produced grandchildren. Fanny was a gentle, obedient girl who lived only to please him: she would marry when he told her to, and as he directed. The trouble was choosing a suitable husband. Someone honest and healthy went without saying; someone who would be kind to little Fanny and make her happy; but it must also be someone whom Wyness could trust to take over the business and run it efficiently when he was no longer, for whatever reason, able to do so himself. There had been a time when he had thought Fergus Adam would fit the bill ideally, with the added advantage of bringing an alliance with the powerful Adam family, but Fergus had blotted his copybook long ago, and even if he had not, since that business over the canal, nothing on this earth would persuade Wyness to marry his daughter to Mungo Adam's son. Adam and Wyness were sworn enemies, and would remain so till death, preferably Adam's.

But Fanny must marry someone, and soon: looking out of his small office window, as he did numerous times a day to check on the various activities of his yard, Wyness felt the old longing which, accommodating itself to the passing years, was no longer a longing for a son, but for a grandson. He saw himself taking the little lad round the yard, holding him by the hand, lifting him over the stream of slurry which poured out of the polishing shed doorways, maybe making him a pair of little glasses, like the men wore, to protect his eyes from flying sparks and splinters as they watched the rings scouring the stone. He'd give him a miniature hammer and chisel and let him try his hand at chipping a block, maybe, and as soon as the lad was old enough, he'd be apprenticed into the yard, to learn the trade from the bottom, as old Wyness himself had done. The fact that his Grandda was boss would not earn him any favouritism, though naturally he'd see the lad came to no harm.

Across the yard, he saw young Lorn Diack, Mhairi's brother, sweeping up the chaff which lay scattered around a newly packed wooden crate. Inside the crate, carefully bedded in straw so that nothing should damage its surface, would be that headstone for London that was promised for the end of the month. The Christie ship would leave on the evening tide with the crate on board and it would reach its destination within the week. Wyness grinned. He prided himself on delivering when promised, if not before, and the London consignment would be no exception. In fact, in recent negotiations he had managed to bargain for a higher price for prompt delivery: the offer of a reduction if delivery were to be delayed invariably smoothed the contract, but so far Wyness had not needed to drop his price for anyone. He and his work-force, including Lorn Diack, saw to that. He was pleased with Lorn, a cheerful, hard-working lad eager to learn and unperturbed by the ribbing he was given by the older men when he first joined the yard, or by the practical jokes. Give him yard-sweeping, measurements, calculations or plain mason's work to do and he tackled each with equal enthusiasm. The Diack lad would go far, like his brothers.

At that moment Wyness heard the rattle of wheels on the cobbles outside and a heavy dray cart, creaking with granite blocks, turned into the yard, Donal Grant at its head and, unusually, his brother Alex beside him.

'Aye, aye,' said Wyness, stepping out of his office into the dirt of the yard. 'And what brings you so far from your work this morning, Alex lad? You'll not have forgotten that order for cassies that I've promised for Friday week?'

'I've not forgotten, Mr Wyness, and I've men working on it now. If they havena doubled their pile by the time I get back to the quarry, they'll have me to answer to. And the rubble all gathered ready for road metal, like you wanted.'

'Good lad. So what's your business? Away with you, Donal,' he interrupted, waving an expressive hand towards Alex's brother. 'There's no call for you to stand waiting while we blether,' but Donal did not move. Instead he jerked a head towards Alex with an expression of suppressed delight which gave Wyness the clue.

'Alex! You're never a father?'

Alex grinned and nodded.

'Well done, lad. Well done!' and Wyness slapped him on the shoulder, then Donal too. 'But wait. You haven't told me. Quine or loon?'

'Loon,' said Alex with bursting pride. 'We'd like to name him "Hamish George", if you've no objection?'

[38]

'Me? Object? You've as much right as any man to call the lad George if you're that way inclined. Not that it's much of a name, mind.' He spoke with a frown which for a moment had Alex worried. Then Wyness grinned. 'Nay, lad, I'm having you on! It's a good job it's young Lorn who's apprentice here and not you or the men'd pull your leg so often you'd walk with a permanent limp. But what am I thinking of? Come away into the office, the pair of you, and we'll toast the lad's health in a dram. Well, well, a wee laddie. And Mhairi's well, is she?'

'Well enough,' said Alex, following Wyness into the office, Donal close behind. A bottle was produced, and glasses, for Wyness kept to the old ways of sealing any business deal with a handshake and a dram and the office was accordingly well stocked. Whisky was poured and glasses raised to Mhairi's new-born son.

'Mrs Wyness will be glad to hear the news,' said Wyness, setting down his empty glass. 'And Fanny, too. She thinks a lot of Mhairi.'

'I know,' said Alex, 'and Mhairi promised Miss Wyness news of the baby's arrival.' He felt in his pocket and produced a note, folded and sealed. 'Would you give this note to her, please?'

'Nay lad, there's no call for folk to be sending notes, when I can tell her for you myself. But she'll be right glad to have it all the same. Now if you've finished your dram, you'd best be off. You've a son to work for now, as well as a wife.'

'Yes, Mr Wyness.' Alex put down his glass with studied care, nodded a dismissal to Donal and, when his brother had closed the door behind him, said, 'And that is why I would like to have a word with you, in confidence, if you could spare me a moment?'

'Aye, lad, as long as your "moment" doesna last all morning. But if you're wanting to apprentice young Hamish George into the yard, come back again in ten years' time and we'll talk about it.'

Alex grinned, but only momentarily, and the smile did not lift the gravity from his eyes. 'Thanks. I'll remember that. But it's something more immediate than ten years' time that troubles me. You remember the agreement you drew up with

Tom and myself . . .?'

It was a full half-hour before Alex emerged from the office, but when he did, the lines of care had lifted from his face as if he had shed a troublesome burden. George Wyness on the other hand looked unusually grave.

'Yon's a fine lad,' he said over and over to his wife that evening. 'As hard a worker as a man would wish for, a good family man and with a responsible head on his shoulders, too. I don't know what came over me, but he talked me into it before I realized. You'll not lose by it, Mr Wyness, I can promise you that, he said, and I reckon he's right, though I hope it'll not come to it for many a year. But I promised the lad I wouldna breathe a word and neither will you, not even to Fanny. Where is she, by the way? I have a note for her, from Mhairi herself.'

But the note was from Tom. *Dear Miss Wyness*, it ran. *Mhairi asked me to write to you to let you know that her little boy was born last night, just after eight o'clock. He is to be named Hamish George and is a fine, strong little lad. If you should have the time to visit Mhairi one day, she would be very pleased to see you and asked me to tell you that you will certainly not be required to wash your own cup and saucer. Your most respectful friend, Thomas Diack.*

Fanny read the note a dozen times before hiding it away in her petticoat drawer, under the muslin lavender bag. He had joked about her washing up, and he had written *Your most respectful friend.* One day, Fanny dreamt, he would be something far closer than that.

'You will marry Niall Burnett,' announced Old Man Adam at breakfast and, looking up from the newspaper, fixed Lettice with an ominous eye.

They had been at Silvercairns for almost three months. The minimal repairs which Mungo had authorized had been quickly done – 'a temporary patching job' as Fergus described it, with moody pessimism – and in early May the household had removed from the Guestrow in the centre of town to the country pleasures of Silvercairns, two miles to the west, on the hillside above the quarry of the same name. The whitewashed patch on the dining-room ceiling was barely noticeable, especially in candlelight, and certainly those guests who had graced their table on various occasions over the past weeks had been far more interested in what the table provided than in the décor overhead. The Burnetts, father and son, had been present at every dinner, as had Amelia Macdonald and her mother, and though Fergus had been left to make what unwilling progress he could in his own time, albeit always with his father's warning eye upon him, Lettice was obviously not to be given the same privilege.

Now, though her heart beat uncomfortably high in her throat, she said with apparent calm, 'No, Papa. I think not.'

'Lettice dear!' cried Aunt Blackwell, who, for once, had joined them for breakfast instead of nibbling on dry toast in the bilious solitude of her room. 'You must not speak to your father like that. Apologize this instant.'

Ignoring the interruption, Lettice reached for the teapot and poured herself another cup with a hand that was almost steady.

'And I say you will,' growled her father. 'Archie Burnett is an old family friend. He gave your brother Hugo letters of introduction for Jamaica when he needed them and I owe him some favour in return.'

'Favour?' cried Lettice. 'You call it a *favour*? Niall will not call it so, I promise you.'

But her father ignored her. 'More important, Burnett is a major shareholder in the Aberdeen railway, besides being exceedingly rich. It is an alliance I need, girl. I have already dropped a discreet word in Burnett's ear and he understands. Niall is the right age, of independent means, and Old Burnett's only possible objection would be that he would prefer to have you himself.'

'Niall Burnett is an odious, supercilious toad.' One look at her father's face told Lettice she was damned, but if she was to be condemned to that particular hell then she would fight all the way. 'I do not like him. I never did and never will. But that aside, Papa, and quite apart from any other objections, he has not asked me.'

'He will, when his father tips him the wink – and when he does, by God, girl, you will accept him or . . . or . . .'

[41]

'Or what, Papa? You will throw me out on to the street?'

'Or you'll take his father instead.'

That silenced Lettice, as he had known it would. She looked down at her plate, lest he see the consternation in her face, or the rebellious defiance which swiftly took its place.

'Is that understood, girl?'

'Yes, Papa.' But if Niall Burnett ever dares to ask me, vowed Lettice, then I will promise him unlimited hell for every hour of every single married day. Her only consolation was the knowledge that he would find the idea as distasteful as she did.

If only she were of age. At twenty-one she would come into the inheritance her mother had left her: little enough to be sure, but enough to give her the power and the bravery to defy her father. As it was she was barely nineteen and whereas poverty might be romantic in stories it was something she knew she could never willingly choose. She was used to comfort, to servants, to new clothes whenever she felt the urge, to good food and wine in an elegant, spacious setting, to a winter house and a summer, to Assemblies and soirées and boxes at the theatre. In fact, she was used to being Mungo Adam's only daughter, and to having what she wanted, when she wanted it. Now, for the first time in her pampered life, it looked as if she might have to renounce those privileges. The idea was appalling, but equally so was the idea of marrying a Burnett, father or son. She tried one last plea.

'I am so happy here with you, Papa. May we not stay as we are for a little while longer? Please?'

'And have you carrying on with the first tradesman who takes your fancy the moment my back is turned?'

'Mr Adam, how can you say such a thing of your own daughter?' cried Aunt Blackwell, deeply shocked, only to bring Adam's fury down around her own ears.

'Quiet, woman. Or leave the room. This is no concern of yours. Lettice understands me, don't you, girl?'

'Yes, Papa.' Her father's reference was to a past misdemeanour which Lettice preferred to forget and apparent obedience seemed the most expedient course until she saw which way he would move next. When he took up his newspaper and resumed reading, she added demurely, 'But I did not

[42]

understand about the Aberdeen railway, Papa. Did you say that Mr Burnett owned it, even though it is not yet built?'

'He owns a large number of the shares,' said her father, his eyes on the financial page, 'and has a seat on the Board. That is all that need concern you. Except that very soon people will be dispersing for the grouse moors or the fishing.' Suddenly he raised his eyes and looked at her with all the force of his powerful will. 'I have already given Fergus his orders regarding Amelia Macdonald, and before the shooting season, my girl, I expect you and Niall to have come to a similar arrangement. Mrs Macdonald's soirée would seem an ideal opportunity for you to indicate your willingness, and I shall be close at hand to see that you do. Or had you forgotten we are engaged to go there in a week's time?'

'No, Papa, I had not forgotten.' But at least at the soirée there would be plenty of other people besides Niall and herself. She might even manage to avoid him for the entire evening. If not, and if her vows of married hell made no impact, she would stipulate a long engagement – as long as possible. Then, with luck, he might get shot on a grouse moor, drown in a river, be thrown from his horse and die. And if luck was against her? To banish that particular unease she said, 'When do you think we can expect to hear from Hugo? He must surely have reached Jamaica by now.'

'Aye, he's reached there, you can be sure of that. As to hearing from the rascal, we can expect a letter when he wants money, and not before.' Adam glowered morosely into his teacup. Not for the world would he confess to anyone that he missed Hugo, hoped with every post to hear from him, scanned the shipping lists daily for news of the *Margaret Ellen* on which his favourite son had sailed, banished by his father in a fit of justifiable rage after one misdemeanour too many on Hugo's part. The matter of the pregnant servant girl was negligible and easily settled, as were the numerous gambling debts, but that business with two of his own workers had been the last straw. Silly young ass. Mungo had had no choice but to discipline the lad. Now his glower hid the usual worry as to Hugo's welfare while he went over in his mind the usual doubts and reassurances. The lad was young and headstrong, but he was intelligent enough to keep out of trouble: he was

[43]

profligate and idle, but he had letters of introduction to the right people and could be charming when he chose. He would do well enough. And if Hugo wrote for money, as sooner or later he was sure to do, Adam would grumble and fume, but he would send it, and gladly.

Sensing something of her father's thoughts, Lettice sought to divert him into calmer channels. 'Where is Fergus this morning? Surely he has not left for work already?'

'Two hours back. I told him we need to use every minute of daylight if we are to keep pace with the orders. Not that Fergus needs telling.' He managed to make it sound more a fault than a virtue.

Poor Fergus, thought Lettice, with rare sympathy. When his friends are still sleeping off the excesses of the night before, Fergus is already hard at work. No wonder he has not the inclination to marry, let alone the time. Aloud, she said only, 'No. The quarry is his life.'

'And so it should be. That hole in the ground is our livelihood, and don't ever forget it.' Adam pushed back his chair and stood up, reminding Lettice yet again what a powerful figure of a man he was, in spite of his years. 'I'll not be back till evening.' Then, with a nod in Aunt Blackwell's direction, he strode from the room.

'Oh dear,' quavered that lady. 'Oh dear, oh dear. Poor Fergus.'

'Why on earth are you sorry for him?' said Lettice in astonishment. 'He at least is happy in his work. I am the one you should be sorry for.'

'But Lettice dear, Niall is really quite a nice boy. Always so well-mannered and polite. Many girls would be delighted to . . .'

With a snort of disgust, Lettice followed her father out of the room.

Lettice had been right when she said the quarry was Fergus Adam's life. Ever since he could remember he had been fascinated by the deepening bowl of jagged rock which his father's workmen laboured endlessly to hack and hammer and gouge out of the earth's very flesh. One day, he used to think in childhood fantasy, they would crack the bottom of that bowl and through the crack would come bubbling up the dark, viscous current of the earth's blood, to fill the bowl to its rough-hewn, sandy, gorse-fringed rim and flow over in a river of black blood which would engulf and destroy everything in its path. But that was sixteen years ago when the quarry was a mere seventy feet deep; now it was almost double that and the bowl was still intact.

Another fantasy was of the quarry as a brooding animal, huge, unpredictable and threatening, which one day, if they overstepped the mark, would turn on its predators and destroy, and the dreadful thing about that particular fantasy was that no one except the quarry itself knew where that boundary mark was. All Fergus knew was that it had something to do with mutual respect, with the line between use and abuse, between expediency and greed. It was a line that Old Man Adam refused to recognize and as Fergus assumed more and more responsibility for the quarry's operation, it formed the basis of every disagreement between them. Old Man Adam was for extracting as much granite as quickly as possible and if that meant applying stronger fuses at closer intervals, then there could be no question in his mind that that was the course to follow. Fergus disagreed.

Unlike his father, he saw the seams behind the rock face, the 'posts' of granite in each new 'bench' they worked, the particular mix of felspar and mica and quartz which made up the layers of rock on rock which the centuries had formed, and the connection between the granite their quarrying had exposed and the rest of the earth's flesh, hidden under its skin of turf and undergrowth and tree. Fergus saw, as his father refused to see, that every blast in Silvercairns Quarry sent vibrations through that connecting flesh and contributed another crack to the structure of Silvercairns House. That leaking dining-room ceiling was only the latest manifestation of something that had been with them for years, something that was not merely the threat to a family house, elegant though that house was, but was an indication of the greater crack to come, or of the vengeful awakening of that sleeping beast. And still Old Man Adam refused to see it. Sometimes, in his bitterness, Fergus wondered if the old man would see it

[45]

even if the house fell about his very ears at the breakfast table, and buried his devilled kidneys under a layer of rubble and settling dust. Profit was the only thing that Old Man Adam recognized, and profit meant a steady stream of pack-horses, labouring up the spiral path from the quarry floor with their loads of granite blocks or paving setts; profit meant selling not only what they had, but what they had not yet got, and blasting open a new seam whenever his father won a new order. Profit meant blasting ever deeper and wider till the journey from quarry floor to surface took half as long again and the strip of land between quarry rim and the gardens of Silvercairns could be measured in yards. And profit meant beating George Wyness.

Since Wyness had had the temerity to lease a quarry of his own, instead of continuing to come cap in hand to Silvercairns for his needs, to hire not only his father's old foreman Mackinnon, but two of his father's best young quarrymen to run it for him, and to declare openly that he meant to 'beat Old Man Adam at his own game', that particular rivalry had become an obsession with Old Man Adam, but it did have one advantage where Fergus was concerned: he was no longer expected to woo Fanny Wyness, to their mutual relief.

He had nothing against Fanny. She was a pleasant enough girl whom he had known for most of her life, as was Amelia Macdonald, his father's latest sacrificial victim. But marriage with either of them would be an empty farce. Fergus had no wish to marry. He had met only one girl who had touched his heart in that way and she was out of the question: his father had threatened to disinherit any child of his who married into the servant classes. The girl's own marriage had fortunately put an end to temptation, but even if she had remained single, he knew to his shame that he could not have forfeited Silvercairns for her sake. Life without Silvercairns was unthinkable.

Now, Fergus checked through the last of the orders which his father had given him that morning and laid it aside. He stretched, yawned and reached forward to strike the brass bell on his desk. It was hours since breakfast. If he was to be as alert as the occasion required, he had better fortify himself with a cup of strong coffee before descending to the floor of the quarry to confer with Bruce. Not for the first time he wished that old Mackinnon was still the foreman. Mackinnon would have stuck out fearlessly for what he knew was right. Mungo Adam could rage and fume and shout till he was purple in the face and Mackinnon would say only, in that quiet, measured way of his, 'Aye, well, Mr Adam. I disagree,' and nothing would shift him. Bruce, the new foreman, was competent enough in his way, but a mite too eager to agree with Adam senior, if it kept the stick from his own back, even if five minutes earlier he had been on Fergus's side. It did not make for confidence.

Fergus was sipping the strong, black coffee which the yard boy had brought him when he remembered a particular item on his father's order list and paused. Thoughtfully he put down the cup and pulled the papers towards him. Yes, there it was. 'To supply granite for the construction of a house for Mr Duffus at Elmbank those blocks necessary for the façade and portico to be squared, dressed and polished and to include two pillars (see attached drawing), measurements as specified, rounded and polished and with pedestals and capitals likewise': the order to be delivered in its entirety by *31st October*!

It was impossible. They had barely three months before delivery date and enough overdue orders as it was without adding to them. All their quarried rock was already spoken for, twice over. If they took on more men, shelved all other work and concentrated only on this, they could perhaps supply the ashlar, but the stone for the façade was a different matter. To choose and cut the columns alone would take time and infinite care: as to the polishing . . . What was his father thinking of to contract for *polished* work? That was the granite yard's province, not the quarry's. The old man must be mad. Before the rift with Headstane Wyness, of course, there would have been no problem: Wyness would have dropped everything and put his entire yard on to the polishing work to accommodate Mungo Adam. Now, the Wyness yard was out of the question. They would have to deal through Macdonald's or one of the smaller, less reliable yards and take their turn. There was nothing for it: he would have to tell his father to cancel the contract, negotiate for ashlar alone and forget the polishing, or add three months at least to the delivery date. It was not an interview to which he looked forward.

But the thought of Macdonald's yard had reminded him of a different meeting to which he looked forward with even less enthusiasm. He wished yet again that his father's plans for business advancement depended on something more scientific than cold-blooded marriage, especially when the marriage in question was his son's rather than his own. Lettice's suggestion that their father should marry Mrs Macdonald was an excellent one, he reflected morosely, and a sacrifice his father should be prepared to make if he expected a similar from his children. Lettice could take care of herself and Fergus had few worries on her behalf. As for Fergus, he would be polite, pleasant, everything etiquette required of him, but he would not marry Amelia Macdonald. And he would not sanction that ridiculous contract for the Duffus house. Mackinnon would agree with him, were he here, and in this case, surely even Bruce would be on Fergus's side?

Gathering up the offending orders, Fergus strode out into the quarry yard, called for the foreman and, when told he was on the quarry floor, set out to join him. Once he had passed the scrubland at the quarry's rim and was on the track which spiralled its tortuous way downwards, clinging to the quarry side as it went, he could see straight into the huge, dusty bowl which reached so far down into the earth that the men working on the quarry floor seemed Lilliputian in their busy activity, the foot of the quarry path no more than a thread. Tiny hammers struck, miniature horses shuffled and stamped as toy bricks were loaded on to toy carts, while voices and hammer blows alike were lost in the vastness of dust and echoing rock. It was a clear July morning, the sun high and warm, but even so much of the quarry still lay in shadow. It would be cool out of the sun.

It was as he walked down the first stony stretch of the track that he recalled with piercing clarity a day three years ago, when a distracted girl had run headlong down that very path, then tripped and fallen, almost at his feet. She had looked up at him in terror, with eyes of a blue he had never seen before or since, and afterwards had fainted in his office. That had been his first meeting with Mhairi Diack and the thought of her had never left him, and would not, he realized, till death. Impatiently he thrust aside the memory. What was the use of dreams? He had work to do.

It was four in the morning when Mhairi woke and already daylight, though the sun had yet to rise. A pink haze hung over the skyline to the east where distant sand dunes met sea in a blur of pale green and shimmering grey, and outside in the yard the grass was dew-drenched and sparkling. Here and there tiny cobwebs caught and held the light in a filigree of silver droplets and in the rowan tree a chaffinch sang. Mhairi breathed deep of the cool, clean air, splashed her face in the morning pail and, refreshed, set about reviving the fire, boiling water, preparing breakfast for the household, lunch boxes for those who needed them, and the dozen other tasks to be done before the working day began. She went about her work softly so as not to waken them before time, but even so Alex stirred in the warm box bed, felt the emptiness beside him where Mhairi should have been, and awoke.

'You are up early, my love,' he whispered, coming up behind her in the tiny scullery and catching her by the waist. He bent his head to kiss her cheek. 'It could not have been wee Hamish who woke you for he is sleeping still.'

'You forget, I am going to the market today. To sell Mrs Macrae's butter and eggs for her. After all Mrs Macrae's kindness to me, it is the least I can do, with her ankle swollen the way it is and needing all the rest she can give it. Annys will come with me and when we have sold our wares, then we will maybe call in at Mitchell's Court and visit friends.'

'And show off wee Hamish?' teased Alex. 'Confess. That is the real reason for this traipse into town, is it not? And me to be deserted, with no welcome after a hard day's work, and no supper awaiting.'

'Poor, neglected husband,' murmured Mhairi, smiling. 'Don't you want our friends to see what a fine wee son you've fathered? And don't you worry about that empty stomach of yours. We will be home again long before you return. Is there anything you would like us to bring back for you from the big city?' she finished, teasing.

[49]

'Only yourself, Mhairi.' He held her quietly, his head resting on hers, for a moment's blessed peace together. Overhead the various brothers still slept, as did Annys in the truckle bed beside wee Hamish's cradle. It was rare for them to have such time together; rare and precious. Through the open door into the yard came the soft purling of a dove from the copse behind the house, and closer at hand the dawn song of a dozen smaller birds, high-voiced and clear. The sun was strengthening now, laying long fingers across the grass where a pair of rabbits lolloped, pausing to chew vigorously on the dew-soft blades before moving on.

'They are away to take the tops off all your kale plants,' he teased and she looked up at him in horror.

'They're not! Quick, let me go. I must chase them away!'

But he held her tight, kissed her gently on each eyelid, then said, 'Hush, my love. I was only teasing. They will have to fight their way through a barricade of netting first. Lorn and I rigged it up last night. But if they do get through,' he finished in mock anger, 'I promise you they die.'

Mhairi laughed, softly so as not to disturb the sleepers, put her arms round his neck and kissed him in a rush of tenderness and love. 'What would I do without you, Alex?' There was a moment's absolute stillness in which joyful, loving trust turned suddenly to fear. Both felt it equally, both shuddered at the bleak gust which swept through their fragile happiness to scatter it piecemeal to the winds. Alex folded his arms tight around her and they clung together with a different need, each seeking at the same time reassurance, and to reassure the other.

'The quarry can be so dangerous, Alex. Promise me you will take care?'

'Would I do otherwise, with a wife and a son who depend on me?' He lifted her chin with his finger, and coaxed her to smile. 'That is better. I will have no frowns on a fine summer morning. And no groundless fears. Promise?' She nodded. 'I love you,' he finished quietly. 'Never forget that, whatever befalls us.'

In the darkened bedroom, the baby stirred and whimpered, then began to cry. 'And I love you,' she said, and added with a determined smile, 'and your noisy, demanding little son who will wake the whole household if he does not get what he wants, the moment he asks for it.'

'Obviously a lad of parts. Like father, like son.'

Mhairi scooped up the baby from the cradle and carried him across the tiny hall to the kitchen where she removed his sodden napkin and bound him up in fresh before putting him to the breast. The rhythmic suckling and the warmth of his tiny head against her skin were both pleasure and reassurance, but when she glanced up to see Alex watching her with a look of thoughtful gravity all her fears came tumbling back. 'What is it, Alex? Is something troubling you?'

He shook his head. 'No. I was merely thinking that you will have burden enough today with the baby to carry without loading yourself up with Mrs Macrae's wares to sell. You must not overtire yourself.'

'Annys will be with me. Besides, we will likely find a lift with a passing cart into Aberdeen and on the way home, the basket will be empty. Unless, of course, I load it with gifts for my dear husband?'

'I told you, I need nothing. But if you should see a length of pretty material that takes your fancy, for a dress maybe, then you are to buy it.'

'Well . . .' began Mhairi uncertainly.

'The quarry is prospering. Come the end of a year, God willing, there'll be a tidy profit to share out. Besides,' he added as she looked unconvinced, 'I like my womenfolk to look pretty and I've been putting a bit by.'

'Well, in that case, I might,' smiled Mhairi. She lifted the baby from one breast and turned him to suckle at the other. 'Annys is growing rather fast at the moment and she could do with . . .'

'Not for Annys, woman! For you. Will you promise me?'

'I will promise to look,' she temporized. 'But not to buy, for there may not be anything suitable.'

'Oh well. I shall just have to buy something for you myself, next time I am in Aberdeen,' he said, with a shrug. 'Though I warn you, I don't know a muslim from a charlatan.'

She laughed, as he had meant her to do. 'Muslin, you idiot. And tarlatan. Though there are charlatans enough around on market days and not always detectable until too late. So I'd best buy my dress length myself.'

'Promise me?' This time she found no escape and when Alex left for the quarry not long after, with a shout up the stair to his brothers to 'Stir a leg, you lazy young stirks,' he was whistling cheerfully, all unease forgotten in the pleasure of the morning. The rest of the quarry workers would not arrive for another hour, but Alex liked to get started early. There was work enough to do and besides, he enjoyed having the place to himself.

Mhairi, however, could not shake off unease so easily. Soon the schools would resume, there would be school money to find for Annys, and in the future for Hamish and any brothers and sisters he might have. Alex had said he had been putting a little money by: suddenly Mhairi knew that somehow she must do the same, not merely for her children's schooling, but for an unknown future.

At that early hour, the road into Aberdeen was deserted until they came to Woodside village and met the first of the factory girls, emerging bleary-eyed and yawning into the morning air. Beside the river to their left the factory chimneys were already smoking above a rolling green swell of summer foliage. Sun glinted from the water and where rocks broke the surface, foamed in a froth of white. There were wild flowers in the hedgerows beside the road – forget-me-nots, buttercups, the seeded whorls of meadow parsley and scented clover – and the verges were powdered with a fine layer of dust scuffed up from the road by passing horse, cart-wheel or foot. Mhairi adjusted the plaid which bound her precious baby safely to her breast and shifted the heavy basket from one hand to the other. As well as several dozen eggs, she had seven pounds of butter to sell and a cheese. It was a small cheese, but heavy.

'Let me carry it,' urged Annys. 'I am big enough.' She was indeed tall for her age, but fragile-looking, with arms and legs, Mhairi often thought anxiously, as thin and as graceful as a bird's. But the child was strong enough, and never ill. Her hair was soft and almost as dark as Mhairi's, her eyes nearer grey than blue, her skin pale as porcelain. Since their mother died three years ago Mhairi had been both sister and mother to

[52]

Annys and she regarded her now with a mother's anxiety.

'I know you are, my love, but I can manage.'

'Then let me carry Hamish for you. I heard you telling Alex that I was going to help you.'

'Did you?' Mhairi was silent as she went over in her mind what else she and Alex had said. They had talked of their love, their anxieties . . .

'Yes,' said Annys gravely. 'You said we would find a lift, but there has been no cart to give us one, so I must help instead.'

'All right,' agreed Mhairi, for the basket was growing heavier with every step. 'Take hold of the handle and share the weight with me. Someone is sure to come soon, for there are always carts travelling into town on market day.'

She was right. Before they reached Kittybrewster they were overtaken by a farm cart in which crates of hens squawked and complained in a flurry of straw and flying feathers.

'If ye dinna mind the company, get in behind, lass. It's a fair way to town wi' a bairn and a babby,' said the driver, reining in his horse, a heavy Clydesdale with feet like upturned buckets. Gratefully, they did, Annys scrambling up first to take the basket and Mhairi following. There they sat amid the straw and hens and rode into Aberdeen, as Mhairi said afterwards, like royalty in an open coach. The driver said nothing beyond 'Watch yoursel's now,' before a particularly nasty bump in the road, or 'Ye'll need to hold tight in this bit.'

They passed through Kittybrewster, followed the canal for a while at Elmbank where there were fields and orchards and lush banks of trees, then they were in the town, with the Wyness granite yard away to the left, and following the old road to the Green.

'Ye'd best get out here,' said their driver at the top of a particularly steep stretch of cobbled road which led down under the Dark Briggie. 'Afore ye shake the teeth from your mou'.'

It was anxiety not so much for her teeth as for the safety of Mrs Macrae's eggs which prompted Mhairi's swift agreement. The cart, though solid enough, had no springs and the wooden wheels sent every jolting vibration straight into any passenger's spine. She hoped the hens were less susceptible.

When they had thanked the driver and waved him on his

[53]

way, Mhairi stood a moment till the trembling had left her legs and she could stand firm again, then, carrying the heavy basket between them, she and Annys followed him down the cobbled track and into the Green.

The Green must once upon a time have echoed its name, but no longer. Any green there was now came from the cabbages and other vegetables which were offered for sale, from the bunches of fresh pot-herbs and the nests of leaves in which countrywomen arranged eggs or pats of butter, the better to set out their wares. Once, the main thoroughfare from the south into the city had passed through the Green, then with the building of the grand new street over the heads of the old, and the further streets which had spread from it, Union Street had become the principal thoroughfare and Holburn Street its route to the south. But in spite of all the new building in the town, the spreading shop-fronts of Union Street, the gracious new terraces and squares, the old Green retained its popularity, as a market-place at least.

Early though it was, the place was already bustling with noisy activity. Mrs Macrae had told them where to take up their stand and what to charge – 'Nae less than ninepence a pound for butter and more if ye can get it, for it's best farm butter and nae yon peely-wally imitation, and them eggs is worth all of tenpence a dozen, but ye'll maybe have to settle for eightpence if there's too many others i' the Green. My stance has aye been on the south side, just afore the fisherwifies frae Cove, so if a'body's taken it, just move them on. Ye'll see a body wi' cabbages, leeks and suchlike, an auld wifie wi' a red shawl. Kirsty's her name and she kens me fine. Tell her you've come in my place and she'll see ye right.'

The Cove fisherwomen were already there, black-shawled and sitting on empty creels or upturned boxes, their murlins and creels of herring ranged in front of them and glinting bright in the morning sunlight. Further down the Green the Torry fisherlassies offered smoked haddock and kippers, strung in pairs and heaped into baskets. Countrywomen from the outlying villages north, west and south of the town came into the square now in a steady stream, most with produce to offer for barter or sale. Some had only a few pitiful bunches of herbs, others heaped baskets of vegetables or fruit. Mhairi saw with dismay that there were already at least a dozen women offering eggs as she was and as many more with butter and cheese.

'Dinna worry, lass,' said old Kirsty with a toothless smile. 'They'll sell well enough. The rich folk are still in their beds, but when the town bestirs itself, you'll see. There'll be that many folk milling and shoving that ye'll wish ye'd stayed home in yer bed. Mind and keep a good eye on your siller for there's light-fingered folk about and there's nought like a crowd for hiding villains. Tie it safe in a bag under yer skirt: it'll need to be a brazen rogue to look for it there! The bairns are the worst,' she went on. 'If ye see a pair of quinies acting innocent-like, ye can be sure they're up to no good. Dinna take yer eyes off them, not for a second, or ye'll find yoursel' a pound of butter short or worse. The lads are as bad, but stay close by me and I'll see ye right. They know old Kirsty and the power o' her arm.' She picked up a hazel switch from beside her basket and brandished it with wicked glee. 'I've tanned many a backside wi' this little beauty,' she cackled. 'And I'll tan a few more afore the day's out. Dinna ye worry, lass. Ye'll be away home wi' yer babby soon enough, for ye'll nay have an egg left by noon.'

Old Kirsty was right about the crowds which came out of nowhere to mill and bargain, shout and push, jostling each other out of the way to handle the merchandise, choosing and rejecting. Annys cradled wee Hamish while Mhairi handled the selling. Remembering her instructions as to the price to ask and the lowest to accept and because she was not selling for herself, but for her friend, Mhairi struck a resolute bargain, but with an air of such apologetic politeness that most customers left well pleased. By eleven they had sold six of the seven pounds of butter, all the cheese and most of the eggs. Mhairi decided that if they were to be home again betimes, it was time for her other errand, to Miss Roberts's shop. Not, however, in Annys's company. Annys could sell the rest of the produce for her and when Mhairi returned from her discreet errand, they would go to Mitchell's Court together and visit the Lennox family and other old friends before setting out for Rainbow Hill.

'I'll take little Hamish with me and Kirsty here will help

you, won't you, Kirsty? You know you are as good with figures as I am, Annys. I'd best leave the egg money here with you, to keep it separate. I will put the little pouch safe under the basket. See you take good care of it and let no one touch it. Remember it is not ours, but Mrs Macrae's. Will you be all right, Annys, till I come back?'

Annys looked up at her with solemn eyes and nodded.

'Good. I'll not be long.' Mhairi adjusted the folds of her shawl around her sleeping child and made her way towards the steps which led upwards into the elegant sweep of Union Street and thence to Crown Court.

Miss Roberts's establishment was on the first floor, up a short flight of steps from the courtyard, which was reached through an archway from the street. Mhairi had been there many times, on one or other errand for the proprietress who enjoyed the patronage of most of the ladies of what she chose to call Best Aberdeen Society. Her Parisian millinery, she claimed, was the most fashionable in the country and she offered a discreet and efficient service whereby last year's models could be sent by steamer to London and returned again, renewed in the latest style. Her French stays were also renowned, but it was not with the ready-made goods, excellent though these were, that Mhairi was concerned. It was with that other seasonally hectic and much-vaunted department, hand-sewed dresses, both day and evening, with peignoirs, mantles, mantelets and any other garment a young lady might wish to buy or have made up for her, to her own measurements, from her own chosen cloth. Miss Roberts had her own seamstresses, of courses, but she employed the minimum and should a rush of orders, for a wedding perhaps or a special Assembly ball, leave her frantic, then she was forced to hire extra help. Mhairi had been that help on more than one occasion. Now, remembering the fears of the morning, the growing needs of her family, and her husband's loving, care-worn face, she adjusted her baby to a less conspicuous position under the folds of her plaid and resolutely mounted the steps. Alex denied it, yet she knew he worried for the future, for his own health and strength, for a time when he may not be able to work as he would wish. She had caught something of his fear in their embrace this morning and had vowed there and then that if Alex worked every daylight hour for her and for their son, then so could she, and together they would put aside a little, every week, against that fearful time, which please God would never come. But if it did, then at least they might have something to put between them and destitution.

She found Miss Roberts in what that lady liked to call her salon, arranging a particularly fetching bonnet of tulle on a little stand. She turned at the sound of the door, a professional smile of welcome on her sharp-featured face. Then the smile vanished, to be replaced by a look of surprise and ill-concealed irritation.

'Oh, it's you, Mhairi Diack. I have not seen you this five months or more. And with a child, too. Well, well . . .' There was the slightest edge of distaste to her voice and Mhairi felt herself begin to flush with anger. She had forgotten how patronizing the woman could be.

'Yes, Miss Roberts,' she managed with careful courtesy. 'I live in the country now, which is why you have not seen me. But today I am in town and I have taken the opportunity to call on you in the hope that you may have work for me? I believe you were well satisfied with the work I did for you in the past?'

'Possibly. But that was in the past. Besides, in the country, and with family obligations . . .' Abruptly she turned back to her work. 'As you see, I am busy at the moment. Another time, perhaps.'

'Certainly I am married, with a child,' said Mhairi with determined politeness though her face was flushed with mortification and rising anger. 'But I have time and skill and for the sake of my child and for his future, I would be glad of any work you can give me. You must be busy at this time of year.'

'I am happy to say that business thrives, as any well-run establishment cannot fail to do,' said the woman, with infuriating complacency. 'But I have no need of jobbing stitchers. If you need work, why not try one of the factories at Donside? Now, if you will excuse me . . .'

Mhairi bit her lip hard to keep back the anger. Jobbing stitcher indeed! She lifted her head, said quietly, with wasted sarcasm, 'Thank you for your help,' and turned for the door just as Lettice Adam entered it, in a rustle of silk petticoats and flowered muslin skirts. She carried a tiny silk parasol with lace edging and there was more lace on her summer bonnet.

'Miss Adam,' cried the proprietress hurrying forward. 'I am honoured, honoured. And what can I do for you today, Miss Adam? I have the latest consignment of the most beautiful little bonnets, quite exquisite, and on your lovely hair they would be perfection itself. Small caps are the height of fashion this season, but should you prefer . . .'

'Who was that?' interrupted Lettice, her eyes on Mhairi's disappearing back.

'I am afraid I don't quite understand . . .'

'That girl who just left, of course. Who else would I mean? Who was she?'

'Merely a girl who used to work for me,' said Miss Roberts, anxious to convey that the plain-clad country girl had appeared uninvited on her premises and would certainly not do so again. She was afraid that Miss Adam had taken umbrage and hastened to placate her valuable customer. 'Do take a chair, Miss Adam. It can be so tiring in the sun, though I am happy to see Madam has her parasol. Very wise. And such a pretty one. Parisian, I believe? Perhaps even, dare I guess, one of mine? But let me show Madam the very latest in . . .'

'Ah . . . now I remember!' cried Lettice, not listening. 'I knew I had seen her before. She delivered my petticoats to Silvercairns. But you said "used to". Does she work for you no longer?'

'She married and moved out of town,' said Miss Roberts warily, uncertain of which way Miss Adam's mind would jump next. The Adam custom was highly valued and she dare not risk offence, however inadvertent. 'It was no longer convenient. My customers require . . .'

'Then why did she come to see you?' said Lettice. 'Surely not to order a dress on her own behalf?' Divining the answer, she supplied it. 'Ah, I have it. She came to you to ask for work and you denied her.' Devilment took over. Lettice had had a tedious morning of it so far and she decided it might be amusing to make this snobbish little despot of a milliner sweat

[58]

a little. 'What a pity. What a great pity. Those petticoats were the most beautifully stitched of any garment I have had from you. In fact,' she elaborated with growing glee, 'I came here expressly to order a pair of dresses, one for evening, one for morning wear, and I was going to insist that they be sewn by the same hand that fashioned such delicate tucking on those humble petticoats of mine. Ah well . . .'

'I assure you, Miss Adam, that my seamstresses are every bit as competent as . . .'

'Of course. You could hardly say less. But no matter, Miss Roberts. Some other time.' She gathered up her skirts in one white-gloved hand and turned for the door.

'You are not leaving, Miss Adam? But you have not ordered . . .'

'No, Miss Roberts, I have not. You see,' she added wickedly, relishing every moment of the woman's discomfiture, 'It has just occurred to me that it would be far more convenient for me to employ the girl myself. And no doubt cheaper into the bargain. Good day, Miss Roberts. I must not keep my brother waiting.' With a serene smile she moved towards the door.

'No, wait!' Miss Roberts scurried round to reach the door ahead of her illustrious customer and bar her exit. 'I am sure I can . . .' Then in desperation she opened the outer door, leant over the steps and, abandoning the veneer of ladylike respectability, shouted in a voice that would not have disgraced a fishwife bawling her wares on the Plainstanes, 'Mhairi Diack! You're wanted! Come back here!'

After the first rush of mortification, pride had stiffened Mhairi's back, slowed her step and given new dignity to her bearing. No mean-spirited snob of a dressmaker with inflated ideas of her own importance was going to make Mhairi slink home in defeat. She was as good a dressmaker as Miss Roberts herself, if not a better. She would find work elsewhere, without difficulty. So, at the foot of the steps, she had deliberately lingered, retrieving courage and looking about her as any countrywoman legitimately might on a day's visit to the town. There were other establishments in Crown Court as well as the hateful Miss Roberts's and no reason why she should not favour them with her attention, if she chose. She was studying a window of snuff boxes and Dutch pipes, wondering if she might see among them something that she could afford as a gift for Alex, when the shrill voice summoned her and she looked up to see Miss Roberts waving imperiously from the doorway of her shop. For a long, cool moment she looked back at her, until the woman knew she came not in answer to the summons but because she chose to do so. Then she walked with slow dignity back up the steps.

'Yes, Miss Roberts? Did I perhaps leave something behind me?'

'Miss Adam wishes to order dresses and would like you to do the stitching of them. Is that not so, Miss Adam? So if you could wait a while until Miss Adam chooses her material, you could start straight away. As you know, I always aim to deliver the work in as short a time as possible, Miss Adam,' she continued, smiling her ingratiating smile once more.

Mhairi could not resist it. 'I understood that I was to do the work, Miss Roberts, but perhaps I misheard?'

Lettice Adam laughed. She had not had such an enjoyable morning for many a day. It served the Roberts woman right and she waited in glee to see what her answer would be. She, however, avoided the issue.

'If you will come this way, Miss Adam, I will show you the latest materials. In the present heat, *mousseline de soie* is proving most popular, unless Madam would prefer a *barege*? White is definitely the thing for evening this season and for the day dress may I recommend this delicate lilac shade?'

But Mhairi was not going to be scorned a second time. 'Before you do that, Miss Roberts, I would be grateful if you could explain to me what you require me to do, how much you will pay me, and what arrangements you will make for the collection or delivery of the finished garments? I do not travel every day into Aberdeen and my time is limited.'

There was a small silence before Miss Roberts said, through tight lips, 'If you will excuse us one moment, Miss Adam? Do please feel free to look about you,' and drew Mhairi angrily into a corner.

'Two dresses, one for day, one for evening. Cut out and ready to sew. The usual terms.'

'I think not. Your terms were for plain stitching. A dress,

and in particular an evening dress, requires double the time and skill, as you very well know.' Then, as the woman frowned in frustration, seeking how to secure the smallest possible terms without losing the whole, Mhairi realized. She had been called back not just to help with sudden extra work – if that had been the case, she would have been given the plain stitching of a dozen different garments – but because Lettice Adam for whatever reason wanted her. The fact that she was an Adam was for a moment disconcerting: the Adams and her own family were sworn enemies. If her husband or brothers found out that she had worked for one of them they would be horror-struck and furious. But Hamish was the only witness and asleep, bless him, while Annys's sharp eyes and attentive ears were safely occupied in the Green. Besides, she told her conscience, it was Miss Roberts she would be working for, Miss Roberts who would pay her. And would pay her well.

'I am sorry,' she said with the new-learnt firmness of her morning's bargaining, 'but unless you pay me half as much again, I shall offer my services direct to Miss Adam. She at least will send a carrier to collect her garments.'

It was an inspired guess. 'Very well, Mhairi,' snapped the woman with ill grace. 'Half as much again.'

'And the carrier?'

'Arrangements will be made.'

'Good,' said Mhairi with private relief. If the Roberts woman had called her bluff, Mhairi would have lost everything, for she could never have carried out her own threat. 'Then in that case, if you will excuse me, I have one or two calls to make before my business in Aberdeen is done. I will return this afternoon to collect my patterns, and material.' With a smile in which there was more than a little triumph, Mhairi left, nodding to Miss Adam the briefest of farewells that politeness required.

She was descending the steps from Union Street to Correction Wynd on her way back to the Green when she was almost knocked to the ground by a gaggle of ragged urchins who bounded up the steps and shoved past her at a squealing run. One of them at least she recognized from her days in Mitchell's Court, but as she clutched at the rail for support with her free hand, she had not the strength to run after and chastise them. She had suffered a shock, her heart beat uncomfortably fast and she was trembling with the thought of what might have been, had she dropped wee Hamish, or fallen. But he was still sleeping soundly in the folds of her plaid and, while she looked down at his sweet, untroubled face, the trembling subsided until she was calm again. Nevertheless, she made a note to give the mother a word or two, and the child more so if she got the chance. Then, her composure restored, she resumed her way back to the Green, and Annys.

Annys was feeling proud and happy. She had sold the butter and had only six eggs left to sell. These she had arranged, with solemn care, in a little bed of leaves, just like a hen's nest, and now she crouched on her heels, admiring the result. They looked so pretty, with their brown speckled shells clean and shining where she had spat on them and rubbed with a leaf, and with part of her mind she wanted no one to buy them so that when Mhairi returned she would see how beautifully Annys had arranged them. With the other part she wanted someone to come and buy them at once, so that Mhairi would come back and find everything sold and be pleased. She knew the money was right, too, though perhaps she had better check it just one more time. She slipped her hand under the basket, withdrew the little bag and tipped the egg money into her lap.

She had almost finished counting it, slipping each coin back into the little leather bag as she did so, when she heard a jeering, once-familiar voice so close at hand that it made her jump. Hastily she thrust the last of the money into the bag, clutched it against her chest and looked up to see two girls of about her own age, barefoot and in grubby homespun dresses, one too big for her, the other too small. The child in her sister's hand-me-downs had a decided squint. The more skimpily clad, the red-headed one, grinned.

'Turned egg-wifie, have ye, Annys Diack? Lay them yersel', maybe?' The girl's companion squealed in delighted laughter which turned suddenly to a squawking parody of a barnyard hen in which the first girl gleefully joined.

'Awa' wi' ye!' said old Kirsty, threatening. 'You'll not put your thieving hands in my basket, nor in the quinie's, neither.'

'But she's a friend,' whined Squinty, with a hidden wink at Annys. 'Used to live down the stair frae Lizzie Lennox afore Lizzie hopped it to yon 'Stralia-placie and afore ye hopped it yoursel', Annys Diack, for the kale-yard and the pigs.' Again, squeals of delighted laughter and a duet of snorting and 'oink-oink'. The girls pushed each other in jostling fun, knocking against first Annys then her basket. Annys clutched the money bag with both hands tight to her chest, her eyes huge with apprehension, while old Kirsty rose creaking to her feet brandishing the switch.

'Awa wi' ye afore I tan yer thieving backsides!' she threatened. One girl put out her tongue while the other, swift as lightning, seized an egg from Annys's basket and threw it at the old woman. It hit her chest and broke open. Annys's horrified eyes were on the glutinous, yellow spreading mass when there was the sound of a new commotion, in the crowds this time. Someone shouted a warning and suddenly, bursting out of the milling throng of marketers, came three small boys at the run.

'Quick,' yelled one, 'they're after us!'

'I see ye, Doddie Henderson!' cried Kirsty. 'And Willy Bruce. Dinna think to escape for I ken fine where ye bide and so do the police!'

The boys skidded to a momentary stop, eyes darting this way and that, then suddenly swirled around the two girls and swept them up in their flight. A moment later all five had disappeared 'like weasels into a dyke', as Annys described it later, and only a momentary flurry, a spilled and rolling cabbage, a shout or a tumbled hat, marked their expert passage through the throng of townsfolk, countryfolk, heaped baskets and the paraphernalia of a busy market.

'I am sorry, Kirsty,' said Annys over and over, her eyes big with anxiety as she watched the egg-stain spread.

'There's nae call for you to be sorry, lass,' said Kirsty grimly, scrubbing at the stain with a handful of leaves. 'It's them as should be sorry, and come sundown they will be, or old Kirsty's nae the woman she was.' She thwacked the hazel switch through the air with whipping venom. 'Wait till I get my hands on one o' they little runts and I'll nae be able to hear mysel' speak for the squealing.'

Suddenly Annys's eyes filled with tears and the old woman looked at her in alarm. 'They didna tak' yer money, lass?'

Annys shook her head.

'Then what are ye greetin' for?'

'They didn't pay for the egg!'

'Of course they didna, ye daft wee . . . Ah, I see what ye're at. Nay, lass, dinna worry. There's nae call for tears. See, here's another, a fine brown egg every bit as big as yours. There, it sits real neat in yon little nest and near enough the same size, too.'

Annys was making her thanks when a gentleman in riding clothes and a tall hat, with pale kid gloves and gleaming leather boots, appeared suddenly in front of her, a small crowd at his back. 'This girl, you say?'

'Aye, yon's the one.' 'Saw her talking wi' them, chattering like, as if they was friends.' '. . . lived on the same stair.' 'Gave it to her, likely, afore they ran off.' 'See, she's clutchin' something to her front.'

'Here, you watch your talk,' said Kirsty, standing over Annys like a mother hen over a chick. 'This quinie's wi' me and has been since sun-up when the likes o' you were still snorin' in yer beds. She's an honest, hard-working lassie and I'll thank you to remember it and leave honest folk in peace. It's them you should be after, throwing eggs at folk.' She scrubbed again at the stain on her front with a wary eye still on the gathering crowd.

'What is that you are holding?' demanded the gentleman of Annys in a voice of quiet authority.

Annys looked up into the man's frowning face, bit her lip with fear and held the little pouch even tighter.

There was something about the child's eyes which he found vaguely disconcerting, but he thrust the thought aside. 'Oh, it's like that, is it? Then if you cannot answer, give it to me.' He held out his hand and Annys summoned all her courage.

'No. I must not. It is Mrs Macrae's egg money.'

'Is it, indeed? And what would Mrs Macrae be doing, giving it to you? Always supposing Mrs Macrae exists.'

''Course she exists,' flared Kirsty. 'And why shouldn't she? Or hasna a body the right to *exist* now wi'out permission from folk like you? I thought this was the Green? I thought we was allowed to bring our goods here to sell and to take money for them? Maybe we're supposed to give 'em away for nothing? Well, if you've come seeking something for nothing, ye can seek elsewhere and leave the poor wee quinie in peace.'

'I merely seek what is mine,' said the gentleman with cold anger, 'and was taken from me not five minutes ago by one of that group of juvenile pickpockets. I intend to find it.'

'Well, ye'll nay find it here so away wi' ye and leave honest folk be.'

'Under the basket, mister,' said a voice from the crowd. 'They was jostlin' and shovin', pretendin' to lark, like. Maybe they've hid it, to come back for later?' 'Aye. Left it wi' their accomplice.'

'We will soon see,' said the gentleman, seizing the basket by the handle.

'No!' cried Annys, scrambling to her feet and clutching its rim. 'You'll break . . .' But he had wrenched it free and lifted it clear of the cobbles where a flurry of torn leaves and straw were all that marked its position.

'Under the eggs, maybe?' said a righteous citizen.

'No!' cried Annys again. 'You must not. They are Mrs Macrae's eggs and Mhairi said . . .'

But someone had pushed through the crowd to the front of the throng, a dark-haired woman with eyes of blue ice. 'What are you doing with my basket?'

Slowly Fergus Adam withdrew his hand from under the leaves and without turning round said, 'Merely looking for something: which it seems I have found.' There was a gasp from the crowd and a mutter of delighted condemnation as he held up the leather pouch by its twisted cord. He turned his head in triumph to confront his challenger and the blood left his face.

Mhairi looked swiftly from Annys, still clutching their own pathetic little bag of coins, to Kirsty, belligerently protective, and then to the accusing crowd.

'In that case, Mr Adam,' she said with the courage of fear and not a tremor in her cool voice, 'I suggest that in future you choose somewhere else in which to practise your conjuring tricks. You have frightened my sister.' She moved to Annys's

[65]

side and, still holding her baby in one arm, put the other protectively round her sister's shoulder. 'And now, if you have quite finished demonstrating your tricks, perhaps you would give us back our basket and leave us? Unless, that is, you wish to buy the last of our eggs? To you, it will be sixpence for the half-dozen.'

Before Fergus Adam could assimilate the turmoil of thoughts which this sudden confrontation with Mhairi Diack had caused and find a suitable answer old Kirsty exploded into jumbled explanation and blame.

'They varmints! I'd never ha' thought it. They get more light-fingered by the minute. One minute they was running, the next skirmishing about wi' the quinies, then ye couldna see them for dust. They kids is heading for the Tolbooth one day, ye can mark my word, or one o' they convict ships to Botany Bay. It's the stick they're needing and Kirsty's the one to give 'em a taste of it and gladly.' She lashed the air with her hazel switch in illustration of intent.

'Am I to understand that you know the children concerned?' said Fergus Adam, addressing the old woman. After the first startled look of recognition he had avoided Mhairi's eye. His face was slightly redder than it had been and his voice had lost the hard edge of authority of five minutes before. He was still, however, the gentleman, son and heir to Mungo Adam, one of the richest and most powerful men in Aberdeen. Kirsty, however, was not to be intimidated. It was one thing for Kirsty herself to apportion blame among her own kind, quite another to betray them to one of the gentry.

'Ye can understand till ye're blue in the face if it takes yer fancy, but there's that many bairns in the town a body'd be hard put to it to tell one from another. They was gone that fast.'

Fergus Adam looked at the lined old countrywoman before him, her black clothing shiny with age and still bearing the glistening traces of broken egg, her faded red shawl worn with dignity over iron grey hair, her sloe eyes unblinking and daring him to challenge her. It was clear that among her own people she knew where justice should fall and meant to see that it did, but it was equally clear that when confronted with authority ranks would close, as they had done now. Beside the

[66]

old woman stood Mhairi, straight-backed and proud, and if there was a hint of fear in those startling blue eyes it was only a hint and merely added to her beauty. Between the two protective women stood the child Annys and he knew now, as he should have known from the start, that her grave, unblinking eyes were a more timid echo of her sister's. In the moment's silence after Kirsty's outburst, the baby stirred and whimpered, Mhairi bent her head to murmur some soft endearment and Fergus Adam felt the old, remembered pain which he had thought conquered for ever.

'Enough,' he said, emotion making his voice unexpectedly harsh. 'It is clear that I will find no co-operation here. However, I am prepared to accept that this child was an inadvertent and unwilling accomplice.' He looked thoughtfully at Annys, noting her pallor, her fragile slenderness, the soft blue-grey of her too-large eyes, and was reminded of the particular tragedies of the family who had lost father and mother in so short a space, tragedies for which the Adam family could not entirely disclaim responsibility. When he spoke again, directly to Mhairi, his voice was quiet and had lost all overtones of superiority. 'I have retrieved what was mine and am grateful. I trust your sister will soon recover from her fright and suffer no ill effects from the day's disturbances.' He looked at her, half hoping for an answer, but after a moment's silent communion with those grave and steady eyes he knew he would find none. He gave the smallest of bows, as to a respected equal, and said, 'I bid you good-day.'

'And good riddance,' said Kirsty with feeling, as soon as the gentleman was a safe distance away. 'But wait till I get my hands on that Doddie Henderson and I'll tan his hide so hard he'll not sit down for a month. And they quinies was as bad.'

'It was Jessie Bruce,' whispered Annys in Mhairi's ear. 'And Evie Lennox, Lizzie's sister.'

'I expected as much,' sighed Mhairi. 'Oh well. I'll mention it to Ma Lennox when we call, but I doubt it will do any good.'

'No, Mhairi, please don't! They'll say I told tales and . . .'

'The whole of the Green saw them,' said Mhairi calmly. 'Besides, would you want them to go from bad to worse for want of a warning word?' Though that warning word was all too likely to fall on deaf ears, thought Mhairi grimly as she packed up their small goods and took her leave of old Kirsty. Jessie, Evie and the others had learnt their tricks at an early age and from an expert: Lizzie Lennox had a lot to answer for.

As for Fergus Adam . . . how dare he accuse Annys of stealing? Her face reddened with remembered anger at the mere thought. But he had withdrawn the charge, in his way, and with courtesy. She remembered those handwritten words on the little pasteboard card at the bottom of her wedding kist: *In friendship*. After all that had happened, friendship was impossible between an Adam and a Diack, but he had not looked at her as at an enemy. Remembering the thoughtful intensity of his regard, Mhairi was reminded of that other Adam, his imperious sister.

'Come, Annys, we have things to do. First we will visit the kirkyard and Ma's grave, and maybe sit somewhere in the quiet while I give wee Hamish his feed. Then I'll buy you a wee loafie at the baker's in Exchequer Row before we go visiting and after that, I've a message to collect and then it's home.'

'Did you buy your pretty material, like Alex told you?' Mhairi had forgotten that particular errand and when she did not immediately answer, Annys said, 'Alex will be cross if you don't.'

'Nonsense. Alex is never cross.' But he would be hurt and disappointed if she came home with nothing. 'As soon as we have been to the kirkyard, we will choose it together.'

They were turning into Mitchell's Court, their errands done, when they heard a loud whisper from somewhere close at hand.

'Hey! Annys Diack. Gi' us the money.'

In the shadows of the archway a group of ragged children lurked. It was Dod Henderson who spoke and he came forward now to bar their way. A freckled lad with sharp, watchful eyes, he was apparently the leader. Annys held tight to Mhairi's arm and did not answer.

'There is no money, Dod,' said Mhairi. 'The gentleman who owned it took it back.'

'That's likely, that is,' he jeered. 'Leastways, unless someone told.'

[68]

'They did, and before you say it, it was not Annys, nor myself, but people in the crowd who saw you.'

'That was our money,' he blustered, though her words had made him glance nervously over his shoulder. 'You'd no right to give it away.'

'And you had no right to steal it. I shall certainly tell your mother, and yours, too, Jessie,' she added as from the corner of her eyes she saw someone put out her tongue. 'Now let me pass.'

Sullenly, the boy slunk back into the shadows of the arch, but not before he had directed a vindictive look in Mhairi's direction. 'You'll be sorry, Mhairi Diack. And yer peely-wally sister wi' her tittle-tattle ways. You always was too stuck up to talk to the likes of us, but we'll pay ye back one day, see if we don't. Then you'll be sorry.'

Annys shivered with apprehension, but Mhairi said quietly, 'Don't worry, Annys, he is young and silly. He will learn better with age.' Then taking her sister by the hand she crossed the yard to the crumbling tenement where they had lived till so short a time ago and, with as much dignity as if she were entering the Town House itself, mounted the steps and went inside.

'I saw your lady friend today,' said Lettice Adam as she and Fergus drove home together along the Silvercairns road. Fergus had been late at their rendezvous, had muttered something about negotiations at the Macdonald yard being worse than useless, that he wished the old man would do his own dirty work and leave others to get on with their lives in peace and that, as if that wasn't enough annoyance for one day, there had been a disturbance in the Green involving pickpockets or some such. He had remained morose and taciturn ever since. It was as they approached the gates of home that Lettice had been reminded of a day in the past when the sewing girl had walked up the drive of Silvercairns with those petticoats in a basket. From the window of the house Lettice had seen her brother on horseback overtake the girl, dismount and walk beside her. She had teased him mercilessly at the time and in the boredom of the moment was preparing

[69]

to do so again. But Fergus made no answer; it was doubtful that he had even heard. Irritated, she said, 'Aren't you going to ask what she was doing?'

'As I have not the slightest idea of whom you are speaking, the subject is of little interest.'

'Well, I will tell you "of whom" as you so grammatically put it, beloved brother mine. The "whom" in question is that Diack girl you fancied till dear Papa warned you off with threats of disinheritance.'

'I would not do anything so crude as to "fancy" anyone, to use your absurd terminology. You must be confusing me with brother Hugo.'

'He at least has blood in his veins,' snapped Lettice in disgust. She had forgotten how boring it was trying to tease Fergus. 'Whereas you have nothing but sheep's whey. Or printer's ink. You talk like a dictionary, and a pedantic one at that. No wonder Flora Burnett threw you over for the Minister. He may be teetotal, but at least he's a red-blooded male.'

Fergus did not deign to answer. His sister's words had brought vividly back to mind his own sight of Mhairi Diack, straight and proud and defiant in defence of her young. She had faced up to him as an equal and he, he realized, had acknowledged and accepted it. Between himself and Mhairi there was an unspoken relationship which he could not hope to explain to anyone, let alone Lettice. He could not even explain it to himself. Damn Mhairi Diack, he thought with sudden vehemence. Why can't she get out of my life and leave me in peace?

'Perhaps you should go to the Minister for advice on how to woo a woman,' said Lettice sweetly as the carriage drew to a halt under the porticoed entrance. She gathered her skirts and stepped elegantly to the ground. In the open doorway she turned for one last barb. 'Of course, it will be a long, uphill struggle for you, brother dear, but there might just be time for you to have enough lessons before the Macdonald soirée.'

Afterwards it was agreed that Mrs Macdonald was to blame. To arrange a soirée in her own home during the summer season was, of course, perfectly legitimate. To invite her friends to join her was likewise both legitimate and generous. After sundry excursions into various parts of the country, near and far, it was pleasant to have the opportunity to compare notes, exchange gossip, winkle out secrets and draw conclusions, as often as not false, from the feast of conversational titbits to be enjoyed at first, second and even third hand as the evening took its happy course. Happy, that is, until the unfortunate social gaffe made itself apparent.

Mrs Macdonald, a respectable and well-favoured widow, had a first-floor apartment in Union Street, on the corner of Back Wynd, and the fine double windows of her drawing-room provided an enviable ring-side view of any civic procession or other such occasion taking place in the street below, a fact which sent her popularity soaring when the time for any such spectacle approached. The side windows of this convenient establishment overlooked the tranquil peace of St Nicholas kirkyard, where many of the tombstones bore witness to the skill of the Macdonald granite yard. One of them, indeed, recalled the sad demise of her own husband, on a splendid double tomb with space reserved for when his wife and sole surviving daughter should be called to join him.

It was in that daughter's honour, though this fact had not been intimated on the invitations, that this particular soirée had been arranged and Amelia herself looked particularly winsome in a dress of what Miss Roberts had assured her mother was the latest Paris fashion. It was of white tarlatan with deep flounces, pinked and ornamented with little blue flowers. On her reddish hair she wore a 'coiffure Louisa' composed of circlets of narrow blue velvet and white lace, and afterwards the matrons agreed over a succession of hastily arranged tea-parties that they had *known* the moment they saw her, dolled up as if she were royalty instead of plain Amelia Macdonald, the granite mannie's daughter.

In the happiness of the moment and oblivious of any social tensions that might ensue, Mrs Macdonald had invited all those of her wide social circle who had known dear Amelia for any or all of her nineteen years, and most had accepted. The fact that Mungo Adam and George Wyness were sworn enemies and had severed all social contact had eluded Mrs

Macdonald's memory, though she knew it perfectly well; and the fact that she knew it had persuaded both the Adam and the Wyness camps to accept on the grounds that she could not possibly have invited the other. Thus it was that, some twenty minutes into the evening's festivities, Lettice Adam, resplendent in flounced yellow taffeta, came unexpectedly face to face with Fanny Wyness, in blue.

'Well, well,' said Lettice, the first to collect her wits. She had remembered that her father was not yet here, having sent Fergus, Aunt Blackwell and herself on ahead while he attended to 'a certain matter', and she realized that when he did arrive, if, as was no doubt the case, Headstane Wyness was also here, sparks would fly. But that was no reason why she, Lettice, should not enjoy herself while she had the chance. In fact, for the family honour, it was the least she could do. 'Well, well,' she said again, barring the other's path. 'If it isn't little Fanny Wyness, crept out from under her stone to take the evening air. I am surprised to see you, Fanny. I had understood that when you needed fresh air, you sought it in the vicinity of Woodside village?'

Fanny blushed furiously and for one dreadful moment could think of no reply.

'I see the country air is good for you,' continued Lettice, with an expression of artless innocence which would have deceived no one but an absolute and slow-witted stranger. 'You have a truly rural complexion.'

'Thank you,' said Fanny, recovering some few shreds of composure. To receive the remark as a compliment was the only dignified defence to a barb like that, at least until she could think of a better, which, to her own astonishment, she did. 'But I see you have been in the country yourself. Those freckles are really quite attractive, when one grows used to them.'

A snort of laughter behind her made Fanny start so that the wine splashed from her glass on to the polished floor, but fortunately no one noticed. Certainly not Lettice who was directing the shaft of her scorn at the newcomer, Niall Burnett, son and heir of the widower Archie Burnett and her father's favourite runner in the 'Marry Lettice' stakes. But Old Man Adam had not yet arrived to cramp Lettice's style.

Or Niall's.

'Fanny's right, by George,' he spluttered. 'Your nose is speckled as a thrush's egg, and the more you stick it up in the air, the speckleder it looks. Very fetching, if I may say so.'

'No, you may not,' snapped Lettice, furious. 'And that inane laugh of yours can have only one explanation: tell me, Niall dear, is the donkey blood on the father's or the mother's side?'

Niall's eyes were as cold as hers. 'I see your wit is particularly dazzling tonight, Lettice dear. Predictable, but dazzling nonetheless, like your delightful ensemble. Allow me to compliment you – or should it be Miss Roberts? – on your corsage. Lilies, I believe? Creamy, freckled lilies.' He bent his head to sniff the posy of flowers on her breast and Lettice slapped his ear, none too gently.

'Keep your snout to yourself. This is not your trough, and never will be.'

Fanny, trembling with apprehension yet not knowing how to escape, thought for one dreadful moment that Niall would strike Lettice back, or swear. Instead he straightened and, catching sight of his father over the heads of the crowd, said smoothly, with a peculiar private smile, 'Come, come, Miss Adam. How am I to woo you as your father wishes, if you will not let me compliment you?'

'I have no objection to compliments, Mr Burnett, merely to insults, and to the people who deliver them.'

'Miss Wyness,' persisted the objectionable Niall, 'I ask you to bear witness to Miss Adam's hardness of heart. Here am I, throwing myself abjectly at her feet, and instead of treating me with the respect and gratitude due to even the humblest suitor, she tramples me viciously into the dirt. I ask you, is that seemly? Is that kind?'

'Much kinder, I assure you, than accepting your absurd proposal, if such it was. Come Fanny,' and, rashly in view of the many potential tale-bearers in the company, Lettice linked her arm through her reluctant companion's. 'I find the air in this part of the room quite stifling and the company more so.' She turned her back on Niall Burnett and, dragging Fanny with her, pushed through the crowd to another part of the room where, the double doors having been opened and the

[73]

chairs cleared, someone was playing the piano for dancing.

To Fanny's consternation, she saw Fergus Adam not five feet away and struggled to disengage her arm.

'Oh, you don't need to worry, Fanny dear,' said Lettice, seeing the direction of her nervous glance. 'You will not be called upon to give my brother the cold shoulder, or the warm one, come to that. He is here after quite a different prey.'

'But he does not . . . I mean . . . surely he does not like to dance?' faltered Fanny, remembering all those painful social occasions before the rift when she had been expected to make conversation with Fergus Adam although neither of them had anything to say.

'What has that to do with it? When my father orders, we obey. Which reminds me, Fanny dear, after your father's outrageous rudeness and disloyalty, I should not be speaking to you and certainly not in public. But before I link arms with a more suitable friend, do tell me about your country wooer?'

The question was so unexpected that for the second time that evening Fanny blushed a mortifying scarlet before stammering, 'I don't know what you mean.'

'Oh yes, you do,' taunted Lettice, delighted with the effect of her words. 'That country bumpkin you are always sneaking off to visit in your father's gig, when he thinks you are taking nourishing soups to the deserving poor. The clodpole with the mason's hammer and the muscles who used to work in the grounds of Silvercairns until we dispensed with his services.'

'You did not,' flared Fanny. 'He left because he chose to do so and I know for a fact that you have not been able to find a better, or anyone even near as good.'

'Well, well,' said Lettice softly. 'So that's the way the wind blows, is it? Fanny Wyness, I am surprised at you, setting your cap at one of your father's workmen.'

'It is none of your business what I do,' cried Fanny, 'and I shall visit whomever I please. I don't have to ask your permission.'

'No, Fanny dear,' said Lettice sweetly. 'But do let me give you a teeny weeny little bit of advice. When a man marries his employer's daughter, you know what the world says, don't you? Not that there is anything wrong with marrying for money. Everybody does it. Very sensible, in fact, especially when you have none yourself. But of course, you won't be thinking of marriage, will you? Just a little dalliance?'

'Tom Diack is an honourable man. He would not marry for money and he certainly would not . . . would not . . . *dally*!' Fanny spoke with unusual spirit and Lettice raised a deliberately languid eyebrow.

'Really, Fanny? You surprise me. As to marriage, you may be right – people are not always as sensible as they seem – but as to dalliance, from my own *observations*, I would have said that he was more than willing. But then people do change with age, so I am told.' With that she directed a charming smile at Fanny and moved gracefully away into the crowd.

Fanny stood dumbstruck, every quivering flower of happiness crushed and stamped into the ground. But above her misery rose a spreading cloud of anger. How dare Lettice spoil things? How dare she slander Tom Diack? How dare she suggest that whoever married Fanny would do so only for her father's money? But worst of all, how dare she insinuate that she and Tom . . . Fanny bit her lip to keep back the cry of despair.

'Was my sister being particularly unpleasant to you?' said a quiet voice at her side and she looked round to see Fergus Adam beside her. Once, not so very long ago, she would have been struck dumb by such attention from someone who for years had been the admiration of every young lady in Aberdeen. Now she turned to him with a look of desolation and said merely, 'Yes.'

'Oh dear.' Now that the eyes of their respective parents were no longer glued to them in expectation of an imminent engagement, Fergus found it surprisingly easy to talk to Fanny Wyness. 'You really must not take seriously what Lettice says. Half the time she does not really mean it, you know. She speaks merely out of boredom, or mischief.'

'Whatever the motive, she wounds just the same.'

Fanny spoke with such misery that Fergus found himself saying, 'Forget whatever Lettice said. Surely you are not going to let her spoil your evening?' and when she looked at him with the pitiful beginnings of a smile, added on impulse, 'Shall we dance? That will show her that you do not care two straws for her opinion.'

[75]

Fergus was already leading Fanny to join the set when he remembered his father. He had forgotten it was Amelia Macdonald he should be partnering, but it was too late now. Besides, his father had not yet arrived and if he did before the dance was over . . . Fergus shrugged. What did it matter anyway? He had enough disagreements with his father already. What was one more?

Mungo Adam was well pleased. The 'certain matter' he had mentioned had been the first ordinary general meeting of the Great North of Scotland Railway Company at which a Board of Directors was to be elected and, due in large measure to private lobbying beforehand, Adam had been included in the chosen few. After the public business of the meeting, there had been a further, most fruitful private meeting at which Adam had picked up useful information regarding the availability of scrip certificates for purchase, not only for the GNSR but for the Eastern Extension, the Alford Valley line and, most interesting of all, the proposed Deeside railway. He remembered conversations in the club, certain paragraphs in the daily press and even that Blackwell woman's inane twitterings. The Queen was coming north to Scotland again this summer, having taken a decided fancy to the place. The Perth papers were as usual gammoning their readers by claiming Her Majesty intended to disembark in the Tay and stay at Blair Atholl, but there had been reliable reports that an innkeeper in Aviemore had received instructions to have ready twenty-six pair of horses to take Her Majesty and suite from Fort William to Ardverikie on Loch Laggan where she was to stay with the Marquis of Abercorn. Her heavy luggage had been forwarded to Inverness already and on its next trip the steamer *Duke of Sutherland* would convey six royal coaches and twelve pair of horses. That ought to cause a rise in the price of oats and make somebody a fortune, thought Adam. It was a pity the Adam empire did not include forage. Someone, however, had tipped him the wink about Deeside and a possible royal interest in the future. Scrip certificates for the proposed Deeside line would be worth buying in. Accordingly he had paid a visit to Duncan Forbes, manager of the Aberdeen bank.

The fellow had been less than enthusiastic: businesses were failing, not only in London but throughout the country, the days of railway mania were past, the climate was no longer right for such speculation, and so on, like the voice of doom. But Old Man Adam had refused to be dissuaded. All right, those North British shares had plummeted in value, but one day they would pay rich dividends and every sensible man knew that the railway was the transport of the future. You had only to look at the Perth to Dundee connection to see that. Before the railway, a one-horse car with three cross-benches had room and to spare on its daily trip between the two towns. Now, tickets sold on Monday alone numbered three thousand. It would have taken the old cart upwards of ten months to carry what the new railway carried in a single day. And that was not the end of it. There would be stations to build, with station hotels, not to mention viaducts, all of good quarried granite, and anyone with shares in the company could expect to gain over and over, the moment the scheme was running profitably. And if there was a branch line with royal connections . . .

Of course, Duncan Forbes had given in in the end. He knew Adam was worth thousands, knew the granite trade had never been better, knew he would get his money back, with interest. The thought of that interest was an annoyance, but the loan was only temporary. Look at the railway profit which was waiting, just around the corner, for bold speculators such as himself, and that other, more solid profit which his own quarry would secure from the building work that the railway would produce. With the right family connections, all the big contracts would be his for the asking. Which reminded him: Fergus and Amelia Macdonald should have forged the vital link by now, and if Lettice had obeyed orders where the Burnetts were concerned, she also should be richly and conveniently affianced. All in all it looked set to be a most profitable day.

With these and similar monetary thoughts multiplying pleasantly in his mind, Mungo Adam arrived at the Macdonald door and was shown into the drawing-room where the dancing was in full swing. He was standing on the threshold, looking over the heads of the crowd for his hostess, when he heard a loud voice at his shoulder.

'Well, well, if it isn't Mungo Adam,' said Fanny's father, slapping Adam on the shoulder with deliberately offensive bonhomie. 'Wasn't expecting to see you here, laddie. How's business these days? Still flourishing?' Before Adam could find a sufficiently annihilating answer, Wyness went on, 'I hear you are trying to buy your way into the railway. I'd be careful if I was you. When it's time to choose from the various tenders you'll not want folks saying as how you bought your way into those too.'

'Are you insinuating . . .' began Adam ominously, but Wyness interrupted.

'I see your laddie and my wee lass are dancing. I hope it doesna give him ideas above his station, for she's not for the likes of him.'

In the sudden silence as the music stopped, Mungo Adam was clearly heard to swear, with vigour, imagination and considerable venom.

'Tut, tut, Mungo, old chap. You are forgetting there's ladies present. You'll need to wash your mouth out.'

'I'll wash yours for you, you blackguard,' growled Adam, and he would have swung his fist at Wyness had not Lettice appeared at his elbow just in time and caught hold of his arm.

'Oh dear, oh dear,' twittered Aunt Blackwell, hovering behind Lettice's shoulder. 'Do be careful, Lettice. You know how your father . . .'

Lettice ignored her. 'Papa, Mrs Macdonald has been trying to make a speech for fully five minutes and the whole room can hear you.'

In the second's pause that followed, Mrs Macdonald's voice sounded suddenly clear above the simmering undertones. 'Ladies and gentlemen, I have an announcement to make. A joyful announcement which I hope will give as much pleasure to all our dear friends gathered here as it does to those most closely concerned.' She stretched out her hands on one side to her daughter Amelia and on the other to Niall Burnett. 'These two young people are today engaged to be married.'

There was a moment's hush before the cheers and in the ensuing babble of excited comment Mungo Adam's voice said

[78]

clearly, 'Where's Burnett, the swindling rat? Just let me get at him and I'll tear him limb from limb.' Aunt Blackwell fell back, stifling a horrified gasp in her scented handkerchief, but Fergus pushed his way hastily through the crowd to join Lettice at their father's side. However, when he tried to calm him, Old Man Adam turned on Fergus, too.

'As for you, you lily-livered pansy, what the blazes were you about letting that mincing fop snatch the girl from under your nose?'

'Miss Macdonald is not a piece of cheese, Father, to be snapped up by the nearest hungry bird. Has it not occurred to you that she might have feelings?'

'Feelings be damned. She has money which is far more to the point. Money which you have deliberately . . .'

But Fergus had had enough. 'If you cannot speak like a gentleman in your hostess's house, Father, then for God's sake hold your tongue. You are an embarrassment.'

'How dare you, sir!' Mungo was purple in the face with rage.

'The lad's right, Mungo,' put in Wyness, applying bellows to the flame. 'I'd hold my tongue if I was you, before ye say something you regret.'

With a roar of strangled fury Adam lunged for his tormentor, dragging Lettice on one side and Fergus on the other half off their feet. But both held their grip on their father's flailing arms while poor Aunt Blackwell looked on in helpless and growing hysteria.

'Hush, Papa, hush,' cried Lettice. 'It really does not matter to us what these people do.'

'Let me get at the blackguard, damn you,' he roared, struggling to break free.

'Well, well,' said an urbane voice, though from a safe distance. 'I had not thought the announcement of our engagement would cause quite such a stir, had you, Amelia? I confess I am flattered. Very much so.' Niall Burnett looked directly at Lettice as he spoke and she felt something of her father's fury as she saw the look in his eye.

'You have every reason to be,' she said, with, under the circumstances, commendable suavity. 'The odds were a hundred to one against any sane girl accepting you, though

[79]

what Amelia's sentiments will be when she wakes up in the marriage bed and realizes just what sort of a verminous rat she has saddled herself with is another matter.'

At the words 'marriage bed' Aunt Blackwell gave a strangled squeal and collapsed with accumulated shock into a convenient chair. The entire company ignored her.

'For myself,' finished Lettice, with monumental contempt, 'I can only say that I am profoundly sorry for the poor, misguided girl.'

'Jealousy,' said Niall calmly, but his eyes had narrowed and there was a suspicious flush to his cheeks. 'My dear Miss Adam, it is plain for all the room to see that you would give a fortune to be in Amelia's place, but there it is. I am afraid the laws of bigamy prevent my marrying both of you and of the two, there can be no question who is superior, in beauty, manners and, dare I say it, disposition.' He turned and kissed Amelia lightly on the cheek.

'She will need all the *disposition* she possesses,' replied Lettice, 'if she is to live with you and survive.'

'It's her money he's after, not her survival,' growled Adam, but before he could add calumny to insult, his son and daughter succeeded in bundling him from the room and outside to the comparative safety of the street.

It was only when they were in the carriage and bowling along Union Street on their way homeward that they remembered Aunt Blackwell.

'Damn the woman,' said Adam. 'She hasn't the brains of a barnyard hen.'

'I will go back for her,' volunteered Fergus, but Adam's pride had returned in full force.

'Dammit, boy, we will all go back for her. This pesky town shall see that the Adam family stands united in pride and glory against the lot of them.'

'I've never heard Aunt Blackwell spoken of in those terms before,' murmured Fergus in Lettice's ear. It was remarkable how the evening had drawn the Adams together in a state of rare family accord.

'And won't again,' whispered Lettice. 'It will be back to the barnyard hen once she is safely in the carriage.'

But when Fergus asked the maid who answered the

Macdonalds' bell if she would kindly tell Miss Blackwell that her carriage awaited her, the maid stared, bit her lip, then broke suddenly into hysterical weeping. Miss Blackwell, it seemed, had suffered a seizure from which no amount of smelling salts had been able to revive her. She was upstairs in the drawing-room, dead.

Part 2

Emmeline Matilda Blackwell was buried with due ceremony and little regret in the kirkyard of St Nicholas three days later. It being more convenient than driving the two miles out to Silvercairns, those mourners who accepted the invitation to share the funeral baked meats – and there were many, for the Adams were still one of the richest and most powerful families in the city – adjourned after the melancholy ceremony to the Adams' town house, hastily opened up for the occasion, where Lettice Adam played undisputed hostess for the first time. She had been hostess before, of course, but always with Aunt Blackwell hovering in the background, a constant reminder of Lettice's youth, inexperience and dependent state. Now, however, Lettice came into her own. She had privately decided that she would run her father's house with a smoothness and efficiency which would outshine even her own best efforts until, before he realized it, she had become indispensable to him. That way she might escape whatever matrimonial fate he thought up for her next, for after his outspoken language on the subject of the Burnetts, father and son, she doubted he would take up that particular threat again.

Old Man Adam for his part was content to let Lettice take over, at least for the moment. Aunt Blackwell's death had relieved him of an increasingly irritating thorn in the flesh, for he had grumbled for a long time that the woman was not worth her keep, and by her spirited rallying to the family flag at that appalling party Lettice had earned her chance to prove her domestic worth. Besides, he needed someone to run his house and preside at his table and why pay out good money for another if Lettice could do the job for nothing? As to her marriage, that could wait. He had other things on his mind.

Fergus too was content, at least where the running of the household was concerned. He had borne Aunt Blackwell no ill will, but the house was a calmer place without her. Lettice was usefully occupied, which meant she had less time and inclination for mischief, and he was generous-hearted enough to be glad that she had escaped an unwelcome marriage, at least for the present. As for himself, with Amelia safely disposed of there was no immediate marital threat on the horizon unless, he thought with amusement, his father decided to renew the Wyness connection. Poor Fanny. She was an artless, good-hearted girl who had been pathetically hurt by his sister's malice. He wished her well. But, marriage apart, his father could do worse than mend the rift with the Wyness camp. After the Macdonald soirée they would be lucky to find preferential treatment in *that* quarter and if they were to fulfil even half of his father's impossible contracts they would need friends in useful places. As expected, Old Man Adam had refused to budge on the Duffus tender and now only a miracle would get them out of that particular corner. The Wyness connection, discreetly handled, might provide that miracle. Mackinnon, Fergus remembered, had come out of retirement to work at the Wyness quarry and Mackinnon had been a good friend to Fergus in the past. That friendship might well prove useful – behind his father's back, of course, and in secret. Otherwise, feathers, and oaths, would inevitably fly. With the prospect of such dangerous waters ahead, Aunt Blackwell, with her palpitations and smelling salts and her gasps of shocked alarm, was well out of it.

The end of the year brought three matters of varying importance. The first was the marriage of Amelia Macdonald and Niall Burnett at a grand society wedding to which the Adam clan was not invited and for which Miss Roberts took in so many orders that Mhairi had all the work she could handle. The second was the long-awaited letter from Hugo Adam, via the mail boat from Jamaica. The climate was oppressive, he wrote, the country in the grip of a severe drought, the sugar cane crops suffering in consequence and everything 'deuced more expensive than I bargained for'. The letters of introduction with which young Hugo had been furnished had secured him the entrée to high society, but little else. He had enjoyed a succession of splendid dinner parties, but had yet to find a job which suited his undoubted abilities. Consequently the meagre funds with which he had been furnished on leaving Scotland had early run out and he would be most grateful for more by the earliest possible means.

Old Man Adam sighed, grumbled, went through elaborate motions of parental disapproval which deceived no one, and rode into Aberdeen without delay to make the necessary arrangements.

The third event, and the one that was to have the most far-reaching consequences, was the arrival a week later, via a different mail boat, of an ill-written letter addressed to Mhairi Diack, care of the Minister.

For if I sent it to the tenement and Ma saw it she'd rip it open nae bother to find out what news I'm sending and raise hell when she saw. The letter had been more than four months in passage from Australia and announced the birth of Lizzie Lennox's illegitimate child, a son, *a couple of months back in May and him a healthy wee loon with a fine pair of lungs and the image of his da. He was a right bastard that one leaving me in the lurch but a good-looking lad and my Leo is his spitting image. You can tell the Adams so and say I'm wanting that money as was promised me when the wee bastard was born safe and well. Melbourne is a right fine place and with a wee bit money to back me I'll be able to set myself up in business nae bother. Ye can tell Ma that there's plenty openings for lassies like our Evie and tell her to put the lads to a trade. There's fortunes to be made easy for them as has a trade. You tell her. So this is what I'm wanting you to do for me Mhairi. You're to tell old Mr Adam or Mr Fergus if you think fit just whichever has the money that Mr Hugo's bastard is alive and well and needing that money I was promised if he's to stay that way. He can send it to me care of the Melbourne bank and the sooner the better. I hope you are well Mhairi. If you get fed up come out here on the next ship. It's a right fine country with plenty sun and greenery and queer animals called kangaroos and funny birds and all but they say as how there's huge empty spaces with nothing in them out back. That's what they call it. Out back. Tell Ma I'm fine but don't tell her about Leo or Da'll be out on the next ship to beat the daylights out of me. And see and send that money real quick. I'm relying on you Mhairi Diack. Your obedient friend Lizzie Lennox.*

Obedient. Mhairi managed a small laugh. Anyone less

[87]

obedient than Lizzie Lennox she could not imagine. Lizzie did exactly what she chose and always had done, regardless. But she had a son, a baby almost the same age as Mhairi's own wee Hamish, and unlike Mhairi she had no husband to support and care for her. Remembering her own protective love for her baby, her heart filled with compassion for Lizzie, so far away from family and friends. . . . *with a wee bit money I'll be able to set myself up in business, nae bother*. Mhairi read and re-read the words, then folded the letter with a trembling hand. What was she to do? It was out of the question to go to Silvercairns, but if she did not go, how was Lizzie to get the money she so obviously needed? Why had Lizzie not written to the Adams herself, from Australia? Surely that would have been the best and quickest way? But of course Mhairi knew why not. Lizzie had been a housemaid in the Adams' employ when Hugo Adam had seduced her, and was understandably nervous in any dealings with Old Man Adam lest he disclaim all responsibility and put the blame firmly on Lizzie herself.

No, as before, it would have to be Mhairi who acted as intermediary. But this time, she could not walk into the quarry office at Silvercairns as if nothing had happened. Perhaps she had better write? To Fergus Adam. Or merely send on Lizzie's letter? But as she looked down at the ill-written, smudged and grubby scrap of paper Mhairi's pride forbade her to do that. She would not expose Lizzie Lennox to the Adam scorn in such a way. But how could she humble her own pride enough to undertake such a journey, and in secret, because both Tom and Alex believed Lizzie Lennox had fled to Australia with a handful of Lettice Adam's jewellery, keeping one step ahead of the law. It would be bad enough if they discovered Mhairi had communicated with the enemy camp: were they to find out the reason, Mhairi dreaded to think what they would do. Tom in particular would be wild: he had his own reasons for hating the Adams, but if he found out that his childhood friend Lizzie had been exploited by one of them, ruined and discarded . . . Mhairi shuddered at the thought.

They would hear about the letter, of course. Such things could not be kept secret, not when it had been brought to the house by the Minister himself. The family had been out at work, but they would hear soon enough from one source or another that the Minister's horse had come up the brae to Rainbow Cottage, bringing a letter that he had had from another Minister, in Aberdeen. Any letter was a rarity, and a letter from abroad unique. They would want to hear the letter read aloud and more than once. Mhairi would be hard put to it to do so, with the judicious omissions and emendations that would be required. But that she could manage, provided she memorized the new version and hid the original safely away afterwards. Or burnt it. But as to visiting the Adams . . .

In the end, of course, she knew she had to go. There was no other way and at least her sewing work for Miss Roberts gave her the perfect excuse. At the end of January there was to be some sort of grand opening ceremony in Montrose, for the new railway line, and many of the town dignitaries would be attending, with their wives. Those wives, naturally, wished to be dressed with suitable originality and distinction and in consequence Miss Roberts was once more rushed off her feet. Since that fortuitous meeting with Lettice Adam in Miss Roberts's shop, Mhairi had been given regular work by that shrewd lady, lest Miss Adam carry out her threat and employ the girl herself, thus depriving the Roberts establishment of much steady custom. In fact, when Lizzie's letter arrived Mhairi had been working on a beautifully flounced and tucked walking dress in deep lavender merino. The moment it was finished she would take it into Aberdeen herself and use the opportunity to call at the Adam town house – for, it being winter, the Adam family had as usual shrouded Silvercairns House in dust sheets and retreated to the warmer confines of the Guestrow.

The shortest day was past, but the mornings were still dark: Mhairi rose by candle-light, crept about her morning duties in the gloom of grumbling firelight and an oil lamp with the wick turned low. Often there was a crust of ice on the water pail, but, the crust broken, the water on her face stung her sharply into wakefulness and set her skin tingling. Alex and Tom insisted on leaving for the quarry long before the sun was up.

'There's lamps, woman, and braziers, and too much work to be done for us to lie idle in our beds.'

But Mhairi worried for them. Both men's hands were chapped and raw, patterned with new cuts and old scars from the rough granite they worked with, and Mhairi worried that one day an infection would creep in and poison the blood. That the dust would get into their lungs as it had done into her father's and choke them slowly to death. She worried that they slept too little and worked too hard. Alex was too thin, his face too drawn, and by the end of a long day even Tom looked weary to the marrow of his bones. They would slump into chairs at the fireside with scarcely the energy to hold young Hamish, let alone play with him, and it was left to Annys, Donal and the younger boys to do that.

Because of the tireless pace of the working week, Sunday was a blessed haven of peace and inactivity. Except that by midday Mhairi could feel the tension rising and knew that were it not for the inviolable sanctity of the seventh day, Alex and Tom would have been away to the quarry the moment the meal was over. But it was no good remonstrating with them. Both Tom and Alex were determined that when George Wyness closed the books for the first year of the quarry's working, the profit should be not merely adequate but outstanding.

As it was, they spent half their Sundays discussing quarry work, even when visitors called: Mrs Macrae from the farm, the Bains, and, increasingly often, Fanny Wyness, sometimes with her mother but as often as not without. Usually she brought a gift: a cheese, a fruit cake, a jar of preserves or a dozen oranges from the market, and once, with obvious pride, a tongue which she had prepared herself.

'I am learning the art of housekeeping,' she explained, 'and Cook showed me exactly how to prepare it. She said I had done it "very well, considering," so I do hope you like it?' Fanny had looked so anxious that Mhairi had carved off a small slice on the spot, tasted and pronounced it excellent. Fanny's smile of relief and simple pride had been radiant. After presenting her gifts, she would sit and talk to Mhairi, play with the baby, insist on helping with any and everything there was to be done, and if Tom was in the room, her eyes never left him. Sometimes Tom would talk to her, walk with her to her conveyance, wave her goodbye, and Mhairi knew without a word from Fanny that these simple acts were the purpose and the crown of her day. About Tom's sentiments Mhairi knew nothing, though she hoped he realized why Fanny called at the house so often. But one thing she did know: both Alex and Tom had thrown heart and soul, twenty-four hours a day, into the quarry venture and if it failed to prosper, it would be through no fault of theirs.

But if their day started before the sun, so did hers. It was still dark when she arrived at the Adam town house on that chill January morning, and she paused a moment in the archway which led from the Guestrow to the Adam courtyard, wondering if she had arrived too soon. There were lights in the kitchen regions and more in the downstairs dining-room, but that might be only the servants, setting the table or seeing to the fire. As she hesitated, a man's figure materialized in the shadows of the courtyard, moved into the light cast by one of the windows, and came towards her. A big man, stooped now with age, and vaguely familiar. Quickly she slipped out of the arch and pressed back under the shadow of a neighbouring doorway. It was bad enough that the Adam servants should witness her visit: she wanted no one else to see her calling at the enemy stronghold lest word filter back to Rainbow Hill.

The old man passed within yards of her and she saw with a thud of shock that it was Mackinnon, the quarry foreman who had come out of retirement to help Alex and Tom run Mr Wyness's quarry. Thank the Lord he had not seen her. He would have stopped, spoken, addressed a jocular word to wee Hamish, asked what she was doing with the lad at this hour in this place . . . and no doubt recounted every detail of the meeting later to Alex and Tom. Her heart raced with the fear of what might have been. It was only when the old man's steps had receded into the darkness of the Gallowgate that it occurred to Mhairi to wonder why he should have been crossing the Adam courtyard. But of course he lived in the area, in one of the nearby tenements, and perhaps it was a short cut? She dismissed the matter as a mercifully narrow escape, slipped back through the archway and made her way to the Adams' door.

When she sent up her name with a request to see Mr Fergus Adam in private, she was admitted immediately and shown

[91]

into a small parlour which she took to be some sort of study. It had a table with books and papers upon it and a chair, and there were more chairs beside the fire which had not long been lit, for it still smoked black at the edges. The papers looked like the sort that Alex had in the quarry office at Rainbow Hill: accounts, specifications for contracts, calculations for tenders. Deliberately Mhairi averted her eyes and walked to the window where she stood with her back to the room, staring out at the darkened courtyard, with, beyond it, the outline of the tenements where she herself had lived until so short a time ago. The street lamps made pale pools in the general gloom and here and there in the dark mass of buildings were rectangles of light from oil lamp, fire or candle where the tenement dwellers were already about the day's work. In the house it was very quiet: only faint domestic sounds from the kitchen regions and, close at hand, the steady ticking of a clock. Then the door opened behind her and someone came in.

'Miss Diack?'

She had not seen him since that confrontation in the market on the Green. His face had been stern then, with anger and apology and the heightened tension which invariably coloured their meetings, rare though these had been. Now he looked at her with an expression of mingled surprise, courtesy and caution. But, with the declared enmity between their two camps, caution was understandable. He was as handsome as she remembered, and immaculately dressed, giving the impression not of having newly risen, which would have been perfectly understandable in a gentleman of his position, but rather of having been up and busily employed for some time. The papers on his desk confirmed this, for he crossed the room quickly, bundled them together, and slipped them into a drawer, as if tidying away something personal on which he had been working and which he would take out again the moment she had gone. Then he turned to face her.

'I understand that you have something you wish to discuss with me, Miss Diack, in private?'

Mhairi did not trouble to correct his use of her name. Instead she took a deep breath, looked him steadily in the eye, and said, 'I have received a letter from my friend, Lizzie

Lennox, via the mail boat from Port Phillip. She asks me to inform you that she gave birth to a healthy son last May and requires the money that was promised her for his upkeep. You will remember that this was the arrangement. As I signed for the first instalment, Lizzie has asked me to do the same for the second. Otherwise, of course, I would not have come.'

There was a small silence. Fergus studied the defiant woman before him with pensive eyes, noting the sheen of her dark hair, the set of her head, her slender neck and straight back, the proudly borne burden of the sleeping infant in her plaid. Her eyes were as incomparably blue as he remembered and despite her marriage to one of his own erstwhile quarrymen, despite her own humble origins, despite all his resolution, she had the same power to speak to his heart. Damn the woman, he thought again. Damn her for her interfering courage. Aloud, because he had been disturbed more than was comfortable, because he wanted only to embrace and kiss her and knew it was forever forbidden, he said with cold hauteur, 'And what proof have I that such a child does indeed exist?'

'None. Except the mother's word.' And knowing Lizzie, thought Mhairi grimly, that word was worthless. But Fergus Adam was not to know that and this time Mhairi believed her friend. Moreover she had anticipated such a question and had her answer ready. 'But as your family is so unwilling to accept responsibility for your brother's bastard I suggest that you arrange for the money to be available at a Melbourne bank, to be handed over to mother and child in person. That way your agent can check that a baby does indeed exist. He could also check the sex of the child, if you doubt that too. Presumably an Adam grandson is worth more than an Adam granddaughter?'

'Such a relationship cannot exist out of wedlock,' said Fergus with prim correctness, though he had flushed under her scorn. 'Nor will the child be entitled to bear the Adam name.'

'I doubt the mother would want that,' flashed Mhairi. 'The name Lennox may be humble but it is at least honourable.'

'You have said enough. The matter will be dealt with, as you suggest, via the Melbourne bank. And now, Miss Diack, I have work to do.'

[93]

This time Mhairi did correct him. 'I am Mrs Grant, as you well know. And I too have work. This matter, as you call it, has taken up too much of my time already. Good-day to you, Mr Adam.' She moved for the door, but something in her words and in the paleness of her face as she spoke them had reproached him and touched his compassion. He remembered that she lived out of town now, must have left home while he was still abed in order to arrive in Aberdeen so early, had the responsibility of a sister and brothers to feed and care for as well as a husband and child; remembered that his family had wronged hers and by so doing had driven a wedge forever between them. Remembered that, had things been otherwise, he would have loved her.

With an effort he suppressed his pride, and said, 'Wait, Mrs Grant. I must apologize for my sluggish hospitality. Will you not take tea before you go? Or coffee if you prefer?'

But there could be no olive branch between a Diack and an Adam and if Mhairi remembered that small pasteboard card with its message of 'friendship' she deliberately pushed the memory aside. Nevertheless she turned to him with grave courtesy and, he thought afterwards, almost a smile. 'Thank you, but I must refuse. Good-day to you, Mr Adam.' She opened the door and closed it softly behind her. Her departing footsteps made no sound on the carpeted passage way and he had to listen hard to hear the thud of the outside door. When he did, he crossed quickly to the window and, though he had not meant to do so, watched the slim, plaid-wrapped figure move through the shadows of the courtyard towards the archway and the Guestrow. Only when she was out of sight did he return to his desk and pull a sheet of paper towards him. He would write at once to the Melbourne bank. Then, he supposed, he had better inform his father that he had a grandson, a bastard to be sure and on the other side of the world, but at the moment the only grandson he was likely to have for some considerable time. It occurred to him that he had not asked what name the infant had been given. Oh well. His father was hardly likely to be interested anyway.

The necessary letter written, Fergus Adam opened the desk drawer, took out the papers on which he had been working earlier and resumed writing: 'House at Elmbank for Mr Duffus: payment to sub-contractors . . .'

The quarry at Rainbow Hill had been operating for well over a year and when, in early April, George Wyness studied the accounts for the first twelve months he was well pleased. From the very first month they had made a profit. After all expenses such as stabling and forage, transport, office supplies and blasting powder had been taken into account, as well as the wages of the steadily increasing work-force, with every month that passed that profit had increased. If they took on more men, production correspondingly rose, and the profit margin steadily grew.

'Aye, well,' said Wyness, beaming across the desk at his assembled business partners. 'I see you've done me proud, Mackinnon, you and your young helpers. There'll be a fine bonus to share between you, after a rare year's work.'

Old Mackinnon sat stiffly erect on the hard wooden chair, Tom and Alex on either side of him and all three looking uncomfortable in their Sunday best, but at George Wyness's words all three men visibly relaxed. 'I'm glad you're pleased, Mr Wyness.' Mackinnon spoke for them all.

'More than pleased. These accounts are excellent.' He drew the ledger towards him and flicked through the pages, savouring the new pleasure of owning his very own quarry. His arch rival Mungo Adam owned a far larger and richer quarry, of course, but he did not own a yard to go with it as Wyness did. Mungo Adam still held the whip hand where the supply of stone was concerned, and would continue to do so as long as he owned Silvercairns Quarry, but he was beginning to overstep the mark and to make enemies. He had offended the Burnetts, for a start, buy his outrageous behaviour at Amelia Macdonald's engagement party, and though because of the long friendship between Archie Burnett and Mungo the rift would eventually be patched over, it would be a flimsy patch and one which the younger generation would certainly not support. Though Burnett was in no way connected with the quarry business, except by his son's marriage, he was an influential shareholder and director of several of the railway boards, including the GNSR, and when it came to allocating contracts, Adam would find opposition.

He had offended the Macdonald camp, too, and though the Macdonald yard would of necessity continue to do business with Silvercairns, Mungo Adam would find it increasingly difficult to secure the favours he had been used to expect. Besides, word had it that Adam had been putting his prices up. Silvercairns granite was certainly the best in Aberdeen, some said the best in the country, but there was other granite very near as good and it did not do to be too greedy. Especially when you needed other folks' good will. If Mungo Adam wanted to be unchallenged despot of the granite trade he should have bought his own yard years ago. Remembering his own foresight, Wyness smiled his satisfaction as he continued to turn the pages of the ledger, beautifully handwritten in careful copper-plate and black ink.

The yard accounts were separate, of course, but there were inevitable overlaps and connections. A particular slab wanted by the yard and ordered from the quarry; a certain building contract that required a portion of polished stone among the unpolished, and sent to the yard accordingly. George Wyness began to look for these items as further proof of his own astuteness and business sense.

There was silence in the room as Wyness ran his finger down the columns, columns which he had checked frequently over the past twelve months. . . . *stone for new walls to the manse at Belhelvie . . . for a cottage on the Inches . . . road-metal for one mile of road at Banchory-Devenick . . . paving stones for London . . . for an addition to the schoolhouse at Lonmay . . . for a viaduct over the water of Cowie . . .*

'Well done, lads, well done. But that reminds me, there's a call for tenders for another viaduct, to span the Den of Logie. I've the specifications somewhere around and I'll let ye have them to take home and mull over. Oh, and there's talk of building a free kirk at Tarland and another at Oyne, with a manse and offices. When I've the details, we'll be offering for those, too.' His eyes returned to the columns, then his finger stopped.

'What's this? *To contract work?*'

Mackinnon pulled the book towards him, glanced at it and

pushed it back to Wyness. 'That was a builder in Elmbank who ran out of stone – did his sums wrong seemingly and contracted for too little. Asked if we'd help out. Only a small order, but we reckoned it was work and all work is worth having.'

'Aye, you're right there. Good man. And here's another similar. *Contract and polishing, via Wyness yard.*'

'Aye. The same builder. Fixed up wi' Macdonalds and couldna wait. We charged him, mind. Told him speed costs money.'

'Good man,' grinned Wyness. 'That's the way to show them. No job too little, no job too large and deadlines always met. I was not going to mention it just yet awhile, but I'm thinking of expanding overseas. There's a certain contract going begging for a homesick Aberdonian who's made a fortune and I've been approached. Not a word to anyone, mind. If Mungo Adam heard he'd try his evil best to steal or scupper it . . . but more of that later. All in all, I'm delighted with the way our first year has progressed. So to celebrate, and to show the world we're prospering, I reckon we'll give a party to all the workers, yard and quarry together. That is, if my fellow directors agree? It'll cut your profits, mind!' At the look on their faces, Wyness laughed aloud. 'Nay, lads, I was only teasing. The party's on me. We'll rig a marquee on Rainbow Hill, wi' braziers to warm the air, whisky to warm the stomach, and dancing to warm the feet. And tell you what!' His eyes lit up with sudden glee. 'We will invite our fellow granite men to celebrate with us. All of them – including His High and Mightiness Mungo Adam. And wouldn't I like to see his face when he opens the invitation!'

'*To celebrate a year's quarrying and a year's outstanding profits.* The man's a liar and a fool!' Mungo Adam thumped the breakfast table so hard with his clenched fist that the cups danced in their saucers and the silver cutlery sang.

'Hardly a liar,' said Fergus rashly. 'It certainly is a year since he leased the Donside quarry. Somewhat over a year, in fact, for I believe it was in . . .'

'Stop quibbling, blast you! You are as inane as that

[97]

Blackwell woman with your witterings. Outstanding profits? Who's he to say what is outstanding and what isn't? A profit's a profit and there's an end to it. The man's a charlatan and a vainglorious, boasting fool.'

'Will you accept, Papa?' said Lettice demurely, avoiding her brother's eye. Fergus had warned her often enough not to provoke their father, for at the best of times his blood pressure ran dangerously high.

'Accept? What do you take me for, girl? I'd sooner accept an invitation from the . . . devil . . . himself.' He stopped, suddenly thoughtful and frowned into his breakfast cup, idly stirring with a silver teaspoon, round and round. It was a large cup of a size suitable for a large man, but even so the blue-patterned china looked incongruously fragile under his massive hand. His children watched him warily, knowing something was forming in his mind, suspecting it would be unwelcome, and gathering strength to resist. But when at last he spoke, Mungo Adam's voice was surprisingly mild. In fact, he was almost smiling.

'I, alas, will have a previous engagement which can on no account be broken. But that is not to say that you will not accept Headstane Wyness's kind invitation, Fergus. Or you, Lettice. In fact, in order to show that we Adams, like royalty, are too dignified and magnanimous to bear grudges towards the lower orders – and to find out exactly what that thieving, devious bastard is up to with his quarries and his polishing yards – *I require you to go*. Is that understood? You will attend, as a gracious favour, and you will mingle. Mingle and listen and learn. Note the names of their key workers, who their principal customers are, where they buy their blasting powder, what is the turnover time at the yard . . .'

'That is a tall order, Father,' interrupted Fergus, 'for an evening's dancing.'

'An order you will carry out, boy, or it will be the worse for you. And if it's dancing that worries you, then you'd best partner the quarry foreman and kill two birds with one stone.'

'Surely I would be best qualified for that particular operation, Papa?' said Lettice sweetly, but Old Man Adam merely glowered.

'None of that, my girl, if you know what's best for you. You

[98]

will dance with Fergus or no one, and confine your mingling to the dinner table and the coffee cups. And when the pair of you come home again I shall require you to produce every detail of that crook Wyness's past contracts, present undertakings and future plans. Then we will set about putting the largest spanner possible in the Wyness works. Do you understand me?'

'Yes, Father,' sighed Fergus.

'Yes, Father,' echoed Lettice. But though both gave the impression of unwilling obedience, both had their private reasons for welcoming the idea of a visit to the Wyness camp. Remembering her own particular reason, Lettice added, while the chance presented itself, 'But of course I shall need a new dress.'

Mhairi could hardly contain her excitement. The party was to be for the whole work-force, Mr Wyness had said, from the humblest stable lad to Headstane Wyness himself, with their wives and families. There would be upwards of two hundred people, one way and another, for rumour had it that Mr Wyness had invited several important guests, 'so they can see just how well we run our business'. There was to be a huge tent, with trestle tables and as much food as anyone could possibly want, and afterwards, dancing to the music of fiddlers and a real accordionist. The day of the party was to be a holiday so that everyone could prepare for the occasion which was to begin at five and go on till midnight. From the moment she heard of it, Mhairi had been able to think of nothing else. As the wife of one of his partners, Mr Wyness had told her, Mhairi would sit at the best table, with Alex and Tom and Old Mackinnon and his wife. Mrs Wyness would be there too, of course, and Fanny. Mhairi wondered whether Fanny would contrive to sit beside Tom and hoped, for her friend's sake, that she would manage it. But who else would be at that table, Mhairi did not know. She had heard only that there would be 'guests'. What those guests would think of sitting down to dine with a humble quarryman's daughter and her quarryman husband she refused to think, but had determined that her whole family should look their best.

The grown men were comparatively easy: clean shirts and their Sunday finery, with well-scrubbed faces, well-brushed hair and a gleam on their shoes that you could see your face in and they would pass. Willy and Lorn were more difficult, with their arms and legs ever lengthening, but she had one or two garments of her father's put away in the kist and she would manage to fit them out somehow. Annys, too young and shy at eight years old to venture out among such a crowd, was to spend the evening with Mrs Macrae at the farm, so she need not worry about her, which left only Mhairi herself. She remembered the material she had bought that time in Aberdeen when Alex had insisted and which she had yet to make up: it was a particularly pretty shade of blue and would be perfect for the occasion, if she could find the time to cut it out and sew it, for she was, as always now, busy with work for Miss Roberts, including yet another dress for Lettice Adam.

'I will help you,' volunteered Fanny Wyness when she called at the cottage one afternoon on one of her increasingly frequent visits. 'I can sew a plain seam perfectly well, and would be happy to do so.'

'Oh no, Fanny, I couldn't ask you,' began Mhairi, embarrassed. 'It would not be fair for you to do my sewing for nothing while I get paid for doing someone else's.'

'But it is not at all the same thing. You get paid for doing a job of work. If that job was, let us say, cheese-making, would you still refuse to let me help you stitch a dress for a special occasion?'

Mhairi laughed. 'Perhaps you are right, Fanny. And this particular "cheese" is certainly taking up far more of my time than I expected.' She indicated the garment on which she had been working when Fanny arrived: a stiff pale green taffeta with a full skirt and neat, pointed waist from which fell in an inverted 'V' a double panel of a darker shade, ornamented from waist to hem with green taffeta bows. 'I have to make another dozen of those wretched bows, each one hand-sewn,' she explained, 'to go down the front of the bodice and around the shoulders at the back. It will look lovely when it is done, of course, but at the moment I wish the customer had chosen a plain cotton shift.'

'Who is the customer?' asked Fanny, curious. She felt the

taffeta between finger and thumb and added, 'It is beautiful material. Very expensive, I expect.'

'Nothing but the best for Miss Roberts,' said Mhairi lightly and added, not altogether truthfully, 'She does all the fittings. I just take what she gives me and follow her instructions. The customer, whoever she might be, is Miss Roberts's business, not mine.' To avoid further questions, Mhairi held the garment up against her front and said, 'What do you think of the style? Do you think a similar would suit me?'

Fanny put her head on one side, considering. 'Yes,' she said at last. 'But without all those bows. They are far too . . . frivolous and silly. I think you should have a row of little buttons instead, or just plain braid.'

'Fanny, you have exquisite taste,' cried Mhairi and Fanny blushed with pleasure. 'And I think you are right. I shall copy the pattern of this dress for my own – without the silly bows.'

'I have some braid at home which I think would be just the shade of blue for your material,' said Fanny. 'I shall bring it next time I come and if it matches, then you shall have it. No, please,' she hurried on as Mhairi began to protest. 'It is some that I had left over and if you do not take it, it will only go to waste. Besides,' she added, 'I should like you to have it. As a token of friendship.' To hide her blushes she bent over the cradle and scooped up little Hamish who was just waking from his afternoon sleep. 'You would like your Mamma to look pretty, wouldn't you, little fellow?'

'Of course he would,' said a cheerful voice. 'But doesn't she always?' Alex Grant dipped his head to negotiate the low doorway and came across the room, to kiss Mhairi lightly on the cheek. 'And how is my pretty wife this afternoon? Busy, I see, as usual, but not too busy, I hope, to find a cup of tea and a piece for a hungry husband?' He nodded a belated greeting to Fanny and added in explanation, 'We've ten minutes to spare while they load the wagons wi' building rubble, then we're away back to clear the floor for the next blasting.' The presence of Fanny Wyness had long ceased to be an embarrassment to Alex: she was Mhairi's friend, that was all. The fact that she was also Mr Wyness's daughter was irrelevant.

It was not, however, to Tom. Now, as he followed Alex into

[101]

the room, he felt the usual conflicting emotions: pleasure at the sight of Fanny, whose sweet face had grown dear to him over the past months, shyness, and a kind of perverse antagonism, which he could not analyse except that he knew it had something to do with pride and the fact that he was her father's employee.

Now as he looked across at Fanny he thought he had never seen her looking prettier. Today she had come unringleted, her heavy hair brushed smoothly over her ears and caught up into a knot at the back under a simple straw bonnet. With baby Hamish in her arms and the dark red dress which suited her so well, she looked like some kind of madonna in a painting, he thought, with unusual poetry. Then Hamish reached up two dimpled hands, clutched the rim of her little bonnet and tugged. As the baby, gurgling with delight, waved his trophy in the air, Fanny's hair tumbled from its pins and fell loose around her shoulders in a shining cascade which reached below her waist. There was a moment's shock before everyone laughed. Everyone, that is, except Tom who could not take his eyes from Fanny as she blushed and laughed and brushed aside Mhairi's apologies, saying, 'Nonsense, the little rascal meant no harm, did you, Hamish?' Nevertheless when Alex took the child from Fanny and held him firmly in his arms, saying, 'Give it back, Hamish. It's not your bonnet, it belongs to the lady,' it took Mhairi a few minutes to disentangle the bonnet from her son's persistent grip.

In those minutes Fanny pushed back the hair from her face, tried awkwardly to bundle it up, then let it fall again and all the time Tom watched her in dawning wonder. She was beautiful. Why had he not realized it before? Beautiful and womanly and . . . Then something made her turn her head in his direction; she saw him looking at her and for once did not look away, but held his gaze with her grave, dark eyes at once timid and inviting. He knew then, as he should have known months back, that he had only to make the approach and she was his. He took a step towards her, hardly knowing what he meant to do, and at that moment Mhairi retrieved the bonnet.

'At last! I do not think he has done it any harm, Fanny. But come with me into the bedroom and we will see what we can do to repair the damage.'

In another moment both girls had disappeared into the room across the little entrance hall, closing the door behind them. It opened again almost immediately for Mhairi to say, 'See the little horror does not touch my sewing, Alex. I will be back in a moment to put it safely away.'

'Go to your uncle,' said Alex, holding out the child to Tom, who seemed not to notice. 'Wake up, brother! You won't get out of your duties by pretending you've seen a vision.'

Abruptly Tom shook his head to clear it, took the child in his arms and made his way into the garden where he hoisted Hamish up on to his shoulder and walked to and fro, entertaining him with some nonsense while his mind went over and over the question of Fanny. They had been friends since the day Hamish was born, over a year ago now. They talked easily together, when they talked at all, but as to anything more, it had not occurred to him. She was his employer's daughter and whereas to marry the employer's daughter might be the height of some men's ambition, it was not so for Tom. The difference between them was a barrier as much of pride as of circumstance. But he was a first-class mason who worked every bit as hard as Headstane Wyness, he told himself defiantly. He was more than worthy of his hire and one day he himself would do the hiring. But in the mean time her father was a hundred times richer than he could ever hope to be and he had no right to think of her at all, however invitingly she looked at him. He would not have the world say that he had married to better himself, and he would not have her father say it either.

Yet seeing her with her hair loose, blushing in embarrassment, vulnerable and womanly and achingly desirable, he had wanted only to empty the house of all others and to have her blissfully to himself, to run his hands through her hair, to embrace and kiss her, to . . . Abruptly he closed the door on imagination. It was a sin to have such thoughts about an innocent girl, his sister's friend and his employer's only daughter. Only. That was one more barrier, for surely Headstane Wyness would want someone of more power and influence than Tom Diack for a son-in-law, to run his empire after him?

He heard Alex calling him to 'Bring my wee son in out of the

[103]

cold, afore ye freeze the toes off his feet,' and realized that the child was barelegged, still clad in the skimpy sleeping shirt of his afternoon rest. He swung the lad down off his shoulder, and went reluctantly inside to find tea made, in the best tea service, Mhairi and Alex drinking it and Fanny Wyness, hair neatly done and bonnet back in place, demurely doing the same. Blushing, he dumped Hamish in Mhairi's lap, grunted some sort of an apology about needing to get back, and fled. It required a composure far beyond his capabilities to join that tranquil tea-party, to sit so close to Fanny Wyness and yet not be able to touch her, to speak as if nothing had happened when it had been the most momentous day of his life. When they would meet again he did not know: but if she did not come to Rainbow Hill before then, he would see her at the quarry party and determined there and then to ask her to dance. After that, he was content to leave matters in the hands of Fate.

It was a gusty April day of sun and showers, but by afternoon the clouds had settled into harmless white billows, high in the sky, and the weather-wise pronounced there would be no more rain. The brisk wind soon dried the worst of the moisture from grass and hedgerow and by four o'clock it was almost dry underfoot. It was barely half a mile to the marquee, but a skirt could collect a lot of mud over such a distance and well-polished shoes could be ruined.

'I could carry you on my back,' offered Alex, when Mhairi speculated yet again whether her new dress would survive the walk. 'Or you could walk there in your shift, and carry your dress over your arm?'

'Alex!' cried Mhairi in outrage, then giggled at the ridiculous picture Alex's words had conjured up. 'But I might well walk there in my sensible boots and carry my little shoes in a bag,' she said, when Annys had been despatched to Mrs Macrae's, with Hamish and strict instructions to 'see he eats up all his brose and do not keep him up all evening, playing, or he'll winge and whine into the small hours.'

'You look lovely,' Annys had said, with awe, when Mhairi appeared in her new dress, the last stitches of which had only been put in that morning. 'Like a princess in a story, going to a ball.'

'I feel like one,' Mhairi had said, smiling, and it was true. She had never been to a public dinner in her life, let alone a dinner with dancing. The only dinners she knew were family ones, the only dances the impromptu kind, and once, long ago, in a public hall after a wedding. There had been no dancing at her own wedding, coming as it did so soon after her father's death. Fanny Wyness, she knew, was well accustomed to such occasions and for Fanny tonight would be nothing out of the ordinary, but for Mhairi it was a glimpse of that fairy-tale world of which she had dreamt long ago.

Fanny had shown her how to do up her hair in a particularly becoming style; Fanny had lent her gloves and a pair of beautiful white stockings which Mhairi had at first refused to accept, until her friend's gentle arguments persuaded her. But no amount of argument would make her accept the loan of any jewellery. Gloves and stockings Alex might have bought for her, had she let him, but jewellery even of the simplest kind was way beyond their means. To borrow Fanny's would be a reproach to her dear husband and a public shame. Besides, her dress alone was finery enough, used as she was to the plainest of garments, and with its neat pointed waist and full skirts, the row of little buttons and braid trim, Mhairi was well pleased.

'You look beautiful,' murmured Alex now, as he put her plaid around her shoulders. 'My wife will be the belle of the ball tonight and I defy any scoundrel to dance with her without my prior permission . . . which I am not at all sure I shall give.'

'And why not,' teased Mhairi, 'when you look so handsome yourself that you will be besieged all evening by damsels clamouring for the honour of your company? You might be glad to have me taken off your hands. But hadn't we better go?' she said, suddenly anxious. 'It would not do to keep Mr Wyness waiting, especially when we are to be guests at his own table.'

'Well, well,' said Lettice Adam, with a soft whistle of surprise. 'Do you see who I see, brother dear? Tonight might not be quite so tedious as we feared.'

[105]

Fergus Adam followed his sister's gaze across the crowded marquee to where Headstane Wyness and his wife were welcoming guests in a group which included, to his astonishment, Mhairi Diack, looking ravishing in some sort of blue thing which even to his untutored eyes looked the height of elegance. She could almost pass for one of us, he thought with wonder. Then, realizing that Lettice was looking at him too intently, he shrugged and said, 'The invitation did say to celebrate the quarry's achievements. Obviously it is one of those democratic affairs that includes everyone, to the youngest stable lad.'

'How too exciting,' began Lettice and was going to say something suitably ironic when Headstane Wyness moved and she saw for the first time the man who had been standing at his left shoulder: Tom Diack, once her own father's employee, who had worked on a broken wall in Silvercairns garden, in his shirt-sleeves and leather mason's apron. Now, he was looking uncomfortable in white shirt and correct dark suit, but just as handsome. Momentarily disconcerted, she said only, 'But confusing, when one sees them out of context.'

'Very,' agreed Fergus, though it was not of Lettice's confusion that he was thinking. Would she sit at the same table? Perhaps even at his own right hand? And if so, how would he address her, or she him? Retreating into rare flippancy, he said, 'We must take care, dear sister, that we do not speak to someone who should on no account be spoken to.'

'On the contrary,' said Lettice, recovering composure, 'you forget Papa's instructions. We are to *mingle*.' She shuddered with pretended distaste. 'And unless you plan to stand in this draughty doorway for the entire evening, I suggest we get it over and begin now . . . Good evening, Mr Wyness. So kind of you to invite us to your company celebrations. And Mrs Wyness.' Smiling graciously as one who bestows favours, she extended a languid hand. 'And dear Fanny.' She leant forward, eyes closed, and offered her cheek for a token kiss. Nothing happened. She jerked her eyes open again to see Fanny looking at her with what she could only call amusement.

'Hello, Lettice,' she said, her eyes taking in every detail of Lettice's new green dress with its array of green taffeta bows, but without her usual awed admiration. 'I did not know you were coming tonight.' Then as her father said a few suitable words to Fergus Adam, Fanny added in a tolerable imitation of her mother's best social manner, 'But do let me introduce you to Papa's new partner and his wife.' Before Lettice realized what was happening, Fanny had steered her neatly past the group to where Mhairi and Alex were standing hand in hand, talking quietly together.

'Mhairi, this is Lettice Adam, though perhaps you recognize her.' She looked first at Mhairi, then pointedly at Lettice's dress. Mhairi felt Alex stiffen beside her and her heart beat painfully fast.

'We have met,' she managed, and added with returning composure, 'Some time ago.'

'Let me see, when was that last fitting?' said Lettice and added airily, 'What fun this is! No one told me I would be dining with my dressmaker.'

Abruptly Alex turned his back and vanished into the enclosing throng.

'Oh dear,' said Lettice innocently. 'And before we had been properly introduced. Did I say something?'

'No more than usual,' said Fanny and added with a surge of liberating anger, 'But diplomacy was never your strong point, was it? Nor, if you will forgive my saying so, Lettice, is taste. All those bows . . . oh dear. Next time Mhairi helps you out with a dress, do ask her advice. She has a natural flair for elegance and I am sure she would not mind, would you, Mhairi?'

But Mhairi too had gone, pushing her way after Alex into the crowd.

'And you, it seems, have a flair for the slums, Fanny my sweet. You must tell me about your new circle of friends sometime, when I am feeling more robust.'

'Must she?' said a new voice as Tom Diack appeared at Fanny's side. 'I thought Miss Wyness had charge of her own life. I didna realize she had to take orders from you.' He looked at her steadily with eyes that were as blue as his sister's, but cold with antagonism.

Lettice gave a pretty little shrug and a coquettish laugh. 'It was not an order, Mr Diack, merely a figure of speech, and

[107]

Fanny is such an old friend. We understand each other perfectly, don't we, Fanny dear?'

'I think we had better move about among our guests, Tom. You promised to introduce me to your new stable-hand, the one who has taken Donal's place, and I have not spoken to Mrs Mackinnon yet.' Taking Tom's arm with a familiarity that brought a frown to Lettice's brow and an unusual disturbance to her self-esteem, silly little Fanny Wyness walked away with the dignity of a duchess, leaving Lettice flouted and alone.

It was her brother who rescued her. After shaking hands dutifully with his host and hostess and exchanging the briefest of diplomatic greetings with Mackinnon, Fergus had looked around him and seen only one figure he was in the least inclined to approach. God, why had he come? Why had he not told his father outright that if he wanted to spy in the Wyness camp he should go himself? Because that was what it amounted to. Fergus had been sent as a spy to find out his host's secrets and use them to do his host down. The idea sickened him and froze any small talk in his throat. How could he talk inanely about the weather, or the prospects for the year's potato crop, or the new Panorama show of the principal towns of Mexico until he had softened up his interlocutor enough to ask, 'What new contracts has old Wyness got in mind and is there any way to scupper them?' It would be not only ungentlemanly, but downright despicable, especially when all he wanted to do was to seek out Mhairi Diack and make his peace with her. He would ask after her sister and her family, beg her to forget past differences, and hope that she would think of him with friendship. But he doubted he had the courage to risk a rebuff. Once, as he stood looking about him in social indecision, he had caught her eye, but before he could move she had looked away and, it seemed to him, deliberately turned her back. He felt an alien, in an enemy camp. So when he noticed Lettice, apparently in the same predicament, he joined her with a sense of relief. 'How is the mingling? Productive?'

'Not as yet, but perhaps it would be easier, Fergus, if we mingled together?'

Easier for one's self-esteem, certainly, thought each independently as together they confronted the nearest couple and opened the first of many short, creaking and awkward conversations.

Dinner was announced. The guests took their places. Those on the high table sought out their names on the little pasteboard place cards and sat dutifully beside them, while those in the body of the marquee had the best of the bargain and found places with their friends. Grace was said and the meal commenced, sedately at first, but with growing animation as the wine flowed. Made bold by the excellent claret to which he was unaccustomed, Tom found Fanny's hand under the tablecloth and held it. Blissfully, she let him, until she required it back to tackle the chicken fricassee. Mhairi, sitting unhappily between George Wyness and Mackinnon, tried over and over to catch Alex's eye across the table and he as persistently avoided it, staring doggedly into his plate, or addressing his neighbour on one side or the other without once glancing in her direction. Just as he had ignored her pleas when she had hurried after him in the crowd. Mhairi knew she had shocked and hurt him to the quick by her deception over that wretched sewing. Why had she not told him from the start that Lettice Adam was one of Miss Roberts's regular customers? Except that if she had, she knew he would have forbidden her to sew one stitch for the woman and it was the best-paid work she could hope to get. And now she had lost not only that valuable source of income, but with it her husband's trust: that was patently clear from Alex's closed, averted face.

From the far end of the table – below the salt, as he put it wryly to himself – Fergus Adam watched her, wondering what it was that had brought that tight, unhappy look to a face which had been radiant an hour ago. Looking beyond his neighbour to her husband, he divined something of the reason, but not the cause. Beside him Mrs Forbes, the banker's wife, ate her way placidly through a succession of excellent dishes without uttering a word beyond asking, after the soup, how his father did, and commiserating over the sad loss of poor Miss Blackwell. 'I miss her dreadfully, you know,' she confided. 'Miss Blackwell was the only person in Aberdeen who shared my interest in our dear Queen who, rumour has it, may well favour our poor little town with her presence this year.' When

Fergus made a less than satisfactory comment on this thrilling prospect, Mrs Forbes returned her attention to her plate. Once, Fergus ventured to introduce the subject of the railway, but Mrs Forbes said only, 'I know nothing of such matters, Mr Adam. I leave all that sort of thing to my husband,' and applied herself once more to the lemon iced cream.

'Talking of railways,' said someone, whose name Fergus had not caught, 'met a chap the other day who claimed he had left London at nine in the morning by express train and arrived in Glasgow at ten o'clock in the evening of *the same day*.'

'If they carry goods wagons,' said someone else, 'that will cut your delivery times down, Wyness. You'll be able to claim an extra bonus.'

'Extra?' said Fergus lightly and either because the provision of claret had been more than generous or because the speaker did not realize who had asked the question, he answered it.

'Aye, on top of the early delivery one. Pity they can't fix a railway to Australia, eh, Wyness?' and everyone laughed. Everyone, that is, who understood the joke.

'Australia?' said Lettice. 'But it is so dreadfully far away.'

There was the smallest of pauses, but enough to tell the Adams that their curiosity was ill advised.

'Aye,' said Mackinnon, with his usual slow deliberation. 'It is that. But then so is New Zealand and there's folks queuing up to emigrate there. Otago's the place, seemingly.'

'Aye, Otago,' agreed someone else. 'Maybe there's good building opportunities there too, eh, Wyness?' Again the laughter, again the exclusion.

'There are plenty here in Aberdeen,' said Lettice. 'I know my father has always found so.'

'So there are, so there are,' agreed Wyness. 'And it's because there are those opportunities and because we know how to use them, that we are all gathered here this evening. Ladies and gentlemen . . .' He pushed back his chair and rose triumphantly to his feet. 'I give you a toast. To granite. May there always be plenty of it.'

'To granite!' echoed the company. They emptied their glasses and cheered.

More toasts followed: to the Wyness quarry, the Wyness

[110]

yard, the railway, various branches of which were mentioned by name, presumably by interested shareholders, to Wyness himself, to the Queen and all the Royal Household, and, most interestingly, 'To our newest venture – overseas.'

Hazarding a throw, Lettice said to her neighbour, the bank manager Duncan Forbes, 'It will be splendid if the Australian venture comes off, won't it?'

'I didn't know your father was planning one.'

'He isn't,' said Lettice sweetly. 'Yet.'

Then it was time for the dancing. Fergus would have taken the opportunity to leave, but Lettice would not hear of it. 'Nonsense, brother. I am just beginning to enjoy myself. Besides, we can't possibly go home at this early hour. What about that mingling father ordered? Unless you have done vastly better than I have, we have nothing with which to feed the old man's curiosity. Let us at least gather one small snippet.'

Fergus had no choice but to give in and when the call came to 'take your partners for the eightsome reel' at her request he led Lettice out to join the nearest set which, he noticed too late, included not only Fanny Wyness and her partner Tom Diack, but Mhairi, partnered by old Wyness himself.

Now was the chance he was waiting for: sooner or later in the intricate patterns of the reel he and Mhairi would come face to face, to dance together. When they did, he resolved not to lose the opportunity, but to speak.

His sister formed the same resolution, though with a different object. She had noted how Fanny's eyes followed Tom wherever he went, how Tom spoke to her with an ease denoting close acquaintance. Whether motivated by envy or merely mischief, Lettice decided to annex him to herself, at least for part of the evening. Virtuously, she told herself it was in the furtherance of her father's orders, quite forgetting that had he known with whom she planned to dance he would have locked her up in the highest available tower on the spot. But when her turn came to link arms with Tom and dance the necessary steps, setting and turning together, all her smiles and blandishments met with the same cold-eyed rebuff. He answered neither smile nor words, except once to say 'Excuse me' when he stepped on her toe.

[111]

'Still the same strong, silent stonemason,' she said teasingly. 'But you need not be so reticent now that you no longer work for us.'

'No?'

His calm indifference brought the colour to Lettice's cheeks, but, aware that Fanny might be watching, she stamped down her annoyance and said, with a deliberately coquettish smile, 'I hope you find more to say to Fanny, poor girl.'

'Aye. I do.'

As they parted to resume their places, she had time to note that Fanny was indeed watching her with an expression of satisfying alarm before her attention was diverted by the realization that the next time they moved up the set, Fergus would be required to partner Mhairi Diack. Knowing Fergus, he would make nothing of the opportunity, but she would watch and tease him just the same.

Alex, who had dutifully led Mrs Wyness out on to the dance floor, also saw the meeting, saw Fergus Adam say something, saw Mhairi answer and smile – only a half-smile, but a smile for all that – and if the music and the spreading gaiety of the evening had begun to soften his displeasure, the sight of his wife smiling up at his enemy reinforced his flagging grievance and nailed the frown firmly to his face. It was still there three dances later, when Mhairi tracked him down at a table in a corner, where he sat with Donal and her brothers, drinking whisky. She slipped her hand into his unwilling one and said, 'Please, Alex? Come outside and talk to me.' For a moment she thought he was going to resist her, but when Donal pushed him, gently but with ummistakable meaning, and her young brothers chorused, 'Go on, Alex. Dinna be so stuffy,' and when Mhairi added, 'Please? I was so looking forward to this evening, together . . .' he shrugged and pushed back his chair. Still frowning, he allowed himself to be led outside into the cool night air and, reluctantly, to the sheltering shadows of a nearby tree.

It was cool under the overhanging branches, and Mhairi shivered, but Alex made no move to put his arm around her shoulders. Then she saw, by the stillness of his face, that the pain of her betrayal consumed him. Her eyes filled with tears of remorse and love.

'I am sorry, Alex. I did not set out to deceive you. But when I realized I would be required to sew for . . . for Miss Adam, I confess I knew you would be angry if I told you. I wanted to spare you that, Alex, and the pay was so good that I could not refuse. Besides, she is not the only customer − I have sewn only three dresses for her in all these months of working − and I do so like to work with beautiful materials.'

'Which I cannot afford to give you.'

'I do not want them for myself, Alex . . . at least, this that you bought me is luxury enough.' She indicated the dress she wore and which earlier in the evening had been such a source of pride to both of them. 'I only meant that I prefer sewing silks to heavy cotton twill. As any seamstress would.'

'There is no need for you to sew anything, except for the needs of the family. Or are my wages not good enough for you?' The hurt in his voice was another reproach, the pride another barrier between them.

Mhairi had not meant to tell him yet, as he had worries enough, but it was her only chance. 'Of course they are enough, Alex, for our present needs. But you said yourself that we should save for the future. You work so hard for us, darling, and I worry that you will make yourself ill. I know I have earned little enough, but with Hamish growing and . . . and now his little brother or sister, I thought . . . I wanted only to help, as best I could.'

That broke through the barrier, as she had hoped it would. 'What did you say?'

'I said . . . oh, Alex, forgive me. I did not mean to hurt you.'

'No.' He looked down at her through the shadows, as if struggling to fight through a bemusing cloud. 'No, not the job. What did you say about Hamish?'

'I did not mean to say it, not tonight. We were supposed to be happy tonight,' she finished with such a wealth of sadness in her voice that he caught her suddenly to him and held her tight against his chest.

'We are happy,' he said softly, leaning his back against the tree trunk and cradling her head against his chest. 'You are my whole world . . .' But when he spoke again, he could not quite conceal the strain. 'We will manage somehow, my love, you

[113]

and I, with our little, growing family.' He stroked her hair gently in silence and as the misery drained out of her, she was content. The marquee was an eerie shape in the half-darkness, its interior lit with a score of oil lamps so that the figures of the dancers leapt and wove and heaved in one intricate silhouette. The sound of the music drifted across the dew-damp grass above the steady chatter of voices, punctuated by sudden exuberant shouts from the dancers, and the doors of the marquee stood open to the night. Couples moved into the light and out again, seeking privacy or merely fresh air, and overhead the sky was prickled with stars. She turned in his arms and kissed him.

'Forgive me, Alex? I love you so much.'

He looked at her gravely, his face in shadow. 'And I love you. But you must not keep such secrets from me again. Promise there will be truth between us, Mhairi. Always.'

'I promise.'

'And the sewing . . .' He hesitated, but before he could choose the words, she supplied them for him.

'Nothing for the Adam family.' Which means, she thought with resignation, the end of Miss Roberts's patronage. But there were other such establishments: she might even, remembering Fanny's praises, set up on her own account. Fanny would recommend her, she knew, and one commission would lead to another. And if it did not, then, as Alex said, they would manage somehow. The important question was that nothing should come between herself and Alex.

'What did he say to you?' asked Alex. The unexpectedness of the question took Mhairi by surprise, though she had no need to ask who he meant.

'Nothing,' she began, then, remembering her promise, added, 'He asked after the family and hoped they were well.'

'He and his sister have been asking a deal too many questions tonight. He did not mention the quarry? Ask how it was doing?'

'No. He was being polite, that's all.'

'You smiled at him.'

'I too was being polite. It was no more than that, Alex. I promise you.' Afterwards her conscience smote her for concealing her visit to the Adam house, but what good would

[114]

it have done to reveal yet another deception, especially now, when they were almost reconciled. 'I could not avoid him,' she went on, when Alex made no comment, but continued to look at her in brooding thought. 'It was the pattern of the dance, and he was very formal and correct. Surely you are not jealous, Alex?'

'And if I was, would it be so ridiculous, and you the best-looking girl in the whole marquee?'

'Yes, it would.'

As he looked down at her upturned, loving face, the last of his hurt and jealousy retreated into the darkness and he bent his head and kissed her.

'But to show the world – and Fergus Adam – that you are mine,' he said later, with a returning frown, 'shall we join the dancers? And let no man come between us if he values his life.'

He slipped a protective arm around her waist and led her back towards the light.

'We must go back,' murmured Fanny, without conviction. 'Papa will wonder where I am.'

'No, he won't. He is far too busy enjoying himself – as I am,' and Tom kissed her yet again. Whether he would have had the courage without the fortification of her father's liquid hospitality is doubtful, though even sober he might well have succumbed to Fanny's open invitation. For when she saw that artful look on Lettice's face, a look she remembered from too many parties in the past, timid Fanny Wyness had decided it was time to fight back. As soon as the dance was over and before Lettice could move in for the kill, she had clutched Tom's arm, brazenly told him she was feeling positively faint after so much exertion and would he please take her outside, quickly, for a little cooling air.

Once outside they had walked decorously up and down for some minutes until their eyes had grown accustomed to the darkness, then, realizing that Tom would be too diffident to do so himself, and fearing to lose her opportunity, Fanny had led Tom deliberately into the deeper darkness of a nearby clump of trees. Here she had turned to face him, put her small hands against the broad strength of his chest and said, 'You will think me dreadfully bold, Tom, but I might never find such a chance again to tell you that . . .'

Here her courage failed her, but the open adoration in her eyes as she looked up at him told Tom more clearly than any words could have done what she wanted to say. For a moment he hesitated, remembering that her father was his host, his employer, a rich and influential citizen way above Tom's sphere, but only for a moment before instinct swept all such intellectual arguments away and he kissed her. He half expected her to push him away, protesting, but instead her hands crept up and round his neck and with the realization that she was offering herself without reservation, Tom forgot Wyness, quarry, social spheres, everything, in the sweetness of their first embrace. At last he broke away, but only to hold her face in his hands and study it with solemn wonder.

'What is the matter?' asked Fanny, breathless. His face was in darkness, but in the sky behind the outline of his head, stars pricked the night with brilliance.

'Nothing, except that I think I am dreaming.'

'You have stars in your hair,' she whispered, 'so perhaps I am dreaming too.'

'You have stars in your eyes,' he said softly and kissed first one eyelid, then the other. 'That is to keep them there.'

'Is it very brazen of me,' she murmured a long time later, 'to say I love you?'

'Very, but I could never resist brazen women.' So they kissed, murmured endearments, kissed again and felt the old world fall away as a new and delightful one took its place. Both lost all track of time until suddenly the awareness of an unnatural silence broke in upon their private happiness and Fanny gasped in horror, 'The music has stopped! The party is ending and Papa will be looking for me. Oh dear, what shall I do?'

'Nothing, my sweet,' grinned Tom, 'except perhaps tidy up your hair where it has come loose at the back.'

'It hasn't?' cried Fanny, appalled. Her hands flew to her hair to probe and twist and secure the escaping strands as best she could, but the lifting of her arms had lifted her bosom most beguilingly and before she knew what he was about, Tom had slipped his arms around her waist and pulled her

[116]

close, and was kissing the skin of her shoulder, her throat, her ear and finally her lips. She struggled to break free, then stopped struggling, and this time there was a new and aching need in their embrace.

Abruptly, Fanny broke away. 'I must go.' With trembling hands she finished pinning up her hair, straightened the folds of her dress and said, in a small voice, 'Do I look all right?'

'Beautiful,' breathed Tom softly. 'My radiant, beautiful love.'

'Oh dear. Do you think Papa will guess?'

'What does it matter if he does guess? Let them all guess if they choose. *I love Fanny Wyness and Fanny loves me.* There, no need for guessing now. I have proclaimed it to the stars and they can tell the whole wide world.'

But in spite of his valiant words Tom knew, as she did, that it would be prudent to keep their secret, at least until they had prepared the way. There were too many obstacles to be overcome, not least the obstacles of pride and circumstance. Soberly, sedately, not touching, they made their way back to the marquee, to mingle unobtrusively with the departing guests.

'Well?' demanded Old Man Adam, confronting his returning children on the steps of Silvercairns, though the time was long past midnight. 'What did you find out?'

'Really, Father,' protested Fergus, handing Lettice down from the carriage. 'You might at least have the consideration to wait until we are inside. We have had a tedious evening and a more than tedious drive home. I do not know about Lettice, but I would appreciate a brandy.'

'Would you, indeed? And I would appreciate an account of your evening, tedious though it might have been. You forget I sent you there, for a specific purpose, and I require to know the result.'

'Come inside, Papa dear,' soothed Lettice, taking his arm and steering him into the hall. 'We cannot talk on the steps in front of the servants. See to the fire in the library,' she ordered one of the latter, 'and send up brandy and a tray of tea. I will just remove my cloak, Papa, then I will join you. What a relief

[117]

it is to be home.'

'Well?' repeated Adam when Lettice had joined them in the library five minutes later.

'Tea, Papa?' said Lettice sweetly. 'Or will you join Fergus in a brandy?'

'Neither, damn you, until you have answered my question.'

'It was a tedious evening, as I believe I have already mentioned,' began Fergus and his father made an explosive noise of mingled disgust and fury, 'but not altogether unproductive . . .'

'Get on with it, man! Speak in plain English and tell me what that crook Wyness is up to.'

'His new quarry is proving successful – very much so, I believe. It is working to its present capacity, but there is talk of hiring extra men in order to step up production.'

'How did you find out that?' said Lettice with surprised approval.

It was pure conjecture on Fergus's part but he was not going to say so. 'There is a policy of economic use of all material,' went on Fergus, freely elaborating now. 'Everything quarried is used for one purpose or another. For the smaller stones they employ causeymen as we do and kerb masons. The rubble goes for building purposes and. . .'

'Yes, yes, we know all that. Every quarry with any sense does the same. But how is he making his money, damn you?'

'As you do, Father,' said Fergus, regarding the irascible old man in the chair across the fireplace from his own with detached curiosity. He had not realized the fanatical extent of his father's enmity towards Wyness, presumably the enmity of the powerful towards a too-threatening contender, and his father must consider Wyness very threatening indeed, for at the moment he might as well have steam coming out of his ears, or flame for breath. But Fergus was not to be intimidated this time. 'From the supply of building stone for as many projects as he can handle. As you do, he tenders for any and everything. As you do, he applies for railway contracts, for the building of viaducts, churches, houses. He sends paving stones to London and, from his polishing yard, tombstones, plinths, and balustrades.'

'*I know all that!*' roared Old Man Adam, thumping the arm

of his chair with a furious fist. 'You don't have to drink the fellow's champagne to find out what the whole town knows already. Tell me the real secrets.'

Fergus looked across the room to where Lettice sat at the tea-table, skirts elegantly draped, and smiling into her teacup at his discomfiture. Deliberately he said, 'Lettice is the one to tell you those, Father. She managed to have some most informative conversations with several unsuspecting gentlemen.' He reached for the brandy decanter, poured himself a refill and settled back in his chair to let his sister extricate herself as best she could. After a look of concentrated venom directed at her brother, she began.

'There was much veiled talk, Papa, of a venture "overseas".'

'Was there indeed?' Adam leant forward in his chair with close attention. 'Well, go on, girl. Go on.'

'Someone mentioned Australia, then saw that we were listening and changed the subject. I tried to find out more, but I am afraid they were uncommunicative and that in itself is suspect. They were happy enough to talk about other things. As Fergus said, they plan to take on more men, and do a lot more blasting.'

'Who told you that?' asked Fergus, surprised. 'Mackinnon?'

'No. It was Tom Diack, actually,' lied Lettice and immediately wished she hadn't, but the expected outburst from her father did not come. Instead he tapped his fingertips together in frowning thought, and she saw with astonishment the beginnings of a private and villainous smile.

'More men,' he repeated softly, 'and more blasting. Well, well. But Silvercairns can out-produce them any day. 'Tell me, Fergus, he said, suddenly brisk and businesslike. 'How is our own blasting going?'

'Very well.' It was barely twenty-four hours since his father had inspected the blastings himself.

'And the men are competent? They know what they are doing?'

'Of course. Really, Father, I do not see . . .'

'Who is the most skilled at making powder charges and setting fuses?'

'All the blasting team are, Father. I would not employ them otherwise.'

'The best, boy. The best.' Old Man Adam snapped his fingers impatiently, a gleam of demonic excitement in his eyes. With a sigh, Fergus began to go through such of the names as he could remember until his father interrupted with an impatient wave of the hand.

'Enough. I did not ask for an inventory of the entire work-force, only for the best. But see those men get to work first thing, and fast: any trouble, and you tell them I'll be down myself before the day is out to see what progress they've made and if it isn't good enough, they are *out*. As for Australia, that villain Wyness will be begging to emigrate there by the time I've finished with him.'

The old man smiled a private smile of satisfaction. 'And now, Fergus, I would appreciate a glass of my own brandy, unless you plan to drink that decanter dry unaided.'

Lettice and Fergus exchanged glances, of curiosity on one side and apprehension on the other. What was Old Man Adam planning?

'Well, don't sit there like a pair of village idiots with your mouths gaping. Tell me more about this fiasco of an evening. Did it rain? Did the marquee spring a leak? Was the boiled mutton on the turn or the butter rancid? And most important, *who was there?*'

When at last they managed to make their excuses and escape to bed, they left Old Man Adam still maniacally awake and obviously plotting.

'What do you think he is up to?' whispered Lettice as they parted on the upstairs landing.

'I have no idea,' sighed her brother, 'but whatever it is, Headstane Wyness had better watch out.'

The last of the guests had made their farewells and departed into the April night, some on foot, some on horseback, and the rest in various kinds of wheeled vehicle from the humblest haycart to the Adams' newest carriage, a glossy black extravagance ornamented with gold. Now the only vehicle remaining was the hired carriage Wyness himself had ordered to drive him and his family home, their own being, as Mrs Wyness had pointed out, a wee bit on the small side to accommodate all of them as well as her own and Fanny's voluminous skirts. Wyness handed his wife up into the well-padded interior, saw her settled with a rug over her knees, then did the same for Fanny. Finally he gave his instructions to the driver, climbed in after them and closed the door.

'Well, Fanny?' said Wyness, when the carriage was safely in motion and bowling along the country lane at a respectable speed. 'Did you enjoy the evening?' The moon was high and bright, making the swaying lanterns superfluous and throwing the sleeping landscape into sharp relief.

'Oh yes, Papa,' she said, with shining eyes. 'It was the most wonderful evening.'

'Really?' Wyness raised an eyebrow in surprise. A dinner for the work-force in a hired marquee was certainly a great night out for them, and the food and wine had been excellent, but Fanny was used to dining in the private houses of Aberdeen society, dancing in their drawing-rooms, or attending those elegant supper and dance things at the Assembly Rooms, with her Aberdeen friends. He had never heard her speak of these occasions as 'wonderful'. 'I am glad to hear it, Fanny. Tell me what you enjoyed the most.'

For once Fanny's tongue was not tied. 'The dancing, I think, Papa. The music was so beautifully played and then to dance inside a marquee, with so many happy people, was . . . was . . . oh, it just made me feel happy too, Papa.'

'And the dinner?' asked her father, watching her shrewdly. 'It was not the sort of food you'd be used to at yon dinners you go to with your friends.'

'Oh no, Papa. It was *much* nicer.' Suddenly noticing the way her father was studying her, with a look of amused speculation, Fanny blushed and said hastily, 'Mhairi enjoyed it too. She told me she had never been to such an evening in her life.'

'No, I don't expect she has. Her father was a causeyman, remember.'

'Oh yes.' Fanny bit her lip. 'How silly of me. But she did enjoy it, just the same.'

'I am glad to hear it, for I thought she was looking a little pale myself, and during dinner she was unusually quiet.'

'Was she? I did not notice.'

'It seems to me, Fanny, that you noticed very little – being far too taken up with, shall we say, a certain person? Your mother remarked upon it too, didn't you, dear?'

But Mrs Wyness, tired after the exertions of the evening and soothed by the motion of the hired carriage which was far better sprung than their own, was dozing in the corner, her head against the studded crimson leather of the seat-back and her mouth very slightly open. Wyness put a warning finger to his lips before tucking the knee rug more cosily around his wife, then he leant across and did the same for his daughter on the seat opposite.

'Well, Fanny?' he whispered. 'What have you to say for yourself?'

But at the prospect of reducing the evening's happiness to mundane words, Fanny's reticence reclaimed her. She wanted Tom and her memories to herself, to dream and sigh blissfully over: she feared he was not among her parents' prospective sons-in-law, feared there would be arguments and opposition, knew they wanted her to marry someone like Fergus Adam – at least, they had done before the rift – and she knew that Tom was the only man she wanted to marry, now or ever. Besides, she thought with superstitious caution, Tom had not yet asked her. It would be time enough for argument when he did. When? Perhaps she should have said 'if'? The awful possibility that he might not, that his objections might be the same as her own father's, that pride and social difference might prove an insurmountable barrier, jolted her happiness into a moment of grey dread. Then she remembered Tom's kisses and knew that, whatever the obstacles, he truly loved her. The thought increased her resolve to keep her memories to herself and in spite of her father's repeated questions and gentle probing she would say no more.

In the end, Wyness gave up. He did not really need her to tell him, for he had noticed with whom she spent the evening, noticed which of his guests was her most persistent dancing partner and who it was she sat with when the dance was over. Had he needed any confirmation, her own face would have given it, aglow as it was with the happiness of whatever private thoughts she was reviewing. And he did not really mind: Fanny could do a lot worse and the lad was hard-working and honest. With Wyness's help he would go far. They were almost at Skene Square and the horses already slowing when he decided to speak.

'If it's Tom Diack you want, lass, then you shall have him. I'll speak to him tomorrow and . . .'

'No!' cried Fanny in horror. 'Please, Papa, I beg of you.' Then, gathering courage from desperation, she said, 'I forbid you to speak to him, Papa. If Tom wishes to marry me he must ask me himself, and with no prompting from you. I will not have you interfering in . . . in . . .' She covered her face in her hands.

'There, there, lass,' soothed Wyness, patting her shoulder. 'I didna mean to upset you, only to tell you that if you fancy the lad it's fine with me. I'll need to be sure he's worthy of you, mind. There's the company at stake, dinna forget that, and wi' Mungo Adam aye looking for a way to do us down whoever marries you will need to be shrewd enough to outsmart the old villain at his own game. Then there's . . .'

But Fanny had stopped her ears. She did not want to listen to her father's prosaic common sense. She was not a parcel of goods for barter, but a young girl in love. She wanted only to think of Tom's face as he had looked down at her and called her beautiful, of the warmth of his arms around her and the melting joy of his kisses.

'Well, lass, here we are.'

Her father's voice broke in upon her thoughts and she realized that the carriage had pulled up at their own front door. In a moment her mother would wake, the door would open and the coachman would be waiting to hand them down the step. 'Promise me, Papa,' she said, with the urgency of desperation. 'Promise you will say nothing to Tom? Please?'

She looked at him with such pleading anguish that Wyness sighed, patted her hand with his own large and comforting one, and said, 'Aye, lass. I promise. Mind you, that doesna mean I'll not be watching you, so mind you behave yourself.'

'I will, Papa, and thank you.' To his surprise and gratification, she leant forward and kissed him on the cheek.

'Thank you, dear,' echoed Mrs Wyness vaguely, waking up

[123]

and looking around her with incomprehension. 'Oh, are we home . . . thank goodness for that. It has been such a long evening and I know poor little Fanny must be tired out.'

On the contrary, poor little Fanny lay happily awake until almost dawn, going over and over in her mind every miraculous detail of the evening, until at last sleep claimed her. When she would see Tom again she did not know, but she had no doubt that somehow they would meet, walk and talk together, kiss . . . somehow, somewhere, and soon.

Tom Diack walked home in a turmoil of emotions of which the uppermost was elation: Fanny Wyness loved him and he loved her. The sobriety of morning would inevitably push elation to one side and bring other emotions to the surface — caution, prudence, and above all, pride — but until it did, he would enjoy the blissful triumph of the moment, untarnished. It was the first time he had fallen in love. There had been girls before, of course. Girls he had talked with, teased, even kissed, but no one like Fanny. Briefly he remembered Lizzie Lennox: but Lizzie was different, more of a sister than a friend, and certainly not in the least like Fanny. Lizzie was wild, brash, loud-mouthed and quite capable of taking care of herself whereas Fanny . . . Fanny was delectably feminine and in need of his protective, loving care.

The moon was high and clear, picking out every detail of the rutted track in eerie monotones of light and shadow. In the distance, he heard the receding hoof-beats of the last departing carriage and could even fancy he heard the creak of wheel and axle as it took the bend at the foot of the brae. That was the Wyness carriage, taking his new love home. Except, he realized, she was not 'new'. Ever since he had first spoken with her in the garden of Silvercairns House they had been friends and now that friendship had subtly changed, in a way which seemed not only inevitable, but right. She had declared herself to him and in a moment swept away all barriers between them. He could have sung aloud. Instead he snapped off a branch from an overhanging rowan and in almost the same movement swept it joyously through the grasses of the hedgerow. An owl lifted from a fence post in silent, wide-winged indignation and he laughed. 'Sorry if I disturbed your supper, old boy, but you'll soon find more.'

Mhairi was waiting up for him. 'You are the last, Tom, and I was beginning to wonder if you were coming home at all.' She looked at him shrewdly and added, 'Has Fanny Wyness gone home?'

'How would I know?' he said, feigning indifference, then seeing her expression he grinned, seized her round the waist, swung her off her feet, and said, 'What business is it of yours anyway, sister mine?'

'None, though I suspect it might just be of interest to you?' she said, laughing as he put her down again. 'And don't make so much din, Tom. The others are asleep.'

'Din? And me being as quiet as a mouse? What are you on about, woman?'

'Oh Tom, it's good to see you so happy. I won't ask about you and Fanny because as you rightly pointed out, it is not my business, but . . . I am glad for you both.'

Suddenly, Tom's elation left him. He leant his head on the mantel and stared down into the glimmering shadows of the banked-up fire, every line of his body proclaiming hopeless dejection. Hesitantly, Mhairi laid a hand on his arm.

'What is it, Tom?'

He did not immediately answer and Mhairi was on the point of leaving him when he said, still staring into the sleeping fire, 'It is no good. I don't know what possessed me to think it possible, even for a minute. It is not like you and Alex.'

'I don't see why not. You are both young and healthy, as we were, and you love each other. Don't you?'

'What has love to do with it? You and Alex were equal, each as poor as the other, whereas . . . Even supposing her father gave his consent, the whole world would say I had married her for her money, to get on in the world, to get myself a partnership.'

'You have a partnership already,' pointed out Mhairi. 'You have as big a stake in the firm as Mr Wyness does. You may not have put in as much money, but you put in every bit as much hard work and more. You need not feel ashamed of that.'

'A working partnership of the smallest kind,' said Tom bitterly. 'A paid labourer with ten per cent of the profits at the end of the year, always supposing there are any profits. How can I offer that to a girl who is used to her own dress allowance and her own carriage?'

'You could try, and I am prepared to bet a week of Alex's wages that she would accept you.'

'I know she would,' moaned Tom, 'and that is the trouble. I cannot ask her to make a sacrifice for me and equally I cannot accept whatever money she brings with her, for I expect there would be some.'

'Undoubtedly. So, in order to preserve your pride, you will reject the girl who loves you and lead a life of worthy bachelordom. Am I right?'

'Dammit, Mhairi, what else can I do?'

He turned to look at her with such bleak despair that she wanted only to put her arms around him and comfort him as she had done when they were little and he had fallen and cut his knee or suffered some similar childish mishap. Instead, she said briskly, 'You can make up your mind to work that quarry so efficiently that your ten per cent is a small fortune. Then perhaps you can bargain for fifteen per cent. After that, twenty. You can determine to be as successful as Old Man Adam.'

At the hated name he jerked upright, as she had known he would.

'That villain? Did you see he'd sent his spies tonight? But if he thinks he can beat us that way, he's mistaken. They found out little enough for all their "innocent" questions and what little they did find will do them no good.'

'And it will do you no good, Tom, to give in before you have begun. If you love her, then fight for her. And you can begin by going to bed, so that in the morning you will be fit for a day's quarrying. And if you will not go to bed for that reason,' she went on as he made some sort of muttered protest, 'then you might at least do so out of consideration for me. I have to get up in the morning, even if you have decided to wallow in self-pity and concede defeat.'

'Who says I have?' Tom straightened and glared at her carefully expressionless face. Then grinning, he shrugged. 'Thanks, Mhairi. I needed that. And you are quite right, as always. I'll need to be up betimes if I'm to beat Old Man

Adam at his own game. So I'll be saying good-night.' Astonishingly, he kissed her on the cheek, a thing he had not done in living memory, and made for the stairs. In the doorway he turned. 'See and call me early, Mhairi. Remember I've a deal of work waiting.'

In the months that followed, there was much work for everyone at Rainbow Hill, though others in the town were not so lucky. For the feared recession in the flax and wool-spinning trade reached Donside and the closure of the mills put three thousand out of work. The soup kitchens flourished, and there was fear of worse unemployment if work on the railways stopped, which seemed all too possible if the Government did not step in, as they were being asked to do, with a Treasury loan. The Aberdeen Railway's capital of £900,000 was almost spent and the work too far gone to abandon, but if the workers were to be paid, let alone the contractors, extra money would have to be raised somehow, if not by private finance, then by public. A petition with seven thousand signatures was submitted to back up the Aberdeen Railway's appeal to the Government, but with no results, except the dubious benefit of permission to raise more capital themselves, if they could find any. In the climate of closing mills and rising unemployment, this was not easy to do, even at a promised six per cent for a five-year loan, and there were disturbing rumbles of take-over offers from other railway companies, in London and Edinburgh.

However, the granite industry continued to thrive. People still built churches, houses and schools, constructed roads which needed road metal, laid kerbstones and setts, and buried their dead under splendid monuments of polished granite stone. The pavements of London swallowed a seemingly endless supply of paving stones, and the buildings of Aberdeen an equally endless supply of granite ashlar and rubble. George Wyness put an advertisement in the *Aberdeen Journal* calling for labourers and skilled workmen, 'good sleeping quarters provided', for his quarry at Rainbow Hill. Mackinnon interviewed several dozen applicants, many of them refugees from Silvercairns, including a man he had worked with in his days as foreman there, George Henderson, called 'Red' as much for the colour of his temper as of his hair, but a good workman for all that. Apparently he had had a disagreement with Old Man Adam over the amount of blasting he could do in a day and had been rash enough to speak his mind. 'I tellt him if he carried on blasting wi' the speed and strength of charge he's been doing, he'd not only blow his own house to bits, but he'd end up wi' a heap o' rubble fit for nought but chuckies. He didna like that. Tell't me to get out afore he kicked me out, on the toe of his boot, and me working in yon quarry nigh on twenty year. Would ye believe it?'

'Aye, I would,' growled Tom, who happened to be in the office with Mackinnon. 'He did the same to my own da. Leastways, it was Mr Fergus who sent my da packing, but one Adam's like another to my way o' thinking.'

'Aye,' agreed Henderson. 'They're all black-hearted, villainous devils. So you think there might be a job for me here, Mr Mackinnon?'

Mackinnon looked a question at Tom, who nodded. Any man who had been sacked by Mungo Adam for no reason except that of trying to do his job and do it well was more than worthy of his hire.

'Aye,' said old Mackinnon, 'there might. Report here tomorrow forenoon at seven thirty and we'll see.'

Red Henderson was only one of many new hands taken on as the quarry at Rainbow Hill steadily expanded. George Wyness travelled up and down Scotland on the look-out for work and as often as not found it. As often as not, too, he came up against Mungo Adam, also on the prowl for contracts, and the competition grew fierce and deadly. Adam won the contract for public buildings in Glasgow, Wyness a similar in Perth. Wyness beat Adam by a hair's breadth for a country mansion near Huntly with polished granite columns, and lost another at Inverurie 'because I wouldna promise what I couldna achieve'. Mungo Adam had no such scruples. Soon it was widely known that if both men tendered, then the price would be rock bottom, for where other men would have come to a private agreement, Adam and Wyness were at daggers drawn. But gradually as the months passed builders noticed that if Wyness promised delivery by a certain date, he delivered, with no lack of quality in the stone provided. Adam on the other hand disregarded the delivery date the moment the contract was signed and on several occasions subcontracted. He had been unchallenged king of the quarries for too long and had grown arrogant. Mungo Adam, it was generally agreed, was overreaching himself and should be taught a lesson. When tenders were called for a row of splendid new houses in Victoria Street, Wyness won the contract though Adam knew for a fact (via a well-paid spy) that his own offer was by far the lowest. But Wyness had promised delivery by the end of the year and Wyness could be relied on. Mungo Adam raged at Fergus, at George Bruce the foreman, at any and everyone who came within range, but it did no good. The contract was lost and that was that.

'Well I, for one, am glad,' said Fergus rashly. 'Now perhaps we will be able to honour the contracts we have instead of breaking all of them in your demented chase after business.'

'Demented?' roared Adam. 'Who built up this business from nothing, tell me that? Who was it turned a mere hole in the ground into the biggest granite quarry in Scotland? Who sent you and your good-for-nothing brother to the best school and the best college and paid your idle sister's dressmaker's bills for all these years? And you dare to call me *demented*?'

'Hush, Papa, you will give yourself apoplexy,' said Lettice, pouring herself another cup of after-dinner coffee. 'Then where would we all be?'

'In the workhouse,' he snarled, though with less heat. 'Where you would have been long ago if your snivelling coward of a brother had his way. You'd be happy if we quarried a child's bucket of pebbles a day,' he sneered, rounding on Fergus, 'with maybe a kerbstone on Sunday, for a treat.'

'Not Sunday,' said Fergus calmly, though his heart had quickened as it always did under his father's anger. 'Sunday is a rest day at the quarry.'

'Aye, and you'd make every day a rest day if you had your way.' He glared morosely into the brandy glass which Lettice put into his hand, but when he next spoke it was on a different tack. 'That villain's bamboozled them all with his talk of

[129]

delivery dates and his promises of this and that and the Rainbow Hill granite not a patch on ours. We've never had to put delivery dates in our contracts before: Silvercairns granite is the best and well worth waiting for. It always was and it always will be. Let him slip up just once and they'll soon see . . . Just once,' he repeated thoughtfully, frowning into his glass. Then the frown lifted.

'I'll be on the quarry floor first thing in the morning to see what progress you've made since I was last down.'

'Two days ago, Father.'

'I know that. But a quarry can spew up a deal of granite in two days. And if it hasn't, I'll want to know the reason why.'

As the days lengthened Tom and Alex rose even earlier and worked later into the evening, often staying on after the rest of the work-force had gone home. Most evenings they came home too weary to do more than drain a mug of ale, eat whatever Mhairi had provided for them and fall exhausted into bed, but on the seventh day there was blessed rest. Mhairi insisted, and though they teased her, calling her a stern old Sabbatarian 'worse than yon fanatics who willna let the trains run on a Sunday', she remained adamant. Sunday was for rest and for the family. 'Otherwise,' she told Alex, in the night-time privacy of their box bed, when, the panelled doors closed, they could almost believe they had the house to themselves instead of sharing their bedroom with Annys and baby Hamish while four assorted brothers slept upstairs, 'otherwise, you will see nothing of your wee son till he's a grown man, and the pair of you'll not recognize each other, even if you meet at your own fireside. As it is, I doubt you'd recognize Annys if you met her in the street, she's grown so much in the last few months. I've had to let her hems down twice.'

'But I would recognize you, my love, in the dark and blindfold,' he murmured, 'every precious, growing inch of you. Here, for instance, and here . . .'

'Sh, Alex, or you will wake . . .' but he stopped her lips with first his finger, then his lips and she never finished the sentence.

In spite of his pretended protests, Tom too was glad of the

[130]

Sunday respite from the quarry. As often as not, after church and the family meal, he would 'take a stroll into Aberdeen' as he airily put it and as often as not he would meet the Wyness phaeton bringing Fanny out to visit them. Sometimes she would send Mackie on ahead and she and Tom would stroll to Rainbow Cottage at their own pace; sometimes Tom would climb up and ride with her; sometimes Mackie, suitably bribed, would wait in a convenient spot while they strolled hand in hand along the river, or pottered beside the canal at Elmbank, or merely disappeared into the woods together, to reappear some time later, Tom nonchalantly whistling, Fanny a little flushed and dishevelled, but bright-eyed and confident.

'Drive on, Mackie,' she would say, with all the self-possession of a duchess, and Mackie, mentally counting the coins such co-operation would bring him, would touch his cap, say 'Certainly, Miss Fanny,' and pass no comment. Not even in the Wyness kitchen at the end of the day, though the effort of withholding such a piece of titillating information was something monstrous. Mackie knew that if he succumbed and fed them even the smallest titbit, the fact would get back to Miss Fanny before the day was out and that would be the end of what had become a steady source of extra income. It was not worth the risk. Whenever the master asked, 'Where is it that you drove Miss Fanny today?' he would say, 'To Rainbow Cottage,' and leave it at that, though sometimes he knew for a fact that the young mistress had scarcely time to say hello to yon Mhairi Diack afore it was goodbye again and home. But then it wasna Mhairi Diack she was visiting, was it?

As the summer progressed, the rumours of a more important visit hardened into solid, indisputable fact. Queen Victoria was coming to Aberdeen. With her husband and children she would embark in the Royal Yacht from Woolwich, sail up the coast and step ashore on Waterloo Quay. The news sent a flurry of excitement through the drawing-rooms of the city and Miss Roberts was besieged with a spate of orders that almost swept her off her capable business feet.

She sent a message to Mhairi Diack to 'Come into town at once. I've work for you.' But Mhairi sent back word that she was sorry she could not spare the time. The Roberts woman offered extra rates but the reply was the same. Mhairi had given her promise to Alex and even double pay would not tempt her. Besides, through Fanny's influence she had built up a small, private clientele of her own and had quite enough work as it was. Miss Roberts fumed and stamped and railed against the ingratitude of people who sewed a dress by special request and ever after thought themselves too good to lift a needle, and she had her work cut out to pacify Miss Adam who did nothing but complain about a stitch here and a tuck there. As if the Queen would notice anyway, with her being on her way to Balmoral Castle and hardly likely to have the time to study the under-petticoats of the populace. Not that that stopped the whole of the female side of Aberdeen society from ordering new clothes and requiring every seamstress in the town to work into the small hours.

But everyone had more than enough work in the weeks leading up to the Queen's visit. Rainbow Hill quarry was working to capacity quarrying the stone for the latest contract, but even Rainbow Hill, in company with the whole of Aberdeen, would shut down on the day of the Queen's visit so that every loyal citizen might be free to cheer Her Majesty as she set foot ashore in Aberdeen harbour and to cheer her again as she started the fifty-mile drive to Balmoral Castle.

Fanny Wyness had great hopes of the day. A public holiday was a rare treat, especially for those whose only rest day otherwise was Sunday, and since she had given her heart to Tom Diack she had learnt the importance of holidays. For her and others like her every leisured day was the same, but for Tom the Queen's visit represented a rare chance to enjoy himself, free from the restrictions of a working day. They were to meet on the quay in time to see the Queen step ashore with her husband and family, at eight o'clock on Friday morning. It would mean an early start for Tom, with the long walk into Aberdeen, but he was used to rising before dawn and the walk was nothing.

They had had a small disagreement about the meeting place: George Wyness as a councillor and prominent local business man had seats reserved in the special stand, with, said Fanny eagerly, room for Tom too, if he wished. Tom did not wish. He had no right, he told her, to a reserved seat and until he had he would find his vantage place as best he could, like the rest of the populace. Nothing Fanny said could shift his resolve and wisely she admitted defeat. Tom would join her when the welcome ceremony was over and the procession had moved on into the town.

On the quay there was to be a town guard, red carpeting, garlands, evergreens and bunting. A welcome committee would present an address, guns would fire suitable salutes, flags would wave and crowds cheer as the royal carriages passed up into the town and westward on the long road to Balmoral. But even after the carriages had passed the mood of holiday would persist and it would be a splendid day for everyone. The formality of the landing ceremony over, Fanny and Tom were to spend it together and by the end of the day Fanny hoped that Tom would have asked her to marry him. She certainly meant to give him every possible encouragement. They would have been 'walking out' together for five months by then and surely that was long enough for him to have collected the courage? She had no doubt that he loved her, but whether that love was strong enough to sweep aside all reservations of pride and social difference she did not know: the day of the Queen's visit would decide.

Mhairi was sitting at the table in the cottage kitchen, putting the last stitches to a dress which Annys would wear for the Queen's visit the next day, when Mrs Bain the blacksmith's wife burst into the kitchen.

'She's come! Sighted off Girdleness not an hour ago and the town in a turmoil with the flags not up and the carpet not down and everything at sixes and sevens. Friday morning we was told and today Thursday and yon Royal Yacht sailing round the Girdleness large as life. And before eight in the morning, with the Provost still in his bed, like as not, and the whole town taken unawares. Would you credit it?'

'Is it true?' said Mhairi, knowing of old the unreliability of rumours.

'True as I'm standing here. The *Victoria and Albert*, which is what yon Royal Yacht is called, seemingly, came sailing in to dock, the royal standard flying from the mast-head and a wee steamer with her to show the way and the whole harbour like an ant hill stirred with a stick. You wouldna credit it, yon mannie said.'

'Which man?' said Mhairi, as much to stem the flow as for information.

'Yon mannie with the horse and him casting a shoe most convenient right by the forge. I mind a day way back, two years past it was or maybe three, when the doctor's horse cast a shoe in that exact place and him on his way to old Mrs McCombie out Persley way, that's old Dr Marshall, not the young one, who's a right handsome young feller and not married neither though with all the girls buzzing around him like bees round a honey pot he'll nay escape long to my way o' thinking. But where was I? Oh aye. Dinna hurry, says Dr Marshall to my Charlie. Dead or alive, she'll bide till I get there, and she did. Dead afore he reached her, and nay likely to move till the last trump. Aye, it's true right enough. Do ye fancy a walk into the town to have a wee keek at Her Majesty?'

'But what about the welcome tomorrow? Is it cancelled?'

'There's nay word of any cancelling. Wi' all yon red carpet and the like and the hiring to be paid for willy-nilly, I reckon they'll have yon welcome whether she's here or gone. Canna waste good bunting and the whole town given a holiday into the bargain. Nay, there'll be junketings tomorrow, lass, dinna fear. Maybe they'll tell her to sail out again and wait i' Nigg Bay till the morning? But I'm away into town to see. Are ye coming? I'll help ye carry the wee one if it's that that's worrying ye,' she added kindly, eyeing Mhairi's girth with a calculating eye. 'Wi' you being seven months gone, I reckon, or nearer eight?'

Mhairi did not answer. She was worried enough about the morrow's festivities as it was without risking tales of women Mrs Bain had known who had given birth in the public street, been trampled underfoot in childbirth, or spawned albino triplets at the feet of visiting royalty.

'Eight-month babies are aye unlucky,' said that cheerful woman. 'See ye dinna bump yourself in the crowds. Ye dinna want to bring it on early like. I knew a woman once, over Grandhome way . . .'

'I'd best stay here,' interrupted Mhairi quickly. 'I've this sewing to finish and then Alex will likely look in and wonder where I am and Annys will be home from the school and wanting her tea. But you go and find out what's happening. You will tell me if anything's changed for tomorrow, won't you?' she said anxiously as her visitor moved for the door.

Mhairi had been looking forward with great anticipation to the Queen's visit and the opportunity it gave her to spend a whole, uninterrupted day in her husband's company. Ever since that party when he had found out about her sewing for Lettice Adam she had been aware of a sadness in his face when he thought he was unobserved. He drove himself harder than ever at the quarry and though she told him over and over that she wanted for nothing, was content as they were, would rather have a healthy husband and a loaf of plain bread than a worn-out one and a side of beef, he took no notice. She knew he worried for the future, wanted to provide for her and their children and would have worked twenty-four hours a day had she let him and had he had the strength. So tomorrow was to be a blessed holiday, a day of relaxation and enjoyment when they would all go into Aberdeen together, to see the Queen.

At least, it was to have been so: but perhaps the Queen would go on to her holiday castle today instead? It would be an empty holiday without the presence of the star. But a holiday nonetheless, she told herself briskly, and it was not only Alex who needed one: Tom had been working just as hard. Tomorrow's holiday would give him the chance to spend much of the day with Fanny Wyness, if he chose, and she hoped with all her heart that he would choose – and choose Fanny for his bride. She knew Fanny wanted it and suspected that Fanny's father would not disapprove for all the differences between them. Tomorrow would be the ideal opportunity for Tom to declare his intentions. At the thought, Mhairi's eyes brightened with anticipation: by tomorrow evening Tom and Fanny might be hand-fast, the wedding day set. Happily, she began to plan the party they would give, to celebrate.

Tom was in the Wyness polishing yard, personally supervising the safe delivery of a particular granite block, when the bells of the city suddenly burst into such a clamorous ringing that it could have but one interpretation.

'She's come!' cried someone, and in a moment all was pandemonium. Mr Wyness appeared at the door of his office, called Tom over and said, 'Look nippy, lad! Find out what's what,' but before Tom could move the word was all over the yard. The royal bartizan was flying from the Town House: that could only mean the Royal Yacht had arrived. Meanwhile the bells continued to ring out their jubilant welcome and in the street outside a growing throng of people flowed past on their way to the harbour, chattering excitedly and sweeping up others in their path. Mr Wyness shrugged, declared the yard closed for the day except for those unnatural enough not to want to see the royal arrival and within five minutes the place was empty, but for the owner and his junior partner. Even young Lorn had gone, deserting the slurry of the polishing shed for the greater attraction of the quay.

'Well, Tom?' said Wyness, slapping his young partner companionably on the shoulder. 'I reckon there'll be little work done in the town today, but we canna gainsay our Queen, especially with her not exactly in the habit of dropping in for a visit. So give me a hand to lock up and we'll join the rest of the skivers.'

He moved away to the row of polishing sheds and Tom followed, closing doors, shooting bolts, checking that everything had been left shipshape.

'Aye, lad,' went on Wyness conversationally as he checked the drawers of his office desk, locking each one afterwards. 'The last time royalty visited these parts was around two hundred years ago, after the Troubles, when Charles II spent a night in the Castlegate at the town's expense, which is no doubt why we havena been able to afford a royal visit since. What a night and what a bill after! Nigh on twelve hundred pounds, by all accounts, and too much of that on dubious females in the royal entourage, and one or two of them brazen local women, I wouldna wonder. But I won't shock your innocent young ears with the details, lad. Did I show you this schedule, by the way? For yon double tomb in London? They're wanting a mixture of pink and blue granite so we'll need to send to Peterhead or Hill o' Fare for that. Donal's away to the kirkyard this morning to get a few ideas. Aye, they didna call him the Merry Monarch without reason, though it was a shocking kind of merriment by all accounts and the ministers of the town mortally affronted, especially when the populace packed the Castlegate to see what they could of the royal goings-on. These figures here, lad,' he said prodding a bundle of papers tied with red string, 'are the estimates for yon Australian business I was telling you of. It's not easy at long distance with it being such a big operation. We could do with a man on the spot to give us the local details, but we'll maybe fix one up one day. Meantime, it's top secret, so mind and dinna breathe a word.' He dropped the bundle into a drawer, slammed it shut and turned the key.

'Aye, yon Merry Monarch was behaving so "merrily" by all accounts that to preserve the morals of the gawping public, the local ministers sent in a Professor of Divinity from the college to remonstrate. He didna have much success, seemingly, for his parting words, heard by all the Castlegate, were, "If you do it, close the windows!" And that's the last of our windows closed, lad, and we'll not need to worry about suchlike immoralities with Queen Victoria and her family, which is a relief. And cheaper for the public purse. Now I'll just turn the key in this door and we'll be away. Can't be too careful these days with Mungo Adam sending his spies everywhere. There, I reckon that's the last, and then ye might as well come with me to the quay and see what's what. I've been wanting the chance of a chat with you for a while, and if you've nought better to do . . .'

'Tomorrow,' said Tom hastily. 'If you will excuse me, Mr Wyness, I have to get back to Rainbow Hill. They'll be wondering where I am.'

'Nonsense, lad. The carter will tell them . . .'

'And I'd best find Donal first and tell him what's going on. He'll not know otherwise.' Before Wyness could detain him, Tom had slipped out into the street and the enclosing crowd.

Had the older man not mentioned that 'chat' Tom might have gone with him: the quarry could wait and Donal was old enough to take care of himself. But lately he had taken to avoiding Mr Wyness's company, especially if there was a likelihood that he might find himself closeted alone with

Fanny's father. He was increasingly aware that Wyness had something to say to him and did not want to hear him say it until he had things clear in his own mind. He loved Fanny: she loved him. That much was simple enough. But he could not support her in anything like the life to which she was accustomed and was afraid that she would not survive a week in the sort of life he had to offer. She had no experience of poverty, of making ends meet, of contriving a meal out of next to nothing, of sleeping three or four to a room. On that first occasion when she had visited Mhairi it was plain that she had no idea how to wash a simple plate, had never done so in her life till then. How would she survive in a but-and-ben, which was all he could hope to provide for her, at least till he'd made his way?

His mind was running over and over the problem as, Donal forgotten, he allowed himself to be carried along with the crowds into the Castlegate, when he heard a remembered voice at his elbow.

'Well, if it isna Tom Diack! And as handsome as ever or my eyes deceive me. My kitchen hasna been the same since you stopped dropping in for a pint of ale and a buttered scone.' A stout woman in black, with a basket over her arm, clutched on to him with her free hand and tried to edge him out of the main stream, into the shelter of the market cross.

'Mrs Gregor,' said Tom in surprise and would have broken free without another word except that justice told him the faults of the Adams did not necessarily rub off on to their cook. In the days when he had worked in the garden of Silvercairns House Ma Gregor had been good to him, making him welcome in her kitchen and always with a plate of something nourishing to put in front of him. 'What are you doing in town?' he finished, with an effort.

'The family's moving back into the Guestrow come the end of the month, and I was in seeing to the cleaning o' the place for they lasses canna be trusted to lift a finger without a stick at their backs. Then I heard the bells ring fit to burst a body's eardrums and thought I'd just take a wee look and see if the Queen's arrived. I'd like fine to see Her Majesty wi' my own two eyes. Was that where you was going?' Tom nodded. 'I'll just walk with ye a little then, if ye dinna mind, and hang on to

[138]

your arm. Yon crowd pushes something terrible and I wouldna want to be trampled underfoot. Meantime, you can tell me how yon brazen hussy of a kitchenmaid is getting on on the other side o' the world.'

'Do you mean Lizzie Lennox?'

'Aye, who else? Not that it was her fault, mind. Yon Mr Hugo was always a devil wi' the girls and Lizzie was a fine-looking lass.'

'Mr Hugo?' Tom's face paled at the name of his old enemy. 'What has he to do with it?' Everyone knew that Lizzie Lennox had left the Adams' employ before she could be pushed, helped herself to a pocketful of Miss Lettice's jewellery and fled to Australia to make her fortune. Hadn't Mhairi had that letter from her?

'What has any man to do with the fathering of a child, ye daft gowk? Though he paid dearly for the pleasure this time. They say yon Jamaica is full o' black people and it's that hot ye canna sleep o' nights for the mosquitoes and the diseases. Malaria and swamp fever and the like. Aye, he paid dearly for his wee bit fun did Mr Hugo, but nay a bad lad for all his faults. He was aye cheerful and lively and the place isna the same wi'out him, though he did lead us all a merry dance when the mood was on him. There's many the night I've had to lock my kitchen lasses into their room wi' my own hands and hide the key. Aye, it wasna all Lizzie's fault and she was a good hand wi' the saucepans for all her complaining. Her black-leading wasna maybe all it could ha been, but nay bad, considering and . . .'

Tom let the words flow over him unheeded as the awful, unsuspected truth took shape in his mind and grew till he felt he would burst with the choking fury of his anger. He was impervious to the cheering crowds, the flags that had appeared everywhere, in windows and doorways and on the masts and yards of the ships in the harbour, even to the splendid sight of the first of the royal carriages being unloaded from the *Black Eagle* at Regent's Quay. He did not notice the splendid welcome arch with its greenery and loyal emblems, the palisaded space where the royal party would land, the wooden gallery for spectators, its structure decorated with shrubs and heather, or the covering of fine sand which had been spread over the route the Queen would take. All he could think of was the villainy of Hugo Adam. He could have whipped the fellow the length of the city till he begged, screaming, for mercy, could have strangled the man with his bare hands. But the villain was safely out of reach in the West Indies and Lizzie was in Australia. He remembered the letter Mhairi had read out, the strangely halting way she had done so, and her unwillingness to show the letter to anyone. Suddenly it made sense. Mhairi knew. She had always known and had deliberately kept the knowledge from him.

'Mind you,' Ma Gregor was saying, 'if he does any fathering where he's gone to, the bairn'll likely be coffee-coloured and he'll have to pay for his folly himself, for Old Man Adam willna fork out again. Ye can be sure o' that.'

'Did he pay Lizzie?' said Tom, with strange quiet, his eyes unseeing on the graceful lines of the Royal Yacht.

'I reckon so. How else did yon brazen hussy get the fare to go to Australia? Oh look! There's the *Victoria and Albert*. And isna that the Queen on the deck? Yon wee woman with the red velvet on her bonnet? Talking to the Lord Provost? Or is it the Town Clerk, Tom? You're taller than I am and I canna quite see.'

Tom did not answer. Instead he shook free of her arm, pushed his way back through the crowd and out into the free air. Then, everything else forgotten, he strode fast for home, and Mhairi.

'Why didn't you tell me?'

Mhairi looked up from her sewing in alarm as the door burst open and Tom almost fell into the room.

'Tell you what, Tom?' she said with composure, though her mind raced with speculation.

'About Lizzie Lennox and yon letter. The letter you read careful bits of out loud and hid the rest. Well, it's the rest I want to see. Where is it?'

Silently Mhairi went to the kist, opened the lid and felt among the layers of folded clothes. She drew out the ill-written, crumpled letter she had not had the heart to destroy and handed it to Tom, watching his face with growing anxiety

[140]

as he read.

'Why did you not tell me?' he said again, more quietly, but with an intensity that frightened her.

'What good would it have done? It would not have undone the harm, merely added to it, and you were in trouble enough as it was.'

'Aye, and on account of the villain himself,' said Tom bitterly, remembering the time he and Alex had spent in jail, accused of robbery with violence by Hugo Adam until the charge had been dropped. 'I'd like to get my hands round the man's throat and . . .'

'Which is why I did not tell you,' interrupted Mhairi. 'Do you think I want a murderer for a brother?'

'It would not be murder – merely retribution.'

'That argument may convince you, but it would not keep the rope from your neck. It is no good, Tom,' she said more gently. 'The matter is over, the child born. Nothing you say or do can undo that and he has been punished for his sin.'

'Punished? You call a life of luxury in the West Indies *punishment*?'

'Yes,' said Mhairi quietly, 'if it means parting from your home and family and friends. And Tom, will you promise me one thing?'

'That depends.'

'Please, Tom? For my sake?'

'Tell me what it is, first.'

'Don't tell Alex? He still believes, as you did, that Lizzie fled before she could be caught, for stealing. He will feel as you do if he finds out and then . . . and then . . . Oh Tom, I could not bear it if anything happened to Alex. I *need* him.' She hid her face in her hands and her shoulders trembled. Tom was instantly contrite.

'Don't worry, Mhairi. I won't tell. Alex has enough to think about already with you and Hamish and the next wee one. But what about Lizzie? With a bairn and no man and miles from her family, who's to think about her?'

'You read her letter,' said Mhairi, recovering composure. 'She has chosen a new life for herself and is enjoying it. The money will have reached her by now and you know Lizzie. Nothing ever gets her down.'

'No,' agreed Tom, but he did not sound convinced. He was remembering the red-haired, fiery-spirited girl who had lived up the stair from them in the Aberdeen tenement and whom he had known all her life. She was maybe not as honest as she should be, but he was fond of her for all that and once, when the town had a holiday, he had chased her up Broad Street and kissed her in a doorway. It was an unfortunate memory, for on that occasion she had been with Hugo Adam until Tom had 'rescued' her, against her will. Remembering, Tom frowned again with a bitter and simmering resentment.

'Don't worry about her,' soothed Mhairi, pouring water into the teapot to make tea for them both. 'She'll be fine. It wouldn't surprise me if she was richer than any of us one day, and you'd not catch her worrying, would you? So why don't you sit down at the table with me and drink a slow cup of tea till you recover your temper? You can tell me what's brought you hot foot back from town when you should be at the quarry with Alex, and most of all, has the Queen come and what is she going to do?'

Reluctantly, Tom did as she said, though his mind still brooded over the shocking revelation that Lizzie had borne his enemy's child. Even a night's short sleep could not shift it. The thought still simmered at the back of his mind and would not leave him, casting a blight over the day that should have been the highlight of the year. For word came that Her Majesty had graciously consented to wait aboard the Royal Yacht in the harbour until the morrow and come ashore exactly as planned.

The town was alive well before dawn, the streets filling rapidly. No one wanted to miss a minute of the momentous day and by seven the streets of the royal route were lined with folk in their party best, jockeying for vantage points from which to watch the royal progress. Every window and balcony was full, every seat in the quayside gallery taken when, at a little before half-past eight, Queen Victoria appeared on the quarterdeck, with Prince Albert and their three children. The populace raised a roar which unseated every pigeon and seagull in the city, waving hats and handkerchiefs and

cheering repeatedly while Her Majesty bowed acknowledgement, smiled or raised her hand. And continued to roar as she
moved to the gangway holding the little Princess Royal's
hand, descended it and stepped ashore, Prince Albert and the
young princes following.

The procession of carriages formed and moved off at a
walking pace along the quay towards the town, while the decks
of the ships in harbour were lined with cheering sailors and the
windows of the houses were similarly lined with cheering
ladies in their finery. The procession turned into Marischal
Street and ascended between two seas of waving flags and
handkerchiefs and a double line of Pensioners. These, under
the command of Captain Munro, fell into step beside the
carriage and formed a guard to the procession as it reached the
Castlegate and turned into the splendid, flag-decked vista of
Union Street.

'But she hasn't a crown,' complained Annys, from her
vantage point on the steps of the Assembly Rooms. 'Or an
ermine cloak or even a sceptre. Just a tartan plaidie and a white
bonnet.'

'With a fine feather,' teased Alex, but Annys would not be
mollified.

Mrs Wyness has a purple dress just like that one. But I like
the princes,' she conceded, brightening. 'And the splendid
coach.'

'And I heard tell that Prince Albert visited the Macdonald
polishing yard yesterday,' said Tom morosely. 'That will
bring them a deal of extra custom.' Tom, for turbulent reasons
of his own, had chosen to watch the procession with his
brothers and sisters rather than with the town dignitaries on
the quay. He would make his way to their trysting place later
and Fanny would wait for him.

'Come another five years and he'll be visiting us,' said Alex,
who refused to be discouraged. He swung his young son up on
to his shoulders, the better to see the horses, and boasted,
'We'll have the best granite business in the north of Scotland
by then, see if we don't.'

'Aye. When we've bought up Macdonald's and the Adam
quarry at Silvercairns.'

'If things go on as they have been, we may well do that,

Tom,' said Alex now, 'in spite of your moaning. You have faith in me, don't you, Mhairi?' and he slipped his arm round her waist and drew her close.

'Not while you're holding that child with only one hand I don't. He's a wee terror for wriggling. Give him to Donal. You know they'll both love that.'

It was true: though Donal could neither hear nor speak, he and his young nephew had a rapport that was delightful to see and the child already knew to touch Donal to attract his attention, to tug at his hand or, if he could reach, to hold Donal's face in his dimpled hands and turn it to his own. They even had a sort of baby's sign language known only to themselves, though Annys was occasionally allowed to share in their secret communications. Now Donal took the baby from Alex and he and Mhairi moved closer together, to watch the remainder of the procession with their arms around each other's waists, in a world of their own as secret as that of Donal and wee Hamish.

Tom saw and envied. He should have been with Fanny, his arm around her waist, and her face looking up into his as Mhairi was looking at Alex. But whenever he thought of Fanny the picture of Lizzie Lennox rose to separate them: Lizzie laughing up into Hugo Adam's face, Lizzie lying to Tom about the stolen necklace at her throat one minute, and kissing him the next. Lizzie swearing and shouting and storming at him in Ma Gregor's kitchen to 'Take yourself off, Tom Diack, and good riddance,' and later, Lizzie vowing she wouldn't spend a night with that bastard Hugo Adam if he were the last man on earth. 'You're worth ten of him any day, ye daft loon,' she had said, before kissing Tom goodbye. 'You've been a good friend,' she had said, but had he? He should have stopped Hugo Adam from the beginning, and now, the harm done, as a 'good friend' he ought to exact retribution. It was no good Mhairi saying everything was over and done with. Lizzie had been as good as one of the family for as long as he could remember and Lizzie had been taken advantage of and then discarded, left to look after her fatherless child as best she could. What would he have done if someone had treated one of his sisters like that? It was all very well for Mhairi to tell him to forget about it, but how could he, with that Hugo Adam roving free and Lizzie suffering who knew what sort of scorn and deprivation?

'Shouldn't you be with Fanny?' said Mhairi at his side. 'I understood you were to meet and watch the procession set out from the quay?' Fanny had told her as much, with great excitement, only two days ago.

Tom shook himself out of his reverie. 'Aye, maybe. But there's no hurry. She knows I'm coming and she'll wait.' Suddenly, as he spoke the words, he saw his way clear. Of course! It was the obvious and only solution. Opposition was inevitable and he would need to think carefully how best to put his case, but he would manage it somehow, and find the courage to carry it through. Deep in new and turbulent thought, he moved off into the enclosing crowd.

Alex and Mhairi exchanged looks, raised an eyebrow, then shrugged. It was Tom's business, not theirs, and it was not every day they got the chance to see a royal procession.

Fanny Wyness waited in her ring-side seat on the quay with determined patience, though the tiers of seats around her were rapidly emptying as the crowd followed the procession on its slow route westward, or dispersed to whatever private jollifications had been arranged to fill the day. Tom had promised to meet her and Tom would keep his word. But as the minutes stretched empty and forlorn in her private pool of loneliness while everyone else laughed and joked and jostled in holiday mood, it took all Fanny's timid courage to keep the tears from her eyes and the smile determinedly in place. If her back straightened and her chin lifted a defiant extra inch, no one noticed, though once her father looked at her with a fleeting frown of puzzlement and twice her mother remarked, 'You are very quiet, Fanny dear.' When she added, with faint reproof, 'I hope you are enjoying this unique and splendid occasion?' Fanny managed a dutiful, 'Yes, Mamma,' with all the enthusiasm she could muster, but the effort left her quivering with threatening tears. Where was Tom? He should have joined her an hour ago and though he had refused to sit with them in the seats of honour facing the fifty-feet-square crimson-carpeted floor, specially constructed to receive the royal feet, he had undertaken to stand in a certain spot behind the fence which kept the populace from encroaching on the royal route, and wave to her. But though she had scanned the crowds from water's edge to Marischal Street, she had failed to see him.

The 93rd Highlanders, in full ceremonial splendour, had patrolled the perimeter of the welcome arena, the boys of the City Grammar School had marched three abreast with equal pride to take up their positions, with children from other city schools, on the quay, and finally the rousing exuberance of the pipers of the 93rd had led the Guard of Honour into position opposite the triumphal arch. The Earl of Aberdeen, in his uniform as Lord Lieutenant of the county and wearing the Order of the Thistle, had arrived with other dignitaries; then the Provost, magistrates and Town Council, in full ceremonial robes of office, and the professors of both King's and Marischal Colleges had taken their places. Finally the royal carriage, drawn by four splendid bays, had drawn up beside the platform, postillions brilliant in scarlet jackets and black velvet caps trimmed with silver, and to complete the picture of loyal welcome, every ship in the harbour was decked with flags and loaded to the gunwales with cheering spectators.

All this Fanny had seen unheeded. For though her eyes ranged over every detail of the dazzling pageant, they sought only one face and failed to find it. The crowds were dense, the sun bright, but she knew with the faith of love that had Tom been there she would have seen him, if not immediately then not long after. He had not come; he had been prevented by some dreadful accident, to himself or to his family; he had been run down on the road by a carriage; he had contracted a deadly fever in the night. She even considered the shameful possibility that he had slept in, unlikely though it was, and had come too late to fight his way to the front of the crowd. But she knew in her heart it was none of these. Tom had not come for some reason of his own. What it was she could only guess at, but the guesses were too dreadful to contemplate: he had changed his mind, no longer loved her, never had done so, wanted to go his own way untrammelled, or, worst of all, had found someone else. Or perhaps, she told herself with small, but determined hope, it was merely that she had misunderstood? It was *after* the ceremony that he was to come to that pre-arranged spot on the quay. Of course, that was the explanation.

So, clinging to that small hope, Fanny had done her best to smile and cheer with the others, waved her handkerchief, cheered again, and when the Queen stepped ashore and the bells of the city simultaneously rang out their clamorous welcome, had risen to her feet with the assembled company to answer the sailors' hearty cheers with an equal vigour.

Finally, the ceremony over, the last of the carriages had departed on its slow route into the city. The crowd was fast dispersing and still she could see no sign of Tom. Fanny's anxiety drained the last of the colour from her face and quickened her pulse to a quivering tension. If he did not come soon, Papa would insist that she go with them to the Town House and she would lose Tom for the rest of the day.

'I will wait a little longer,' she said now, with an edge of obstinacy to her voice which surprised her mother. 'I gave Tom my word and would not like to break it.'

'Aye, well,' said her father, frowning. 'I gave my word to be at the Town House, with your mother.'

'Then I will wait here alone.'

'With the town full o' sailors with nought else to do but pester the girls? You will come with your mother and me, lass, or you'll go home.'

Before Fanny could reply she glimpsed the face she had been waiting for and the change to her own was miraculous. 'Tom!' she cried, springing to her feet, most precariously on the timbered gallery, and waving her hand. 'Over here!' She scrambled to the ground and would have run towards him had not her mother caught her daughter's arm and restrained her.

'And not before time,' muttered Wyness, who was too shrewd a man not to have noticed the recent efforts Tom Diack had made to avoid his company. This time, however, it was his turn to be taken aback.

'Good morning, Mrs Wyness, and Mr Wyness,' said Tom, with grave-faced courtesy. Then he turned to Fanny. 'I hope I have not kept you waiting too long, but the crowd was that dense I had to fight my way through it. I was by the Assembly Rooms,' he added, sensing the need for explanation, 'with

Mhairi and the others.'

'Aye, well,' said Wyness, still frowning, 'I was about to take Fanny with me.' He drew a gold repeater out of his waistcoat pocket, consulted it and dropped it back into place. 'As I thought: we should have been at the Town House ten minutes back.'

'I am sorry if I kept you waiting. And, Mr Wyness . . .' To the older man's astonishment, Tom took his arm and steered him a little way from the others. 'I would be grateful if you could spare me ten minutes of your time before the day is out? There is something I wish to ask you, in private.'

'Is there indeed? Well, well.' Wyness beamed his approval, all rancour forgotten. 'Then if you take care of my daughter for a whilie and show her the town, you can maybe bring her home around five? You can take a bite of dinner with us and then we can have our wee talk after.'

'Thank you, Mr Wyness, but I would prefer to talk before, if that is possible.'

'Wanting to get it over with, so you can enjoy your meal? If you're nervous, there's no call to be, I can tell you that now. But as you wish . . .' He slapped Tom companionably on the shoulder. 'Take good care of her, mind.' He winked as one man to another. 'And see ye behave!' Then he took his wife's arm and led her, mildly protesting, away.

Fanny had seen her father's change of expression, noticed the conspiratorial bonhomie, and when Tom told her they were to spend the day together before he took her home, to have dinner with them, her heart threw off the last shred of anxiety and she looked up at him with adoring eyes. He was going to 'speak' to her father at last and she had no doubt at all what the outcome would be.

'I thought we'd wander along Union Street for a bit,' Tom was saying. 'Once the crowds have dispersed we'll be able to see the decorations better. There's a splendid one at the Royal Hotel. "God Save the Queen" in gold letters a mile high and the front smothered so thick in laurels and flowers and flags ye can hardly see the windows. They'll maybe sell us a cup of coffee, too.'

It was on the tip of Fanny's tongue to protest that coffee was too expensive for Tom's purse, but she stopped herself in time. Instead, she said, 'That would be lovely, Tom, but I am not sure I want to drink a cup of the Royal's coffee. Mamma says they boil the dregs over and over.' This was pure fabrication on Fanny's part, but once she had embarked on the lie it came easily. 'You never know what you're drinking, Mamma says, and the Royal is not the only hotel to scrape the dregs from the cups and use them again. So if we feel tired and in need of coffee, we'll go home to Skene Square for it. Everyone will be out, so we will have the place to ourselves and I will make it for you myself, in the kitchen.'

Tom was both surprised and intrigued by the eagerness in her voice. At the mention of Skene Square all his defences had come rushing to the fore: he had anticipated an uncomfortable ten-minute wait in the intimidating drawing-room while a servant girl scurried off to do Fanny's bidding. It would have emphasized the social gulf between them and soured his day, whereas he had saved carefully for today so that they could sit together at some restaurant table and drink coffee or hot chocolate with maybe a wee cake or suchlike for Fanny and enjoy themselves as equals. But the picture of Fanny surreptitiously raiding the kitchen behind the servants' backs was at the same time endearing and curious.

'All right,' he grinned, slipping his arm around her waist and drawing her close. 'But not till we have walked as far as Holburn and the city boundary. That will give me a thirst to do justice to a whole vat of coffee.'

'And afterwards, when we have covered all traces of our illicit drinking,' giggled Fanny, 'we will walk out again into the town, and maybe to the canal? We might see one of my father's barges,' she said, pretending innocence, but they both knew that a stroll along the canal bank on a day of holiday was a stroll for lovers.

But her words had reminded Tom of the coming interview with her father and he felt panic threaten.

'Is anything the matter?' Fanny asked hesitantly when he did not respond, but continued to walk in silence, apparently in private thought.

'No.' With an effort, he added, 'It is just that today is a holiday. I want to forget all about work – and that includes your father's barges and everything in them. No disrespect to

[149]

your father, but I want today to be for you and me, alone.'

'Of course, and I am sorry.' Smiling her relief, Fanny prepared to enjoy the blissful, precious day, by the end of which Tom would have declared his love and they would be formally engaged.

'Isn't this fun?' she said some time later when they had let themselves into the deserted kitchen at the Skene Square house and she was busying herself, surprisingly competently, with the paraphernalia of coffee-making. 'I like this room so much better than the drawing-room, don't you? When the coffee is ready we will sit here and drink it at the kitchen table, just as if it were our own kitchen in our own little house and Cook were not coming back to shoo us out and take charge. I used to be afraid of Cook,' she confided, setting out cups, cream jug and sugar. 'She always seemed so red-faced and fierce, but she is really quite nice, when you get to know her.'

'And you have?' teased Tom.

'Oh yes. She has taught me so many things I did not know before. Like how to make coffee.' She carried the jug carefully to the table, then slid into the seat beside Tom. Solemn-faced, she poured. 'Is the coffee all right?' she asked anxiously, watching Tom's face as he drank. When he pronounced it perfect her face broke into a radiant smile. 'Good. I thought I had done it properly. I have been learning,' she said shyly, 'so that when I marry, I will not be a disgrace to my husband.'

'How could you ever disgrace anyone, you silly little darling,' and Tom kissed the end of her nose. Blushing with pleasure, Fanny scrambled out of her seat again, disappeared into the larder and reappeared a moment later with a fruit cake on a plate.

'Would you like a slice of this cake, Tom? I am afraid it is all that this particular hotel can offer, but it is highly recommended.'

'Well, if you insist,' he grinned, and she cut him a healthy slab. 'Hmm . . . it's excellent. Mhairi could not make a better, though do not tell her I said so.'

Fanny stood beside his chair, watching anxiously as he ate. 'Do you really like it? Really truly?'

'See my plate? Isn't that testimony enough? You may convey my compliments to your cook.'

'I made it,' said Fanny and blushed. 'Cook told me how, but I made it all by myself and no one helped me. I can make broth, too, with a mutton bone, and I know how to boil a hen and make a rabbit stew.'

'You will make a fine little wife for someone, one day,' he said, not thinking, and the next minute she was standing so close to him that he could almost feel her heart beat.

'Do you think so?'

Her hand rested lightly on his shoulder and she looked at him with such open invitation that the only answer was to pull her down on to his knee and kiss her and, when her hands crept up and round his neck, to kiss her again with a melting, lingering sweetness which almost vanquished his resolve. But he had promised himself to wait till this evening and he would keep his promise: today was too precious and fleeting to waste on the sober practicalities of tomorrow. Instead, he kissed the end of her upturned nose and said, 'I think you are the most delightful and provocative little waitress I have ever come across.'

'I am glad we did not go to the Royal Hotel,' she murmured, snuggling closer.

'And I. The coffee here is so much better. Besides, I am not at all sure they would approve of such unladylike behaviour among their customers.'

Fanny giggled. 'Nor would Cook.'

'Then we had better make our escape, before they come back.' He stood up, swinging her high in the air before setting her down again, laughing. He was still holding her by the waist and was bending his head for one last kiss when there was the sound of voices outside: someone was coming down the area steps.

'Quick!' whispered Fanny in agitation. 'Cook's coming.' She seized Tom's hand and pulled him towards the inner door and the servants' passage. 'We'll escape through the house and the front door.' Smothering their laughter, they sped through the back regions to the green baize door which separated servants from masters, pushed it open and slipped through into the carpeted silence of the hall.

'Phew!' gasped Fanny, laughing. 'That was a narrow escape. And we left the cake on the table! They will think there have been burglars!'

'Perhaps you ought to tell them?'

'And spoil their fun? Certainly not. They will spend the rest of the day speculating who the dreadful intruders could have been. The truth would be far too tedious.' She paused, listened with her head on one side, then whispered, 'Good. That was the door closing. It will be safe to go outside now.'

She opened the heavy front door, easing it back with cautious care and closing it with equal caution after them. Then, hand in hand, they ran silently down the steps and did not stop running till they had turned the corner of the street. There they skidded to a stop, fell laughing together against the nearest railings, and suddenly Tom's arms were tight around her and his lips on hers.

Breathless, Fanny broke away, flustered and blushing. 'Not in the street, Tom! Suppose one of Papa's friends comes along?'

'Then they should do the gentlemanly thing and look the other way!' but he took her hand and tucked it decorously under his arm. 'There, is that better? And now, Miss Wyness, if you have the time, perhaps you would allow me to show you the sights of the city? I know a particularly attractive grassy path beside the canal . . .'

It was calm beside the canal, all barges moored for the day, the locks closed and the waters unruffled except by the spreading ripples of a trio of gliding ducks. The sounds of the city were far behind them beyond Castle Hill, with the flag-decked bustle of the harbour and the warehouses of the quay. The grassy path beside the man-made canal was empty of the packmen whose route it was to the Aulton two miles north, as well as of barge horses, lock-keepers and the like: all gone, like the rest of Aberdeen, to see the Queen. All, that is, except couples like themselves, seeking privacy and each other's company. Tom put his arm around Fanny's waist and after only a moment's hesitation she slipped her gloved hand under his jacket and did the same. Their steps slowed, stopped, moved on again, and when they came upon a convenient grassy bank which no one else had claimed, Tom spread his jacket on the ground to protect her skirts and they sat down together, to watch the sunlight on the water, the meandering progress of an aimless duck, a late butterfly on a nearby flower. Fanny's head was on Tom's shoulder and his arm around her waist.

'Happy?' murmured Tom after a silence in which neither dared to speak, lest the moment should be spoilt.

'Very.' She looked up at him, her eyes brimming with love. 'And you?'

'I think I might be happier', he murmured, 'like this,' and he stretched full length on the grass, pulling her down beside him. 'And if you are afraid that someone might see you,' he said as she half struggled, laughing, to sit up again, 'there is no one for miles around, except those ducks, and us.'

'But I would not want . . .'

She never finished the sentence, for Tom kissed her and whatever protest she had been going to make was forgotten.

'What were you going to say?' he teased, a long time later.

'Only that . . . oh Tom, I love you.' She put her arms round his neck and pulled his face down till her lips found his. 'There, you said you could not resist a brazen woman.'

'And I can't . . . but you cannot say I didn't warn you.' So they kissed, their lips teasing and meeting again, with joy and playful laughter, until suddenly playfulness receded to be replaced by a deepening, yearning hunger compounded of mutual and growing need.

But when, against all resolution, and weak with longing, she murmured, 'Do you truly love me, Tom?' his hands halted in their gentle exploration of her body as the memory of her father sprang up, huge and chilling, between them. He pushed her abruptly away, sat up and, head in hands, groaned quietly to himself.

'What is the matter?' she asked, laying a hesitant hand on his shoulder.

'Everything!' he said, with a vehemence that frightened her. 'You ask if I truly love you. Yes, I love you, Fanny, but I have no right. I can offer you *nothing*.'

'I want nothing! Only you.'

'You say so now, but when you are worn out with drudgery, with a handful of children clamouring at your skirts and no money for food and clothes, let alone the dominie, what will you say then?'

'I will say I love you,' she said with a quietness that went straight to his heart. 'I will say I love my children because you gave them to me, and if there is no money for the school, then I will teach the children myself. I will love the house you provide, be it only one small room. I will love everything about my life, provided I share it with the man I love.'

'You don't know what you are saying,' cried Tom, jumping to his feet and striding up and down in an emotional turmoil. 'You speak pretty, romantic words, but there is no romance in a cold hearth and an empty belly. Believe me, I know.'

'It would not be cold if you were there,' she said in a small voice, but he hardly heard. 'Besides, I have a little . . .'

'Don't say it! I will not live on someone else's money.'

'I was not going to say money,' she lied. She tucked her feet under her and stood up, brushing the grass from her skirts and setting her hair to rights. 'I was merely going to say that I have a little housekeeping skill – you said so yourself, Tom – and I will soon learn more. I will cook and clean and mend for us, and do so gladly.'

'No.' He turned his back and stood staring across the canal towards the links and the sea. 'I love you too much for that. I want to be able to cherish you as your father has done, not to wear you out before your time. Besides . . .' He stopped suddenly, brought up short by his own realization as much as by caution.

'Besides what, my love?' She laid a gentle hand on his arm, but he shook free.

'Nothing. Just that there is something I need to straighten out in my mind. Can you wait just a little longer?'

'Oh yes, Tom. For you.'

There was a moment's absolute silence between them as if both looked into an awesome chasm at their feet, then Tom turned, pulled her towards him and clasped her tight against his chest, murmuring soothing words and stroking her hair with his hand. 'I am sorry, Fanny. You are a dear, sweet, generous girl and I am making you miserable. Today of all days when we should be gloriously happy together. Forgive me? It will be all right one day, my love. You will see.'

[154]

But at his words all Fanny's returning joy left her. One day, he said, as if talking of some far distant and unattainable future. She had given him every opportunity, shown him how much she loved him, promised to wait for him and still he had not asked her in as many words to be his wife. Suddenly she felt deflated, rejected and ashamed. Gathering what few shreds of dignity she could, she turned her back and moved, erect and desolate, along the path towards the town.

'Fanny, wait! I did not mean to hurt you.'

'I am not hurt,' she said, without turning her head. 'Merely a little tired. If you will excuse me I think I will go home.'

But Tom had blocked her path. 'You will do nothing of the kind, you silly little madam. You will kiss me and be friends again or . . . or I will pick you up and hold you by your feet over the canal until you promise to be good.'

'You wouldn't!' she cried in horror.

'Wouldn't I?' He seized her by the waist and lifted her high. 'Wouldn't I?' he said again, standing on the very edge of the canal bank, and lifting her higher.

'No,' she shrieked, half terrified, half laughing. 'You wouldn't dare because . . . because . . . No, Tom, don't! I'll be good. I'll do anything you say, just put me down again . . . please!'

Grinning, he did, but not without teasing her a little first, so that she squirmed and begged for mercy. 'Let that be a lesson to you, Miss Wyness,' he said, finally setting her down on the path. 'Not to waste the day in squabbling with your betters.'

'I was not squabbling.'

'No?' He lifted her chin with his forefinger and looked earnestly into her face until reluctantly she smiled.

'That is better.' Gently he kissed her forehead and drew her hand through the crook of his arm. 'Now shall we walk back into town, my love?'

But though they walked as lovers, stopping now and then to kiss before they reached the Castlegate where decorum intervened, both were aware of things left unsaid.

'What did you mean when you said "one day"?' she asked him as they turned into the flag-decked bustle of Union Street.

'Oh, nothing. Just something I want to talk over, with your

[155]

father.'

One day. The words sounded like a death knell. But Tom had said he loved her and this evening he was going to speak to her father. Wait a little longer, he had said, and she would. Until this evening. She pushed away the last shred of misgiving and allowed the thought to fill her with a spreading glow of happiness: by tonight, everything would be gloriously, blissfully settled.

'Well, lad,' said Wyness genially, his arm around Tom's shoulder as he led him into the study and closed the door behind him. 'You've no call to be nervous. I think I know what your business is and I'll not bite your head off when you speak. In fact, I've been thinking these some weeks back that it was time you upped and spoke out.'

'Have you, sir?' Tom looked at the older man with wary surprise. 'Then you'll know what I'm trying to say.'

'Aye, but you'd best say it yourself just the same, though I can tell you now that my answer will be yes.'

'Yes? Then that's all right.' Tom brushed his forehead with the back of a hand in an expression of relief. 'I was afraid you would think I was leaving you all in the lurch, evading responsibility, pursuing some kind of dream.'

'I'm sorry lad. You've lost me there. Maybe it was that reception at the Town House: I've never seen such massive inroads made into the Common Good fund. You only had to blink an eye to have your glass refilled twice over and it was a wonder anyone was left on their feet by the end of it. No, after a do like that I'm afraid you'll have to explain in plain language and words of one syllable. And dinna be too long about it. I'm needing my dinner. It is about Fanny, isn't it?'

'Yes, sir.'

'Well, get on with it, man. Speak out.'

'First of all, Mr Wyness,' began Tom haltingly, then with gathering fluency as he spoke, 'if you will forgive the impertinence, I want you to know that I love Fanny and I believe she loves me. I know as well as you do that I am not yet in a position to provide for her as she deserves, but I will be one day, you can be sure of that.'

'Aye, lad, I believe you, and if it's any help to you, I can tell you now that when Fanny marries, she'll not come empty-handed.'

'What Fanny owns, or might own in the future, is her concern, not mine,' said Tom fiercely, then, in case he had offended her father, he added more quietly, 'You have been more than kind to me already, giving me a job in the quarry with a share of the profits, but I don't want to be dependent always on the generosity of someone else. I want the chance to prove myself by my own efforts, to make my own way unaided, for Fanny's sake as well as for my own. I want to be worthy . . . I am not explaining myself very well, but I hope you understand?'

'Aye, lad,' sighed Wyness, 'I think I do. You're mad and proud and pig-headed and you want to support a wife on your own tuppence or not at all. You'll not see reason, but I think I understand. I don't suppose it is any good to offer you more money? No, I thought not. I wouldna have respected you if you'd accepted, and as to proving yourself, I'd be delighted to know that Fanny's husband is capable of standing on his own two feet, if only so he can run the firm when I'm gone. Not that I ever had any doubts where you were concerned.'

'Thank you, sir. But I need to prove it to myself, too.'

'And how do you intend to do that? I can tell ye here and now that I have no intention of retiring yet awhile nor, God willing, of going to the great polishing yard in the sky. I want to see my grandsons afore I go. Well?' he demanded as Tom made no answer. 'What is this proving you keep talking about and where do you propose to do it?'

'I want the chance to prove that I can work, and succeed, alone, but I would not like to break my connection with Rainbow Quarry,' began Tom hesitantly. 'Then when you were locking up the polishing yard yesterday you said something which set me thinking and this morning I made up my mind.'

'And asked for a private word with me. At last we're getting to it. Well, go on, lad, what is it that you want to ask me? I told you I wouldna bite your head off, but I might if you keep me waiting much longer, so speak out.'

Summoning all his courage, Tom did.

'*What?*' His roar lifted the dust from the bookshelves and set the chandelier tinkling as far away as the drawing-room. 'Am I to understand', growled Wyness when he had recovered enough to speak in something approaching a normal voice, 'that you sought me out to ask me *that*?'

'Yes, Mr Wyness.'

'And here's me thinking you wanted to marry Fanny.'

'I do.'

'Then you've a strange way of asking. What has got into you, boy? Are you mad?'

'No, Mr Wyness. Leastways, I don't think so. There are always opportunities for good tradesmen and besides, you said yourself that the firm would benefit from a man on the spot. I would like to be that man.'

'And what about my daughter? You have played with her affections for long enough, lad, and I'll not have you breaking her heart.'

'I have no wish to do so, Mr Wyness. On the contrary. But you know as well as I do that I cannot offer her anything like what she is used to and until I can, I will offer her nothing.'

'Nay, lad, pride never got a body anywhere. My Fanny, when she marries, will bring her husband a tidy sum, to be sure, but she's a girl who can live on little enough. She's not a one for extravagant spending, like some we could mention, and she'll not live beyond her means. Besides, I like you, lad. You're a hard worker and you'll do well for the firm. Fanny couldn't make a better choice and to show I'm all in favour, I've decided that when she marries, she'll take half my shares in the company with her. Now I can't say fairer than that, can I, lad?'

'No, Mr Wyness. You are very generous. But I prefer to support my own wife, just the same, and until I can, I'll wait . . .'

'And what does Fanny say about it?'

'I have not asked her yet. I thought it best to speak to you first.'

'Did you, indeed? Well, now that you have, I reckon you'll have a bit of explaining to do.'

'She told me she would wait for me,' said Tom uncertainly.

'Aye, maybe. But did you tell her why?' Tom shook his

head. 'Then we'll call her in and you can tell her now.' Wyness crossed to the doorway and tugged the bell. 'Tell Miss Fanny I want a word with her,' he told the servant who answered, then he and Tom waited in silence till they heard the drawing-room door open and quick, light steps hurry in their direction. There was a brief tap at the study door before it opened and Fanny stood there, breathless and bright-eyed with expectation.

'Yes, Papa? You called me?'

'Come in, lass,' sighed her father, 'and I reckon you'd best sit down. Tom has something to say to you.' He motioned her to a chair where she dutifully sat, but on the edge of the seat, hands clasped in her lap, her whole attitude that of suppressed excitement and bubbling joy. 'Well, go on, lad, or do you expect me to do your proposing for you?'

Tom gulped, reddened, lowered his eyes deliberately so as not to see her face and said, 'I have told your father that I want to marry you.' She half started from her seat, but before she could control her happiness enough to speak, he hurried on. 'And I have told him that first I want the chance to prove that I can work and succeed alone. I explained my reasons and I think he understood.'

'Aye, I did,' sighed Wyness, 'though whether poor little Fanny will is another matter. But I'd best leave you two alone to sort things out together.' Abruptly, he strode out of the room, closing the door behind him.

At the sight of her father's grave expression Fanny's heart had begun to beat uncomfortably fast, and now the happiness that had flared up at Tom's first words died away to leave only an all-embracing, hopeless dread. She sat unnaturally straight-backed in her chair, bit her bottom lip hard and clenched her small hands together to keep them from trembling, while her eyes remained fixed on Tom's flushed, evasive face.

'You had better tell me,' she said at last when the silence became intolerable.

'I have decided to leave Aberdeen and work elsewhere,' he managed, still not looking at her, 'I hope as your father's agent as well as for myself. I cannot say how long I will be away, only that I will come back as soon as I have earned enough to

[159]

support a wife and family. I hope you will be waiting for me, as you promised?'

He crossed to her chair, took one of her hands in his and said gently, 'Do not be sad, my love. It is not the end of the world. I will come back.'

When she said nothing, but continued to stare at him with haunted, desolate eyes, he said, 'I thought you would understand. And wait for me, as you said you would.' When she still said nothing, but stared straight ahead of her, the tears welling in her eyes, he pulled her roughly to her feet and kissed her with a passion and a tenderness that left her breathless. 'Now will you believe that I love you?'

'If you loved me, you would take me with you.' The bleak words hung like an accusation between them. After a moment, when he did not speak, Fanny said quietly, 'Where will you go? To Glasgow? Or to London?'

'Neither,' he said and added, more brusquely then he had intended, 'I shall find passage on the *Wuzeer* bound next week for Australia.'

With a cry of despair, she twisted out of his arms and ran weeping from the room.

'Australia?' Mhairi was appalled. 'But you can't, Tom. What about Fanny?'

'It is because of Fanny that I am going. In Australia a good tradesman can make his fortune far quicker than here: when I've made mine, I will come back.'

Mhairi looked at him shrewdly: the words he had used had reminded her of the letter which had caused all the trouble and with the reminder came a new suspicion. 'Are you sure you are going because of Fanny?' she said quietly. 'It couldn't be because of Lizzie Lennox, by any chance?'

'I don't know what you're talking about. I've told you: I want to make my fortune so I can marry Fanny.'

'You could do that here, where you are needed.'

'I'm not indispensable. Alex and the others will manage fine. They'll take care of you and the wee ones.'

'Is that how you salve your conscience?' said Mhairi with deliberate brutality. 'It doesn't matter that you have obligations if there is someone else you can shift them on to?'

'I have no obligations, except to myself. You have a husband to look after you, Lorn and Willy are old enough now to fend for themselves and Annys is not a baby any more. I want to live my own life for once, for myself alone.'

'And Fanny?'

'She understands,' blustered Tom. 'She knows how I feel about things and she has promised to wait.'

'Does she know how you feel about Lizzie Lennox?' The unexpected question stripped Tom of all defences. For a moment he looked hunted and shamefaced, until belligerence took over.

'That is my affair and no one else's,' he blustered. 'Besides, how I feel about Lizzie Lennox has nothing to do with how I feel about Fanny.'

'She may think it has.'

'Then she would be wrong. Besides,' he said, with a hint of anxiety in his voice, 'she doesn't know, and will not unless someone tells her.' He looked hard at Mhairi, whom he knew to be Fanny's confidante and friend. 'You wouldn't tell her, would you, Mhairi?'

'That depends on what you are going to tell me,' she said calmly, sitting down in the armchair beside the fire and taking up her sewing – a small garment in white cambric which she was hemming in readiness for the birth of her second child. As it was Saturday Annys was not at school and had taken her infant nephew out into the garden to play. The others were at the quarry, of course, where Tom should have been, except that after his decision he seemed to have given himself the right to work or not, as he chose. 'You may fetch me a glass of water while you are choosing your words,' she went on relentlessly. 'For you will need to choose them very carefully.'

'I don't need to choose,' muttered Tom, as he went into the scullery, to reappear again with Mhairi's drink. Then, his back to her and facing the little window, his gaze apparently fixed on a distant tree, he said, 'It is simple enough: I just want to make sure she is all right, that is all.'

'And how do you propose to do that?'

'See her, of course.'

'If you can find her,' said Mhairi drily: she had a shrewd

idea of how Lizzie intended to use the money Old Man Adam had sent out for her, but let Tom find that out for himself. 'Besides, won't you be too busy making that fortune you were boasting of?'

Tom swore. It was a rare enough occurrence for Mhairi to raise an eyebrow in surprise, but she made no comment.

'You none of you believe in me, do you? You all think I'm skiving off to enjoy myself and leave you to do all the work. Evading responsibility. Running away. Well, it's not like that. I meant it about the fortune – maybe not a great fortune, just enough to set me up in a wee house fit for Fanny to live in. Mr Wyness needs a man out there, to look after the big contract and find others for him, so why not me? And as I'm there, why shouldn't I seek out an old friend, especially one who's been hard done by and deserves someone to stand up for her seeing as how her own family will not lift a finger.'

'No reason,' sighed Mhairi, 'except that you know in your heart it is an excuse. Otherwise, why the bluster? You are acting because of some sort of misplaced pride and against your true nature and you'll not find peace again until you recognize it. As to poor Fanny, she may understand as you claim she does, but I doubt it. All she understands is that you could have chosen life here with her and have chosen the other side of the world instead. But don't be surprised if she grows tired of this waiting you keep boasting of and marries someone else. There,' she finished, snapping off her thread with more than necessary force, 'that's done. If there is anything you want mended before you set out on this trip of yours you'd best give it to me now. I may not be in the mood later. I've a new baby due any minute, and a houseful of working men to see after, in case you had forgotten.'

Tom bit his lip in remorse: he had been so taken up with the devastating decisions of the last twenty-four hours that he had forgotten everything except his own affairs. Mhairi's child was due in a few weeks. Then there was the quarry and the Victoria Street contract. Mhairi was right: he ought to be helping here, not flitting half across the world. Then obstinate pride reasserted itself. He had made his decision, the whole town would know it by now, and he was not going to lose face by backing down because his sister was expecting a baby. It wasn't fair to ask it of him. He'd spent his life being responsible for his brothers and sisters and it was time he broke free of them and lived his own life.

'Thanks,' he said stiffly. 'But I'm not needing any mending done. I'll maybe learn how to darn a sock on the voyage. The sailors are right good at it, seemingly, and it'll help pass the time. We'll be five months at sea.'

There was silence as both realized the implications of the long and hazardous voyage. The voyage safely over, even supposing Tom made his talked-of fortune within a year, he could not expect to be home again until at least two years from now, more likely three.

'I will miss you,' said Mhairi in a small voice, all disapproval forgotten.

'And I you.' He moved to her chair and when she held out her hand, took it and squeezed it hard, trying to convey love, encouragement and reassurance together. 'Don't worry, Mhairi,' he said when she looked up at him with tear-filled eyes. 'I promise I'll come back. And if anything happens and you need me before then, you are to send for me at once and I will come. Understand?'

But Tom's own eyes were moist when, a week later, he stood at the gangplank on the quay, not far from the spot where only a week ago the city had welcomed its Queen with such carefree jubilance and enthusiasm. His brothers and sisters were with him, Lorn and Willy unusually solemn, Annys alternately tearful and excited, Alex protecting Mhairi from the bustle of the quayside and Donal beside him, wee Hamish on his shoulders. Fanny Wyness stood a little apart, with her parents. They had not wanted her to come, but she had insisted, hoping even to the last minute that something would change Tom's mind. Her face was white and strained, but her eyes were dry. She had vowed that Tom should see she was not the weak and helpless little woman he thought she was, but instead was strong enough to survive any vicissitude. At home in her room, when the ship had sailed away with her lover, she would cry as many oceans of tears as she chose, but here on the quayside she would be brave as any Spartan woman, sending her menfolk into war.

'Goodbye, lads,' said Tom, ruffling his younger brothers'

hair then clapping them lightly on the shoulder. 'See and keep an eye on Mhairi – and behave yourselves. When I come back I'm not wanting to hear tales of mischief or devilment. As for you, young Annys,' he said, picking her up by the waist and lifting her till her face was level with his own, 'see and dinna grow too tall while I'm gone. And be good. You're to do as Mhairi says, and help her. Goodbye, Alex.' He gripped his friend's hand in awkward affection. 'I'll be back home again afore you know it. See and look after yourself.'

'You too, you young devil,' said Alex gruffly. The friends had not been parted since childhood when they had attended the Frederick Street school together.

Then it was Mhairi's turn. Tom could not remember a time when Mhairi had not been there, helping his mother with the housework and the children, caring for their widowed father and, when he in turn died, taking over responsibility for the orphaned family. Tom had given his word to share that responsibility: the memory stabbed him with guilt, but he pushed the thought aside. He was going away only to come back again, rich and prosperous, and while he was away, he could send them money. They would not miss him. They would manage fine.

'Goodbye, Mhairi,' he said, and bent to kiss her on the cheek. When she put her arms round him and hugged him tight, not speaking but conveying in that rare embrace all her love and fear for him, his eyes swam suddenly with tears. She was cumbersome with child and he was reminded with heart-stopping clarity of their mother whose final childbed had been her death-bed.

'Look after yourself, Mhairi, and write the moment the next wee horror is born. Promise?'

'I promise,' she managed, brushing the tears from her eyes.

'See and take good care of my sister,' he grunted, turning to Alex and attempting to cover his emotion with a frown. Quickly, he brushed the back of his hand across his eyes and prepared for the last and most difficult farewell.

'Goodbye, Mrs Wyness,' he said, extending a hand. 'Goodbye, sir. I will execute all your commissions as soon as I can and send you word.'

'Aye. See that you do. And while you're at it, you can add a few of your own. You've got the samples?' Wyness had assembled a small collection of polished granite of various colours and styles, some with lettering, some without, for Tom to use to drum up custom.

'Yes, sir. They are safe in the hold.'

'Then as long as they don't wear a hole through the hull and sink the ship to the bottom, you're all set to make that fortune of yours. See and make it fast.'

'Yes, sir. I will do my best.'

'Well, don't just stand there. Say goodbye to my daughter and get it over with. We've better things to do than hang around the quay all day with the seagulls pestering and the wind threatening to snatch the hair from our heads.'

'Yes, sir.' Tom looked awkwardly at Fanny, embarrassed by the presence of her parents and the host of other citizens who had gathered on the quay to wave the ship on its way. Fanny looked steadily back at him. She was unnaturally pale, her eyes strangely fixed and her lips set. Suddenly he realized: she was rigid not with hurt affront as he had first thought, but with bravery. Forgetting Wyness, his own family, everyone, he stepped forward, drew her into his arms and kissed her. At first she held herself stiff, even her lips unyielding, then suddenly she put her arms round his neck as she had done that day on the canal bank and it was as if they were alone on a fragile, blissful island, in an achingly beautiful sea.

'Goodbye, my darling,' he whispered at last. 'Remember I love you.'

She did not answer, but he felt her shudder as the unnatural stiffness returned and when he stepped back to take his final leave he saw the rigid mask was back in place. His own eyes, in contrast, were unashamedly wet.

He gave a curt bow, swung the canvas kitbag on to his shoulder and strode up the gangplank without a backward glance.

The bosun's whistle sounded, sails flapped, yards rattled and cracked in the brisk offshore wind, hawsers were loosed, tug boats hooted their busy warnings and finally the *Wuzeer* was under way. The quay was loud with cheers and a host of last-minute messages lost on the wind. Handkerchiefs and hats were waved in salutation and answered in similar fashion

[165]

from the crowded gunwales as the ship edged her careful way out into the mainstream and on towards the narrow arms of the harbour mouth.

Mhairi's group moved imperceptibly closer to Fanny's till they merged into one, Mhairi and Fanny side by side and holding hands. Together they watched until Tom's brave figure was a mere speck in the crowds of departing adventurers on deck, watched until the ship reached the open sea, hoisted sail and changed course, watched till the graceful outline was lost behind the green bluff of the Girdleness. Then the small, forlorn group split into its separate parts and turned at last for home.

Part 3

The Queen's visit had left more than the aftermath of a holiday for the public to mull over: in certain circles it had left the conviction of future gain. Her Majesty was well pleased with Deeside and there were rumours that in the new castle she had leased at Balmoral she had found the Scottish retreat she had long been looking for. If that proved to be the case, then the proposed Deeside railway could not fail to profit, and with it the city of Aberdeen.

In the library of his house at Silvercairns, in his favourite chair beside a fine wood fire, the day's paper laid aside and a glass of best brandy in his hands, Mungo Adam mentally counted over the number of scrip certificates he had collected for the vital line and could not keep the smile from his face. Never mind the temporary difficulties of the Aberdeen Railway and its failure to win funds; never mind the rumours of take-overs and suchlike. Mungo Adam would fight any such suggestion to the last ditch to ensure that those future profits stayed firmly in Aberdeen, where they belonged. Adam rolled the brandy round his tongue with particular enjoyment and refilled his glass. It was an excellent vintage. He must remember to order more. In fact, it was time he restocked his entire cellar and never mind the cost. When the Deeside line was built and in operation dividends would shower thick and fast into the Adam coffers. The Aberdeen line would be equally profitable and if the freight service proved as beneficial as Fergus had suggested it might, then the quarry, too, would thrive. It was a happy thought.

But that was in the future and there were more immediate matters to occupy him, in particular the outrageous progress of George Headstane Wyness. Remembering the fellow's overweening arrogance, Adam's self-satisfied expression changed to one of pure malevolence. The whole city knew how the man was prospering and to see him at the Queen's Welcome, sitting in a seat every bit as good as Adam's own and smirking and smiling as if he was royalty himself, would have made a stronger man than Mungo Adam sick with fury: as it was, the only thing that had kept Mungo sane was the thought of the brevity of the man's triumph, for brief it would undoubtedly be. Mungo Adam would see to that. He had already laid his plans and laid them so carefully and cautiously, biding his time till all suspicion was lulled, that when he struck, as he fully meant to strike, no possible suspicion would fall on him.

Adam already knew all about the workings of the Rainbow Hill quarry: who made up the boring teams, who prepared the fuses and the powder charges, who gave the final orders, who were the quarry's best and most experienced men – and now he had just heard that one of those men had upped and left for Australia, without warning. A mere week after the Queen's visit. Waved off from the quayside by Headstane Wyness himself so the fellow had not left without the Wyness blessing and that could only mean one thing: those rumours Fergus and Lettice had brought back from the Wyness party were true. The blackguard was indeed planning to extend his trade beyond the seas. But that particular effrontery could be dealt with later: Adam would be kept informed of every detail so that when the time came, suitable steps could be taken. More important was to put a stop to the man at home.

Thoughtfully Adam reviewed the many outrages perpetrated by Wyness until he came to the latest and most outrageous of all. Wyness had tendered for a contract that Adam had wanted, bribed for and fully expected to get – an elegant crescent of houses near Bon Accord Street, including five pairs of polished columns for five elegant porticoes. Fergus had complained about the columns, of course, but Fergus had been overruled. And now Adam's whole tender had been overruled in favour of *George Wyness*.

Reliable rumour had it, as confirmed by Adam's own spy, that if the contract was fulfilled by May, in time for the summer building season, the bounder would secure a second and better contract for the next development, without even going through the motions of a tender which might at least have given Adam a chance to win. They had started on the blasting programme already. They would continue with it, no doubt congratulating themselves on their own cleverness and efficiency, patting themselves on the back for being well within schedule, smiling and joking, all unsuspecting, until...

Old Man Adam frowned in long and devious thought, but at last the frown was replaced by a slow smile of satisfaction. He stood up, crossed to the leather-topped desk, opened a drawer and took out a sheet of paper. Then he sat down at the desk, pulled blotter and ink-well towards him, picked up his pen and began to write. The note finished, he folded it, sealed it with wax and his own signet ring, then rang the bell.

'See this is delivered tonight,' he told the servant, 'and not a word to a soul. It is strictly business, but business that the opposite camp must not get wind of. Understood?'

'Yes, sir.' His understanding further encouraged by a suitable coin, the servant left to execute his orders, just as the dressing bell boomed its timely warning from the depths of the hall.

'That should fix him,' said Adam to the empty room. 'Headstane Wyness shall learn that he challenges Silvercairns at his peril.' He drained his glass, smacked his lips with particular satisfaction and made his way upstairs, to dress for a celebratory dinner.

Work at Rainbow Hill steadily progressed. At first, Tom's departure left a noticeable gap, but very soon the pattern readjusted itself and settled down without him. More men were hired, more granite blasted and prepared for transfer to whatever destination awaited, whether the Wyness polishing sheds or the building site of one or other of the many contracts Wyness had secured for them, and all the time a small group of men of whom Alex was one worked on the special stone required for the new 'Crescent' contract as it had become known. The stone for the columns had to be chosen with particular care and blasted from the rock with even more, for if the chosen rock was split or broken the work would have to start all over again, and the process was a long and complicated one.

First of all Mackinnon, as experienced quarry-master, with Alex close at his side, would inspect the walls of the quarry, noting the way the posts lay, and finally selecting the block to be blasted from the bedrock. Together they would inspect the chosen stone for cracks and joints, feeling with their hands, eyeing it from all possible angles, judging whether it would take the blast up the bed or against it, discussing every point together, until Mackinnon had satisfied himself exactly where the hole should be bored and how deep. Then they would discuss the amount of force needed, the depth and circumference of the boring hole, the length of the fuse and exact amount of powder, and which tamping to use. Only when every detail was settled to Mackinnon's satisfaction would the team assemble and boring start.

The block successfully broken away from the bedrock, it would be chipped roughly to size on the spot before being loaded on to one of the quarry carts and carefully transported, either by road or canal, to the polishing yard. There, masons using hammer and chisel would prepare it for the polishing mill. When it had been suitably punched and fine-axed, the stone would be placed on a wagon which would move slowly to and fro under flat cast-iron rings attached to vertical spindles. These rings, lubricated by a constant supply of fine sea sand, would polish the surface until the required shine was achieved, and any fine detail or special moulding which the rings could not negotiate would be carried out laboriously by hand. It was a long and tedious process, but the result would be a polished column of enduring beauty and strength. And Wyness had contracted for five matching pairs, with a deadline which must on no account be missed.

With Tom gone, Alex felt the burden of such a responsibility heavy on his shoulders and decided that in case there should ever be an occasion when he could not consult Mackinnon, or when he himself might not be immediately available for advice, a detailed schedule should be drawn up of the blasting programme.

Mackinnon took to coming home to the cottage with him and together they would pore over endless sketches of Rainbow Quarry, showing side elevations and quarry floor, which they parcelled out into sections and numbered. Often, after a day's on-the-spot inspection, they would spend the evening revising the previous day's sketches and on at least

[172]

two occasions they tore the whole thing up and started again. But at last they had it parcelled out to their mutual satisfaction. Then Mackinnon pin-pointed possible bore positions, and even drew up a sort of reference scale which compared depth of bore hole with strength of charge required, 'Though ye canna rely on it absolutely, for every rock's different and so much depends on the angle and the size of the posts.'

Together they drew up a programme, listing the order of sections to be quarried; they revised it, criss-crossed it so many times with alterations that they had to redraw a clean and then a final copy. Donal was in silent attendance throughout these discussions, following the written diagrams intently, often pointing out areas the others had forgotten, or adding his comments to the calculations. Willy and Lorn showed equal interest so that often the kitchen table was so covered with papers that the five heads almost touched as they pored over them and poor Annys could find no place to put the supper plates.

Mhairi did not mind. She was fond of Mr Mackinnon and knew that Alex valued his advice. Besides, her second child was imminent and she welcomed the diversion to keep them all from worrying on her behalf. So she fed them, kept them well supplied with ale and saw that the lamps were bright, then she sat contentedly at the fireside, sewing, while across the hearth Annys played with Hamish until his bedtime, then read a school-book or did some small task for Mhairi, such as peeling vegetables or setting the dough to rise, to save her time in the morning when Annys was at school. Those were useful, contented evenings which Mhairi was to look back on with gratitude. Later, when Mackinnon had gone home and the household was abed, Alex would put his arms around her in the darkness of their box bed and they would curl together for warmth, murmuring quietly of the doings of the day or of plans for the morrow, until Alex slept.

Mhairi would lie awake long into the night, too cumbersome and uncomfortable to sleep for long at a time herself, but content to know her family was peacefully sleeping, especially Alex who worked so hard for them all and whose arm lay protectively across her breast as if even in sleep he would defend her against all trouble. She would listen to his regular breathing beside her, to the small whimpers and sighs from her little son's cradle, to the night sounds from the hill: an owl calling, or the sharp bark of a fox, until the first birds trilled in the twilight and others answered them in growing chorus as the sky lightened to dawn. Then she would ease her way very carefully from the bed, so as not to disturb Alex, tiptoe out to the back scullery and begin preparations for a new day.

On a morning in October, some five weeks after Tom's departure, Alex came up behind her unawares as she stood at the scullery sink and slipped his arms round where her waist used to be.

'If you grow much bigger,' he teased, 'I shall not be able to reach round . . .' Then he stopped, absolutely still for a wondering moment before saying in awe, 'I felt the wee one move. Will it be today?'

Mhairi shook her head. 'I don't think so. In another week, perhaps?' She turned her head to smile up at him over her shoulder. 'Don't worry, Alex. I know what to expect now and I'll be fine. Annys is staying at home to help me and to run messages, and I have good neighbours. So take that frown off your face,' she said softly, turning towards him and tracing the lines on his forehead with a loving finger. 'It does not suit you.'

'How can I help worrying, my love,' he murmured, holding her tight. 'You are my whole world, Mhairi. Where would I be without you?'

'You would be late for work,' she teased, trying to push him away, but her eyes were moist and she bit her lip against the emotion which flooded through her. 'I thought you said you were going to start that precious blasting today?'

'So we are.'

'Then you'd best get that porridge inside you to add strength to your arm, and there's a slice of good pickled beef for your sandwich.' Suddenly, valour left her and she clung to him shivering, her face against the reassuring strength of his shoulder. 'I don't know what I would do without you, Alex. Promise you will take care?'

'And would I do otherwise, woman, with a wife and a family to support?' He took her face in his hands and looked solemnly into her eyes. 'Listen to me carefully. While I am gone, you are to be calm and quiet and strong, as you always are. For my sake, and for our children. If you feel your spirits failing, remember that I love you. Promise?'

'I promise.' She drew away from him and attempted a smile.

'Good. Now, where's that porridge you were boasting of, woman? Or has wee Hamish eaten the lot while my back's been turned?'

Ten minutes later he kissed her goodbye on the doorstep. 'Remember what I said, Mhairi love, and don't worry. I will be home at midday, to see how you are. Till then, take care of yourself, for me?'

He kissed her again, swung his tool-bag on to his shoulder and strode whistling up the track towards the quarry. Mhairi watched till he reached the rowan tree where he turned and waved before disappearing beyond the hedge. Smiling, she closed the door, took up a pan lid, banged it vigorously with a ladle and called up the stairway, 'Breakfast's on the table, boys. But if you're not downstairs in five minutes you'll be away to your work without any.' Then she went into the bedroom to pick up Hamish from his cradle.

Alex and the rest of the team had been working on the bore hole since Monday and the drilling had gone so well that Mackinnon hoped to be able to lay the fuse today. As always, Alex wished Tom was still here instead of on his way to the other side of the world. It was all very well to say they had men just as skilled to call on, but it was one thing to work with a man you knew, quite another to team up with a stranger, and the sooner those blessed pillars were safely quarried, cut to shape and handed over to the polishers in the yard, the better he would be pleased. It had taken them long enough to find a good, uncracked post, for they needed a height of at least twelve feet and the granite of Rainbow Hill was not as regular as that of Silvercairns. After consulting their master plan it had taken several hours' inspection and the most detailed investigation of every crack and cranny in the quarry's surface before Mackinnon had made his choice.

'I'll bore the hole myself,' Alex had said, 'with Robbie.'

Robbie Bruce was the third of the three-man team which, until his sudden departure, had also included Tom. But Tom's departure had left a gap.

Red Henderson had offered. 'If you're looking for a strong arm and a steady hammer, I'm your man,' His hair greyed over with granite dust, his leather apron similarly dusted and a hammer swinging nonchalantly from an undoubtedly muscular arm, he had laid a testing hand against the rock and felt its surface, moving his hand slowly up and down and then across. 'Is this the place you've chosen? There's a wee fissure here, but nay suitable for a charge, I dinna think. Had it been bigger, maybe. Saves a deal o' trouble if you can tip your powder down a crack. Seen it done in Cornwall when I was a lad. You tip the charge down, then make a fuse with a lump of moistened powder tied on wi' string. A "spit devil" they calls it. Blows the rock apart as neat and clean as a man could wish and beautiful to see. But this crack's nay big enough. You'll need a bore hole, maybe two. Here?' and he had indicated the exact spot which Mackinnon had already chosen.

'As you seem to know what you're talking about better than most, Red, you can join the team,' Mackinnon had decided, 'and the sooner we start, the better.'

It was slow and arduous work: one man of the three held the steel drill in place while the other two walloped it alternately with their eight-pound hammers, until, after twenty minutes or so, it was time for the idler to take his turn. That way each man had twenty minutes' comparative rest in the hour, but it was a tough job, for tough men. Four feet in twice as many hours was a great achievement and, depending on the rock and the men, the job could take much longer. As it was, by that Thursday midday Mackinnon was satisfied.

'I was beginning to think we'd have to wait till tomorrow morning, but looking round the quarry I reckon there's nought the men can't leave and the sooner we fire it the better. I've the powder and fuses ready in the office. Nip along and fetch them, Robbie, while I just see . . .' The old man lowered the drill into the hole and tested the depth. 'Aye, that's fine. Alex, you'd best tell the lads to start moving the horses and carts out of the quarry and send a lad round to warn the men, will you? We'll need a long fuse for this one, I'm thinking.'

'Which way will you lay it? North or north-east?' The old man turned to look behind him over the floor of the quarry, wetted a finger and held it up to test the wind. Behind him, Red squatted beside the bore hole, dusting its edges and smoothing away the grit.

'Nay wind to speak of, but we'll make it north-east. There'll be no difference once the flame's taken hold.'

Robbie reappeared at the run, with a bundle of twisted hemp and a metal can.

'What powder are you using?' asked Red, peering into the can.

'Cruickshank's best. The medium, nay the coarse. Can you make a fuse?'

'Twisted hemp, with space to pour the powder in? Aye.'

'Then get to work on this one and mind and leave plenty of length. Robbie, you take the ramrod and make sure the powder goes right to the bottom when I pour. Not too hard, mind, or you'll blow us all to kingdom come.'

Alex reappeared. 'All set. They'll shift when they hear the warning whistle.'

'So will we,' said Mackinnon, 'so mind and make that fuse long enough. I'm nay as young as I was.'

'What about the tamping?' asked Red.

'Over there.' The old man pointed to a bucket which he had set by earlier. 'You'd best fetch it. We're just about ready.'

Mackinnon tipped the powder in a steady stream into the bore hole. The fuse was lowered, more powder added, Robbie wielded the wooden ramrod to pack everything tight. Red added the tamping of broken stone and moistened quarry dust while Alex saw that the fuse was not carried down into the hole with the rest. Finally the whole was well tamped down, the fuse laid out along the ground and the whistle blew its warning. Instantly the quarry emptied until only Mackinnon and his three helpers were left.

'You too, Robbie,' said Alex, jerking his head. 'And you, Red.' The two retreated across the quarry floor and behind a jutting rock. 'There's no need for you to stay,' he said to Mackinnon. 'You get back with the others. I'll light the fuse fine on my own and I can run faster than you.'

'I've never laid a fuse I havena lit, not in all my working

life,' said the older man, 'and I dinna plan to start now. If you insist, you can watch so as to learn the knack, but you'll run when I say. You've a wife and a son, remember, who need ye.'

'And what about you, you old fraud? Mrs Mackinnon doesna need you, I suppose?'

Mackinnon grinned. 'All right. I'll be honest wi' ye, Alex lad. I canna abide anyone else doing the best bit o' the whole process. Lighting that fuse is a thrill I wouldna miss for the world.'

'You'd best get on with it, then, afore the powder gets damp.'

'Blow your whistle.' Alex did, with two shrill blasts. Mackinnon cast his eye for the last time over the deserted quarry, took a tinder box from his pocket and crouched on one knee. 'Remember, as soon as the flame's taken hold, put your head down and run for yon rock. Now, I strike the spark, take the tinder and hold it to the end of the fuse, like this, making sure both strands catch. There . . . they're alight . . . now *run!*'

They were almost at the rock when a low rumbling shook the earth under their feet, the noise crescendoed to a thunderous, ear-splitting crash and the air sprang alive with flying rocks of every size from boulders to mere granite chips, their edges sharp as knife blades. Then dense smoke billowed up from the jagged wound to obliterate everything in choking swirls of powder fumes. In the quivering emptiness which followed the explosion the intermittent patter and thud of falling stones sounded strangely muffled through the masking smoke, then that too ceased and there was a silence which seemed to stretch into infinity.

Gradually the smoke lifted until the quarry floor was visible under its pall of acrid grey and the first of the quarry workers ventured out from his prudent shelter. What he saw stopped him in his tracks. On the floor of the quarry was a shingle beach of broken stones fit for nothing but building rubble and at its fringe, half buried under that rubble, the motionless figures of old Mackinnon and young Alex Grant.

At Rainbow Cottage the explosion rattled the windows in their frames and set Mhairi's heart thumping hard with fear.

She snatched a plaid from the back of the door, thrust Hamish into Annys's arms, cried, 'Stay here!' and ran, stumbling and gasping, as fast as her heavy figure allowed up the path towards the quarry. Others overtook her, farm labourers, the blacksmith, men from the stables, and the moving stream of people was more terrifying than the explosion had been. Into Mhairi's mind rushed the memory of the day her father had died, killed by the collapsing arch of the viaduct on which he was working. Crowds had flowed to the scene of that accident just as these people were doing. Dust had lain thick everywhere, coating grass, tree, dyke with a layer of grey, just as the grass was layered now. And when she had reached the scene of the viaduct collapse it had been a waste of rubble, just as this quarry floor was. They had searched among the fallen masonry, brushing off stones and dust to reveal the lifeless figures of the workmen, inert and caked in dust just as these figures were. Two figures, stretched full length and twisted, as if thrown from a distance. Someone, the Woodside doctor, was crouching on one knee beside the first, feeling for a pulse beat, listening, gently probing. A second, younger man was attending similarly to the other. Then the doctor lifted his head, called to someone for a blanket and when it came, turned his patient gently on to his back and covered him with it, pulling the edge up and over the dead face. The second man sat back on his heels and snapped his fingers, though what he was summoning Mhairi never knew. For the dust-caked body on the ground stirred, half raised itself on one elbow and turned its blood-streaked mask of a face in her direction before falling back again inert.

'Alex!'

After the first anguished shriek, she pushed her way through the parting crowd with the strength of ten, and heedless of the broken stones under her knees, the torn skin of her hand, of the doctors and onlookers and quarry workers, threw herself to the ground beside her husband. There she knelt for a timeless moment, staring at her husband's dust-covered face, the closed eyes, the gaping gash in his forehead from which blood oozed thick and bright, the twisted way his beloved body lay, before she clutched up a handful of her petticoat skirts and tried tenderly to staunch the wound with

[179]

it, murmuring, 'It's all right, Alex, my love, it's all right,' while her eyes grew dark with terror and her heart beat so hard she thought it would burst her rib-cage.

Alex moaned, stirred, said something that could have been 'Mhairi?' though the word, if it was a word, was faint as a breath of wind in summer grass.

'I'm here, darling. I'm here.' She took his hand gently in her own, felt the skin which should have been warm and strong frighteningly cold against hers. 'I will look after you, Alex darling. Lie still, my love and . . . and . . .' But tears choked her throat and she could not speak. For the first time she looked up at the doctor who was standing silently beside her, but he gave the smallest shake of the head. Very well. If he would not help, she would care for Alex herself, nurse him back to health and strength and . . . Fighting against hysteria, she crouched over him, the tight mound of her womb forgotten, and murmured, 'You will be well again very soon, my love.' She kissed him tenderly on the forehead where the blood still oozed, then, still whispering endearments, she kissed his cheek and, with infinite gentleness, his closed eyes. Miraculously, they opened and he looked at her with full and loving recognition, but when he tried to speak Mhairi could hardly make out the words.

'I'm . . . sorry . . . my . . . love . . .' Then the light left his eyes and his hand which she still held lovingly in hers lost what little life remained.

'Alex!'

Annys, still standing fearfully in the doorway where Mhairi had left her, wee Hamish clutched tight against her chest, heard the cry as far away as Rainbow Cottage and trembled with dread.

'Alex! Don't leave me. *Please*!' Mhairi threw herself weeping on to his chest, heedless of the dust and grit and blood, and clung to him so tightly that even the doctor and his unknown assistant together could not move her. Then from somewhere in the quarry precincts her young brother Willy appeared, ashen-faced and aged in the space of a morning far beyond his fifteen years.

'Mhairi, let the doctor do what has to be done,' he said quietly, standing over her with new authority. 'Remember

[180]

your baby. Alex's baby.'

Be calm and quiet and strong . . . for my sake . . . She heard Alex's voice clearly across the stillness and her own voice, answering, *I promise.* With a long shudder she drew herself up to a kneeling position, lovingly set Alex's dishevelled clothes to rights, smoothed the hair back from his battered forehead, and finally laid gentle fingers over his sightless eyes.

Then Willy stretched out his hand and at last she allowed herself to be helped, trembling, to her feet. Her face was ashen, streaked with tears and dust and her husband's blood, but set in an expression of new calm. There was more blood on her shapeless clothes and her hair had come loose in places from its pins, but she carried her cumbersome body with dignity and her dishevelment with pride. *Be calm and quiet and strong.* But when she looked a question at her brother he saw such desolation in her eyes that he had to gulp hard to keep back his own tears.

'They will bring Alex home for us,' he said quietly. 'The others have been sent for. Put your arm through mine and we will go on ahead to make everything ready.'

'Very well.' The crowd parted in silence for them as together they walked, dry-eyed and desolate, back to Rainbow Cottage and Alex's little, fatherless son.

Lettice Adam adjusted the veil of her black straw bonnet and from under its concealing screen inspected that section of the congregation which her eyes could encompass without too unseemly a twisting of the head. They were all there, as was to be expected: the quarry owners, the Council, the Trades. You would think they had been royalty instead of merely an old quarry foreman who after a lifetime's service at Silvercairns had come out of retirement to join the enemy camp and a young quarry worker no one had heard of. Fergus had behaved in an extraordinary manner when the news came, shutting himself away in his room and refusing to speak to anyone, and even her father had looked shocked, muttering, 'Damned unfortunate. Bungling fool who caused it should be shot.' But apparently the fuse had been prepared, laid and lit by Mackinnon himself. Mackinnon, who had never bungled anything in fifty years of quarry work, had obviously lost his touch. 'Too old . . .' 'Never should have gone back . . .' 'Wyness should have known better than to ask it of him.' Subtly the blame was laid at George Wyness's door: he had given a dangerous job to an old man who could no longer cope and had paid accordingly. As the old man had paid, with his own life and that of his young friend.

Across the aisle in the front pew Lettice Adam saw the black-clad and dignified figure of the old widow, small, rotund and shapeless in her layers of mourning, and beside her the equally shapeless but taller, straight-backed figure of the young one, her face a white oval in a sea of black. They said she was expecting a child at any moment, poor thing. But momentary sympathy was lost in a shudder of distaste. That class bred like rabbits.

Beside old Mrs Mackinnon on the aisle side stood the brother, Donal Grant, looking well-scrubbed and pale, but really quite handsome. He, she remembered, was the deaf and dumb one who had worked with the Silvercairns horses until he too had deserted to the Wyness camp, and those two younger boys on the other side of the Grant widow were presumably Diack relatives of some kind. They had the same dark hair and colouring. Wasn't there a younger sister, too, and a child? But presumably they had been left at home.

In the pew behind the chief mourners were George Wyness and his family. Fanny, Lettice noted, looked particularly pale and wan, but then black was not a kind colour for a girl of Fanny's complexion. Lettice herself, on the contrary, knew she was in particularly good looks today. Black set off her flaxen hair to perfection.

Her eyes roved the congregation, looking for a new face among the tedious old ones and, just when she was resigning herself to the same old dreary collection, she found one. Next to old Dr Marshall, whose side-whiskers looked more in need of pruning every time she saw him, was an unknown young man, clean-shaven and decidedly pleasing to the eye.

Lettice had kept house for her father most competently for more than a year now and was growing restless. The dinner parties they gave were no longer a challenge and although her father grumbled regularly about the bills, she knew she could

[182]

buy what she wanted whenever she wanted it. But what was the point of giving the most sumptuously elaborate dinners, dressing in the most stylish and becoming dresses, talking wittily in the most entertaining way, if it was only for the benefit of the same boring clientele? She dare not say anything to her father, of course, or he would instantly resurrect the marry-off-Lettice idea which, mercifully, he seemed to have forgotten. But she would make discreet inquiries; find out who the new man was. Perhaps she should try an experimental faint, now, in church, so that Dr Marshall would rush to her side to revive her, followed, of course, by his solicitous companion? But no doubt Fergus would heave her outside single-handed, or Mrs Macdonald would pounce from the pew behind and thrust smelling salts up her nose. Regretfully, Lettice abandoned the idea: if she planned to engineer an introduction to the unknown gentleman, then old Mackinnon's funeral was hardly the place.

'Who was the dashing young fellow with Dr Marshall?' she inquired of Fergus as, the funeral over and their due commiserations offered, they made their way towards the waiting carriage. Old Man Adam had stopped to speak to a business acquaintance, and Lettice had seized her opportunity, brief though it would be. They had not accepted the general invitation to join the sorrowing families for suitable refreshment: George Wyness was presiding over that particular function and Mungo Adam had his own reasons for shunning his arch rival's company. As for Fergus, his emotions were in turmoil enough as it was without facing another such ordeal.

'Who?' he said now, startled out of his sombre reverie. He had felt a deep and grateful affection for old Mackinnon who had taught him all he knew about quarry management, as well as being a straight and honourable man. Fergus would miss him, and so, he thought wryly, would Silvercairns. But it would be time to face that particular problem when it arose, as it inevitably would sooner or later. For the moment his grief was for Mackinnon himself, and for his widow. As to the other widow . . . she was more beautiful than ever in sorrow. Seeing her surrounded and supported by her loving and solicitous family, he had wanted only to whisk her up and carry her away to some secret bower where he would comfort and cosset and cherish her till the sorrow left her face and she looked at him with as much love as she had given that dead quarryman. He remembered her face as he had taken her black-gloved hand, bowed, offered the conventional words of sympathy. Remembered the white skin, paler than ever against the black which enfolded her, the dark lashes and strangely unseeing blue of her eyes. She had looked at him with the same impassive dignity, thanked him quietly for his attendance in the same expressionless voice as she gave to those before and after him. He doubted she even saw that he was there. When they got home, he would write to her, offer his sympathy as a friend. But, oh God, if what he feared was true . . .

'The Beau Brummell with the over-large cravat and the over-new suit.' Lettice's voice, light with mockery, broke in upon his thoughts. 'The young fop who is so proud of his new hat that he held it on his knee and stroked it like a cat all through the service. The one with Dr Marshall,' she finished in exasperation as Fergus looked increasingly bemused.

'Really, Lettice, must you always be so relentlessly frivolous, even at a funeral?'

'Yes, brother dear, when you are so relentlessly tedious!' flashed Lettice, though she had the grace to look shamefaced. '*Who is he?*'

'That is Dr Marshall's nephew David, newly qualified and learning the ropes from his uncle so he can take over the practice one day, when he has found a respectable woman to marry.'

'Then he is only an apprentice medicine-man?' said Lettice, disappointed. She had hoped for better than that.

'So it seems. Dr Marshall was called to the quarry when the accident happened and his nephew went along too, for the experience.'

But Fergus had lost what little interest he had in the subject. He could think only of Mhairi, remote and proud and achingly brave, but with such desolation in her eyes. If only she would let him, he could help her, care for her, love her . . . Quickly he slammed that dangerous door and turned his mind instead to a simpler sadness: poor old Mackinnon, killed by his own blast. The thought was strangely disturbing to Fergus who had always thought of Mackinnon as the safest man he knew where quarry blasting was concerned. If it was a question of estimating the strength of charge, the old man invariably underestimated, 'to be on the safe side', as he had told Fergus over and over. If it was a question of the length of fuse, the old man was equally cautious. 'If in doubt, Mr Fergus, make it longer than necessary.' If the cause had been the position of the bore hole, Fergus was equally baffled: Mackinnon had an extraordinary rapport with the granite and knew by instinct where each hole should be made. Fergus would not believe he had lost his grip enough to make a wrong choice. But the fact remained: something had gone wrong. For some reason Fergus found the idea disturbing.

When he had said as much to his father, Mungo Adam had growled, 'Isn't it enough that the old man is dead without you raking over the ashes looking for scandal? Accidents happen and that was one of them, and a damned unfortunate one for George Wyness.'

That was something else that worried Fergus, but he had the prudence not to say so aloud. Now he found Lettice's interest in the young doctor who had examined the dust-caked and battered victims both callous and irritating.

'Here comes Father,' he warned. 'I suggest you drop the subject. You know how disturbing he has found the whole episode and I advise you to keep quiet, or talk safely about the weather.'

'I notice the leaves are beginning to fall, Papa,' said Lettice sweetly, as the carriage drew away from the churchyard and headed west along Union Street towards Holburn and eventually Silvercairns. 'Soon we must be thinking about removing into town for the winter.'

'Soon? Why soon? The weather is still good, the shooting excellent. Why should we move back *soon*?'

With an inward sigh, Lettice set out to mollify him. 'I am sorry, Papa. I was merely thinking aloud. It is a question of domestic arrangements, of no concern to you, but needing much careful planning if the transfer is to be made smoothly, with no disruption to the kitchen, or the family meals. Laundering linen and packing china is no concern of yours, Papa, and I am sorry I spoke unthinkingly. I should have asked instead whether you were planning any particularly important dinners in the coming weeks? For one of your railway friends, perhaps?' It was common knowledge that when the Queen had returned south by land instead of sea, the weather being too rough, she had taken the train from Montrose to Perth and thence to London and had pronounced the journey both comfortable and convenient. Thus the embryo Aberdeen line had been given royal approval, albeit unofficial as yet, and the anti-take-over lobby of which her father was leader was understandably buoyant. But even this lure did not tempt him out of ill humour.

'When I am, I will inform you,' he snapped and returned to his brooding contemplation of the passing scene.

Behind his back Lettice made a face at Fergus, who ignored her. They rode in silence for some minutes until Fergus, to make some sort of conversation, said, 'It should not be long before the mail boat arrives from the West Indies. Mr Burnett is expecting imminent word from his relations – reading between the lines I suspect he has invested in the business out there and in view of the recent devastating drought is worried about the fate of his money.'

'Aren't we all?' muttered his father into the upturned collar of his greatcoat. The wind on the open road could be chill.

'I wonder if there will be any news of Hugo?' said Lettice. 'Possibly even a letter in his own inimitable hand?' She missed her brother and, when hostessing her father's tedious dinners proved particularly trying, for two pins would have taken ship to Jamaica to join him.

Her father visibly brightened. The quarryman did not matter, but Mackinnon's death had come as an unpleasant shock and he could not get the thought of it out of his mind. But the name of his favourite son banished gloom to the wings, at least for the moment. Besides, hadn't Mackinnon's death meant the defeat of Adam's arch enemy and opened the way to future profit? He leant forward and told the coachman to 'Get a bit more life into those horses, damn you. It's not a hearse they're pulling. The funeral is over now so look lively, or I'll come up on that box and drive the thing myself.'

As a result, they trotted up the long drive of Silvercairns House in splendid style, dust flying from the wheels and the horses' manes streaming, for all the world like conquerors returning triumphant to their castle.

The family kitchen at Rainbow Cottage was grey and silent on that cheerless autumn Sunday. Even the fire seemed to have caught the general air of mourning and simmered suitably muted and subdued. In a chair beside the fire sat Mhairi, staring unseeing at the cast-iron kettle on its chain over the grumbling peats. She was motionless, even the hand which held her sewing needle lay still on the cambric garment which made a small white pool in the darkness of her black-clad lap, mirroring the white oval of her face.

At the table Willy and Lorn whispered together with anxious, worried expressions, while Donal worked away at yet another sketch for a monument. No one needed to ask for whom the monument was to be designed. After Mhairi, Donal of all of them suffered the most. Not only had he lost the brother who had brought him up from infancy with unfailing love and protective care, but also old Mackinnon who, throughout their childhood when they lived on the same tenement stair, had been like a benevolent uncle to the orphaned brothers whose own uncle gave them grudging house-room and little else. Ever since the funeral he had worked at sketch after sketch with a sort of frenzied energy while the others watched in helpless silence, unable to comfort him and knowing that only such activity could ease his grief. Today all three of them were dressed once more in their sober best for in spite of yesterday's funeral, Mhairi had made them all go to church – 'If only to please me, and to pray for Alex's soul.'

Across the hearth, on her creepie stool, Annys was feeding Hamish gruel, one careful spoonful at a time. She and the child were the only ones in the room who did not wear black. Now she bit her lip, looked anxiously at Mhairi then at Lorn who answered her with a warning shake of the head. He knew instinctively that Mhairi wanted no one to attempt comfort.

Suddenly through the silence came the sound of carriage wheels approaching until they drew up at the cottage gate. Men's voices, footsteps on the path, then Willy opened the door to Mr Wyness, sober-faced as they were and similarly clad in black.

'Fanny wanted to come with me,' he told Mhairi when she had answered his greeting with a dutiful but lifeless 'Please come in.' 'I told her she'd best wait till tomorrow. With the funeral over, we have business matters to discuss and the sooner we get them over, the better. But she sends you her loving sympathy and hopes you will find comfort in the love you still have in plenty all around you.'

When Mhairi made no answer, but continued to stare bleakly into nowhere, Wyness looked at her shrewdly for a moment, then said, 'Aye, well. It's a sad time for all of us. She sent you a basket of provisions, too. Mackie's taken it round to the scullery, but there's a haunch of venison among other things so you'd best get some of your women friends to deal with it if you haven't the strength yourself, Mhairi. Nought like a good piece of meat to build a man's muscles and we're all going to need a deal of muscle in the weeks to come. The fruit is for you, Mhairi, and I think Fanny said there was a calves-foot jelly, too, so see you eat that yourself, for the baby's sake.'

'Thank you,' said Mhairi, in the same dead voice. 'Please thank Fanny, too.'

'Now, what about making us all a cup of tea, Annys, when you've finished feeding young Hamish?' said Wyness. 'Then we'd best get down to business.'

'A mere six months ago,' he said later, when they were gathered round the table ready for the 'business' meeting, 'we were celebrating a year's successful operation and a year's profits.'

Annys had produced tea of sorts, with a glass of whisky for Mr Wyness, and another, privately requested, for Mackie in the back yard. She had found biscuits, too, and in the basket on the kitchen table, home-made shortbread which Mr Wyness told them Fanny herself had baked. 'So see you eat some, Mhairi, and keep your strength up.'

But after the first dutiful bite, the shortbread lay untouched on the plate in Mhairi's lap.

'I had three working partners then,' continued Wyness. 'Now I have none.'

'There's still Tom,' began Lorn, but Wyness waved him

to silence.

'We'll come to Tom later. First, there are matters to discuss. Business matters, concerning this.' He took a sealed letter from his pocket and laid it on the table in front of them. It was inscribed in careful black copper-plate *Alexander Grant*.

There was silence as they all stared at the letter, then Wyness said, 'You'd best open it, Mhairi. Mrs Mackinnon gave it to me. She told me what was in it, too, and because her husband died before young Alex did she assures me it is legal. And even if it wasn't, she told me she would write it all over again herself. A fine woman, Mrs Mackinnon.'

With trembling fingers Mhairi slit open the letter with a table knife, unfolded it and handed it to Donal. 'He must read it first,' she said, with the first sign of animation in her voice since Alex's death.

They watched Donal read it through once, then a second time, while surprise, shock, gratitude and grief lit up his face as vividly as if he had spoken the words aloud. Finally, his eyes glistening with unshed tears, he handed the letter back to Mhairi, then sat with his head in his hands.

Mhairi began to read it for herself, but when she gasped and bit her lip, Lorn and Willy together cried, 'Read it aloud!'

She began in a faltering voice. 'Mr Mackinnon writes that in the event of his death he leaves his shares in the Rainbow Hill quarry to Alex. *Because Alex is the nearest thing to a son that I have had, because I know that Alex will continue to care for his brother Donal as he has always done, with love and understanding, and because . . .*' Here Mhairi's voice trembled for a moment before she steadied it enough to finish, '*because Alex will be as good a quarryman one day as any man could wish . . . to . . . see.*'

There was a moment's awed silence, then Mhairi said bleakly, 'And he would have been, had he lived.'

'But Alex is dead,' said Lorn, and Willy added, 'So what does it mean, Mr Wyness?'

'It means that the shares in the quarry belong to Mhairi. With Mr Mackinnon's twenty per cent and Alex's own ten per cent, that means Mhairi has a thirty per cent stake in the enterprise, for herself and for that son of hers. And before you ask, Alex came to see me himself about it long ago, the day after wee Hamish was born. "If anything happens to me," he said, "I want your assurance that my share goes to Mhairi and the boy." Alex was a fine man, with a responsible head on his shoulders.'

'But what about Mrs Mackinnon?' faltered Mhairi. 'Will she have enough to live on? I would not want to think that we had taken what was rightly hers.'

'I look after my workers, lass,' said George Wyness. 'Unlike some we could mention. Funeral expenses paid and a wee pension for the widow, like your Alex suggested. Cheeky young stirk, I thought, telling me my job, but he was right. It takes a weight off a man's mind knowing his widow will not starve. So there'll be something for you too, Mhairi. As to Mrs Mackinnon, she'll be fine, leastways she will be if she can see her lad now and again, eh, Donal?'

Quickly they explained to Donal in a mixture of carefully enunciated words and sign language and he nodded understanding. But his face was worried. He wrote quickly on his sketch pad and pushed it towards George Wyness.

Mackinnon was a good workman. Why did the accident happen?

'Aye, lad. You may well ask. We'll need to find out every detail and piece it together as best we can. I've had a word with Robbie Bruce already and Red Henderson. In fact, I've heard their tale over and over, and it just doesn't fit. Leastways, it doesn't fit with yon explosion . . . We need Alex's and old Mackinnon's own version to complete the picture and we'll not get that this side of the grave, God rest their souls. But we owe it to their memory to keep on trying and maybe one day we'll fathom it somehow. Meantime, we'll need to find a new foreman for the quarry, until Tom gets back. You'll be writing to him, naturally, and telling him he's needed?'

'No!' Mhairi's cry startled them all, not so much by its volume as by its contrast to her demeanour till that moment. 'I forbid it! He cannot even have reached Australia yet. What is the use of sailing all that way to find a letter waiting which summons you home again?'

'But with Alex dead, Mhairi, he will need to . . .'

'No!' Mhairi's unnatural lassitude had completely left her

and she half rose to her feet, holding the table edge for support but unwavering in her vehemence. She was remembering her last meeting with Tom before he left, his protests that he had done enough for his brothers and sisters, that he wanted to live his own life for once, that he needed to make his own way and his own fortune. 'Tom promised he would come if I should need him, and I know he would take ship the moment he read my letter. He is the best of brothers and I love him dearly. And because of that *I will not have him called back*. He left for reasons of his own, and must come back by his own choice, in his own time, or he will never be at peace. Alex is dead and the funeral over. Tom's coming will not change that.'

'Maybe,' said Wyness into the silence which followed her words. 'But he is entitled to be told. Alex was his friend, after all.'

'He will be told, one day, but please, Mr Wyness, not yet? Give him at least a year to do whatever it is he needs to do in Australia? Alex left all his plans and calculations for the quarry. He and Mr Mackinnon had everything worked out, even to the order in which the sections must be quarried. If you will oversee the work I am sure we can manage somehow between us, with Donal and Lorn and Willy, and there are good workmen at the quarry, loyal workmen who know their job. Robbie and Red and the others. Let Tom come home in his own time, Mr Wyness, please?'

Wyness looked at her with a mixture of admiration and compassion and something else she could not define. Then he sighed. 'That's all right, then. If I hadn't known it to be impossible I would have said you and Fanny had put your heads together and composed that speech between you, for she said exactly the same. Tom must come home of his own free will, she said, or not at all. Poor lass. I dared not bring her with me today till I'd seen which way the wind blew in these quarters, but it seems you women are determined to martyr yourselves and we menfolk will just have to do as we're told, eh, lads?' and he winked at Lorn and Willy. 'So first, we get our story straight. Not a word in any letters to Tom about the explosion. We tell him Mr Mackinnon died of a heart attack, at the quarry, and left his shares to Alex. That is all. So that's settled. Now to the next thing: we'll need a new foreman.'

'Not wi' us around,' said Willy stoutly, and Lorn echoed, 'Not wi' us ready and willing to help wherever we're needed. We may be only apprentices, but we can do a man's work just the same. Then there's Donal here.' Willy put an arm across the other's shoulders. 'He'll help, won't you? So you see, Mr Wyness, you've plenty of menfolk to rely on, without hiring strangers.'

'Maybe you're right,' said Wyness thoughtfully. 'But you'll still need someone.'

'Appointed from inside,' warned Lorn.

'Aye,' said Willy. 'We're not needing a stranger coming in to tell us how to run things and maybe telling the rest of Aberdeen too.'

'I will fetch the papers at once, Mr Wyness,' said Mhairi. 'Then you will see how everything is meticulously planned. You could supervise the work yourself, without difficulty, and I could do the paperwork and see to the men's pay. If I own thirty per cent of the shares, then I must work to deserve them.'

'And what about Hamish, and the next wee one? Who will look after them?'

'I will, with Annys. Don't you see, Mr Wyness,' she finished, pleading, 'I *need* to do something to help, for Alex's sake. Annys, pour more tea and Willy, fetch more whisky for Mr Wyness. I will be back in a minute.'

Mhairi hurried across the tiny passage into the bedroom to reappear with a bundle of papers and the first signs of colour in her face since Alex's death. 'There you are, Mr Wyness. You will find everything written down: the powder charges, the length of fuses, where to start the blasting, everything. The boys will explain.'

So Wyness bent over the papers as old Mackinnon had done, and the others crowded round him, pointing, explaining. Lorn and Willy and Donal. Only Alex was missing. Then Hamish, who had been playing under the table with a building block, scrambled up on to Donal's knee and after looking round the other faces to see what game they were playing, bent his own small head over the papers in exact imitation of theirs.

'Don't cry, Mhairi,' said Annys quietly, slipping her hand into Mhairi's own. 'One day it will be all right again, you'll see.

Remember what Ma said? Never lose hope?'

With a long shudder, Mhairi managed the first promise of a smile.

Two days later, Mhairi's second child was born, with little fuss and the sympathetic ministrations of Mrs Macrae and Jessie Bain. As she laboured in childbirth, Mhairi had no thought for the child, only for its father whom she would never see again this side of the grave. She welcomed the pain as a means of sharing his pain, and at last, when his child was born, she felt only a kind of hopeless desolation: until they put the little scrap into her arms and she saw Alex's eyes looking out at her. Hamish had her own dark hair and blue-eyed colouring, but this one was Alex in miniature. Looking at the tiny child Mhairi felt overwhelming love flow through her, then her eyes filled with tears of exhaustion, gratitude and grief.

'There, there, lass,' soothed the women, 'you've menfolk still to help you and as fine a pair of bairns as a body could wish for.'

'I know, and thank you. But I wish . . . I wish Alex was here . . .' And the healing tears flowed freely and unchecked. The women watched her, nodded to each other in satisfaction, knowing her weakness and her need. Soon they would bring hot milk and whisky and steer Mhairi kindly but firmly along the first stretch of the road to recovery.

In the family kitchen, the others waited, until the bedroom door opened and closed again and Mrs Bain crossed the tiny hall to join them.

'Annys, your sister wants you. She's needing to tell you about cooking and that so away in and dinna make a noise. The baby's newly asleep. Ye can take wee Hamish with you and give him a keek at his new sister. Poor wee runt,' she continued when Annys had scurried across the hall and into Mhairi's room, closing the door behind her. 'But then I tellt Mhairi, a shock like that and you've got trouble and yon drive into Aberdeen for the funeral didna help. She was lucky the bairn didna interrupt the service. And such a skinny wee scrap of a thing. Like a new-born rabbit. But a wee quinie, which isna so

[193]

bad, though without her man she was maybe wanting another loon? But you canna be doing wi' a runt for a son, nay if he's to earn his keep. I was telling Mhairi about my sister's husband's cousin . . .'

'Would you like a dram, Mrs Bain?' interrupted Willy, recollecting the duties of a host. 'You've been hours in there with Mhairi and you must be tired.'

'Aye, I wouldn't say no,' said that lady, subsiding into a chair. 'But only for a minute, mind. I've a home o' my own to go to. Poor wee lass, I'm that sorry for her, losing her man like that. Thrown half across the quarry, my man said, and every bone in his body broken. It's nay right, and her left wi' two wee bairns to bring up alone.' She drained her glass and when Willy refilled it said, 'Thanks, lad. Right good this whisky is. Sets a body up and no mistake and we're all needing a bit o' cheering, wi' Alex gone and him so young. But it's dangerous work is quarrying,' she went on, settling into her chair. 'Puts me in mind o' that laddie over Kemnay way, or was it Peterhead? No, I mind now, it was at yon quarry on Paradise Hill and they was blasting like your Alex was doing. Well, they'd bored the hole and put in the powder, like, and whatever they was using for the packing, then this laddie took his ramrod and was tamping the stuff down when whoomf! – it blew up in his face. Shot his own ramrod clean through his forehead. You'd ha' thought that would ha' killed him, but no. He gets to his feet, right as rain, and walks home nae bother, wi' the ramrod stuck through his head, like a spit through a chicken. They doctors couldna believe it. You should have been dead, they tellt him, but he wasna. Lived to be ninety-three. Pity really,' she finished. 'He was a miserable old devil. Folks said as how they'd mixed the tamping wrong. Tipped it in from the wrong bucket, or somesuch, but it was a miracle just the same. Should have been dead and wasn't. Not like your Alex, more's the pity. A fine lad he was, always a cheerful word and a warm welcome.'

But Willy had had enough. 'Your family will be expecting you, Mrs Bain,' he said, standing up. 'And you have done more than enough for us already.'

'Aye, well, she's a good neighbour is Mhairi and we're all that sorry for her. Mrs Macrae will stay a while longer, to see your Annys right, and I'll be in again myself tomorrow. Don't you be worrying her with talk of yon explosion,' she warned. 'Why this, why that, on and on. It was an accident, and no more to be said. There's accidents I could tell you of that . . .' but Willy had ushered her firmly to the door and opened it.

'It is growing late, Mrs Bain. Your husband will be worrying.'

'Him? He wouldna worry if I was away for a week and carried home feet first. "Oh, there you are, Jessie," he'd say. "Where's my tea?" There was that time a couple of years back . . .'

'I will walk you home,' interrupted Willy, and closed the door behind them.

Old Man Adam stood with his back to the generously blazing fire in the Silvercairns drawing-room and lifted his coat-tails to the heat with particular pleasure. 'Too late now,' he said, beaming. 'By the time they've sorted themselves out again and found the stone they need, the deadline will have passed and they'll have lost the contract. Sheer incompetence from start to finish. You'd best start thinking about a tender of our own, Fergus, so we have it ready to offer when the time comes.'

Fergus Adam did not immediately answer. The family had adjourned to the drawing-room after an excellent dinner, for once without any extraneous guests, and while Lettice busied herself with the coffee-pot he had sat down at the writing-table to write a note which his heart had been urging him to write ever since the funeral. So far, however, he had not progressed beyond *Dear Mrs Grant*, and at his father's words what little inspiration had been flowing dried up completely. He prudently concealed the page under the blotter, laid aside his pen and, taking the offered coffee-cup from Lettice, half turned in his chair.

'I have been meaning to ask you, Father,' some demon prompted him to say. 'Has it not occurred to you that that unfortunate explosion at Rainbow Hill was really most convenient for us? Perhaps *too* convenient?'

'What are you suggesting, damn you?' Adam's face was red, but that could just as well have been caused by anger or by

[195]

heat from the fire.

'I am suggesting nothing,' said Fergus. 'Merely pointing out a fact.'

'The fact being that that grasping crook overreached himself, as everyone knew he would do sooner or later. Damned incompetent, bungling fool. The man should have stuck to his polishing yard instead of meddling in quarry work about which he knows less than nothing.'

'Which, presumably, is why he employed men who did know to do his work for him? You could not have found a better quarryman than Mackinnon.' Remembering the old man's years of kindness and patient instruction when Fergus was a raw novice at Silvercairns, his natural rapport with the rock and his calm integrity of purpose, Fergus knew with cold certainty that there had been dirty work somewhere. The thought chilled his heart. And now Mackinnon was dead, blasted to death by one of his own powder charges, and Alex Grant with him, leaving Mhairi widowed with a young son and an infant daughter to support as best she could. They said the new-born child was puny, though it had managed to survive, so far . . .

The thought of Mhairi's pain and suffering and the hardship her growing family would inevitably endure filled him with guilt and compassion. He could ease that hardship with a mere stroke of the pen, but remembering her pride when she had come to him to plead on her friend's behalf for support for Hugo's bastard, he knew that it would be useless to send her money. She would merely return it, with a suitably scathing message. He would like to select a bunch of perfect grapes for her, from the Silvercairns hothouse, arrange them on a bed of their own leaves in a little wicker basket and take them to her himself. But were he to call at the house, with grapes or wine or even a brace of grouse, would she accept those impersonal gifts in the spirit in which they were given? In friendship and concern? He doubted it. And of course she would be right. How could he hope to meet her in friendship when her family had suffered such misfortune at the hands of his? But his father's blustering voice broke in upon his thoughts.

'Once, maybe. Once upon a time old Mackinnon was an

expert, I grant you that. But he retired from Silvercairns because he was growing past it, and I reckon old age caught up with him. He made his fuse too short and couldna run fast enough.'

'And the explosion, Father? They say it shattered the rock into road metal. I've never known Mackinnon err except on the cautious side.'

'Senility,' blustered Old Man Adam. 'Weighed his powder twice over maybe, and doubled it by mistake. But whatever mistake he made he paid for it, God rest his soul.' Here Adam half turned to lean an arm on the mantelpiece and glare into the fire. Truth to tell, his conscience was not easy about old Mackinnon. He had been a descent fellow and a loyal workman. Still, he would have died sooner or later, one way or another. As for the other fellow, it was his bad luck – besides, wasn't he one of the two who had been the cause of that fracas after which Adam had had no choice but to banish his own son Hugo to Jamaica? Deliberately Adam stamped down his conscience and concentrated instead on future success.

'By all accounts it will take Wyness a while to clear away the damage and start up again. Which is where we step in, Fergus. Back into our rightful place. And before you start to whinge and whine about how they've suffered, just remember it's our livelihood we're talking about. Folk who have the impudence to set up in opposition to Silvercairns deserve all they get. There's no room for sentiment in this business, Fergus, and the sooner you recognize it the better. His loss is our gain and I mean to make the most of it. So you'll map out a few figures for that row of houses and let me have them by morning?'

'Yes, Father,' sighed Fergus, but a phrase of his father's lodged in his mind and would not leave him. People who oppose Silvercairns, he had said, 'deserve all they get'. Suspicion hardened into certainty. He did not know how, but he was as sure as if his father had told him in as many words that Mungo Adam was responsible for the Rainbow Hill explosion and, indirectly, for old Mackinnon's death. With that knowledge on his conscience, how could he hope to write even the simplest message to Mhairi Diack? Whatever his own feelings in the matter, his father's action had destroyed all hope of reconciliation between the Adam and the Wyness camps, for ever.

Deliberately, Fergus extracted the paper from beneath the blotter and tore it into tiny pieces till even the carefully written name was destroyed.

In spite of the enthusiasm engendered by Queen Victoria's visit the previous autumn and the hopes it had renewed of good fortune for the Aberdeen Railway, work on the line was virtually at a standstill. With resources drained almost to the last penny, by land compensation way beyond the original estimate as much as by the cost of laying the line, and with no new source of capital, the company was in a sorry state. It could pay neither workers nor contractors and the threats from the larger and more prosperous English lines became more pressing. It was well known that the Edinburgh and Northern, backed by the great North British, was after the Aberdeen Railway and so was the London and North-western. The Board of Directors was split into three violently disagreeing camps, two favouring one or the other of the bidding companies and the third resisting both.

'If that grasping blackguard Burnett had not demanded so much compensation for his wretched agricultural land, we'd be £10,000 better off!' stormed Adam.

'And if some we could mention had not charged through the nose for stone for viaducts and the like, we'd have another £10,000 to play about with,' countered Burnett. Burnett was accused of using his new family connection with the Macdonalds to milk the company and swell the family purse. Adam in his turn was charged with speculating with company money to line his own pockets. Fur and feathers flew and the meeting had to be adjourned. Another acrimonious seven-hour session a month later produced a fresh barrage of insults and a major reshuffle in which both Burnett and Adam lost their seats. It was little comfort to either to know that the other was in the same boat. Meanwhile the new Board considered, and rejected, each of the take-over bids, and settled instead for the issue of new preference shares to existing shareholders, the money to be used exclusively to finish the line to the banks of the Dee and thus connect Aberdeen with the south.

'Damn stupid idea,' stormed Adam, ranging up and down the library of the Adam town house and thumping any piece of furniture that came within reach of his fist. 'I am to have the privilege of shelling out another £17 for each £50 I've spent already, with no hope of seeing my money back till God knows when. The money raised by this damn fool issue of so-called preference shares can't even be used to pay the company bills! They owe us a small fortune already, what with all the stone they have had from us in the past year alone for viaducts and cuttings and the like. We have had to pay our workers just the same, but do they think of that? Oh no. It is our privilege to be out of pocket while they sit back and count the money coming in. But they'll get no more from me until I'm paid what's owed me. How am I expected to run my business otherwise, eh? Tell me that.'

Fergus did not even attempt to do so. His father's rhetoric had become familiar over the past months, as had his constant bullying for more and more production, at an ever faster rate. Fergus had learnt long ago that any answer was useless. It was best to ignore his father until the old man had run out of steam. Consequently, he returned his attention to the book he was reading and avoided comment.

Unwisely, as it happened, for the thought of money lost never improved his father's temper. 'Listen to me when I talk to you, boy!' ordered Old Man Adam. 'I don't pay you to sit there reading novels and drinking my brandy without a care in the world. We have a quarry to run and a profit to make. Where's that order for the Free Kirk?'

'It will be ready by the end of the month, Father,' sighed Fergus.

'The end of the month? What sort of efficiency is that? I promised it for the beginning, not the end.'

'Then perhaps you should have consulted me first,' said Fergus, deliberately turning the page.

'I don't consult you, boy!' roared Old Man Adam. He snatched the book from Fergus's hands and hurled it across the room. 'I order you, blast it, and I ordered you to complete that consignment by the first of the month.'

'If you order the impossible, you can hardly complain if you do not get it.'

'Impossible? Why impossible, when you have an able-bodied work-force and enough rock to last you till doomsday?'

'There are only twenty-four hours in a day, Father, and too many of them are in darkness, particularly at this time of year.'

'What are lamps for? Dammit, boy, there's no excuse for laziness. The only cure for that is the whip and for two pins I'd take it to you myself, you impudent, bone-idle puppy . . .'

But Fergus had had enough. He rose to his feet and stood, fists clenched at his side, his face unusually white. 'I will not be spoken to like that by anyone, even by my father,' he said quietly. 'I require an apology.'

'You can require till you're blue in the face, but you'll find none, you snivelling little runt. You'll get out to that quarry and earn your keep if I have to drive you there myself, with my own riding crop,' roared Old Man Adam, taking a menacing step towards his son. Had the whip in question been handy, Fergus had no doubt his father would have used it and his own anger burst its filial bonds.

'Run your own blasted quarry and go to the devil!' With that he strode from the room and out of the house. Where he would go he had no notion, but until he could form some sort of plan, where better place to find solace than a tavern, and the nearer the better?

Fergus was sitting morosely in a secluded corner of the Lemon Tree, glowering into his third bumper of claret and wondering yet again why he had had to be saddled with such a villainous tyrant of a father, when he heard a familiar voice at his side.

'I thought it was you, Fergus. Is family enmity still set against me, or may I join you?'

Fergus looked up to see Archie Burnett, Niall Burnett's father and his own father's one-time friend. The man had a brimming glass in his hand and an expression which Fergus could not fathom. It was almost pitying, but not in any patronizing way, and Fergus could see no hint of ill-will. He nodded assent and made space on the bench beside him.

'You look down in the dumps,' began Burnett. 'Anything in particular?'

Fergus hesitated, remembering old rivalries, the Niall-Amelia business and most recently his father's boardroom tales. But the final memory brought with it the picture of Old Man Adam threatening him with the whip and the last thread of caution snapped.

'No more than usual. Only that my father is a tyrannical old bastard with the temper of a pit bull-terrier. He should have been shot long ago,' finished Fergus with unusual bitterness.

For some reason Burnett looked relieved. 'Ah, is that all? I had wondered for a moment if perhaps . . . but of course you couldn't have heard. The letter arrived only this morning, and I am afraid I have been rather cowardly, but things being as they are between your father and myself, you will understand my hesitation.'

Fergus's courtesy and patience had been exhausted by that interview with his father and not yet replenished. 'I understand nothing when you talk in that convoluted fashion. For God's sake, say what you mean or hold your tongue. I have no patience tonight for puzzles.'

Burnett swallowed, paled slightly, but did not react with the outrage to which he was fully entitled and which Fergus had half expected. Instead he said after a moment, 'You are quite right. Give me a moment and I will choose my words.'

They sat in silence while the rest of the tavern pulsed with lamplight, cigar smoke and convivial laughter. A big man at the bar was telling an interminable joke, interrupted at every sentence by his own laughter and egged on with patient geniality by a trio of similarly jocular friends. At a table near the door a group of farmers in from the country compared cattle prices in a fog of cigar smoke and ale-induced contentment. By the end of the evening they would not have a care in the world and when the innkeeper put them out into the street, reflected Fergus with envy, their horses would find the way home for them, no bother. Whereas he had no home to go to. Nothing would induce him to return to the house in the Guestrow and as for his beloved Silvercairns, he had renounced that for ever. Though perhaps he would ride out there in the moonlight, to have one last look at the sleeping quarry before leaving it, never to return? Then he would go abroad somewhere. It did not matter where. He was weighing the merits of Canada against Australia and finding both equally dreary when Burnett cleared his throat in a nervous

[201]

way which caught and held Fergus's attention.

'You will remember that my family has connections in the West Indies,' he began, with dry precision, 'through whose kind offices your brother Hugo was introduced to suitable circles of influence?' Fergus grunted assent. 'I had letters from them this morning, enclosing a personal one for your father.'

'From Hugo?' said Fergus, brightening. News from Hugo, whatever it might be, would cure his father's temper as nothing else would.

'I regret not. In fact the contents are of such a nature that I thought it best to withhold delivery until I had thought things over. Your father is an old friend and though recently relationships have been strained, I still feel a certain affection and concern for him. I am glad to have met you tonight because whereas I know the matter will be of equal concern to you, you are young and resilient whereas your father is old and all too choleric. You will know better than I how to go about this painful matter.'

'Painful?' Fergus looked at the older man warily. Was it some money matter? Some further embarrassing entanglement of Hugo's? Another bastard, perhaps? Or worse? Fergus was so engrossed in private speculation that he was totally unprepared for the revelation when it came.

'Very painful,' said Burnett and took a fortifying swig from his glass. 'The fact is . . .' and at last, in words of brutal simplicity, he told him.

Fergus sat stunned, all colour drained from his face and his heart beating painfully hard. Oh God. Oh dear God. He reached for his glass and drained it. Burnett leant back in his chair and summoned a refill which Fergus accepted without a word. When he had drained that too, he said, in a voice which was less than steady, 'How are we to tell him?'

'How indeed? If it helps, I have the letter here.' He handed over a parchment packet, the seal unbroken. 'The contents, I can assure you, are as I said. My cousin wrote in the fullest terms.'

'Tonight?' said Fergus aloud.

'Or tomorrow. What is one more day? But no more than one, for there were other letters by the same mail and word will inevitably spread. You will deliver the letter for me?'

'I will. If not tonight, then in the morning.'

'Thank you. You are a good lad, Fergus,' and Burnett laid a comforting hand on his shoulder. 'You have taken a weight off my mind. Poor old Mungo, he will take it hard.'

As will we all, thought Fergus, the weight of grief already heavy on his heart. The sooner the deed was done, the better.

But when he let himself into the darkened house some time later, he found the household already retired for the night and his father with them. The relief was overwhelming: tomorrow would bring turmoil enough, but tonight was for his own grief, in blessed silence and alone.

'So you decided to come back, did you?' growled Mungo when Fergus appeared at the breakfast table, earlier than usual but not early enough to precede his father. 'Couldn't face the big wide world alone, eh? Realized when you were well off? Well, don't think you can stick your feet under my table as if nothing had happened, because I've been up several hours already and I've found out a thing or two about your so-called business management.'

With resignation Fergus accepted the inevitable. He had known his father would discover one day, but why today of all days? Except that once his father read the letter, nothing else would matter.

'What exactly do you mean, Father?'

'What *exactly*? I'll tell you what exactly. Payments to sub-contractors I've never heard of. Payments to polishing yards that don't exist. And what is this "via M" that crops up all over the place? I'll tell you what it is, my lad. You've been lining your pockets at my expense. No wonder you can't be bothered to complete contracts on time. You've salted away a tidy sum by now and plan to run away abroad and live on it in idleness, like your brother in the West Indies. No wonder the profit's down. No wonder I'm up to the oxters in debt, and I've my own son to thank for it. What have you to say for yourself, you thieving, four-eyed blackguard, before I have you thrown into the Tolbooth for systematic swindling and downright theft?'

Oh God, sighed Fergus with pity. The poor, misguided,

[203]

vulnerable old man. '"Via M" means through Mackinnon, Father. It was the only way we could begin to keep up with the business you kept contracting for. Mackinnon helped out with building work and with polishing. He put our work through the Wyness yard.'

'He did *what*? You mean to tell me that Wyness was doing us a favour and we've been paying him for it?'

'No, Father. Wyness knew nothing about it. It was a private arrangement between Mackinnon and myself though not, as you so scurrilously suggested, with any motive of private profit, on either side. All transactions were perfectly proper and above board, except that neither you nor Wyness knew of them, for obvious reasons. Which is why we are so behindhand with our orders now. With Mackinnon's death all arrangements in that quarter naturally came to an end.'

'Naturally,' mimicked Adam with fury. 'But not before you and he between you had made me the laughing stock of Aberdeen, going cap in hand to Wyness of all people to help us out.'

'I told you, Father, Wyness knew nothing about it, and still doesn't.'

'Unless he's gone through his own books with a toothcomb and found the same discrepancies as I have. Then what, eh? Then what?'

'Mackinnon is dead, Father. No one else knows.'

'So you say, but there are spies everywhere, lad, don't you forget it. As for you, you devious, swindling crook. I'll not have you going to my enemies behind my back and begging for favours. If that's your way of doing business then you can get out. Leave me to run my own quarry as you so kindly offered to do last night.'

His father's words flowed over Fergus's head unheeded for he could think only of the letter which, once read, would alter his father's life for ever. He must give it to the old man, but oh God, must it be yet?

'Nothing to say for yourself, eh? No excuses ready? What's become of your two-faced diplomacy now, or are you working out how to ask me for money, like your brother?'

That gave Fergus the hint he needed.

'No, Father. I am waiting for a suitable opportunity to give

[204]

you this letter,' and he took it from his pocket and held it out towards the old man. 'But I should warn you that Mr Burnett said . . .'

'Burnett? Burnett? What has he to do with my letters?' Mungo snatched it from Fergus's hand, said, 'I'll deal with you later, sir,' and strode from the room. A moment later Fergus heard the library door open and slam shut again.

'Whatever was all that about, brother dear?' said Lettice, descending the stairs and crossing the hall to join him in the breakfast room. 'I could hear the shouting from my bedroom. Is Papa in one of his moods again?'

Fergus did not answer. He was waiting with dread for what must inevitably come and before Lettice could repeat her question they heard a noise which neither had heard before and hoped never to hear again – an animal howl of anguish followed by the sound of their father sobbing.

'I am sorry, Lettice,' said Fergus, putting his arm around her in brotherly comfort. 'A letter has arrived from the West Indies. Hugo is dead.'

It was retribution of course. Mungo Adam knew that at once. A death for a death. But no one had meant anyone to die. It had been an accident, that was all. An unfortunate accident. And now Hugo was dead. Caught a fever and died within two days, the letter said. A virulent swamp fever of a kind prevalent in those parts. Why had no one told him of the danger? He would have sent Hugo to Canada instead, or to Australia. Anywhere to keep him safe. The grieving old man laid his head on his arms and openly wept.

He did not hear the door open behind him, did not turn his head as the steps approached.

'I am sorry, Father,' said Fergus, his own eyes moist. He laid an awkward hand on Adam's shoulder.

'Poor Hugo,' said Lettice, her eyes brimming over. 'I loved him.'

'Aye, lass,' said her father. 'We all did.' With a long shudder he sat up, brushed a hand across his eyes and, without speaking, handed the letter to Fergus. Then he held out his arms to Lettice and they clung together in wordless grief, waiting till Fergus had read to the end. For his part, Fergus knew that his grief was to be separate and ignored: he was expected to take charge now, all differences forgotten, and to mark the passing of his father's favourite son with suitable reverence and glory. Hugo had died, therefore Fergus was forgiven, but no one could ever take Hugo's place.

'The quarry must be closed, Father,' he said quietly. 'As a mark of respect. I will see the Minister at once and arrange a service of remembrance. I will tell the work-force that everyone is expected to attend, and I will send a message to the *Journal*'s office, announcing our sad news. Is there anything else you would like me to do?'

'No, lad,' said his father wearily. 'Just leave me alone, to grieve in peace.'

Gently, Fergus put his hand around his sister's shoulders and led her, weeping, from the room. As the door closed behind him, he heard the unmistakable sound of his father's muffled sobs and at last his own tears flowed unchecked. Hugo had been irresponsible, annoying, even at times downright decadent, but he had been his brother, after all.

'I will ring for brandy,' he said, when they regained the breakfast room. He wiped his eyes impatiently with a large linen handkerchief then offered it to Lettice. 'You could do with some and so could I. Besides, it will give me the opportunity to tell the servants, if they have not already guessed . . .'

By the following morning the whole of Aberdeen knew that young Hugo Adam, who had been sent to the West Indies in disgrace, had caught one o' they tropical fevers and had upped and died.

When Mhairi heard the news her first reaction was satisfaction. She was instantly ashamed of herself, but in spite of all efforts the feeling remained. She had wished Hugo Adam no ill, but after the way he had treated her friend Lizzie Lennox she could not help feeling that he had found his just deserts. As for Old Man Adam, she knew instinctively that he was behind the accident which had killed her own dear Alex and whereas she was sorry for any man who lost a son before his proper time she remembered that Hugo had been her husband's enemy, that he and Alex were much of an age, and could not help thinking that justice had been done. It was a sad justice and she prayed God to ease the old man's grief, but it was justice just the same. She would write at once to Tom, care of the bank in Melbourne which was the only address they had for him, and tell him the news. It would not be easy to conceal her own still all-consuming grief, but she would do it. Besides, when Tom read of Hugo Adam's death he might give up his needless worrying about Lizzie and come home, by his own choice, to Fanny Wyness and Rainbow Hill, where he belonged.

Mr Wyness would be going to the memorial service, with his wife and daughter, but no one else from Rainbow Hill. The quarry would be working as usual, for since the explosion they had such a backlog of work to catch up with that they spent every available daylight hour at the quarry and many more by lamplight. But because Mhairi was not going did not mean she felt no sympathy for at least one of the grieving family. She knew the black depths of grief into which her own loss had plunged her and which still enveloped her day and night, and could not help remembering the kindness and sympathy in Fergus Adam's eyes when he had offered his condolences at dear Alex's funeral. He was not responsible for his father's sins and he had lost a brother. Mhairi knew how she would feel if her brother Tom were to die.

When the menfolk were safely away to work and Annys busy with little Catriona, Mhairi found a clean sheet of writing-paper and a pen. She sat a long time in frowning thought, before finally writing, *Dear Mr Adam, I write to offer you and your family my deepest sympathy in your time of trouble. The loss of a dear brother is always hard to bear and the more so when distance has separated one from another. I pray that God in His kindness will bring you peace and comfort in your grief.* She signed it simply *Mhairi Diack Grant*. It was little enough, but the best she could do. Mhairi folded, sealed it and wrote *Fergus Adam, Esquire* on the cover. Then she slipped it into her deepest pocket until such time as she might deliver it without arousing her family's suspicion. There were some things that were best kept hidden, for everyone's sake.

[207]

The church of St Nicholas was packed for the service: in spite of his profligate habits, Hugo Adam had been a popular lad with many friends. The Silvercairns household turned out *en masse* and the weeping of the assembled housemaids, led by Mrs Gregor herself in voluminous black, almost drowned out the Minister's words when he paid tribute to the 'fair-featured, blithe-natured and talented young man whom all who knew him remember with affection in this, their hour of loss'. The quarry workers, too, attended in full force, and so did Aberdeen society, old enmities forgotten in the tragedy of the moment. Fergus noted the Wyness family, the Burnetts, the Macdonalds and even a handful of professors from Marischal College where Hugo had briefly been a less than satisfactory student. Afterwards, when they had stood in grim-faced line to receive the company's condolences and give suitable thanks, Fergus and Lettice took an arm each and led their father, stumbling, home. Mungo Adam had aged in the hours since the arrival of that fateful letter. From an upright and vigorous gentleman of advancing years he had become a stooped and broken old man. Fergus saw and grieved for him, but was helpless to lift the weight of sorrow from his father's heart: at least, until a chance word in the library, where the trio had removed for a glass of restorative Madeira and dry cake. Lettice had ordered similar refreshment to be served in the servants' kitchen, but had thought it prudent to conceal that particular extravagance.

'What is the use of anything any more?' groaned Mungo Adam, addressing no one in particular. 'My son is dead.'

'You have us, Papa,' said Lettice, attempting comfort, but her father brushed her aside.

'There is no one to follow after me. What is the use of going on?'

'There is Fergus,' pointed out Lettice, with some asperity. 'Even if you choose to ignore my existence, you can hardly deny that Fergus is an Adam.'

'Hugo was the only one of you with any spirit,' mourned the old man. 'At least he had red blood in his veins, and now he is dead. I work and slave all my life to build up the richest business in the city and for what? To see my son die childless and no one to follow after me.'

'To put the record straight, Father,' said Fergus who, in spite of his expressionless face, had been deeply hurt by his father's remarks, 'Hugo did not die childless. I am ignorant of what children, if any, he fathered in Jamaica, though knowing my brother, I expect there are several, but he has at least one son that we know of and can vouch for, at present in Australia. The child is illegitimate, of course, but a bastard is better than no child at all, especially when it is *Hugo's* bastard. If you are so in need of grandchildren I suggest you look there.'

There was a long silence. Lettice looked uneasily at Fergus but he shook his head. Already he was regretting his ill-judged sarcasm, but they had given their father too much indulgence as it was. Let the old man work out his own salvation. Fergus refilled their glasses and resumed his seat. When at last Mungo Adam spoke it was, to their surprise, with something of his old vigour and irascibility.

'You may be right, Fergus. If I wait for you or your sister to produce offspring I could wait till doomsday. I'd have better luck with a gooseberry bush. But a son, you say? And vouched for? I remember now, we paid out money to some wench a couple of summers ago. How old is the child?'

'Approaching two years, I think.'

'Hmm. Young enough not to have picked up bad habits. Old enough not to keep the whole house awake at nights. Buy him.'

'I beg your pardon, Father? I don't think I quite heard . . .'

'I said, "Buy him." Send word to that bank manager fellow in Melbourne to find the child and look him over. See he has the right number of arms and legs and so on; no squints or rickets or anything like that. Tell the fellow to make sure the lad is a good, healthy specimen, to give the mother £50 or whatever he thinks he can get away with, and to ship the child home in the care of a suitable person. Someone who is travelling anyway, so we'll not have the cost of her passage on our bill.'

Lettice and Fergus exchanged glances of equal horror. It was Lettice who spoke first.

'But, Papa, you can't just buy somebody else's child, just like that.'

'Why not? The girl made enough fuss when she was pregnant, demanding this, that and the other. Now we're offering to take the brat off her hands. What could be fairer than that?'

'Has it occurred to you, Father, that the mother might feel some measure of affection for the little fellow?'

'If she does, £50 will fix it. Make it £75 if she proves difficult, but we'll have the lad's keep for the next twenty years, remember. You can tell that bank manager to remind her of that if she plays hard to get. £100 is my last offer, and that only if the lad is particularly well favoured and healthy. If she quibbles, then the deal's off. But you can take my word for it, a girl like that will jump at the chance of the money. She'll have a couple more little bastards by now, like as not, and be glad to see the back of our one. What's his name, by the way?'

'I have no idea,' said Fergus with cold contempt.

'No matter,' said Mungo Adam. 'We can always change it.'

But Fergus had had enough. His flippant attempt to divert his father's attention from introspective grief had succeeded beyond imagining. 'You cannot buy a child like a horse or a gun dog, Father. A child needs loving care. Who will look after the boy and see that the poor little chap is happy?'

'Lettice will.'

'Papa!' cried Lettice, aghast. 'I don't want to look after . . .'

'I've told you often enough it's time you were married, girl, and as you persist in staying single, you can acquire a child the easy way. I've made up my mind so I will hear no more protests. Away you go, Fergus, and write that letter. Send it express, mind. It will take long enough for the lad to be shipped home and I don't want to die of old age before he gets here.'

'Suppose you do not like the boy when he arrives?' said Fergus with weary sarcasm. 'Are we to post him back again?'

'And who do you suggest pays the passage? No, if he is not suitable for above stairs, we'll send him below. Cook or someone can find a place for him till he's old enough to earn his keep. Well, what are you waiting for? Away with you and write that letter, or do I have to do it myself?'

'Dottled,' whispered Lettice as Fergus passed her. 'Soft in

[210]

the head.'

But whether Old Man Adam was dottled or not, he had set his mind on buying Hugo's bastard. At least that way his son was not entirely lost to him and besides, there was the chance that by some blessed dispensation the child might actually resemble its father. It was a hope that dried the old man's eyes and put the life back into his step.

As for Fergus, he regretted ever mentioning the poor little bastard, but the harm was done now. The least he could do was see that the child came to no harm, unless, of course, the mother acted like any normal mother and refused to sell him? It was a hope that Fergus clung to as the months passed and no word came. But it was a five-month voyage to Australia and another five months back again and before anything could be arranged the manager of the Melbourne bank would have to find the child. It might be a year before they heard and in that time anything could happen.

The news of the failure of the Banking Company of Aberdeen fell like a revenging thunderbolt into the sunlit tranquillity of the Silvercairns breakfast room. Old Man Adam, opening his morning paper on that fateful June morning in expectation of nothing in particular, saw the paragraph and gasped aloud. He reached for his teacup with a hand that trembled, but the usually fortifying brew failed to reduce the shock. The bank had failed. He knew all too well what happened in such circumstances: those who had lent money would lose it, and those who had borrowed money . . . ?

Dear God. It was retribution. There was no other explanation. He was being punished for Mackinnon's death. First Hugo, and now this. With dread he remembered that loan he had negotiated, the railway scrip he had bought in expectation of future profit and which he would now have to sell, before the line was even laid, or hand over to the bank in lieu. Unless he could raise money in some other way? The quarry was still profitable, of course, but since the competition with Wyness had hotted up, the profit margin had been cut and besides that, there were many bills unpaid. Which might remain unpaid, if his creditors had entrusted their money to the Aberdeen bank.

'Is anything the matter, Papa?' asked Lettice, alarmed by the grey colour of his normally ruddy face and by the soft but persistent rattle of cup against saucer as he replaced them on the table.

'The Aberdeen bank has failed.'

Lettice was taken by surprise. It was rare enough for her to receive a straight answer from her father, without patronizing comment or sly dig, and rarer still for him to reveal fear, as he was doing now. For a moment she could think of nothing to say, then she ventured, 'Duncan Forbes's bank, in Castle Street?'

'You could call it his. It will be no one's now, except the debt collectors' and the bankruptcy court's.'

'What will it mean, Papa?' she asked, his fear reflected in her own voice. The way he had pronounced the word 'bankruptcy' had had a frightening effect on her complacency. Then with relief and a twinge of shame, she remembered that she would soon be twenty-one and whether her father was bankrupt or not, she would have at least a little money of her own.

'What will it mean? It will mean, my lass, that too many folk who were rich yesterday will be poor today. Where's Fergus?'

'At the quarry, Papa. You know he is always gone before eight in the morning.'

'Then I'd best ride into town myself and see exactly what's going on.'

But at that moment, there was a discreet knock at the door and a servant entered with a letter on a silver tray. 'For you, Mr Adam, sir. By hand. The messenger is waiting for a reply.'

Adam broke the seal, unfolded the paper and read. 'Damned impertinence!' he roared. 'My lawyer shall see about this. Have my horse brought at once. Well, what are you waiting for? Get out, damn you.'

'And the reply, sir?' said the servant, standing his ground. 'What am I to tell the messenger?'

'Tell him to go to the devil.'

As it transpired, Mungo Adam's worst fears were unjustified. The Aberdeen bank had certainly failed: riddled with debt for some years, with a massive loan to a local mill which, with the recent recession, it had no hope of ever recovering, it had over-issued notes to more than ten times the value of its assets. Were only half the bearers to present those notes for payment, the bank would be ruined. The Union Bank of Glasgow had seen its opportunity and bought up the Aberdeen bank, debts and all, with the vital note-circulation which hitherto it had not had access to in the north-east. But those who had borrowed in Duncan Forbes's day found themselves called to account by the new owners, their debts reviewed and their securities checked. Mungo Adam was one of many who received that 'damned impertinent' letter, but unlike most he did not approach the interview in conciliatory mood. In his eyes it was a privilege to lend to an Adam and anyone who did not see it was a fool. Unfortunately, by Mungo's reasoning, the new manager proved to be just that. He saw no reason why Mungo should not pay back at least some of his debt, and certainly the interest which had accrued and which Mungo had chosen to ignore.

'Or I am afraid, Mr Adam, that we shall have no choice but to recall the whole of the amount loaned. You will understand that we are making every endeavour to re-establish the bank on a firm footing and to rid ourselves of bad debts, large or small.'

'Bad debts?' exploded Adam. 'How dare you, sir! First you summon me like some office menial to jump to your bidding – *me*, Mungo Adam of Silvercairns – then you insult me a second time by demanding payment. You are no better than a common usurer, an extortioner of blood-money, a blackmailing, blood-sucking Shylock who should be whipped in the market-place as a public example. I will have you know, sir, that the Adams *are* this town. This town is built with Silvercairns stone, its workers paid with Silvercairns money, and I'll not be dictated to by some ignorant, snivelling wee Glasgow mannie who does not know his betters when he meets them. Do I make myself clear, *sir*?'

'Perfectly. You wish to repay the loan and take your custom elsewhere.' The 'wee Glasgow mannie', who was indeed small of stature, regarded Mungo Adam with a steely antagonism which goaded Mungo into rash defiance.

'Exactly. As any right-thinking Aberdonian will do. You

[213]

will hear from me again.'

'I sincerely hope so, Mr Adam, and before the week is out. Otherwise I shall have no course but to take further measures.'

'Take what you like and be damned to you,' roared Adam and with a final volley of insults of a more or less personal nature, relating to Glasgow in general and its male offspring in particular, slammed out of the room and the building, leaving the heavy door resonating in its frame behind him.

However, in the calm sunlight of the city street, his rage receded and in its place came a creeping dread of what he had done. He had burnt his boats beyond repair in that quarter. Pride demanded that the wretched fellow get his payment with the shortest possible delay, interest included. But practicalities demanded that in order to do that, even were he successfully to call in all the moneys owed to him, he must borrow from somewhere else. Give for security his house or his railway shares, always supposing he could find a bank which would accept the latter as surety, or sell the shares themselves.

Mungo Adam strode along Union Street, looking neither to right nor left, intent only on solving the impossible problem with the least damage to dignity or purse. Shares or house? If house, then town or Silvercairns? The town house was in an enviable position, solidly built to last for generations, a gentleman's house of stability and stature, befitting a gentleman of distinction. He could not envisage anyone but an Adam living in it. It would be more than his pride could stand to part with it, even as a surety which may never be claimed. But Silvercairns was equally bound up with the Adam pride and interests. An elegant mansion set in elegant grounds of formal garden and parkland, with stables, dairy and every other appurtenance the country gentleman's life required, it was the perfect country retreat, the perfect setting for business dinners and influential weekends, and so convenient for the quarry. If Adam remembered his children's warnings of cracking stonework and tilting walls, he brushed them aside. Silvercairns was perfect, and as much a part of the Adam empire as the house in the Guestrow.

But if not the house, then it must be the quarry, or shares? The quarry, of course, was out of the question. No one but an utter fool would pledge the source of his livelihood. Which left his sizeable holding of railway stock, in the GNSR as well as the Aberdeen Railway. Dividends were still non-existent and the value of his initial holding had fallen to a point which he preferred to forget, but since the last issue of preference shares, the Aberdeen Railway was looking up. Work had resumed on the line and there was every chance of its reaching the city by the end of the year. In fact, there was already talk of a grand opening ceremony in the spring. The price of shares in the company had risen accordingly and whereas he would not make anything approaching what he had paid for the things, Mungo might do reasonably well if he sold them, and better than he had hoped. But he did not want to sell them. He wanted to hang on to his stake in the company so that one day he would win his way back on to the Board and have power and influence to run the line himself. Besides, the Deeside line was part of the same company and if he sold out, he would lose his stake in that too. It was common knowledge that Queen Victoria had favoured the railway with her custom from Perth to London last year, and equally well known that Her Royal Highness was to spend the summer once more at Balmoral. When the railway reached all the way from London to Aberdeen and then along the Dee valley, who was to say that the Queen would not make the entire journey by rail? With patronage like that, the line could not fail to prosper, and its shareholders likewise.

No, it would be foolish to part with his holding at this stage, just when it looked as if he would see a return on his money at last. But he feared that the days when banks would give a loan on railway stock were past. At the back of his mind he cursed the day he had embarked on railway speculation, but it was a brief treachery, soon squashed. Mungo Adam did not admit mistakes, or make them.

He had reached this point in his thoughts when he found himself, by some oversight, in the Green, the noisy turmoil of the market-place all around him, with housewives bargaining for the daily produce, fishwives bawling their wares, countrywomen adding their distinctive voices to the general turmoil and the air thick with the smell of fish, cabbage leaves, fresh herbs and cheeses, and an underlying odour of horse

[215]

dung, rotting vegetables and sweat. Mungo Adam was about to turn away in fastidious disgust and make his way back to Union Street and civilization, when a voice at his elbow bellowed, 'Lemons, ripe lemons, landed this morning from across the sea . . . Valencia oranges, straight from the sunny south . . .' and simultaneously, like an omen, in green and gold lettering on a red signboard above a doorway across the street, he read *The Bon Accord Investment Company, Aberdeen and Australia, Ltd.* Australia, land of promise, where he had an unknown little bastard grandson who would be found sooner or later and sent to him, to carry on the business after he was dead.

If he still had a business. Remembering, Mungo Adam set his jaw in determination as he re-read the words of the newly painted sign. Then for the first time he saw, in smaller letters underneath, *Loans negotiated, large or small*. He pushed his way through the throng to the newly painted door, opened it and went inside.

'Wasn't that Mr Adam?' murmured Fanny Wyness in surprise. Mhairi turned her head to follow her friend's gaze, but could see no one resembling the handsome, well-dressed figure of Fergus Adam among the crowd. Mhairi herself still wore mourning for Alex, and the white of her infant daughter's clothes against Mhairi's black-clad arm made a startling contrast.

'I do not see him,' she said, turning back to her marketing. 'But then I would hardly expect Mr Fergus to walk about among the common folk, would you?'

'Oh no, not Fergus,' said Fanny, who had become quite friendly with that gentleman in the months since Tom's departure, though they seldom met except by chance. The enmity between their two families saw to that. 'I meant Mr Mungo Adam.'

'Surely not?' Mhairi looked round a second time, with greater curiosity. To see Fergus Adam would have been astonishment enough, but to see his father . . . Old Mungo Adam rarely went beyond the area of his house, his club, and the better parts of Union Street. To see him in the common market-place would presage nothing less than the end of the world.

'There are not two men so large and black and intimidating in the whole of Aberdeenshire,' confided Fanny, 'and I know I am right. He went into that door over there. The Bon Accord Investment Company, Aberdeen and Australia,' she read aloud, her voice dying away on the last word. It was three months since they had had any word from Tom and that only a brief note from the Cape.

'Do not despair,' said Mhairi gently. 'There will be letters soon. And remember, he will not receive ours till after he reaches Port Phillip.'

They had all written in the weeks following Tom's departure and even Annys had added her message to the family letter, which had been carefully vetted by Mhairi lest any hint of Alex's death slip through. 'I am perfectly well,' she had told them vehemently when they had tried yet again to persuade her to call Tom home. And she was well, physically. Thinner, paler, but well. Despite all Mrs Bain's gloomy forebodings, her little daughter survived, as she herself did, without Alex, but Catriona had never known Alex's love whereas she herself still wept secretly into her pillow each night, in the lonely darkness of her bed. But she would not have Tom told. He could help at the quarry, perhaps, but he could not help her assimilate her husband's death. Only she herself could do that, somehow, with time.

Of Fanny's letters, naturally, she knew nothing, but now Mhairi wondered yet again if Fanny had broken her promise and mentioned the quarry accident to Tom. They had discussed it together over and over, Mhairi convinced that under no circumstances should Tom be told lest family obligation put undue pressure on him to come home, Fanny agreeing, yet pointing out that Tom as both shareholder and family member had every right to hear about their setbacks as well as their triumphs.

'I do not want him to come home for my sake, Mhairi,' she had explained, with wide-eyed seriousness, 'before he has achieved what he set out to do, but nor do I want him to feel excluded. You see, I promised I would tell him everything that happened.'

'Everything except what will disturb him unnecessarily, and long after the event. If you write to him of the explosion, by the time he reads your letter the quarry will have retrieved its losses and be back on the way to profit. Where is the point in troubling him with something that is over and done with?'

'And Alex?' Fanny had pointed out. 'Should not Tom be told of the death of his lifelong friend?'

'No. At least, not yet . . . Promise me, Fanny, as a friend?' She had promised, but with reluctance, and ever since Mhairi had been unsure.

The months after the explosion had been hard: endless days of endless toil for all of them from before dawn till after sunset, week after week, month after month, but they had welcomed the physical exhaustion as a means of forgetting their grief for Alex. And now at last, as Mhairi had predicted, they were beginning to break even again. The past six months would show no profit, but no loss either and for that alone she was grateful. Somehow they would manage until the quarry clawed its way back to profit. With Fanny's help she had found enough dressmaking to earn a little extra and now, with the summer months upon them, the results of her labours in their small plot of land had produced enough to supply the family pot as well as fill a weekly basket for sale in the Green. She adjusted the weight of baby Catriona, eight months old now but still small for her age, and glanced down with maternal pride at Hamish, a sturdy two-year-old, with soft dark hair and his mother's clear blue eyes. He held Fanny Wyness's hand with the familiarity of long acquaintance and Mhairi knew that he was safe in her care. Fanny was a dear friend and had been Mhairi's best support in the empty months of her new widowhood. But Fanny too was a 'widow' in a way. She had been brave on the quay on the day of Tom's departure, but Mhairi had read her grief and wept silently for her, as she still did when she caught her friend unawares and saw the loneliness in her face.

Now she said briskly, 'Do not forget that Tom is not in Edinburgh or even London. Even if he wrote the very day he landed in Port Phillip, I doubt we could have heard by now.'

'No,' said Fanny gratefully. 'Perhaps you are right.'

'I know I am. As I was right when I told Annys she would

surely sell all our produce by noon. See, there she sits beside old Kirsty, her empty basket on her knee and for all the world like an old woman herself.'

Poor Annys, thought Mhairi with a rush of tenderness. The child's fear showed in her face, though she sat bravely enough, head high. Ever since that occasion when Fergus Adam had had his purse stolen and had 'found' it under Annys's market basket, Annys had been afraid that 'they young varmints' as Kirsty called them would return to torment her. Mhairi had told her gently but firmly that she could not stay at home the rest of her life just because Evie Lennox, Jessie Bruce and friends had chosen to pester her on that one occasion long ago. 'I need you to help me, Annys love. With Alex gone, we all have to do what we can now, and with Hamish and Catriona to see after as well as the garden and the quarry I have not the time to spend all morning in the Green. I have my sewing to see to and my clients. I'll take you and fetch you, but you'll need to be a brave girl and sell the eggs and vegetables yourself. Besides, Evie and Jessie will have learnt their lesson long ago. They'll not come back. And if they do,' she had added, unwittingly cancelling her own argument, 'then Kirsty will see you right, won't you, Kirsty?'

'Aye, I will that. Let they varmints so much as show a nose in these parts and I'll slice it off and pickle it afore they can say "eggs". I havena forgiven yon lassie for spoiling my best gownie and she knows it. Nay, Annys, you'll be safe enough wi' auld Kirsty. You just stay close and I'll see ye right.'

Now, as she watched her sister's brave and unsuspecting face, Mhairi felt her heart twist with tenderness and pity. Poor Annys, in the nine years of her life she had known little happiness. She had been only four when her mother died and not much older when her father followed. Since then it had been nothing but struggle and toil and in the past months, since Alex's death and Catriona's birth, Annys had had to stay away from her beloved school, to help in the house. Mhairi had promised her that she could go back again, as soon as Catriona was older, maybe even after the summer: Mhairi had promised her mother on her death-bed that she would see Annys 'grew up right' and she *would*. Somehow she would manage, somehow find the money to send her back to school.

[219]

'Have you sold everything, Annys?' she asked when she and Fanny reached the spot where Kirsty always sat.

'Yes, an hour ago.' Annys smiled up at Mhairi with pride.

'Me! Me!' cried Hamish, tugging at the basket, then he scrambled into it and sat triumphantly bouncing up and down while Annys laughed and asked if he was a cabbage or an egg or a farmhouse cheese. Seeing them together, Mhairi's anxiety eased: Annys might have lost her parents, but she had found love enough in the family that remained, and would continue to do so. Mhairi watched, smiling, while Fanny went through the pantomime of buying a cheese, 'A little, plump cheese that likes to be tickled', until Hamish had been retrieved from the market basket and they could all turn their steps for home.

Mhairi, as usual, refused Fanny's offer of a lift in the Wyness carriage, and it was not until they were parting at the door of the Wyness yard, where Fanny was to join her father, that Mhairi remembered Mungo Adam.

'If it was him, I wonder what he was doing in the Green?' she asked Fanny as they kissed cheeks in parting.

'I cannot imagine.' Then Fanny added with a hint of mischief, 'But I will tell Papa. He is sure to be interested and he might even know the answer.'

But if he did, George Wyness did not tell his daughter. He said only, 'Well, well. The Bon Accord Investment Company. So that's the way the wind blows.' He was in exceptionally good humour for the rest of the day, though neither his wife nor his daughter could begin to fathom why.

It was two months before the longed-for letters arrived, but after that they came often. Tom was doing well. On the boat out he had met a Mr Leslie who was going to Australia to join his brother. The brother was a pastoralist who had already made a fortune and the Leslies had proved a valuable contact. With their help Tom was establishing himself in business, and they had even suggested that he build them a mansion house one day. Tom gave details of building contracts he had undertaken and, to George Wyness, of investment opportunities *which cannot fail to succeed*, and of the successful progress of that other, secret mission which must not be mentioned. He

[220]

wrote of the bright-coloured birds and fishes he had seen, the flowers and trees and strange animals and of the native people *who are called aborigines and who live on the land until it is taken from them by the settlers, when they move away to live somewhere else. Sometimes, if they will not go, they are killed. The pastoralists who do this are not good men, but greed for land makes them forget how to behave as a good Christian should. I am happy to say that Mr Leslie did not get his land by killing . . .* He wrote of ships arrived from 'home', of Scots men and women he had met, but nowhere did he mention Lizzie Lennox, or her child. Mhairi wondered if he did not write of her out of concern for Fanny, or because he had not found her, and as the months passed her curiosity grew.

Towards the end of the year, a month or so after her first birthday, Catriona woke crying and when Mhairi inspected her, she was horrified to see the baby was covered in a rash of tiny red spots. Her first thought was scarlet fever — two of her own sisters and a brother had died of that disease in infancy — and her heart raced with terror. Her children were all that remained to her of Alex: how could she bear it if they too were taken from her? But when Dr Marshall came in answer to her frantic message, he pronounced it nothing worse than measles, and the false kind at that. 'Were it the other kind,' he told her kindly, 'you would have need for anxiety, but your daughter has been wise enough to catch only the hybrid variety, for which I can prescribe nothing but patience, and care.'

Hamish, who had never had a day's illness in his short life, caught it too, then Fanny Wyness: 'For the second time,' said her mother in disapproval. 'I know she had the illness in childhood which you would have thought would be enough for any girl, but no, dear Fanny must catch it twice.' She spoke tetchily, as if her daughter had caught the disease deliberately to spite her, but she had had a tiring day at the Soup Kitchen Committee and her headache was bothering her as a result. 'It seems to me,' she told her daughter when she looked in to Fanny's sick-room to bid her good-night, 'that you had better stop visiting that cottage on Rainbow Hill. There is no call for it, no call for it at all. Your father pays the widow a generous enough pension and it is not as if the family were unemployed or destitute. Besides, they are not even in our parish.'

'Mhairi is a friend of mine,' protested Fanny weakly from her pillows.

'Then I suggest you find your friends elsewhere. Amelia Burnett, for instance, or one of those nice girls you used to meet at dancing class in Belmont Street. One of those girls would be far more suitable.'

Her head ached and her throat was remarkably sore, but this did not prevent Fanny from saying, 'There is nothing "unsuitable" about Mhairi, Mamma. She is a dear, kind friend to me and I value her company most highly.'

'Humph!' said her mother, or a sound very like it. 'It is her brother you value and think to keep him through her friendship. Do not think I cannot see through your wiles. But it will do you no good to wear out your health with these country visits. It will not bring him back. Only time, and his own inclination, can do that.' When Fanny did not answer, but turned away her head, Mrs Wyness sat down on the edge of the bed, took her daughter's unwilling hand in hers and said, more gently, 'I speak only for your own good, Fanny dear. You know as well as I do that Tom Diack cannot be depended upon. Your father gave him every encouragement, as I suspect you did yourself, and still he would not commit himself. A man like that is neither trustworthy nor reliable. Why, in that last letter he talked of buying land himself. *Good building land* was his phrase, *on which to build a solid family house.* Ask yourself who that house was for, Fanny. It is my opinion that Tom may well find the life in New South Wales so much to his liking that he settles there for ever, and you have no formal engagement. Be sensible, my dear. Remember you are twenty-one and a girl of that age who is still unmarried had best begin to look about her, unless she wishes to remain a spinster all her life. Amelia is giving a dance next week,' she added wistfully. 'Now, of course, you will not be able to go. Such a pity. You might have met that charming young doctor again, Dr David, old Dr Marshall's nephew. He is quite taken with you, I know he is. Your father said the same and Dr David is such a charming young man. You could do a great deal worse than marry him, Fanny dear.'

'I do not wish to marry him!' cried Fanny, tormented

[222]

beyond endurance. 'I will marry Tom or no one. Now go away and leave me in peace.' She buried her face in her pillow and kept it there until she heard the door close behind her mother's outraged figure. Then she gave herself up to weeping. She did not believe a word her mother said, but she wished Tom would write to her and say he was coming home.

In spite of all setbacks, the new and expanding railway network continued to attract support from both investors and those without whom even the best-laid tracks and most elegant engines could find no profit. Someone with pages of figures and time to spare computed that the number of trips taken on the railways in the past year was equal to two trips a year for every man, woman and child in Great Britain and Ireland, and the effect on the habits of the nation was enormous. Moreover the safety record was excellent and though occasional accidents might shake the public's confidence, the fact remained that the odds were six million to one in favour of travelling in safety. All in all a reassuring prospect, and in spite of the lingering distrust of the railways as an investment, they were beginning to pay reasonable dividends at last, and at a higher rate of interest than many other investments.

'Four and even five per cent in some cases,' said the Chairman at the board meeting of the Great North of Scotland Railway. 'And though the price of shares might have fallen a little here and there, if proper measures are taken this can soon be remedied.'

'Proper measures,' grumbled a voice from the body of the room. 'What we need is proper progress.' Mungo Adam's money had lain idle long enough. He wanted profit and he wanted it now.

'With proper measures,' persisted the Chairman, 'we can achieve reasonable returns for a reasonable investment.'

'Aye, that's all very well,' challenged Old Man Adam, rising to his feet in the second row. 'But we can expect no profit on a line that isn't built. Though when you think who the Board in their wisdom awarded the building contract to, such lazy incompetence is not surprising. How long is it going to be, Mr

Chairman,' he shouted above the tumult of protest, 'before the line runs north from Aberdeen? Tell me that! It's been long enough in the planning, and no return on investors' money that I can see.'

'Very soon, very soon,' came the murmur of placating voices. 'It is a question mainly of the canal . . .'

In order to eliminate rivalry the directors of the GNSR had arranged to buy up the canal, and to use its bed for at least part of the planned route.

'Work cannot start until the canal is emptied . . .'

'Which cannot be done until all legitimate traffic has ceased . . .'

'Unless we wish to be saddled with huge claims for compensation . . .'

'Then I suggest', said Mungo with ill-contained annoyance, 'that you take steps to sweep the thing clean of your so-called "traffic" *immediately*. Or someone may take such steps for you.' With that he slammed out of the meeting, leaving a sigh of relief behind him. Now, at last, they could get down to work.

In the spring of 1850 the railway to Aberdeen from the south was finally opened. Though public celebration was postponed till a better time of year, neither ice nor tempest could prevent the directors and major shareholders from marking the occasion with a private celebratory dinner in the Assembly Rooms. Fanny Wyness was of the number, with her parents, and so were the Adams, Mungo, Fergus and Lettice. For though he loathed and despised the man, Mungo Adam had no intention of leaving George Wyness a clear field. Fergus spoke to Fanny Wyness and earned himself his father's displeasure. Wyness spoke to Adam and was ignored. Lettice saw Mrs Wyness and Fanny in conversation with young Dr Marshall, joined the party and was ignored in her turn, until she said deliberately, 'Do introduce me to the doctor, Fanny dear,' and Fanny had no recourse but to do so, mumbling quickly, 'Lettice Adam, who used to be a friend of mine.'

'Used to?' said Dr David, raising an eyebrow. Eighteen months had passed since that funeral when she had first seen him. Their paths had not recrossed and after her first idle curiosity Lettice had forgotten him. Now she saw that he was looking particularly sophisticated and debonair for a country doctor. His dark hair and green-flecked eyes, though not conventionally handsome, were pleasing enough and he had a certain air about him, as of a lively spirit dutifully suppressed. In answer to his question she smiled prettily and shrugged.

'You know how it is, Dr Marshall. People take different paths and in consequence seldom meet.'

'Even in a town as small as Aberdeen? I thought everyone met practically every day?'

'Now you are teasing us for being provincial.'

'Not at all, Miss Adam. By that reckoning I am provincial myself, for though I trained in Edinburgh and London I am a Buchan man by birth. Did not my uncle tell you?'

'I have not the pleasure of acquaintance with your uncle,' said Lettice. 'Our doctor is Dr Mackenzie, whom perhaps you know? If you do, you will realize that he is old enough to have brought me into the world, which indeed he did. He has been our family doctor for too many years to change now.'

'That is just as well, Miss Adam. Were you to change to my uncle's practice, then I fear my Hippocratic oath would prevent closer acquaintance between us.'

'Really, doctor? And were you thinking of closer acquaintance?'

But Mrs Wyness had had enough. 'I thought you had joined us to renew an old friendship, not to engineer a new,' she said, with acidity. 'The doctor and Fanny were about to dance.'

Dr Marshall looked startled, but was too much of a gentleman to deny it. 'Certainly we were,' he said, offering Fanny his arm. 'Perhaps we will meet later in the evening, Miss Adam? In the mean time, I hope you will excuse me?'

Then to Lettice's annoyance he led Fanny to join the nearest set and left her standing beside the odious Mrs Wyness. Lettice turned on her heel and walked away. But behind her anger she felt a new chagrin tinged with definite jealousy. Little Fanny Wyness did not deserve anyone as masculine or as compelling as Dr David and surely he could not find anything of interest in her? Of course, if what her brother Fergus said was true and Dr David was still seeking a respectable woman to marry, then Fanny Wyness would certainly fit the bill. Someone dull, dependable, meek and obedient, who would smooth the anxieties of hysterical patients and calm the tempers of the irate, including, if necessary, her husband. Fanny Wyness would certainly do all that, and if he was after money to set himself up in a decent practice, then she had more than enough of that too. The thought was vaguely unsettling.

All her life Lettice had been in the habit of considering herself superior in all things to everyone, and to discover, albeit in private, that in spite of her own undoubtedly superior beauty, breeding and wealth, Fanny might be regarded by young Dr Marshall as a better match than herself shook her confidence as nothing else had done. Niall Burnett's choice of Amelia Macdonald had been nothing, made as it was because the gentleman in question knew he had no hope of securing Lettice's favour. Dr Marshall was quite a different matter. He was less rich, less well bred, even less handsome than the odious Niall, but in spite of that he had an air of male confidence and straightforward charm that stripped away Lettice's defences and disarmed social prejudice. He was a Buchan lad made good and proud of it and his manners, certainly, could take him anywhere. Lettice hoped Dr David would seek her out before the evening was over, and pursue that closer acquaintance he had mentioned. If he did not . . . but that was an eventuality she did not choose to contemplate. Then she noticed her brother Fergus approaching.

'I saw that fellow snub you,' said Fergus, 'and came to your rescue. Care to dance?'

'There was no need for rescue,' she said, accepting his offer with lofty disdain. 'And no snub. A prior engagement, that is all.'

'Really?' Fergus raised a quizzical eyebrow, but his sister was in no mood for confidences.

'Really,' she said. 'And if you are going to continue to step on my toes, I would prefer to sit out this particular reel.'

'Thank goodness for that,' he said, subsiding into the nearest chair. 'I confess I am quite exhausted. I tried to escape to the card room but was hauled back by the collar by some well-meaning matron. Since then I have danced dutifully with every elderly dowager in the room. As to the younger, I dare not ask them for fear a father appears out of the woodwork brandishing a shot-gun and forces me to the altar.'

'You must have an extraordinary way of dancing, brother dear,' said Lettice, sinking into the chair beside him.

'Not at all. Just incredibly bad luck. Talking of which, have you seen Father lately? I had thought the opening of his beloved railway would have lifted his depression, but it seems to have done the opposite. I don't know what old Wyness said to him, but it turned him grey about the gills.'

'Grey?' said Lettice, puzzled. 'Are you sure you don't mean purple?' Her father had grown increasingly choleric in the months since the take-over of the Aberdeen bank.

'That I could have understood. It was the grey colour that worried me. As if he had suffered an unpleasant shock.'

'Probably something to do with the quarry,' said Lettice. 'You know what rivals they are. I expect Wyness told him of some new contract he had settled over the turtle soup, no doubt with a second, better one signed in gravy over the pigeon pie.'

'Perhaps,' agreed her brother. But Silvercairns Quarry already had all the work it could handle and since Hugo's death Old Man Adam had been more amenable to the arguments of common sense. He no longer demanded the impossible or talked of blasting great chunks out of the quarry sides, but seemed prepared to follow Fergus's plan of judicious and careful quarrying to achieve a steady and regular supply. In fact, in the past year Fergus had felt happier than ever before. He sensed that he and his beloved quarry were at one, working together to gather in the earth's benison, with respect and care. The work-force seemed happier too and had achieved a steady rhythm of production that seemed almost self-perpetuating. Without consulting his father, Fergus had increased the men's pay throughout the quarry, not by much, but by enough for them to see the difference at the end of a week's work. When his father eventually discovered it, Fergus had not faced the torrent of abuse he had expected: instead Mungo Adam had said only, 'It seems a wicked waste of good money to me, but if it brings results, I suppose it's inevitable.

[227]

We don't want that rat Wyness luring our best men away, as he has been known to do in the past.' Hugo's death had certainly chastened the old man and made him almost human. Which made Mungo's outburst the moment they were inside their carriage and bound for home all the more startling.

'The rat! The evil, maggot-ridden, putrefying rat! But I will beat him at his own game yet. He'll not grind me into the dirt, oh no. Damn him for a . . .' and there ensued a torrent of oaths which made Lettice turn away her head in blushing shame while even Fergus looked shocked. He was well acquainted with his father's colourful vocabulary, but tonight's offering was particularly rich.

'Enough, Father,' he ventured, as the old man paused for breath. 'Remember there is a lady present.'

'Not for long there won't be, not if that venomous, sneaking toad has his way. We'll all be in the poorhouse and you'll find no "ladies" there.'

'What do you mean, Papa?' cried Lettice in genuine alarm. She had been reflecting on the iniquities of young doctors who did not seek people out when people hoped they would, and who instead let themselves be led astray by designing older women with daughters, when her father's words triggered a childhood memory of accompanying her mother on a charitable visit to a poorhouse. It was a memory compounded of misery, poverty and the smell of despair and drove the elusive Dr Marshall quite from her mind.

But though she repeated the question with growing anxiety, her father did not answer. Instead he sat in glowering thought until they reached the Guestrow and the carriage turned in under the arch to pull up at their own front door. The lamp was lit above the entrance and the sight of the heavy oak door with its iron bosses and bars and its huge iron keyhole was strangely reassuring. Lettice was gathering her skirts together ready for descending the step when the old man finally spoke.

'Be at breakfast by six, Fergus. We'll drive to the quarry together. You've kept things jogging along at a snail's pace for long enough. It is time to double production, if not treble it.'

'But, Father!' protested Fergus, appalled. 'It is not poss . . .'

'But nothing,' interrupted the old man, pushing him aside and hammering on his own front door until it was opened by a terrified and obviously newly wakened servant. 'If you can't do it, then I'll do it myself and to hell with the lot of you. Brandy!' he bellowed into the dark-panelled shadows. 'At the double if you know what's good for you!' Then he strode across the hall and into the library, slamming the door behind him, only to throw it open again on a roar of displeasure. 'The fire's out! What sort of a house do you keep, woman, with no fire in the grate when it's wanted?' This to Lettice who had barely time to open her mouth to point out that it was past midnight and the servants all abed before he went on, 'Light it, damn you, and if it's not blazing high in five minutes, I'll see you chop the wood yourself and lay the twigs with your bare hands. I've had enough of blood-sucking parasites and I'll not tolerate them in my own house. Is that understood?'

'Yes, Papa,' said Lettice, hurriedly throwing off her bonnet and cloak and scurrying for the kitchen. Behind her, she heard Fergus attempt to remonstrate with the old man and be told to go to hell for his pains. She had thought the opening of the railway an occasion for self-congratulation and rejoicing: that had certainly been her father's mood at the beginning of the evening. He had been delighted with his own foresight in investing in the railways and on the way to the dinner had been talking of the profits which would come rolling in now that the link was finally made between Aberdeen and London. During the dinner itself he had seemed jovial enough, and it was not until afterwards, she realized, when George Wyness had said something to him, that her father's mood had changed.

What had George Wyness said? She dare not ask, for fear of driving her father into apoplexy, but whatever it was it had certainly had a devastating effect on her father's temper. Poor Fergus. Lettice knew how he felt about his quarry, knew how happy he had been lately, and knew that that halcyon time was at an end. When she escorted the terrified kitchen-maid into the library, bearing a shovel of hot coals from the kitchen fire, with candle-ends, newspaper and similar reviving agents, she found her father sitting upright in the high-backed leather armchair beside the empty grate, an untouched brandy glass in his hands and his frowning eyes staring unblinking into space. For a moment she thought he had had some sort of seizure, then she saw his eyes move.

'Get on with it. Then get out.'

In silence Lettice and her helper did. They found Fergus waiting outside the door and when Lettice had sent the kitchen-maid scuttling back to the warm safety of her bed beneath the kitchen table, he took her arm and led her upstairs. At her bedroom door he stopped and said, 'Have you any idea what has got into the old man?'

Lettice shook her head. 'None at all.' They were both whispering, in spite of the distance between library and bedroom. 'But it must be something pretty terrible and probably concerning money. He mentioned the poorhouse, remember.'

'So he did.' Fergus sighed, remembering what else his father had said. 'But I had better say good-night, sister, if I am to be up in time to prevent him blowing my quarry to smithereens.'

Prevent him. Lying sleepless into the small hours Fergus knew he would try his best to do so and knew, with dread, that he would inevitably fail. Whatever had got hold of Old Man Adam had got him by the throat and would not easily let go.

In the darkened library below, Mungo Adam sat immobile while the fire died away and the night air, with the moonlight, crept insidiously through the room to fill it with an eerie chill. He had forgotten fire, bed, everything except those cheerful, taunting words.

'Nice to see you again, Mungo old boy.' Then, as if that was not insult enough, with the back-slapping that went with it, the fellow had added, with a grin that reached from ear to ear, 'I hear my new investment company lent you money. Always glad to oblige, of course, but mind you keep up the payments. We don't take kindly to bad debtors.'

'You should have seen his face,' chortled Wyness for the twentieth time over breakfast the following morning. 'It was worth every pennyworth of capital I laid out just to see it. And the company is doing well on top of that. Young Tom was right. Property is the thing, whether the building, the buying or the leasing of it. And property in a new, developing land is best of all. A shrewd lad, that one. He'll go far.'

'He has done already,' pointed out his wife, who had had another 'difficult' interview with Fanny. 'Australia is far enough for anyone, and a deal too far, if you ask my opinion, for a marrying kind of man. Fanny will be lucky to see him again.' When her husband made no comment, but concentrated on his breakfast porridge, she added, 'Dr David Marshall is such a charming young man. When he and Fanny danced a reel last night they looked so "right" together. Didn't you think so, dear?'

'I can't say I noticed one way or the other. But if you are angling for the doctor as a husband for Fanny, you'd best forget it. He's a nice enough lad, but she will not look at him, for one, and I will not, for another. What sort of use would a doctor mannie be to my polishing yard? Except maybe to take the splinters out of the lads' eyes now and then, and young Donal is fine at doing that already. You couldna find a better eye-doctor even if he had a string of letters to his name. Props them against a doorpost, takes a sharpened wood splinter or maybe a needle, and has the grit out, smooth and easy, afore you can say "Eye Institute". He's a good lad, is Donal. That design he's done for his brother's tomb is the best yet. It's sure to be a favourite in our pattern book and we're planning to send it out with the others, to Tom. Minus the lettering of course. I've two lads working on the templates now.'

'You talk as if Tom Diack is well settled there.'

'He is, lass, he is. But that's not to say he'll not come back, when he's done what he went out to do.'

In fact, had it not been for Fanny, Wyness would have been happy for Tom to stay out there indefinitely. In spite of their anxieties on her behalf, poor Mhairi could not have done more valiantly in her widowhood had Tom come racing home to be at her side. Though it upset Wyness to see the sadness in her face, he told himself it was only natural: Alex had been a good husband to the lass and she had loved him. But the children were a comfort to her and with her family about her she had not lacked for company or for love, so when she asked it, Wyness readily agreed to postpone the sending of the fateful letter. The quarry, too, had survived under his nominal management, though the Diack lads between them had put him right on more than one occasion, and Tom was doing

[231]

excellent work on their behalf in Melbourne. The progress of the secret contract was slow but steady and with Tom on the spot to report every stage Wyness knew that when the big moment came, they would be ready. He also believed that when the contract was completed, Tom would come home. Unfortunately, Mrs Wyness did not share his confidence.

'Then I hope he hurries up about it, before Fanny is a sour and shrivelled old maid. I declare she irritates me beyond endurance sometimes with her martyrdom and her patience, but I tell her she is not growing any younger and it would serve him right if she forgot all about him and married someone else. She does not listen, of course, but it would be so very pleasant if she could be married in the summer and really she has waited quite long enough. It is a full eighteen months since he sailed.'

'Yes, dear, I am sure you are right,' soothed Wyness, hardly listening. He was wondering how large a slice of the yard's profits to invest in the new company which Tom Diack had recommended, and how long it would be before Old Man Adam defaulted on his payments. Because when he did . . . but that triumph lay in the future. Meanwhile, the present held pleasures enough for him.

'If there is another kipper to follow this one, my dear,' he said, beaming, 'I would greatly appreciate it. I have rarely tasted better, and superbly cooked.'

That same morning marked the end of what Fergus thought of ever after as the halcyon days at Silvercairns. Breakfast was scarcely over before Old Man Adam announced that he had urgent work to attend to in Glasgow. In his absence the household was summarily ordered to pack up and remove to the country, though it was a month before the normal time 'and the beds not aired nor the chimneys swept' as Ma Gregor complained to anyone who would listen. But it was a two-mile ride from town house to quarry and though the house at Silvercairns still bore the signs of winter's damp, it stood on the quarry's doorstep and that was all that mattered if every minute of every day was to be put to productive use, as Old Man Adam meant it to be. For when Old Man Adam returned from Glasgow he was like a man possessed: up before dawn, raging unjustly at Fergus for being a 'bone-idle wastrel with the drive of a jellyfish and the business acumen of a sheep', striding about the quarry floor at all hours terrorizing the work-force, countermanding not only every order Fergus gave but most of his own as well, until the foreman Bruce took Fergus aside and begged him to 'Do something about Mr Adam, sir, afore the entire force downs tools and walks out.' White-faced, but resolute, Fergus did.

He chose his moment, after dinner in his father's library at Silvercairns. The fire was smoking, no doubt because of the bird's nest Lettice suspected in the chimney, there were damp patches above the window frame and more in the corner of the ceiling which adjoined the dining-room, but apart from these minor blemishes, the room was comfortable enough and the dinner Lettice had provided had been excellent and made up, as Fergus had suggested, of all their father's favourite dishes. Fergus had taken Lettice into his confidence, but when she had offered to stay with him in the library, to give moral support and 'join in the fun', he had refused. Now she had reluctantly removed to the drawing-room on a pre-arranged pretext, 'to write an urgent letter', and the moment had come.

Fergus drained his brandy glass in one and said, without preamble, 'I must ask you, Father, to keep away from the quarry floor. You unsettle the men.'

'*Unsettle?*' His father's roar shook every crystal of the drawing-room chandelier and lifted the dust as far away as the attic. At the same time he struck the arm of his chair a blow that would have crippled a weaker man's hand and shot to his feet to tower over Fergus in bristling rage. 'If seeing they do what I pay them to do is unsettling, boy, then I'll do a deal more of it and anyone who does not like it can go to the devil. Including you.'

Fergus looked into his father's eyes without flinching. 'Thank you, sir, for your confidence.'

His father had never liked him and never would: that was a fact he had accepted long ago. Nevertheless he had hoped, naïvely, for due recognition of his achievements. Now he realized with chilling certainty that nothing he did could ever make him acceptable in his father's sight. Even if he doubled the quarry's production overnight it would merely be to be told he should have trebled it. But in spite of that implacable dislike Fergus remained Adam's elder, and now only, son and heir and he would not stand by and see his father destroy his inheritance. Cold sarcasm gave way to a rush of liberating, white-hot rage. His eyes narrowed, though without leaving his father's, and he assumed an air of deliberate and insolent ease, hands hanging loose over the arms of his chair, outstretched ankles crossed.

'If your aim is to destroy the quarry, Father, you are certainly going the right way about it. If you look at the production figures alone you will see that since your personal supervision, as you so proudly call it, they have fallen. Disastrously. And no wonder, when you spend your days undoing whatever I and my foreman have done . . .'

'*Your* foreman?' interrupted Adam, who had been momentarily incoherent with fury. He aimed a kick at the firebucket which overturned to spill its contents across the floor. 'Mine, damn you, just as the quarry is mine to run as I choose.'

'And destroy as you choose? As you choose to destroy that Persian rug? Because I warn you, Father, one more outburst from you on the quarry floor and I have it on the best authority that the entire work-force will walk out – and before you say good riddance to them, may I remind you that ours is not the only quarry in Aberdeen and there are others ready and waiting to take on as many skilled workers as they can lay their hands on. If you choose to send your best quarrymen straight into George Wyness's camp, by all means do so, though I should be glad to hear how you plan to replace them. With Orkney fishermen, perhaps?'

Old Man Adam had opened his mouth to shout Fergus down, but at the mention of George Wyness, changed his mind. Instead he began to pace the room, muttering incoherent oaths and striking or kicking out at anything in his path. In the fractional pause this gave him, Fergus resumed the attack. He had burnt his boats to the last splinter now and had no more to lose.

'Or perhaps you plan to don a leather apron yourself, Father, and do the work of fifty with one hand behind your back? You have told me often enough that I am useless, ignorant, lazy, not worth my keep, and can go to the devil. I'm tired of it, Father. I might just take you at your word, only it's not the devil I'll go to. It's George Wyness. I've no doubt he'll take me on, too. I am a good quarry manager, though you refuse to see it, and trained by one of the best men in the business, but that's not why he'll take me on. It will be to show the whole of Aberdeen that he is powerful enough to hire an Adam to work for him.'

'Work for George Wyness?' That stopped Old Man Adam in his tracks as Fergus had known it would. He whirled round from the window where his pacings had taken him and snarled, 'I'll see you in hell first!'

'I was not planning to go there, Father. Merely to Rainbow Hill.'

'And take all the family secrets with you? I forbid it, damn you. I . . .' He stopped, a strange look on his face, and suddenly Fergus knew beyond all doubt that what he had long suspected was true.

'Secrets, Father?' he said, very softly. 'I did not realize there were any, unless of course you are referring to, shall we call it the Mackinnon affair? People who oppose Silvercairns, you said, deserve all they get. And you make your arrangements accordingly. Yes, Father, I understand your misgivings. George Wyness cannot fail to be most interested in that particular secret, should I choose to tell.'

There was a long pause during which Fergus stood up, walked to the side-table and refilled his brandy glass. His father watched him in silence, then slowly made his way to the high-backed chair on the other side of the fire, and lowered himself into it.

'Brandy, Father?'

Old Man Adam made no answer. Fergus refilled his father's glass, placing it on a low table beside him, then resumed his seat and waited. Let him sweat, thought Fergus with satisfaction, then as he watched his father's face satisfaction gave way to the first stirrings of remorse and even a reluctant pity. He had won the contest, but it was an empty victory, devoid of pleasure. He had meant to sway his father by reasoned argument and instead had sunk to blackmail, inadvertent but no less shameful for that. The fact that his

[235]

suspicions about the Rainbow Hill explosion had been confirmed merely increased the shame. He had sunk to his father's level: he ought to make his father confess, admit responsibility and make what retribution he could. Instead he knew he would use the knowledge merely to restrain his father and to increase his own power over the quarry he loved. He had meant not to speak again until Old Man Adam spoke, but instead, to bring the life back into his father's face, he heard himself saying, 'I wonder when we will hear news of Hugo's child?'

'Hugo's child?' Adam looked at him in puzzlement and Fergus realized that his father's thoughts had been further away than he knew. For a moment he wondered if his father could have had some sort of turn, a minor stroke perhaps? But when the old man spoke again he sounded all too like himself.

'You'll not go to work for Wyness, because your place is here, in Silvercairns, keeping the place going for the next generation. Don't think I don't know what store you set by that quarry you choose to call yours. You love it like a mistress, which is why you've never had time for a flesh-and-blood woman, leastways not that I've heard and I hear most things. So you'll stay and work that quarry and as long as I'm satisfied with the profits, I'll undertake not to interfere.' This, Fergus realized, was all the capitulation or apology he was likely to receive. 'But you'll increase output by a third and hire no extra men to do it and before you ask why, I'll tell you. For two reasons: first, I've debts to be paid off, never mind what or to whom, but unless they are paid, we stand to lose more than your precious Silvercairns, and secondly, I'm expecting my grandson from abroad. When Hugo's son arrives, I want him to find the richest quarry in Scotland waiting for him.'

No mention of Mackinnon, no admission of guilt, no explanation or apology; merely the threat of destitution if impossible profits were not achieved, and even if they were, of disinheritance in favour of Hugo's unknown by-blow, a mere child of three. Whether such disinheritance of a legitimate in favour of an illegitimate heir was possible in law Fergus neither knew nor cared. All that mattered was that he had the quarry in his own hands again, and he meant to keep it there. Whatever bland ignorance his father pretended, Fergus had a weapon with which to fight the old man and would not hesitate to use it.

To confirm the point, he said mildly, 'Yes, Father. Mackinnon always said the quarry, properly managed, would last for generations.'

As to Hugo's child, Fergus would deal with that problem when the time came.

Part 4

Tom Diack had done well. Looking back over his first fifteen months he could not help but be proud of his achievements: he had taken orders for as many headstones as the Wyness yard could send, had negotiated most favourable terms for the big contract which was referred to in all letters merely as 'the job' to preserve secrecy, and had also built up a small but profitable business on his own account. Had it not been for his failure to find any trace of Lizzie Lennox and his undiminished longing for Aberdeen and those he loved at home, he would have been well pleased.

That fortuitous meeting on board ship during the tedious voyage out had given him the contact he needed and young Mr Leslie had been true to his word. The Leslie brothers had been delighted with his sketches for a gentleman's mansion – sketches which were based on Mr Wyness's house in Skene Square – and had undertaken to find a reliable architect to produce detailed plans. That done, Tom had set to work at once to recruit the workmen he needed. The house was well on the way to completion and Tom had tentative inquiries for two similar mansions, in Burra Burra and Geelong, and a preliminary inquiry for a Presbyterian church in Melbourne itself. As a result of that introduction to Mr Robert Leslie, well-established and prosperous sheep farmers from all over the Geelong area had talked to him about building ideas, all too often in some unspecified future, but one or two of them had more immediate plans, and as a result, Tom had undertaken to build a schoolhouse for one, a family house with verandahs for another, and even a house for a sentimental German immigrant who wanted an exact replica of the home he had left behind him in the fatherland. Eventually after many hours of bargaining, practical on Tom's part and emotional on Herr Hoffman's, they had arrived at an acceptable compromise which took account of the terrain, the local materials, and Tom's particular expertise.

This last had evolved rapidly as circumstances required: with the confidence of knowing that he possessed an enviable skill which was in short supply in this emerging frontier country, where everything was new and developing, where there were no long-established overlords like Mungo Adam to sap a man's confidence, Tom had spread his wings and set no limits to his daring. If he could not do a particular job himself, he undertook to find someone who could, to oversee the work and guarantee its standard – in short, to act as middle man. In fifteen months, from a quarryman used to hewing and working with granite alone, he had become a building contractor, willing to undertake and organize the construction of practically anything, and to work with pick and hammer alongside the men he hired wherever necessary. He knew who to approach for the best bricks and building stone, who to turn to for roof joists and timberwork, and become adept at putting together a building team from the first survey of the chosen plot, through the plans and diagrams, to the fitting of the window glass and the locking of the great front door. Through his building work, he learnt where land was available and which was of most value, for building or farmland, and reported accordingly, both to George Wyness and to the newly appointed manager of the Australian branch of the Bon Accord Investment Company. He was paid well for his pains and spent little, so that his savings steadily grew, as did his building business. Had he been able to find the workmen he needed, when he needed them, Tom would have been content. But skilled workmen like himself were few and quickly snapped up.

It was in order to do some of that snapping that Tom had come to the docks to meet the latest ship from home. As always, he had called at the bank with his usual inquiry: as always they had given him the same answer. No, they could tell him nothing of Miss Lennox. No, they could not give him an address. If he cared to leave his card they would give it to her if she called, but they could undertake no more than that.

Tom had emerged into the glaring sunlight with the usual sense of frustration and disappointment. It was months since that momentous letter had arrived from Mhairi, telling him of

[242]

Hugo Adam's death, but while the news had removed one obligation it had merely strengthened the other: there was no longer the need to punish the offender, God had done that for him, but the victim needed his solicitous attention and concern even more than before. However, until he could find the girl, he could do nothing and she seemed determined not to be found. But Lizzie had always been a wayward lass, obstinate and defiant. Remembering those long-ago childhood days in Aberdeen Tom turned his steps towards the quayside with the usual wave of homesickness gripping his heart. He wanted buildings of granite instead of wood, old-established buildings where people's fathers and grandfathers had worked before them, not all these anonymous shacks which sprang up out of nowhere overnight. He would be ashamed to put his name to one of those buildings, he grumbled to himself as he made his way to the quayside. Hen hutches with balconies. One honest Aberdeen gale and they'd be fit for nought but a bonfire for the Queen's birthday.

But the thought of a gale changed sour criticism to longing, pure and unashamed. He wanted the crisp sea breeze of home in his face, the cold at his fingers, and under his feet the iron-hard feel of turf after a night's frost. Here there was only sun and warmth and the sort of sea that was no sea at all to his way of thinking, but a blue silky bowl with froth on it. In *winter*, for June was winter here. At home, winter meant ice on the pail in the morning, frost patterns on the window pane, the sky a clear ice-blue and one's breath a white puff of cloud with every word. Winter meant a kale-pot always simmering on the peat fire for a warming dinner, and in the dark of morning, before they set out for work, a fine dish of porridge, steaming hot and comforting. He'd had porridge since he left, of course, but it was not the same. You needed a crisp Scottish morning to appreciate it properly. As on every day since he had sailed from Aberdeen, he wondered what they were all doing, Alex and Mhairi and his family, and then, with a different homesickness, he thought of Fanny Wyness.

But he had no right to think of her, or of anyone, when he should be concentrating on the job in hand, which was to find, and hire, a clutch of good tradesmen to help fulfil his ever-increasing building contracts.

[243]

So, with growing impatience, he waited in the crowds for the port authorities to finish whatever formalities had to be gone through before the passengers could set foot ashore, and made desultory conversation with his immediate neighbours. It was in this way that one heard of suitable immigrants: joiners, masons, bricklayers who could be approached with the firm offer of a job. But today his neighbours on one side were meeting female relatives from the Highlands who hoped for good domestic work, and on the other side, a married man from Alloa with wife and family who hoped for a job on a sheep farm. Tom had no work for either, but wished them both well, and it was while he was looking around him in restless frustration and silently cursing the harbour doctor or the customs men or whoever was taking such a devil of a time to give the passengers clearance that he saw, not ten yards away in the waiting crowds, the unmistakable figure of Lizzie Lennox. Her hair was as red and unruly as he remembered under its pert straw bonnet and the bright emerald green of her dress stood out vividly in the crowd. But she had no child with her that he could see: only another girl of her own age, with yellow ringlets and dressed in a bright orange dress and a yellow shawl. Tom struggled to push his way towards her through the milling throng, shouting, 'Lizzie! Lizzie Lennox!' but his voice was lost in the cheers and cries of greeting as the first of the passengers came ashore and the next moment Lizzie herself was lost to view in the general mêlée.

Tom swore under his breath, pushed and elbowed his way to where he had last seen her, but with no success. But he had seen her, that was something. She was not dead as he had sometimes feared, nor, apparently, had she disappeared into the middle of nowhere on some sheep farm. Neither was she starving and poverty-stricken, bowed down by the burden of a fatherless child. On the contrary, she had looked healthy and well fed and was obviously not without friends. As to the child, that could well be at home, with some servant or elderly person. As soon as he had scanned the groups of newly embarked passengers, spoken to the likely, asked his questions and given his name and address to the most promising, he would begin his search. His business would not take long and in that time, she could not travel far. If she was not to be found

[244]

in Melbourne, then he would seek her further afield. Somehow he would find her.

It was many hours later when Tom, footsore, weary and dejected, at last gave in. He had scoured every inch of Melbourne, trailing up and down the endless grid of so-called streets, many no more than trodden dirt and many more malodorous with rotting refuse and decay. He had peered through windows, into gardens, entered every kind of inn, eating house or hostelry but without success. She had eluded him. Disappeared like a weasel into a dyke. The comparison brought a rush of longing for Fanny which made him bite his lip against the surge of anger and frustration and homesickness for those he loved. What was he doing walking an unknown street in an unknown town, looking for someone who had no doubt forgotten he existed, when most of the inhabitants of that town were asleep in their beds, as he should be in his? Most, for there were still some solitary travellers, like himself walking aimlessly alone in the darkness. Dammit, he'd looked long enough. It was time to go home, if he could find his way out of this labyrinth of murky roads with no lamp and no moon to see by.

Trying to pick up his bearings, he turned the corner of a wide street into another, smaller street of trodden stones and dirt edged with wooden hen-coop houses, an occasional bush or tree and the usual dreary patches of sun-scorched grass and dust. A mean street in a mean part of town. Tom caught the glint of water somewhere to his right, knew it to be the harbour and lengthened his stride. His lodgings were away on the far side of town, in the wholesome suburbs. The night air, scented with blossom and an undercurrent of less-welcome human odours, was unnaturally warm on his cheeks, the scent of night-soil stronger as he passed between the huddled wooden houses. He was wishing with the usual longing for a breath of cold northern air to cool his face and cleanse his lungs when a voice from close at hand said, 'All alone, are you, laddie? It's a dark night to be walking alone. Woudn't you like company?'

Tom stopped, turned his head, and saw a small figure

leaning her elbows on the rail of the wooden fence which formed a sort of verandah on the front of the nearest building. It was a one-storey affair of slatted wood, but with a good pitched roof and a chimney. The door to the house was open as were the windows on either side of it, one of them in darkness, and in the other the dim glow of an oil lamp with the wick turned low. The night air was loud with crickets. Then from somewhere beyond the settlement a dingo bayed the moon with a howl that brought a shiver to Tom's spine and a sudden wish for company. He had meant to ignore the woman, as he usually did, but something in the voice made him hesitate and she spoke again.

'I'm thinking you are a stranger in these parts. Maybe arrived on yon ship this morning and with nowhere to go? Well, I've room and to spare in my wee house if you're looking for a bed. If you care to step up here a while I'll make you right welcome, and not bankrupt you, neither.'

There was something vaguely familiar about the voice and as Tom still hesitated, she spoke again. 'I've a pot of coffee brewing, if you need to keep your strength up. Or maybe something stronger?'

Tom took a step towards her and as he did so the moon came out from behind a cloud and flooded the scene in eerie light.

'Tom Diack!' The girl gave a strangled scream of alarm, quickly stifled. 'Lord help us if it isn't Tom Diack large as life and twice as handsome. Who'd ha' thought to see you here, you young devil, sneaking up on folk and frightening them near out of their wits. Lord love us but you gave me a right turn, you did.'

'Lizzie?' Tom could not believe it. In the half-light he had seen only a shape, two-dimensional and without colour, a paleness of face and arms against a darker blur made up of hair and garments and the shadowed wall of the house. 'Lizzie Lennox?'

'Who else would it be, ye daft gowk, and me calling you by your name? Or are you that well acquaint with all the ladies of Melbourne? Well, don't just stand there like a dummy wi' only a ha'p'orth in the shilling. Come away in afore ye rouse the neighbours. And dinna make a noise while you're doing it.

[246]

My friend's in there.' She jerked her head towards the darkened room. 'Well, well, Tom Diack,' she went on, drawing him into the lamp-lit room and turning up the wick. 'Who'd have thought it. And what brought you to these parts, or shouldn't I ask?'

'Work,' said Tom, struggling with the thought of Lizzie, in her too-bright dress and too-pert manner, with the unknown friend asleep beyond the thin plank wall. He noticed there was a bed in the room, with a cleanish pillow and a patchwork bedspread, a large heart-shaped patch in bright red calico in its centre. For some reason the sight of it made him blush.

'Well sit down, laddie. I'll not bite ye.' She indicated a straw-bottomed chair beside the empty grate in which a pleated paper fan wilted under its layer of dust. 'I'm right glad it was you, Tom, and not some stranger.' She sat on the edge of the bed, slipped off her shoes and wiggled her bare toes in relief. 'I'm nay in the mood to be sociable tonight.'

'No, I realize it is late,' said Tom awkwardly, 'and you have no doubt had a busy day, with a child to care for.' He paused, then said in a rush, 'You had a child, didn't you? Hugo Adam's child?'

'That's my business, nay yours, Tom Diack, but then you always was an interfering young stirk, poking your nose where it wasna wanted.'

'You lied to me, Lizzie, and I believed you. You should have told me the truth, then I'd have killed that bastard,' said Tom with concentrated venom.

'Aye, well. I didna, did I, and a good thing too. You'd have been hanged, else. You should be grateful to me, instead of going on at me as if you was my father. Which reminds me, how is the old bastard?'

'Still alive, when I last saw him which was a while back. And don't change the subject. I was talking about Hugo Adam.'

'Not to me, you wasn't. He's away.'

'What do you mean, "away"?'

'Dead, snuffed it, popped his clogs, gone to the great gambling den in the sky.' She lay back on the bed in an attitude of embarrassing abandon and kicked one bare foot in the air.

[247]

Tom was shocked. He remembered Lizzie Lennox as quick-witted, sharp-tongued, volatile and cheerfully amoral, but there was a new, taunting edge to her voice which he did not care for and was unsure how to take. When he had received Mhairi's letter telling him of Hugo Adam's death his first reaction had been annoyance: he had felt vaguely cheated of the chance to bring a villain to justice, but later he had felt relief at an unwelcome obligation gone, and then a reluctant pity for the man, dead at twenty-one, before he had achieved anything in life except notoriety. Lizzie seemed to feel nothing.

'Lizzie! You must not speak so disrespectfully of the dead.'

'Don't see why not.' She sat up, slipped her feet back into her shoes, tossed her head and turned her back. Then she began to inspect her appearance in the small, blotched looking-glass which hung on a nail above the fireplace. She took out a tortoiseshell hair comb and put it back again, in a different place. Then, sensing his disapproval, she said, 'He was a right bastard, that one. I reckon the West Indies was too hot for him. Though where he's gone now is maybe just as hot.' She laughed, but when Tom did not join in, her laughter died and she snapped, 'You're as bad as my father, Tom Diack, wi' your piety and your long face. And for what? Hugo Adam caught a fever and dropped dead, and serve him right. You didna like him alive so why the difference now? He was a nice lad when I met him,' she added wistfully and for the first time Tom saw a glimpse of the old Lizzie whom he had last seen almost four years ago in Aberdeen. 'Right handsome he was, too, and wi' such a winning tongue in his head.' Then, recollecting, she brushed sentiment aside. 'Pity he didna stay that way. He should have paid what he owed.'

That reminded Tom. 'His family paid, I hope?'

'Where do you think I got the money for this place? It's nay rented, you know. It's mine. Leastways, come Christmas it will be. It's nay big enough, mind, but it'll do meantime, till I've got myself established, like. One day I'll have more rooms and a parlour, wi' chairs and that, for my visitors. Me and Rosabel, we've got it all worked out. But you wouldna be wanting to know about that,' she said, suddenly wary. 'Tell me about home. How's Ma and our Evie?'

[248]

'I've been away more than eighteen months, but they were well when I left them. Who is Rosabel?' He knew, before she answered, that it must be the girl with the yellow ringlets.

'Just a friend.' Lizzie shrugged. 'She works wi' me.'

A door opened across the passage and there was the sound of low voices, male and female, steps on the verandah and then a door closing.

'Who was that?' said Tom, half rising from his chair.

'No one. Just one of Rosabel's friends, that's all.'

'At this time of night?'

'We're nay in Aberdeen now, Tom Diack. Folk dinna have to turn out the lamp at nine and sleep if they dinna want to. Here, we stay up talking and that till morning, if the fancy takes us.'

'And what about the child, Leo?' said Tom, recollecting. 'That's not the right sort of life for a child.' He was remembering Mhairi's firm but loving discipline of young Hamish who went to bed when he was told to do so, and stayed there.

'I've got no child.' Again Lizzie turned away, this time making for the door. 'I'll get that coffee I promised you, then we can have a proper talk.'

But Tom reached the door before her. 'Don't lie to me again, Lizzie. I saw that letter you wrote to Mhairi, about wanting money for "a fine, healthy boy". You got it, too. And before you tell me any more lies, I know because Mhairi told me. You had to take the lad to the bank manager and prove he was alive.'

'Sanctimonious bastard,' said Lizzie with feeling. 'He kept going on about "proof of paternity" till I tellt him it was Hugo Adam he should be examining if that was what he was looking for, though I hadna heard it called "paternity" before.' At her suggestive wink Tom blushed. 'Fetched a doctor mannie in, too, to poke my Leo about and inspect his credentials, then he looked in his ears and that, picked over his hair for lice and poked a wooden stick thing in his mouth. Leo bit him,' she added with a reminiscent grin. 'Served yon doctor mannie right.'

'So they gave you money?'

'It was my money what was promised me when that bastard

[249]

upped and left me. And not enough of it, neither. Move out of the way, Tom Diack,' she said in sudden exasperation. 'Can't you see I'm wanting out?'

'Not until you tell me about the child. Where is he?'

'Gone.' Again she tried to push past him, but he caught hold of her arm and gripped it tight.

'Gone where?'

'Where do you think?' she said, avoiding his eye. 'There's fevers here as well as in them West Indies, and nae wonder with no proper scaffies and all that filth rotting in the streets. That breeds diseases, that does. Folks is always dying, expecially bairns.'

Tom was horrified. 'But you wrote that he was such a strong laddie, healthy you said . . . Oh Lizzie, I'm so sorry.' He tried to put his arm around her with the idea of offering her comfort, but she pushed him away.

'Leave me be, Tom Diack. It's no business of yours.' She averted her face as she spoke, pushed roughly past him and closed the door quickly after her so that he could not follow.

Left alone in the room Tom stood where she had left him, immobile. The child was dead. It was a possibility that had not once occurred to him, but now that she had said so it seemed inevitable. Poor Lizzie. She had spoken so bravely and perhaps after all it was for the best. A girl with a bastard child would find life hard enough, even here. Now she would have only herself to support. He moved to the window and stood looking out over the darkened town, but the moon had gone in again and he saw only blackness, alien and hostile. He closed the wooden shutters and turned back into the room.

It was neat enough, he supposed. A plain wooden floor, bare whitewashed walls and, as well as that looking-glass, a picture in a wooden frame. It was of a plain-faced woman in a dark dress, with a white ruff round her neck and a little dog.

At that moment the door opened again and Lizzie came back in, frowning, 'Silly cow. I put the pot of coffee on specially and she's drunk the lot. But it willna take long to brew up again. For God's sake, sit down, can't you? You give me the creeps, hovering.'

'I am so sorry, Lizzie. Sorry about your little boy, I mean. It must have been . . .'

'Shut up about it, can't you?' she shouted. 'Do you think I want to hear you going on and on like . . .'

The door behind Tom opened and a yellow-ringleted head peered round. 'Are you all right, Lizzie? I thought I heard shouting and . . . Oh.'

'Aye, I'm all right. Leastways, I was till this interfering gowk appeared.' Lizzie jerked her head derisively at Tom.

'Making trouble, is he? I've just had one like that. The things he wanted me to do. I told him it was double rates for antics like that, but he . . .'

'Tom is a friend from home,' interrupted Lizzie loudly and went through a pantomime of warning grimaces which left Rosabel baffled.

'From home?' Rosabel pushed the door open wider and stood, one hand on the doorknob, studying Tom from top to toe. She wore the same bright orange dress she had worn on the quay, but seen close to it looked even brighter and decidedly cheap. Her cheeks were unnaturally red and her hair like yellow straw. She ran her eyes over Tom with an intimacy that made him blush, then she winked and grinned. 'Wish I had a friend like him. Has he brought you news of your Leo?'

'Hell!' said Lizzie, with fury. 'What did you have to say that for, you stupid bitch?'

'Who are you calling stupid? There's nought stupid about asking a civil question when . . .'

'Shut up, you daft cow! You've said enough! Who asked you to come in here anyway? He's my visitor, nay yours. So you can get out.'

'Wait!' said Tom, catching hold of Rosabel's hand. 'What did you mean, "news of Leo"?'

'Ask her,' said Rosabel, glaring at Lizzie. 'Not that she'll tell you, the lying bitch. A fine way to treat a friend, that is, and me coming in to see if she was all right, like the arrangement is. Next time I'll not bother. She can get beaten black and blue for all I care and serve her right. Let me go, can't you!' She struggled to break free, but Tom held on.

'What did you mean by "news of Leo"? Lizzie said he was dead.'

'Dead?' Rosabel threw back her head and laughed. It was one of the most unpleasant sounds Tom had heard in his life.

'Fancy her telling you that. Though I suppose in a way of speaking he is dead to her, poor little bastard.'

'Shut your mouth!' shouted Lizzie. 'I warn you I'll . . .'

'Warn away,' taunted Rosabel, 'but it will do you no good. Not with your friend here wanting an answer to his question. What's it worth then, mister?' she said, looking coyly up at Tom. 'Make it worth my while, will you?'

'Leave him alone, you filthy cow. He's not like that. And I thought I told you to get out?' Lizzie pushed Rosabel hard in the well-rounded chest.

'All right, all right, I'm going.' Rosabel hitched up one shoulder of her dress where it had slipped, lifted her hands to her hair and adjusted a ringlet, then with a wink at Tom and a smile that chilled his blood, flounced out of the room, closing the door behind her. She opened it a moment later to say, 'If you really want to know, Mr Stranger-from-home, she sold the poor little bastard. Cheery-bye.'

The door closed on a silence which stretched and stretched. Then Tom said, very quietly, 'You did *what*?'

'Why shouldn't I take money if they was offering me it?' Lizzie turned her back and made great play of straightening the bedcover and the pillow. Then she sat down in the one and only chair, in a position of studied languor. 'Besides, my Leo will be fine where he's gone to. He'll be brought up like a gentleman, he will. He'll live in Silvercairns and have his own pony, like his Da before him. Bring him up like he was their own, the mannie said.'

'Which man?' For one dreadful moment Tom thought that, like Leo, Hugo Adam was not dead after all, but had sent to claim his son.

'The bank mannie, of course. Him as poked my Leo about the first time, afore he would hand over the money as was owed me. Said they'd offered to take him off my hands and why not? I'd had the feeding of him for long enough and it was time yon Adams took their turn. Cost a lot, babies do, and he was right strong and healthy was my Leo. You should have seen him wi' a mutton bone. Stripped it clean afore you could say knife. That's why I tellt them £50 was nowhere near enough. £50, I said, for a fine strong lad like my Leo? There's farming folk out back would give me double, any day of the week. They pastorals is always looking for strong lads, I tellt them, and if yon Mr Adam wants his wee grandson bad enough he can pay proper money for him. They gave me £80 in the end,' she finished, with a note of pride.

'£80.' Tom closed his eyes and leant his head against the door. 'I can't believe what I'm hearing.'

'Aye, well. I strike a hard bargain, I do. I get another twenty when the lad arrives safe and well,' she added, expecting praise.

'How could you, Lizzie?' Tom thumped the door once, in concentrated fury, then began to pace the room in a turmoil of helpless emotion. He was appalled, shocked, angry and ashamed – of Lizzie for behaving as she had done, and of himself for being so naïvely taken in. 'How could you? Sell your own son for £80 . . . Oh God,' and Tom buried his face in his hands.

'I tellt ye, I get another twenty when he arrives. That makes a hundred, that does, and right useful it will be, too.' She sounded well content with her bargain.

'And little Leo? Did you never think how he might feel?' Tom thought of his nephew Hamish and could not imagine Mhairi selling him, even if the whole family was starving, even for a king's ransom. As to sending the little fellow among strangers . . . He shuddered with horror at the thought.

But Lizzie had not Tom's imagination. 'He'll be fine where he's going to, will my Leo,' she said defiantly. 'He'll be a gent, he will, and one day, when he's a grown lad, I'll maybe visit him in Silvercairns. I right fancy a meal in yon dining-room, wi' silver forks and that. I'll be rich myself by then and I'll buy a tiara specially. Take that look off your face, Tom Diack!' she cried as he made no answering comment. 'You're nay a preacher and it doesna suit you. And for pity's sake sit down. It fair gives me the creeps to see you striding about like that. Besides, the room's nay big enough and you'll likely break something. Sit on the bed, can't you? I'll not threaten your precious virtue, if that's what you're thinking.'

Tom shuddered. Nothing would induce him to go near that bed with its tawdry calico heart. But he stopped his pacing and leant his back once more against the door. 'I prefer to stand.'

'Have it your own way,' sighed Lizzie, leaning back in her

chair and letting her arms hang loose on either side. 'I've had a busy day and I havena the strength to argue.' She closed her eyes, but only long enough to gather strength for the next attack. 'You've no right coming in here and lecturing me, Tom Diack. What do you know about it anyway? It's my business what I do wi' my own son and no one else's. I've done the best for Leo, I have. Besides, he was getting in the way here, always popping up where he wasna wanted, coming into the room and crying "Ma!" when I was busy. Some of my men friends didna like it. Put them off their stroke, it did. No, no. He's best where he is. But I miss the little bastard, just the same.'

Suddenly there was a vulnerable edge to her defiance, but only for a moment before the brittle hardness returned. 'Well, now you've satisfied your curiosity, Tom Diack, about what's none of your business, you can satisfy mine. Tell me about Ma and our Evie and the folks in the tenement. But first, I'll get that coffee, afore it boils away.' She stood up and moved for the door. 'You'd maybe like a dram with it, too, seeing as how it's late? You can sit in that chair while you're waiting and I'll fetch another from . . .'

'No, thank you,' interrupted Tom. 'I must go.'

'What? Leave when you've only just come and me having all they questions you havena answered yet? That's not neighbourly, that isn't. You'll bide here and drink a cup wi' me, Tom Diack, till you've tellt me all I want to know.'

Instead, Tom pushed roughly past her and out of the house, almost falling down the steps in his haste to be outside in the clear air again, to get the smell of her out of his nostrils and the sound of her out of his ears. God, he'd been a fool. All those months he had worried over her, persuaded himself she needed his help and protection, built up a picture in his mind of a poor, suffering mother, bravely struggling to support her fatherless child, and all the time . . . God, it made him sick to think of it. Sick and angry and mortified and soiled.

He heard her shout after him, insults or pleas, he did not know which and did not care. He wanted only to blow the memory out of his mind and be clean again. He wanted the wholesome, loving comfort of Rainbow Cottage, among his brothers and sisters, and suddenly, heart-stoppingly, he wanted Fanny Wyness, with her sweet-faced innocence and gentle, loving heart. If only that precious college was finished he could wind up his various enterprises, collect his savings and take the next ship home. As it was ... Pray God she would wait for him just a little longer – and pray God that poor little bastard Leo would come to no harm.

Part 5

Work at Rainbow Hill went steadily forward. In the eighteen months since Alex had died, they had clawed their way back from the brink of disaster until once more they had a steady stream of orders for building work in the town as well as further afield. With the railway contract and the big Australian order they had enough work to keep the quarry busy seven days a week, had a seven-day working week been permitted. As it was, they contrived to cram the work of seven days into six, and spent a good deal of the seventh planning work for the week ahead.

True to her promise, Mhairi had taken over much of the bookwork and accounts. As often as not, three-year-old Hamish came with her to the quarry office and whenever Willy had a spare moment, he would take the lad outside into the quarry yard and show him how to chip away at a block of granite with a little hammer.

'You will be apprenticing him into the yard before he can read or write,' Mhairi protested, half-serious, but Willy merely grinned.

'Aye, I will, if I can sneak him off with me before you and Annys whisk him away to yon school. A waste of time, schooling, when there's man's work to be done.'

'Willy! How can you say such a thing when . . .' Then seeing the expression on his face she laughed. 'But you must not tease me like that in front of the child. Suppose he thinks you are serious?'

'He won't, will you, little fellow?' and Willy picked up his small nephew under the armpits and swung him up on to the office desk. 'You listen to me, lad,' he said, his own face on a level with the boy's. 'You will go to school when your ma says, like I had to do, and then when you've learnt all that reading and writing she sets such store by, you will come to work with me. That is, if you want to be a quarryman like your da was.'

Hamish looked at his young uncle with solemn eyes,

without speaking.

'Well, lad, what do you say?' said Willy, with a wink at Mhairi.

'Can I go on the boatie?'

'You mean the barge? With the stones?' Hamish nodded. 'Aye, I expect so, lad.'

'Can I drive the cartie?'

'With the horses? Like Donal used to do? Aye, maybe. When you're bigger.'

'I'm big now!' boasted Hamish, standing tall.

'But not now,' countered Willy, lifting him off the desk and back on to the floor. 'You'd not be able to see over the horses' heads to tell them where to go. Besides, you have to be strong to lead horses or they go their own ways, and to be strong you need muscles, like this.'

Willy flexed his biceps and Hamish stared goggle-eyed at the moving knot of muscles. Solemnly he flexed his own arm and studied the soft, plump baby flesh. 'I'm nearly strong,' he said and Willy gravely nodded.

Watching them, Mhairi felt a stab of poignant grief for her dead husband: it was he who should have been here, playing with Hamish, not Willy. Then grief was replaced by love, for her brother who, like the rest of them, tried so hard to make it up to her for Alex's death, for her son, her family, all those who were so dear to her, and then suddenly, like a cruel echo of that love, came fear. Already she had lost Alex. Suppose . . .? Dear God, she prayed silently inside her head. Please keep them safe.

That evening, Willy came home later than usual, but beaming. 'We cut the last of those slabs for Tom's Brisbane order today,' he said, subsiding into a chair with a sigh of content and taking the brimming mug that Mhairi put into his hands. 'Two weeks ahead of time. We'll send them in to the yard tomorrow first thing, eh, Lorn? And catch Mr Wyness on the hop.' He drank deeply. 'My, but that's good, Mhairi. And that pot smells appetizing. What is it?'

'Only a boiling fowl. The one that hadn't laid an egg all summer.'

'You see, lads,' said Willy with a wink at Lorn and Donal. 'We'll need to watch out. Anyone who doesn't earn his keep is for the chop. She's a hard woman, is Mhairi.' He grinned and dodged her playful smack, before settling back into his chair, feet outstretched to the fire.

'Hewed the first of the Huntly order today, too,' he said with pride. 'Two wagonloads of ashlar sent on their way already. We'll maybe ship the bulk of it by barge up the canal to Inverurie. What do you think, Lorn?' Without waiting for an answer, Willy continued, 'You can maybe mention it to Mr Wyness in the morning and see when the barges will be free. Then we'll need to get to work on the stuff for the Free Kirk order. There's one or two big blocks needed for that. I'll remind Robbie Bruce about it tomorrow.'

'Yes, dear brother,' said Mhairi, 'but tonight perhaps you could forget the quarry for a while and enjoy this hen before it boils away to nothing.'

Obediently Willy drained his mug and joined the rest of them at the table. He had seen her involuntary shudder, and knew how she felt whenever a name was mentioned that had the smallest connection with the explosion that had killed Alex and Mackinnon. Robbie Bruce had been one of the fated team.

Unlike Mhairi, Robbie himself seemed to have recovered from any lingering shock caused by the accident, as had Red Henderson, and both were among the quarry's most trusted workers. There had been a time when Mr Wyness, Mhairi and her brothers had suspected everyone connected with the explosion of some sort of double-dealing, but with the vital testimony forever unobtainable, they in company with the rest of Aberdeen had settled to the reluctant conclusion that Mackinnon's skill had slipped with age and the fault, if it was a fault, lay in the grave with the victims.

The aftermath of that shattering explosion had been wagonload after wagonload of road metal to be disposed of as best they could, with one or two loads of building rubble for which they found takers enough, though little reward. But George Wyness was not in the business for building rubble: his pride lay in larger blocks for columns, pedestals, arches and lintels, a pride shared by most of the men and, though he was still a mere apprentice, by Willy Diack. To find and quarry such blocks entire was an achievement which never failed to fill him with a warm satisfaction, and the spoiling of

[261]

one such, by a careless crack or corner chip, was not merely an economic loss, but a personal failure. Since that shattering explosion with its deadly aftermath, Wyness had ordered most particular care to be taken over every powder charge and fuse. Every ounce of powder was weighed, checked and accounted for, every inch of fuse recorded. Mhairi kept the record book herself, and became adept at entering both the charges used and the result in tonnage of quarried rock.

'That's no job for a woman,' Mr Wyness had protested when she first offered herself, but he soon saw her usefulness and accepted the situation. Besides, she was not there all the time, merely a couple of hours a day. After that, she had sewing to do for the rich ladies of the town. But Mhairi almost preferred the quarry, in spite of the dust and dirt. To work where Alex used to work helped her grief and at least in the quarry office she was working for the family business. Now, looking round the faces at the supper table – Alex's brother Donal, her brothers Lorn and Willy, young Annys with Hamish on her knee – Mhairi felt a glow of well-being which banished anxiety. Her infant daughter was happily asleep in the next room, she had her family around her and food on the table. For the first time since Alex's death Mhairi felt that all was right with the world. Only Tom was missing, but he was doing well for himself by all accounts and soon he would come home again, where he belonged.

'This is the best hen we've had for many a day,' she said, smiling. 'Would anyone like any more? There's plenty in the pot.'

George Wyness, too, was pleased with the quarry's progress. The Australian order was well under way now and all that remained was the most important part of all. But they could not embark on that until plans were finalized and the model delivered. Tom had written that the choice had been made, and as soon as it was completed the model would be sent, but sea passage being what it was, that might take months. When it did arrive, though, they would have to put all their most experienced hands on the job. There was a deadline for this particular order which must on no account be missed.

Professional pride alone required it, but on top of that, and to make prompt delivery doubly sure, there was, for understandable reasons, a large financial penalty for failure, a penalty which George Wyness had no intention of paying.

'So see no one gets wind of it,' he warned Lorn over and over. 'There's enemies everywhere so dinna trust even the toe in your own sock. I'm not wanting the Adam camp to hear the smallest whisper of what we're at so mind and say nothing to anyone. Donal's the one who'll be in charge when the model arrives, but Donal will not let on to a soul, will you, lad?' and Wyness clapped Donal companionably on the shoulder. The three were in the office at the polishing yard, the door firmly shut against all comers and Tom's latest letter, with its sketches, on the desk in front of them. Donal had studied both letter and sketches and knew as well as any of them what was afoot. He grinned, winked and gave a cheerful thumbs-up sign.

'Good man, Donal. It's the chance you've been waiting for, lad, and I know you'll not let me down. All we need is for that blessed ship to arrive.'

But when at last it did, in early September, it brought, as well as the large, carefully packed and doubly sealed packing-case which George Wyness was expecting, a smaller and more ragged packet, with a shock of tangled red hair, a pair of hand-me-down breeches, heavy boots two sizes too large for the wearer, and a label round its dirty neck: *Leo Lennox. To be collected.*

'You say the ship has been sighted?' Mungo Adam looked up from his breakfast plate of devilled kidneys and tried with scant success to keep the eagerness from his voice. It would not do for Fergus to suspect.

'Yes, Father.' After two hours spent already at the quarry Fergus had come home to Silvercairns on purpose to deliver the message. 'Sighted off Girdleness an hour ago. There will be formalities, of course, but by midday we can expect the passengers to come ashore.'

'By midday . . .' After the briefest of grins, quickly hidden, Mungo Adam was quiet, lost in his own thoughts.

Fergus waited, expecting an answer, but when he realized that there would be none, at least not immediately, he subsided into a convenient chair and poured himself a cup of tea. As he drank, he watched his father and wondered, as always, what was going through the old man's mind. It was an exercise which had become familiar to him over the months since what he thought of as their confrontation, months during which Old Man Adam had paid lip service to his promise not to 'interfere' but had done so nevertheless in a hundred different devious and meddlesome ways.

So Fergus watched him warily, wondering as always how long he would be able to keep his father's grasping ideas under control. His latest had been to note the time lost by men who had to vacate the quarry while a charge was fired; he had suggested to Fergus that they enter this as 'idle' time and dock it from the men's wages, an outrageous suggestion with which Fergus did not bother to argue. If he could work out a way to do it without time-wasting injury to his own work-force, thought Fergus morosely, his father would order the men to keep at their work while the powder blew up beside them. The thought sent a shiver up his spine and reminded him once again of the explosion that had widowed Mhairi Diack. He had glimpsed her occasionally in the town, looking pale-faced and achingly beautiful in her widow's black, but had not attempted to speak to her. The knowledge of his father's guilt prevented that.

The thought brought another, equally unwelcome. Fergus knew that his father had become increasingly obsessed by the need to find out George Wyness's affairs. He was almost sure the old man paid spies to report to him, though he had no evidence on which to base the suspicion except one occasion when he had surprised his father handing money to a servant with what he thought was a sealed note and another when he was almost sure he saw an unknown boy of ten or so scurrying through the shadows of the drive and not long after his father had appeared, claiming to have been 'taking a bit of fresh air to clear the head'. Small things in themselves and possibly harmless, but there was no doubt in Fergus's mind that his father was up to something. On too many occasions Fergus had looked up to find his father's eyes on him and always Old

Man Adam looked quickly away, but not before Fergus had caught the sly expression and the look of cunning. It was as if the old man knew Fergus had a hold over him and was plotting something criminally devious behind his back in order to turn the tables. The thought made him increasingly uneasy, as he was now, waiting for his father to speak.

Fergus was nearer the mark than he thought. Old Man Adam stole a look at his son from under carefully frowning brows and looked quickly down again. So Hugo's boy had arrived. He must not let Fergus see the glee in his eyes, or the different glee at the thought of his plans for the Wyness downfall.

Ever since the night of the Wyness party when Lettice had told him of the rumoured Australian order, Mungo Adam had brooded over the possibility that George Wyness might be establishing a trade link with Australia until it had become an obsession with him. But try as he might he had been able to find out little more. Some said Headstane Wyness had the contract to bury all the dead in Van Diemen's Land, with Brisbane, Melbourne and Sydney thrown in; others that he was to build a mausoleum for the king of the aborigines, or a palace for the governor of the prison, with portcullis, moat and dungeon included. They were cheerful rumours, cheerfully embellished, and left Old Man Adam none the wiser, until he found his spy. Remembering what that spy had told him, Adam's eyes gleamed bright with malice. A big order, for a public building, with a grand opening ceremony the date of which was immovably set, and failure to deliver on time earned a spectacular penalty.

Adam had not forgiven George Wyness for that back-slapping remark at the railway opening: the revelation that he, Mungo Adam, had borrowed money from a firm of which Wyness was a partner had been almost enough to choke him with impotent fury. He had payed it back the next day, of course, with interest. But ever since, Mungo's ambition had been to ruin Wyness, utterly and completely, by whatever means possible. The Australian order was the perfect opportunity. There was only one piece of information missing – the vital delivery date. There must be papers somewhere and if there were, he would buy a reading of them. As he had bought himself a grandson.

Old Man Adam thought of Hugo, his dear, dead son, and of the unknown and unofficial grandchild from Australia. Hugo's son, who was to cheer and sustain him and give him a reason for living. Hugo's son, who was one day to inherit Silvercairns over Fergus's head and pay Fergus back for his pious, censorious, mean-spirited ways. And Fergus said the ship had been sighted: Mungo could hardly contain his excitement, but he must do so at all costs. It would not do for Fergus to suspect.

The child must be three or even four by now, no longer an infant but a boy. He would have a look of Hugo – how could he help it, with Hugo for a father – and would have the same lively spirit and quick intelligence. Mungo would train him up from the start to take over one day, train him to be shrewd and hard and ruthless as Mungo himself was. There should be none of Fergus's romantic sentimentality where the quarry was concerned, but a hard-headed, practical approach which would consolidate their riches and bring them more . . .

Day-dreaming, Mungo Adam forgot the worries of the moment and saw only the future, rosy with the promise of youth and hope.

'Would you like me to go to the quay to meet him?' Fergus's voice broke in upon his father's thoughts.

It was on the tip of Adam's tongue to say certainly not, he would meet the boy himself, when he recollected. Too much eagerness and he would give himself away. 'I had thought of sending Lettice, the child being young, but you might as well go with her. If you can spare the time.'

It was cold on the quay: a brisk onshore wind whipped the surface of the harbour water and rocked the ships at their moorings, gulls wheeled and swirled, darting and swooping over the debris of the fishing boats and the detritus of the ship which had newly arrived from the other side of the world. The quayside bustled with activity as derricks swung over the open hold, shore porters hurried this way and that, trundling barrows piled with cabin trunks, or catching the nets of assorted bundles as they swung up from the belly of the ship

[266]

and out over the quay. One crate caused particular attention, being all of twelve feet long and four feet square and stuck all over with labels warning handlers to *Take Care*.

'Mind you dinna drop that,' warned George Wyness who was on the quay to receive the mysterious crate himself. 'One crack and I'll do you for the full insurance.'

'What you got in there, eh? An Egyptian mummy?' called one wag, but even his own work-force at the yard was not allowed to see. Wyness closeted himself in the room that had been specially set aside for the purpose, with Donal and young Lorn, and they unpacked the crate between them behind locked doors. Afterwards, George Wyness and Lorn came out, but Donal stayed inside for the rest of the day, the door locked on the inside. Various of the men in the yard strolled past with an eye to seeing through a crack maybe, or a knothole in the woodwork, but even the newest yard boy could see nothing and when Wyness caught him with his eye to the keyhole, he got a hot ear for his pains and the threat that 'If I catch you again with your eye to what's none of your business, you'll be out of here on the end of my boot, and I'll not trouble to open the gate first.'

But the mystery of George Wyness's crate was soon forgotten in the excitement of the second mystery of the day: a small boy with no luggage to speak of and a label round his neck saying *To be collected*. In no time at all the word was all over town that one of Hugo Adam's by-blows had come home to roost and by evening it was generally agreed, though prudently out of her father's hearing, that Lizzie Lennox was the girl in question. After all, you had only to look at that hair.

'Good God!' murmured Fergus and heard Lettice beside him groan a more ladylike 'Oh dear.'

'This is the child for the Adam household?' he asked, hoping for some mistake, but the sailor shrugged, spat, said, 'Aye, that's the one, and a real little devil he is, too.'

Together Lettice and Fergus studied the child who stood in an attitude of pathetic belligerence, his chin jutting forward and his feet in their enormous boots planted one a little in front of the other. His ragged, sawn-off breeches hung from string braces and more string tied in the extra folds of cloth at the waist. His face was dirty and his red hair worse.

'Why has he no clothes that fit?' said Lettice, with a shudder of aversion.

'He grew, didn't he? That's a long voyage, that is, from Port Phillip and on account of us feeding him so well, he grew.' The sailor eyed the lady and gentleman, swiftly pricing the hand-stitched leather of the gentleman's boots, the kid gloves and immaculate waistcoat, and the fur-trimmed folds of the lady's velvet travelling cloak. 'Fed him real well, we did,' he said, ingratiatingly. 'When the woman what was in charge of him died of the flux, we looked after him like one of our own, didn't we, little lad? He got his tot of rum with the rest of us, and his biscuit. You can't say fairer than that now, can you?'

With a sigh, Fergus felt in his pocket for a suitable coin and when the man hovered, added another. He sought out the purser, the ship's doctor, and finally the quarantine officer but all was in order. This dirty little urchin was indeed the child they had been sent to meet and he was, officially anyway, free from disease, and ready for immediate collection.

'But we can't take him home like that!' said Lettice, staring at the boy in undisguised distaste. 'He may have fleas or lice or . . . or . . . anything.'

'We'll take him to the Guestrow,' decided Fergus. 'Get the maid to scrub him. Burn his clothing. Cut his fingernails and his hair. Send out for new clothes from somewhere. Then perhaps he will begin to be presentable. Come along, Leo. You are going to live with us now.' He reached out a hand. The child jerked back, looked fearfully to either side of him, then without warning ducked under Fergus's arm and ran.

He didn't get far, of course. One of the sailors cornered him, picked him up under one arm and carried him squirming and kicking to the Adam carriage where Fergus held him firmly down until the doors were closed and the carriage on its way.

'It is no good struggling, Leo. We are your family now and you have nowhere else to go. There is really no need to be frightened. We will not harm you.'

'Do you think he can speak?' said Lettice doubtfully. She wrinkled her nose in distaste and pulled her skirts out of reach of the still-kicking legs. If this was the child her father

[268]

expected her to 'adopt' it was an appalling prospect.

'I expect so. You can speak, can't you, Leo?'

For reply the child swore, with all the colourful variety of a well-seasoned and imaginative tar. After the first appalled silence, first Lettice and then Fergus burst into sputtering laughter while the child looked uncertainly from one to the other.

'It serves Papa right,' managed Lettice at last through tears of glee. 'Whatever will he say when he sees him?'

Before Fergus could answer, Leo did so for him. Seeing the astonishing success of his new if limited vocabulary, he repeated it with variations, and this time led the laughter.

Later, when the boy had been duly scrubbed, trimmed, disinfected and reclothed, Fergus sent for young Dr Marshall who was helping out at the vaccination clinic nearby 'to look the child over'. He came within the hour.

'Too thin, of course, but his chest is sound. Nothing wrong with him that I can find, but you had better see he has the necessary vaccination without delay. Bring him round to the clinic and I will do it at once.'

'Thank you, but another time,' said Lettice quickly. What better opportunity to further their acquaintance than to take the wretched child to Dr David's clinic? 'We will make an appointment,' and before Fergus could protest she added, 'My father is expecting us and we are late already.'

'Very well, Miss Adam, as you wish. But I would warn you most strongly against delay.'

'Yes, yes, I quite understand. I promise we will not fail in our duty.' Here Lettice gave him her most dazzling smile before turning to Leo. 'Come, Leo dear, it is time for you to meet your Grandpapa.'

They found Old Man Adam in his library, pretending indifference. When the door opened, he clambered to his feet and stood, back to the fire and hands lifting his coat-tails behind him.

'Well, don't stand in the doorway like a bunch of cowering servants. Come in where I can see you. So this is the boy.' If he was dismayed he did not show it, though he stared in silence for so long that Fergus began to wonder if he would ever speak. Then he saw that Leo was staring back at Old Man

Adam with unflinching eyes and for the first time he saw a resemblance to his dead brother.

'Well,' said Old Man Adam at last, 'what have you to say for yourself, young man?'

'I don't like you,' said Leo in his high child's voice. 'Your face is too red and your whiskers are too fierce.'

For a dreadful moment both Fergus and Lettice thought their father would explode with rage, but instead he gave a shout of laughter, slapped his thigh and roared, 'Damn the boy for his impertinence. He's a true son of his father, by George. A true son of his father.'

By May of the following year, the mysterious undertaking at the Wyness polishing yard was approaching completion, still shrouded in the strictest secrecy. Those who worked on the project had been told the reason and sworn to silence. The merchandise was to mark a particular anniversary and unless it was in place by a particular date it was absolutely worthless and they would forfeit the fee for the entire enterprise. No wonder the door was kept permanently locked and opened only to let one or other of the workers in or out. Wyness himself kept the key, though it was rumoured that the dumb fellow, Donal Grant, had another: he was in charge of the operation, whatever it was, and the various workmen took their orders directly from him. 'Written down, maybe?' said one hopeful, thinking of the money such a paper might fetch in the right market. But if they were written down, any notes were immediately destroyed. Certainly they did not find their way out of the Wyness yard.

George Wyness was well pleased. When the project was finished and safely despatched to its destination he would be more so. As long as his deadline was met, what happened when it reached Australia was not his business. Tom Diack or his deputy would handle that end of things and all Wyness need do was wait for the money and the praises which he had no doubt would come his way and lead inevitably to fame and further orders of a similar kind. Yes, Tom Diack had arranged everything admirably. If he could arrange his own life equally well and come home, Wyness would have no complaints.

For some reason the thought of Australia brought vividly to mind that wild, red-headed urchin who had arrived on the quay from the same boat as the Wyness goods. They said he was Hugo Adam's son, born in foreign parts to that Lennox girl who had once been a servant in Silvercairns. If anyone had told Wyness that one day Old Man Adam would adopt the bastard child of a servant girl as his own kith and kin, Wyness would not have believed it. But by all accounts it was true. Mrs Wyness had heard it from Mrs Macdonald who heard it from Amelia who heard it straight from Lettice Adam herself.

'They say the old man treats the lad like his own grandson,' said Mrs Wyness over the breakfast table. 'Even though the child is wild as a mountain cat by all accounts and his language not fit for respectable company.'

'Maybe there is some good in Mungo Adam after all.' George Wyness stirred his tea round and round and stared morosely into the swirling liquid. He felt an unexpected twinge of jealousy, not the usual professional envy of a business rival, but a different, more personal emotion. It was time he, George Wyness, had a grandson. What was the use of building up his business otherwise? What was the use of the secrecy, the planning, the hard work and vigilance if there was no one to share it after him? Of course Mhairi, his young partner, had a son and a fine, bright little lad he was too, but Wyness wanted to see that dreamt-of sign over his yard door before he died: *Wyness and Grandson* in letters of gold.

He looked across the table at his daughter and for the first time felt some of his wife's exasperation. Tom Diack was a good lad, a hard worker and an honest craftsman who would do fine as a son-in-law – if he ever came home again to claim a wife. Perhaps it had been a mistake not to tell him of young Alex Grant's death? At least then he would have been home by now. It would be three years come September since he'd left and it was neither fair nor natural to expect a girl to wait that long for a man. Fanny was twenty-two and practically 'on the shelf' as his wife lost no opportunity to remind him. Faithfulness was all very well, but to some it could look like plain obstinacy. Besides, who was to say the lad would ever come back? He'd done well for himself, by all accounts, with a flourishing building business and a sizeable investment of his own in the Bon Accord Investment Company. Now he was busy building a mansion, he wrote, as near enough a copy of Mungo Adam's Silvercairns as he could manage from memory. For a sheep farmer who had made a hefty fortune. But Tom Diack sounded well on the way to making a small fortune of his own and who was to say he would not build himself a mansion, find himself a wife from among those wealthy sheep farmers of his acquaintance and settle down for good in the land of promise? At the thought George Wyness sighed aloud.

'What is the matter, dear?' asked his wife with solicitude. 'If it is indigestion again let me . . .'

'It is not indigestion! Can't a man sigh at his own breakfast table without the doctor being fetched at the run and the entire medicine cabinet tipped down his throat?'

'Then what is the matter, dear? If you do not tell me, how can I be expected to know?'

'You are not expected to . . . Oh, what is the use? You will plague me with your fussing till I tell you. *I want a grandson.*'

There was a moment's astounded silence before Fanny pushed back her chair and ran from the room.

It was not fair, she said over and over behind the safety of her locked bedroom door. She wanted Tom and if she could not have him, then she wanted no one. They had no right to expect her to marry and breed like some sort of farmyard animal to 'ensure the succession'. She had actually heard her mother say that, as if they were royalty, instead of merely tradesfolk who had done better than most. It was not fair. If her father wanted a grandson as badly as that why couldn't he buy himself one, like Old Man Adam had done, instead of expecting her to produce one for him, to order? Ever since she was fifteen she had been aware of her mother looking over the young men of their acquaintance with Fanny's possible husband in mind, as if Fanny herself had no say in the matter. 'Fanny is a docile, obedient child,' she had overheard them say too often not to believe it was their firm opinion of her. The implied corollary to that was 'Fanny will do as she is told.' But I will not, vowed Fanny, over and over. I will wait for Tom, and if he does not come, I . . . But that alternative was too

[272]

dreadful to contemplate. Tom would come back, one day, she was sure of it. He had given her his word.

'You promised!' cried Hamish, jumping up and down in his excitement. 'You promised, Uncle Willy. You did. When the boatie goes, you said I could go with you. Didn't he, Ma? Didn't he promise?'

Mhairi looked across at Willy and shrugged. 'Aye, well,' grinned her brother, 'maybe I did. How old are you now, laddie?'

'Four and a bit. A big bit.'

'All right. You can come. But you'll need to do just what I tell you. I don't want to be jumping in and out of the canal fishing you out of the water when you've fallen in.'

Mhairi smothered a cry of alarm and Willy laid a reassuring hand on her arm. 'No need to worry, Mhairi. I'll take good care of him. I'll maybe tie him on, for safety. Like the best sailors tie themselves on in a rough sea,' he added quickly, seeing his nephew's mortified face. 'Maybe when you and Annys have done your messages in the town, you can meet us at the Wyness yard? You might even get a peep at the great Secret if you're lucky,' he added with a wink.

'Donal's secret,' said Hamish, nodding his small head. 'And mine. I promised not to tell, God's-honour-hope-to-die-if-I-tell-a-lie.'

Over the boy's head Willy raised a questioning eyebrow, but Mhairi merely shrugged. She knew no more than he did about the strange friendship between wee Hamish and his uncle Donal. Only that they enjoyed each other's company and that she trusted Donal absolutely, to guard and cherish her son as she would do herself, and as Willy would do on the morrow.

Nevertheless when she watched them set out in the early light of a fine summer morning, she could not quite suppress a twinge of anxiety. Willy and a fellow quarry worker were to travel with a barge-load of slabs from the quarry, conveyed by cart to the nearest landing-stage, and thence follow the canal to where it skirted the Wyness yard. Here they would unload the slabs and reload with a different cargo, to be transported

[273]

direct to the harbour. Although the slabs were part of a current order and legitimate cargo, the merchandise for the second part of the canal trip could easily have gone by road, as was the usual practice. But Donal and George Wyness had begun to plan the transport of the precious Australian contract and Willy was to time the journey by barge, note any possible hazards or drawbacks, watch the water line, the locks (of which there were many), the other water traffic and canal-path users: in fact, generally to anticipate obstacles to speed, safety and, most important, security. Naturally, no one but those concerned must know the true purpose of the journey and, as Wyness pointed out to his wife in private, what better cover than a small boy, accompanying his apprentice uncle on an unimportant river delivery of a few unpolished slabs for tombstones and the uplifting of more of the polished variety for shipment to their respective graves?

But as Mhairi waved them goodbye from the gate of Rainbow Cottage, she felt the familiar anxiety and inside her head said a quick prayer for their safety. Then she turned back into the house to assemble eggs, herbs and various other garden produce for the morning's market. Annys was already feeding wee Catriona who, though almost three, was still small enough to be carried without difficulty, but who preferred the independence of her own two feet. However, it was a long way for small legs, and a burdensome one with baskets alone, without the added weight of a child to carry, and though Annys was eleven now and a willing help, Mhairi hoped, as always, for the timely aid of a passing farm cart.

As usual, she was lucky. After the first hour or so she left Annys in charge of the market basket and, taking Catriona with her, went about her various errands in the town. When their marketing was over for the day, she and Annys walked in Union Street for a while, admiring the shops and the grand carriages that bowled up and down the wide sweep of the street, and finally paid their usual visit to the kirkyard of St Nicholas. Alex had been buried here, beside her parents' grave, and Mhairi never failed to lay a posy of flowers on his grave and sit a while in sadness, remembering. The words of her mother's song would sing sweetly in her mind and bring tears to her eyes, for her parents as well as for her own dear

Alex: *There's nae sorrow there, John, there's neither cold nor care, John, the day's aye prayer in the Land o' the Leal* . . . Then she would remember her promise to Alex, to be calm and quiet and strong, for their children's sake. I am trying my best, she would tell him secretly, but I miss you so dreadfully . . .

Here Fanny Wyness joined them, as she often did when they spent a market day in town, and they went into the Royal Hotel together, to restore Mhairi's spirits with tea and a scone. But at last it was time to make their way to the Wyness polishing yard where they were to meet Willy and Hamish on their return from the harbour.

'We may be a little early,' said Mhairi, 'but Mr Wyness will not mind. Catriona has had enough exercise for the day and we can sit in the office and rest our legs till the barge arrives.'

'But it is such a lovely day,' said Fanny wistfully. 'And I am sure Annys is not tired, are you, dear? Why don't we walk to the yard along the canal bank? I will take turns to carry Catriona and the path is so pretty at this time of year, with the wild flowers and the grasses, and there may be ducks on the water, or little moorhens. Besides, we will see the barge much better from there.'

Poor Fanny, thought Mhairi with the usual compassion: she knew the canal path had been a favourite walk before Tom had left. If only her brother would come home. He had been gone long enough.

'Please, Mhairi, do let's?' pleaded Annys, interrupting her thoughts. 'I am not in the least tired, truly I am not.'

'Maybe,' smiled Mhairi. 'There will be time enough to decide when we reach the Castlegate.' She picked up her market basket in one hand and, taking Catriona's hand in the other, made her way out of the hotel and into the street. Here Annys took the child's other hand and, with Fanny walking beside them, the little group set out towards the Castlegate, their shadows long in front of them and the splendour of the summer sun at their backs. Her sister's shadow, Mhairi noticed, was almost as long as her own.

Annys had grown tall in the last year and though still a child she would not be so for much longer. Already there was a new roundness about her hips and her dress was increasingly tight across the chest. Mhairi could see what a beautiful woman she would one day be and felt a glow of secret pride, quite devoid of jealousy. Mhairi had brought her little sister up since she was four and was proud of the result. Annys was a good girl, too, and though Mhairi had not been able to give her all the schooling she would have wished, the child had never complained. Mhairi had taught her herself at home, whenever she could, and Fanny Wyness had lent her books and talked to her about history and places across the sea, especially that huge and unexplored continent called Australia where Tom had gone to work. Annys could read and write as fluently as Mhairi herself and was quicker than Mhairi at adding up the figures for the quarry books. Yes, thought Mhairi with a mother's pride, Annys was not only pretty, but she was intelligent and conscientious; if at times she was too timid, it was a better fault than its opposite and she would learn confidence with age.

Watching her sister as they walked eastward along Union Street, each holding one of Catriona's little hands and now and again swinging her up off the ground amid squeals of glee, Mhairi caught herself wondering who Annys would marry and hoping that whoever he was he would be gentle with her and kind. She shook her head impatiently and smiled at her own sentimentality. Annys was eleven years old – time enough to think of marriage in ten years' time.

'Why are you smiling?' asked Annys, turning her solemn eyes on Mhairi.

'No reason. At least . . .' She looked over Catriona's head at her sister. 'Wouldn't it be funny if this precious secret of Fanny's father's that we might just be allowed to see today, if we are good, turned out to be one of those emusses that Tom wrote to us about? Or a kangaroo, stuffed and mounted on a polished granite pedestal?'

'Not stuffed!' cried Annys in alarm and Mhairi hastily corrected herself.

'Of course not. I meant to say a statue of a kangaroo. A likeness in stone maybe, life-size and with a little pocket on its front, like Tom described to us in his letter.'

'I hope it is,' said Annys. 'With a kangaroo baby in the pocket. Is it, Fanny? Have you seen it?'

But Fanny merely shrugged and shook her head. 'If I had

seen it, I would not be allowed to say,' she said. 'But I have not. Many a time I have been sorely tempted to steal my father's key, to tiptoe in one night and have a look. Except that I think I should be frightened of the dark.'

'You might be even more frightened of what you saw,' said Annys earnestly. 'It might be a dreadful Gorgon or a monster that would strike you blind for your curiosity.'

'My father would not make a statue of a monster!' said Fanny indignantly, and immediately bit her lip and looked quickly over her shoulder as if Union Street were thick with spies.

Well, well, thought Mhairi, looking curiously at her friend. I believe Fanny for all her demure innocence knows a little more than she pretends. Aloud she said, 'We are almost at the Castlegate and I for one intend to go straight to Mr Wyness's yard and beg a seat in his office and perhaps another cup of tea. I will take Catriona with me as she is almost asleep on her feet, though she will not admit it, will you, my love?' and she whisked the child up to sit across the natural shelf of her hip. In answer her daughter put her thumb in her mouth, laid her head on her mother's shoulder and closed her eyes.

Fanny laughed. 'Very well, but Annys is not in the least tired, are you, Annys? We two will walk the canal path while you two take the shorter, town route and we will see who finds the barge first.' With a wave of her gloved hand, Fanny tucked her arm into Annys's and the two girls walked away into the Castlegate, to pick up the canal path where it wound up from the harbour and on behind Castle Hill.

Mr Wyness met Mhairi at the gate of the yard, under the painted sign which curved high over the entrance to allow the free passage of loaded wagons, and proclaimed in letters a foot high, *George Wyness, Granite Merchant*.

'Saw you coming,' he explained. 'I was just telling that new lad a thing or two . . . Where is he, the young skiver, he was here a minute ago . . . Ah, there he is, over yonder.' He jerked his head in the direction of the polishing sheds where Mhairi could just make out the back view of a boy with a sweeping brush in his hands, vigorously doing battle against the slurry which ran from the open doorway in a steady stream. 'Had the nerve to tell me he couldna wield a besom on account of having

[277]

a bad back! At his age! Bad back, my eye. If there's ought wrong with that one it's a disease called laziness. But you'll not be wanting to hear about him, will you, Mhairi? I know what you've come for,' and he gave an elaborate wink. 'Let's just say to satisfy a little curiosity, eh?'

Mhairi smiled. 'Not a bit, Mr Wyness. I came to meet Willy, that's all, and to retrieve my son. That is, if the little fellow hasn't taken the opportunity to jump barge and run away to sea. His latest ambition is to be a sea captain and sail away to Australia to visit his uncle Tom.'

'Aye, well,' said Wyness. 'I could tell you of someone else with the same ambition, but I'd maybe best not. No news, I suppose?'

Mhairi shook her head.

'No, I thought not, and it's no good me telling you to write that blessed letter, is it? But obstinate wee lass though you are, Mhairi, you'll be tired after a day in town, so you'll take a cup of tea while you're waiting. I'll just give the lad a shout.'

Wyness went out of the room, closing the door behind him, and while she waited, Mhairi looked out idly over the Wyness yard with its jumble of granite in all stages of polishing, the lettered headstones and the raw granite blocks still waiting to be shaped. The door to the nearest polishing shed was open and from it came the grating whirr of disc driving sand against stone. The discs were lubricated with water and from the doorway oozed a constant sludge of mingled water, sand and dirt. Beyond the shed, across the yard, Mhairi noticed the loaded sand cart, newly back from the shore with the next delivery. Idly her eyes ran over the other buildings, the old polishing sheds, the new, the loading bay for the wagons, and beside it what had once been some sort of office and was now Donal's domain. Mhairi noted the new wood on the door, the strong timber frame and what looked even from this distance like a new and formidable lock. She wondered who was working in there with him today? She knew he worked with two other men, sometimes three, and that Lorn was often called to lend his developing skill to whatever work was afoot behind those locked doors. She was speculating whether Lorn was in there now, or somewhere about the yard, when her eye was caught by a movement: the yard boy, brush in hand,

[278]

but not brushing. Instead, he seemed to have his eye to the hinge of the door which at that very moment opened a foot or so to let a man out before swiftly closing again. In the short time it took Mhairi to glance at the man and see that it was neither Donal nor Lorn, the lad had put several yards between himself and the shed door and was again busily sweeping.

Mhairi was still frowning at the incident and wondering whether she had imagined it when George Wyness came back, followed by a different yard lad bearing a tray of tea and shortbread.

'Not as good as yours, Mhairi, my dear, but edible. Put it on that table, Eddie, and away with you. Mind and get that packing done afore the carrier arrives.'

'Who was that?' asked Mhairi, pouring tea. 'I have not seen him before.'

'No, you wouldn't have. Eddie's only been with me a month, but he's shaping well.'

'And the other? The slurry boy? What is his name?'

Wyness followed the direction of her eyes to where the boy in question was still sweeping with a great deal of ostentation and little result.

'George. But he'll not be slurry boy much longer, I'm thinking. Lazy young stirk. Why the interest?'

'It may be nothing and perhaps I have become over-cautious since . . . since the accident, but there is something vaguely familiar about him. And while you were out of the room I would swear he had his eye to the door of your special shed.'

'Did he indeed?' He strode to the door, flung it open and bellowed, 'Boy! In my office, at the double!'

'I don't expect he saw anything,' said Mhairi hastily, at the same time trying to soothe Catriona who had been jerked awake by George Wyness's roar. 'Someone came out and he moved away.'

'You want me, Mr Wyness?' said a voice from the yard. Mr Wyness stepped to one side to draw the lad inside and for the first time Mhairi saw him, face to face.

'But that's Dod Henderson from . . .'

But the boy recognized her at the same moment and before Mhairi could finish her denouncement, he had tossed away his

[279]

broom, jumped the two steps to the ground and was running for the gate as if the hounds of hell were after him.

'Stop that boy!' If Wyness's first bellow had raised the pigeons from the neighbouring chimney pots, his second lifted every perching bird in the city. A clutch of masons who had been chipping away at a double monument moved as one man to block the gate and the boy skidded to a stop, darted, dipped, shot this way and that, while more and more men downed tools and joined in the diversion. But Dod Henderson had been trained in a good school. After the crowded market on the Green, a granite yard was nothing, and before anyone realized what he was planning, he had dodged, feinted, dodged again and sped straight for the newly arrived sand cart, with, behind it, the still-gaping back gate and the distant freedom of the canal path.

For Fanny Wyness the canal path, as always, brought back memories both sad and sweet and as she and Annys walked in silence beside the flat pathways of the water, Fanny relived the last time she and Tom had walked there together. He had told her he loved her, asked her to wait 'just a little longer'. 'It will be all right one day,' he had promised, but when would that day be? She had waited almost three years already and the thought of waiting 'just a little longer' held all the dreary hopelessness of life imprisonment: for locked as she was in her self-made cell of loyalty she had indeed made a prison for herself. Her mother was always telling her so and lately her father had begun to say so too. Look at that remark he had made about wanting a grandson. I will give him one and gladly, she thought, if only Tom will come home and marry me. But if he does not come home soon, I am not sure I can endure much longer.

It was not the constant needling of her mother's plaintive remarks, nor her father's silent frowns, but the absence of Tom which wore down her spirits: he wrote too rarely and when he did, Fanny found his letters like the first forkful of a longed-for meal of which the rest was snatched away before hunger could be satisfied. Sometimes there was no letter for months and then two or three together, but when that

[280]

happened it was no better. There might be more of Tom, but there was also more of Melbourne, of the people he had met and the things he had done. She felt that Tom was drifting further and further away from her, being sucked deeper into that other life on the other side of the world about which she knew only what little he chose to tell her, that he was forgetting her, had already forgotten her, except as a name to which to address a letter, the content of which was dictated more by duty than by the heart. In his last, he had written at length about the plans of the local Caledonian Society and the building of a college, but instead of making her feel she shared in his life, it had had the opposite effect and left her feeling excluded and rejected. Remembering, Fanny had to fight to blot out that memory with a sweeter one, and to fight again to keep the tears from her eyes.

'Tom will come home soon,' said Annys quietly, and slipped her hand into Fanny's in reassurance. 'I know it.'

'How?' protested Fanny, smiling in spite of herself. 'When even my father does not?'

'Because I wrote to him. I did not tell him anything I shouldn't, about Alex, I mean. I just told him that you were growing sad and lonely and that if he did not hurry home, someone else would marry you.'

'You didn't!' Fanny was appalled.

'Yes, I did, and it is true. Dr David is very nice, but I would rather you married Tom, so I wrote and told him so. You don't mind, do you?'

'Oh Annys, you are incorrigible,' laughed Fanny, blushing and flustered and at the same time secretly glad. A young sister could write things that she herself could never write and whereas she had no closer feelings for Dr David than those of easy acquaintanceship, he was pleasant company and she knew that, with her own mother's connivance, possibly even at her instigation, tongues were wagging behind her back in the drawing-rooms of Aberdeen. She also knew, and the knowledge gave her secret satisfaction, that the rumour had reached Lettice Adam and had put her pert little nose decidedly out of joint. But suppose Tom believed the rumour? Decided Fanny had given him up? Instead of bringing him racing home, it might make him settle in Australia forever, out of pride. 'You should not have done it, Annys,' she said in sudden fear. 'It was very naughty of you to write such falsehoods.'

'They are not falsehoods. It is wicked to tell lies and I wrote only the truth. You *are* sad and lonely, just as Mhairi is, and someone else *might* marry you. To comfort and look after you.'

'Pigs might fly,' retorted Fanny. 'And if you are going to continue to talk nonsense I shall not listen. There,' she said, loosing Annys's hand, 'I shall walk on ahead and leave you.'

'No, please, Fanny! I did not mean . . .' Annys scrambled to keep up with her companion, for as well as not wishing to offend Fanny, she had a dread of being left on the path alone. Some of the barges were drawn by horses, some by men, and some by noisy, squabbling gangs of small boys, pushing and jostling for path-room, and jostling again for the tossed coins of reward. Ever since that incident in the market Annys had had a horror of such groups of urchins in case they should contain her enemies of the Green. Now she quickened her step to catch up with Fanny who was striding ahead with surprising speed, considering the heavy folds of her skirts and the uneven surface of the towpath.

'Wait, Fanny, please!' But at that moment they rounded the curve beyond Mounthooly and there in the distance ahead of them lay the barge, low in the water, its outline broken by the standing figure of a man and beside him a small child. Though it was still some distance away they could see the tow rope curving between boat and path where one of the Wyness horses plodded, patient head down and powerful shoulders taking the strain of the rope. Someone walked at the horse's head: a quarryman, perhaps? Or one of the yard boys?

'That is what Hamish wanted to do,' said Annys, taking advantage of her companion's momentary pause to catch up with her and take hold of her hand. 'But Mhairi would not let him because of the water.'

'And the size of the horse,' pointed out Fanny. 'The little lad would scarcely reach to the animal's knees.'

'I don't think a small point like that would deter Hamish,' said Annys. 'He has no fear of horses, nor of anything else that I can think of,' she finished, with a note of puzzlement. Annys herself was afraid of so many things that she could not imagine

[282]

a state in which no such anxieties existed. Even now she had only to glance down and to her right where a mere fringe of grass separated path from water to feel herself shudder with alarm, though she knew perfectly well the water was no more than four feet deep. She saw her own sturdy boots, reassuringly firm on the dirt path, the tufts of thistle and celandine among the meadow grasses, the clover and campion and here and there the bright blue sparkle of forget-me-nots, and beyond that pretty, flower-studded strip the green treachery that was the water. Not flowing river water, but artificial water, trapped for eighteen miles between man-made banks, with locks for steps, and eyebrows of bridges – fifty-six of them, they said, though Annys had not seen even half that number. Moorhens skimmed the water, with ducks of multifarious plumage, and the plop and stir of the rushes as they passed indicated the presence of smaller creatures such as water voles or frogs. Annys knew they were harmless, knew the water would not reach above her shoulders, but her fear did not respond to reason, and never had. She envied Hamish his untroubled courage.

'Yes,' agreed Fanny. 'It can be worrying sometimes, especially for anyone trying to keep the little fellow out of mischief. Can you see if he is tied on? Mhairi told me Willy promised to tether him all the way to the harbour and back.'

But they were not close enough to see into the body of the barge and contented themselves with quickening their steps on the grassy towpath. The walk had been further than Fanny remembered, but then when she had walked it with Tom, she had noticed neither distance nor fatigue. Now she stamped firmly on the memory of that other time, raised her arm to wave and called, 'Hello!'

'Should it not be "Ahoy there"?' said Annys earnestly. 'Or perhaps "Barge ahoy?"'

But before Fanny could call out either of these nautical alternatives there was a sudden swirl of commotion ahead of them and a confused crescendo of shouting which reached the bellowing clarity of 'Stop him!' just as a small figure burst into view on the path ahead, ducked under the arm of whoever was leading the horse, dodged the horse itself and came skidding towards them.

[283]

'*Stop him*!' hung like a banner on the wind and Fanny instinctively spread her arms to bar his way. Beside her Annys stood rigid with terror, her eyes on that panting face which, though older now, held the same vindictive purpose as it came pounding down the narrow path. The boy dodged to the left, to the right again, then made as if to duck under Fanny's arm on the landward side where scrubland and bushes edged the path. Fanny lunged for a hand-hold on his jacket, but the lad twisted, swerved, then before anyone realized what he meant to do he had placed both hands against Annys's chest and pushed with all his strength.

Fanny turned in horror and as if in slow motion saw Annys, mouth open and eyes wide with terror, fall backwards, slap spread-eagled on to the water's surface in an arching shower of spray, lie there for one astonished moment then, as the water closed over her gasping face, begin to struggle and squirm in a frenzied maelstrom of bubbles and rapidly water-logging clothing.

In the moment's shock which followed, the taunting voice came high on the wind from the far freedom of the open towpath.

'Serve you right, Annys Diack, for a tell-tale-tit!'

Willy saw the splash from the barge, whirled on Hamish with a fierce 'Stay where you are!', paused momentarily to add a gentler 'You are captain of the ship now, young fellow, so stay at your post,' then leapt for the shore. Before Fanny had recovered enough even to begin to think what to do, Will was chest-deep in the water and fighting to control the gasping, bubbling convulsions of his young sister. But somehow he managed to heave her upright and Fanny had one glimpse of the girl's streaming face, hair and waterweed obliterating all but the black holes of her terrified eyes before he had tipped her forward over his arm, to choke and gurgle and expel what canal water she could before he reached the bank and heaved her water-logged body up into the outstretched arms of those who had come running to help. Then Will himself climbed out, shook himself like a dog and, seeing that Annys was in good hands, hurried back to the barge and his nephew.

'Anything to report, Captain?' he said, with a rush of relief that the boy had indeed done as he was told and stayed put.

'Man overboard, sir,' grinned Hamish and saluted. Then he amended, 'I mean lady overboard. She made a lovely splash, didn't she?'

'She did indeed, you little horror. But we'd best get her home, as fast as we can, and into dry clothes. Out you come, lad, or we'll have your mother after us, for dawdling.'

He swung Hamish ashore, just as Mhairi herself burst on to the scene, white-faced and anxious. She swept Hamish up into her arms and held him tight, burying her face in the soft warmth of his neck.

'Thank God he's safe,' she said, looking over the boy's head at Willy. 'I thought he had fallen in.'

'Would I let him do a thing like that? Where's your faith, woman?'

'But I heard a splash and shouting and . . . Willy! Your clothes are wet!' Still holding Hamish tight in her arms, she looked this way and that and finally at the huddle of figures on the towpath some twenty yards away. He answered her question before she spoke it.

'Annys fell in. At least, it would be more accurate to say she was pushed.'

'Pushed?' Mhairi looked at him in bewilderment.

'Aye, by some wee devil who came scooting out of the Wyness yard as if all the hounds in hell were after him. Up to no good and caught at it, likely.'

'Dod Henderson,' said Mhairi quietly. 'And you are right. Poor Annys. I must go to her.' She thrust Hamish back into Willy's hands and hurried towards the little group on the path to find Annys, a rug round her shoulders and a puddle rapidly spreading at her feet, shivering and choking and saying over and over, 'I'm all right.' But when Mhairi pushed through the crowd to her side and put her arms around her, Annys laid her sodden head on her sister's shoulders and burst into convulsive weeping.

It was not until much later, when Annys had been whisked into the Wyness office, discreetly stripped of every stitch she had on, rubbed briskly with a rough towel, bundled up in blankets, and coddled with hot tea laced with whisky while the

[285]

Wyness carriage was sent for, that Mhairi remembered the state of Willy's clothes and cried out in horror.

'Don't fuss, woman,' he said. 'I'll be home directly, and you're nae exactly dry yourself. See, here's the Wyness carriage now and there's Donal wi' the quarry cart to take the rest of us.'

Nevertheless, when Annys was safely in Mhairi's own bed in the cottage on Rainbow Hill, hot stones wrapped in flannel at her feet and a warming hot toddy inside her, Mhairi fussed over Willy with all the solicitude of a mother for a sickly child. When the children were in bed, she made him strip in front of the kitchen fire, filled the zinc bath with hot water and ordered him into it, and would have sent him to bed too, had he not rebelled.

'It may be bedtime for the bairns, but I'm nay a child any more, Mhairi. I'm man of the house, bar Donal, and there's two hours of good twilight left and maybe three. So bring me fresh clothes, woman, and let me about my work.'

'But Willy, you . . .'

'Exercise will warm me quicker than anything,' he interrupted and then, at the look on her face, added, 'but I'll take a cup of that broth if you can spare it, afore I go.'

It was as she ladled the broth from the heavy iron pot that she remembered. 'Dod Henderson was working in the Wyness yard. Newly taken on, Mr Wyness said. I saw him with his eye to a crack in the door of Donal's shed and when I told Mr Wyness and he sent for the boy, Dod took one look at me and ran. Why should he do that?'

'Habit?' suggested Willy over the rim of his spoon. 'He always was a mischievous wee devil.'

'Or guilt? After all, he was spying.'

'What boy wouldn't spy if he had the chance, with a mysterious locked shed on his doorstep? He ran because he'd been found out and didn't want to face the punishment. But I'll give him punishment when I lay my hands on the young varmint,' finished Willy with a frown. 'My sister might have been drowned.'

'Yes.' Mhairi bit her lip in dread at the thought of what might have been. 'Thank you, Willy, for rescuing her so swiftly, before she had time to swallow half the canal. As it was, she managed to drink more than her share of it. But she seems to be sleeping peacefully enough now,' she finished. 'Maybe I need not ask the doctor to call in after all?'

'Never mind the money,' said Willy. 'If it makes you easier in your mind, and stops your fussing, then send for him. And now I'd best be on my way. I can't have young Lorn accusing me of slacking.' He pushed back his chair, waved Mhairi goodbye, and strode out into the cool evening air, turning up the collar of his jacket as he did so and pulling it tighter across his chest. It was chill when the sun went down.

'Mind and keep warm!' Mhairi called after him. 'Or I'll need to call the doctor for *you*.'

In the morning Mhairi did indeed send for Dr Marshall, but not on Willy's account. At some time in the early hours of morning, Mhairi was awakened by the unnatural rasp of her sister's breathing. She slipped quickly from bed, wrapped a plaid around herself and, bending over Annys, laid a gentle hand on her forehead, only to snatch it quickly away: the skin was burning. Her heart thudded fast with terror and she sped into the scullery where the first pale light of morning strung monochromes of shadow from every jutting edge and corner, found a pail and slipped out into the yard. Rabbits scattered, but only to the sidelines to await her return inside, and the dawn sky was already pink along the edges. Close at hand a robin sang and another answered it, from the rowan tree. Mhairi noticed none of it, but pumped in a frenzy of fear till the bucket spilled over, then scurried back inside. Should she wake her? Sponge her down with cooling water? Or was it best to let sleeping patients lie? For she was a patient, Mhairi had no doubt of that, Annys who had never had a day's illness in her life. Now, some kind of fever had gripped the child in the night and had her by the throat. Oh God. How soon could she legitimately send for the doctor?

By the time Mhairi had washed, dressed and bundled up her hair with less than her usual care, she had made up her mind. She mounted the steps to the loft, shook Lorn awake and told him to 'Run for Dr David quick as you can and fetch him back with you. Annys is ill. If the doctor is not at the house, then find where he is and follow him. It is urgent!'

That done, Mhairi found a rag, wrung it out in cold water

[287]

and began to sponge her sister's face and wrists, while Annys moaned and tossed and sank further into unconsciousness. 'Please God,' Mhairi prayed over and over in mounting anxiety, 'ease the fever and make her well again. Please God, don't let the infection spread. Please God . . .'

Within twenty-four hours the news was all over town. One of George Wyness's yard boys, running for his life with old Headstane close on his heels and lusting for blood, had pushed Annys Diack into the canal. Her brother had fished her out again, but though she had not drowned, she had swallowed foul canal water and with it a fever which was like to kill her. How and why the girl had been pushed were details which varied with the teller, from the tediously accurate to the wildly inventive, but apart from the question of whether Annys Diack would die or not and how long it would take her to do so if she did, the real interest was in what the lad had seen in the locked shed, the seeing of which had brought such wrath upon his head.

'Word has it he was spying, for someone else,' said Lettice.

Fergus looked up quickly, his eyes on his father's face. Like everyone else, Fergus had heard of Annys Diack's illness and his heart ached with compassion for Mhairi and for the young sister who so touchingly resembled her. He remembered the child's frightened eyes as she had looked up at him in the market-place, the pathetic bravery with which she had clung to that pitiful basket of eggs. And now she was gravely ill, even dying, and by the hand of that same young scallywag who had stolen Fergus's purse. He longed to write to Mhairi, to call at the house with baskets of hothouse fruit and flowers, to take her in his arms and comfort her, till her burden was eased. But the barrier between Diack and Adam was higher than ever. For as Lettice said, hadn't the boy been spying? Fergus awaited his father's answer with more than usual interest.

The family was at dinner in the Silvercairns dining-room, though without guests. Had Old Man Adam had his way, young Leo would have dined with them, in the place of honour at his grandfather's right hand, but Fergus and Lettice combined to oppose the idea with such implacable logic and

[288]

determination that Mungo had to give in. It was past the child's bedtime, no child his age ever dined with his elders and betters, and furthermore Leo's table manners were disgusting. His language was little better and until he was even remotely civilized he should be kept discreetly out of sight, certainly at meal times. Old Man Adam grumbled and argued, but allowed himself to be talked down. After all, he had plenty of time during the day to enjoy his grandson's tempestuous language and behaviour, and enjoy it he did. He had only to think of Leo taking over the quarry in Fergus's stead to chortle silently with glee. That would take the smug look off the fellow's face and wipe out that air of sanctimonious virtue for ever. Serve him right for carping and scrimping all these years, for not blasting open the quarry seams as he should have done, for treating the quarry with niminy-piminy kid gloves when he should have walloped into it with the biggest hammer available and blasted it to the skies long ago. But Leo would be a quarryman after his own heart one day. Already he had asked to see an explosion, and talked of setting one off himself, 'When I'm big.' Adam would see that he did, too, and maybe sooner than anyone thought. Young Leo would have no mean-spirited scruples of the kind Fergus delighted in and was displaying now, with his fastidiously curled lip.

'Spying?' the old man repeated, with none of his son's distaste. 'Then I hope he found something worth the trouble. What does the town in its wisdom think the enterprising lad saw?'

'Below stairs believes it was a corpse,' said Lettice with amusement. 'Wrapped up in cloth like an Egyptian mummy and Headstane Wyness busy boxing it into a stone sarcophagus to conceal the crime. Half the town is terrified to pass by the Wyness yard, especially at night, lest the poor unhappy ghost leap out and haunt them.'

'And what does the other half of the town believe?' said her father, a strange and private look in his eye.

'Perhaps they know the real explanation, as you undoubtedly do,' said Fergus. 'Unless, of course, you have sent good money after bad.' When his father fixed him with a venomous glare, Fergus did not lower his eyes.

'I know it, do I? Then perhaps you will be so good as to tell me what it is that I know, as I don't seem to know it myself, sir.'

But Fergus had noted the evasive look, the flicker of alarm quickly smothered. His father knew all right, and believed his own secret safe. The simmering anger of months boiled up in Fergus and spilled over.

'If you have so quickly forgotten the private information of your own spy, you are more senile than I had thought, Father.'

'How dare you, sir!' Old Man Adam gripped the table edge and half rose from his seat, his face dangerously purple.

'Fergus,' warned Lettice in alarm. 'You must not upset Papa when you know he is . . .'

'Upset? If telling the truth is "upsetting" then he should have been upset years ago and the better for all concerned.'

'I'll have you horse-whipped . . .'

'In character as always, Father. That at least is reassuring. You find yourself in a corner with no escape so you resort to violence and bluster. And, of course, lies. But then we should be used to that by now.'

Suddenly, without warning, Adam collapsed into his chair, all the bluster drained out of him. In the small silence that followed, Lettice leant anxiously towards him, laid a hand on his arm and said, 'Are you all right, Papa?'

Impatiently he shook off her hand, but his own when he snatched up his glass and drank was less than steady. Whatever the cause of that tremor, Lettice could have sworn that the look in his eyes was one of private gloating, rather than of shock.

Then he spoke. 'Fergus is right. I do know what that old villain is up to, but if George Wyness thinks to find fame and fortune that way, he's mistaken. I've put a spoke in his wheel before now and will do so again and no mean-spirited, traitorous, snake-in-the-grass is going to stop me.' He met Fergus's eyes in open challenge, his own gleaming with triumph. 'Yes, Fergus, I know his precious secret, and I have made my plans. Plans which neither you nor anyone else will prevent me carrying out, when the time comes.'

There was an ominous pause in which Lettice and Fergus exchanged apprehensive glances, hers tinged with sympathy, his with alarm, before the old man finished. 'And if I should need any help, there is at least one member of the family on whom I can rely. Young Leo will support me, to the death.'

He pushed back his chair and stood up. 'Send my coffee to the library, Lettice. I have work to do. Which reminds me, Fergus. I know we've orders enough to keep the men busy twenty-four hours a day, but profits are up and with the longest day past I've been thinking. It's throwing away good money to pay men to work when they can't see what they're doing and lamps don't burn for nothing, so I have decided to close the quarry at six from now on, and that means the office as well.'

Fergus raised an eyebrow in surprise: it was not dark till nine and in the past his father had insisted on utilizing every glimmer of daylight, often till the sun sank well below the hill. Perhaps he was learning sense in his old age? He shrugged. 'Very well, Father, if you think it best.'

'I do. Beginning tomorrow.'

'We will need to ship our cargo by the end of the week,' said Wyness, slipping through the door and pulling it quickly shut behind him.

That business of the Henderson boy had shaken his confidence: you thought you ran a loyal yard, with every man one hundred per cent behind you, and then out from the woodwork crawled a poisonous little worm like that one. Admittedly he was new, but Wyness had done the usual checks, asked about among the men, and the lad had seemed honest enough. Lazy, maybe, but honest. Perhaps he was honest in his way and only ran because he thought Mhairi would tell about his thieving activities in the market, only pushed Annys like that because she was in his way and he had vowed to pay her back, but in his heart Wyness doubted it. The boy was corrupt and Wyness had not realized. As a result of his misplaced trust, young Annys was lying on what might be her death-bed. Wyness felt guilt and compassion tear at his heart. He had only to look at the faces around him to feel the anxiety, like a constant pain. Donal for one would far rather be at Annys's bedside than here in the polishing shed and had it not been for the urgency of the work, Wyness knew he would have stayed at home. Lorn, too, and Willy, who had been brought from the quarry to lend a hand: there were men in the yard more skilled and able to do the work required, but Wyness had had enough of treachery and dared take no further risk.

As for Mhairi, Wyness could not bear to meet her eyes, though he called daily at the cottage to ask after Annys and to leave what material comforts he could: wee jellies Fanny had made, fortifying syrups of this and that, with custards and the like. Whether Annys ate any of them Wyness doubted, but if not they might just do Mhairi good, poor lass. At least she did not have to worry about wee Hamish and Catriona. Fanny had removed them to the Wyness household. 'To guard them from infection, Papa,' and though her mother had protested that 'We are not a public orphanage, to take in any waif and stray that takes your fancy,' George Wyness was wholeheartedly in favour and she had been easily overruled. Besides, it had occurred to her that the health of the children might require regular inspection by 'that nice Dr David' and the sight of Fanny in such a touchingly domestic situation might well prompt him to ask the vital question.

It was a different question that troubled Wyness now as he stood in the locked confines of the polishing shed and studied the work in progress.

'Will it be finished in time? I realize you must do every single inch by hand, but you know Tom said the Grand Opening is set for 2nd February and if we dinna catch the Christie ship . . .'

'Aye,' said Lorn, straightening. In the four years since he had come to the yard he had grown from a skinny schoolboy, all elbows and knees, into a youth, still skinny, but with the spare strength of muscle and bone and as tall as Wyness himself. Now his clear eyes, blue as all the Diacks' eyes were blue, looked straight into Wyness's own. 'We'll finish it, Mr Wyness. It'll be ready for when the ship sails.'

'It'll need to be well packed, mind,' said the older man, allowing at least one anxiety to be stilled. 'Then there'll be the transport to the docks.'

Willy and Lorn murmured together, then Lorn looked a question at Donal, made a few hasty sketches on a scrap of paper and thrust it into Donal's hands. Donal studied it, frowning, for some time, added a sketch or two of his own, then handed it back, finger pointing at the first of the drawings.

'That way will be best,' translated Lorn. 'Smoother, less risk of jolting. It's maybe quicker by road, but there's aye a risk of a broken axle with such a heavy load and if we allow time for those pesky locks and take suitable precautions, the canal will be safe enough. Then once the crate is in the Christie hold, matters are out of our hands.'

'Aye,' agreed Wyness, smiling now. 'When a Christie promises, he delivers. Like we do, lad, like we do. Especially when we lose more than I care to think of if we fail. But enough of that. Tell me, how is young Annys today?'

Mhairi sat in the half-darkness of the cottage bedroom, hands loose in her lap and eyes unblinking on her sister's unconscious face. She had sponged her fevered body with tepid water half an hour back, as young Dr David had told her to do, but though it had eased her burning skin for a while, she knew without the confirmation of touch that the fever raged as fiercely as ever. 'Dear God,' she prayed as she had prayed over and over ever since that first, dreadful morning, 'please God, keep her safe from harm. Please make her better, restore her, bring her back to me whole and well again. Dear God, help me . . . help her . . .'

Through her head, over and over, went a different verse of that song of her mother's: *Our bonnie bairnie's there, John, she was both good and fair, John, and oh we grudged her sair* . . . For the first time she faced the unthinkable: what would she do if Annys were to die? Dear little Annys who was more daughter to her than sister, who had clung to her for comfort when their mother died, whom she had promised her mother she would 'bring up right'. 'Oh God, please let me keep her,' she prayed over and over in growing desperation as she watched the child moan and burn and shrink to fragile bones and dry skin and was helpless to alleviate her suffering. 'Please God, you have taken Alex from me, leave me my little sister. Please?'

But the memory of Alex brought an overwhelming need.

[293]

Alex would have shared the burden, comforted and strengthened her, helped her when her faith faltered. The others did their best: her young brothers with their touching protectiveness and care: Donal with his silent love and loyalty. But it was Alex she wanted, to put his arms around her, to strengthen and sustain her, to help her bear the unbearable. But Alex was lost to her for ever, in the Land o' the Leal, and she must bear her burden alone.

She had no awareness of the measurement of time: it could have been yesterday, a week ago, or even a year ago when she waved Willy and her son so happily on their way to the canal: ever since she had woken to find Annys in the grip of this dreadful fever, time had expanded to embrace the world and at the same time dwindled to enclose only herself and Annys in the trembling intensity of her fear. She knew the others came and went, ate, slept, worked, knew her children were safe, but she had no real awareness of them: all she knew was that Annys trembled on the edge of death and she was powerless to do anything but will her with all her love and strength and being not to slip over that edge and into oblivion.

Occasionally she allowed herself to sleep, but unwillingly and only if someone took her place at the bedside and promised to wake her at the smallest sign of change. Should Annys speak, Mhairi must be there, should she turn her head or open her eyes, she must be close at her side. But the child neither moved nor spoke: only lay burning while the flesh shrank from her bones and her strength dwindled before their eyes. Mhairi watched helpless while fear spread through her and choked her heart. Her own flesh fell away as Annys's had done, her eyes were huge in their sockets and haunted with dread.

She was praying over and over inside her head, watching her sister's face and waiting till it was time to sponge her again, when she heard the sound of hoofs on the trodden path outside, men's voices, then steps in the hall. Dr David had called for his daily visit and, as usual now, had brought his uncle with him. She knew it to be a measure of the seriousness of Annys's condition yet she rose from her chair with the usual mixture of hope and relief. For a few moments at least her responsibility was lifted: the doctors, old and young together, would know what to do, would be able to help Annys better than she could, and make her well.

'I am sorry, Mrs Grant,' said Dr David with an air of grave kindliness which his uncle noted with surprise and secretly applauded. This nephew of his would be a worthy successor one day. 'I can detect no measure of improvement and it would be wrong of me to raise false hopes. However, I will say that there is some small cause for optimism. Had the infection spread as we feared it might, then there would have been signs of which there are fortunately none. That in itself is encouraging.'

'You mean Annys is no better, but no worse?' said Mhairi with bleak simplicity.

'Precisely. The fever is still too high, the delirium unabated, but your sister's constitution is strong and fighting back. Do not lose hope, Mrs Grant. With your loving care there is still a chance of recovery.'

Mhairi turned her ashen face to Dr Marshall, who looked at her in silent compassion before nodding his agreement.

Oh God, thought Mhairi. Still a chance. That meant there was little or none . . . Annys was going to die, as Alex had done. Her family was leaving her, one by one. *And suppose the fever were to spread*? To Hamish, or Catriona? At the thought she felt her body shake with cold terror. Then through her darkness came the memory of another sick-bed, and her own mother's dying words. 'Never lose hope, Mhairi,' she had said. 'Hope makes everything bearable. Remember that and ye'll survive.' And I will, vowed Mhairi fiercely inside her head. *I will*.

Mrs Macrae called, with Mrs Bain and other neighbours, to help out where they could with cooking, washing and the like, for every waking moment of Mhairi's time was spent at her little sister's bedside. During their visits they tried to persuade Mhairi to sleep, but she dare not lest she miss the moment when Annys cried out for her.

'Mrs Macrae is right,' said Mrs Bain, when that lady called one afternoon to see how the patient did and to deliver a present of eggs 'to keep your strength up'. Mrs Bain was hardly inside the door before she had hauled Mhairi out of the sick-room, leaving the door ajar, and into the family kitchen.

'You'll be propping your eyelids open wi' fence posts if you go on as you are doing. A body needs sleep and a worried body needs more than most. So you do as Mrs Macrae says, Mhairi lass, and take what rest you can. I canna stay long myself wi' my man needing his tea and the hen not plucked, but Mrs Macrae said to tell you she'll be along later to give you a wee break. How is that lass o' yours today?'

'The same,' said Mhairi, and added quickly, 'but no worse.'

'Aye, well, that's one mercy anyway, and come morning you'll have no more need to worry.' Mrs Bain nodded sagely and made straight for the kettle. 'A cup of tea's what you're needing and there's no call to keep casting your eye towards the bedroom door. We'll hear soon enough if the lassie stirs.' She busied herself in Mhairi's scullery, spooning tea and setting out scones on a plate. 'Baked them myself, specially,' she said over her shoulder. 'There's nought like a good scone and a fly cup to cheer a body when she's down. I brought a wee peck o' jam, too. There now,' she continued, setting down the tray on the kitchen table and settling into the nearest chair. 'We're all set for a nice wee chat. I was only saying to Mrs Macrae this morning as how it must be awful lonely for you up here on your own wi' only Annys for company. She's a nice wee lass, your Annys, but quiet like at the best of times and now, well she's nay exactly lively, is she? Not with her lying dumb as a statue when she's not moaning and tossing wi' the fever. Talking of statues, have you heard what George Wyness has got in his shed?'

'No,' said Mhairi, her heart suddenly cold with apprehension. She knew George Wyness wanted absolute secrecy, knew too much depended on safe delivery of the precious 'secret' to risk subversion from the Adam quarter. Carefully, without expression, she said, 'What?'

Mrs Bain leant across the table and mouthed, 'A dead man. One o' they corpses what the medical students used to dig up for experiments. No wonder old Wyness willna let folk in to look. But Doddie Henderson saw it clear as daylight through a crack in the wall. A dead man, all grey and cold, with a little grey beard and stuff all over him, like those Egyptians use, to keep him from rotting away. Hundreds of years they can keep a corpse, can they Egyptians: they tie all the bits together, seemingly, with oils and ointments and strips of cloth. So there's no saying how long old Wyness has had that corpse, maybe years. I mind there was a man went missing one Christmas a few years back. Set out from Woodside to see his sister at Kittybrewster and never hair nor hide of him seen since. Mind you, there was folks said he'd hopped it, his wife being too free with her tongue and too mean with everything else, and there was a ship leaving for Australia that week, sure enough, but maybe he didna get as far as Australia? Maybe he got no further than yon shed? If you ask me, Headstane Wyness needs to be careful or he'll find himself haunted. Our Ina said as how old Lennox from the tenements saw a ghost only last week, hovering and wailing. Sobered him up quick as anything, it did. Gave him such a fright he ran a mile wi'out pausing for breath.'

'Shall I pour the tea?' interrupted Mhairi quickly. 'I expect it is ready by now.' She had a dread of Mrs Bain's stories at the best of times, but now, with Annys so ill . . .

'Fevers is strange things,' said that cheerful lady. 'Take scarlet fever, that's a killer, that is. Whole families dropping dead like flies. Then there's that enteric that turns a man's guts to water, and cholera. Dreadful, is cholera. There's a whole street in Edinburgh, seemingly, walled up and buried with all the dead folk still in their houses on account of them all having cholera. Leastways, I think it was cholera, but maybe it was that foreign plague folks used to drop dead with, years back? Hugo Adam, he died of a foreign fever, didn't he? Aye, wicked things is fevers.' She sipped thoughtfully at her tea, but before Mhairi could think of anything that would be safe from sick-bed connotations, she was off again.

'Holloway's pills. That's what your Annys needs. There was a man on his deathbed wi' fever, just like your Annys, when in comes his wife. Eat these, she says, and when he opens his mouth to say he isna hungry, tips a handful of they Holloway's pills down his throat. He was out of his bed afore nightfall and pawing the ground to be let back to his work. There was a man in the Green yesterday, telling all about it. You wouldna believe the cures they pills has done. Better than

[297]

any doctor, the mannie said, so I says to myself, Jessie, I says, if there's anything that's going to cure Mhairi's Annys, it's they pills. I wasna going to say till I'd had my tea, but I bought some for you.' Triumphantly, she produced the packet from a pocket in her skirts and laid it on the table. 'There now. You'd best give them to her straight, lass, so they can work the quicker.'

Tears sprang to Mhairi's eyes: tears of mirth and sorrow and gratitude and despair. 'Thank you, Jessie,' she managed before her control snapped and the tears flowed unchecked.

'There, there, lass, there, there,' soothed Mrs Bain, her arm around Mhairi's shoulder. 'Your wee Annys will be right as rain in no time. There's no call to be sobbing your heart out yet awhile. They pills canna fail. The mannie said so himself and him wi' a great bag o' letters from folk what would have been dead if they hadna had the Help of Holloway's. So, away to your Annys and give her them now.'

With a shudder, Mhairi pulled herself together, pushed back her hair and managed a smile. 'I will. Next time I sponge her down. It seems a shame to wake her specially when she's sleeping.' Seeing the disappointment in Mrs Bain's face, she added hastily, 'I'll put them by her bed ready, with a glass of water so she can take them the moment she stirs.'

'Aye, lass, that'll be best. Mind and hold her head up, though. There was an old wifie over Grandholme way choked to death on a pill when it went down wrong way, stuck in her windpipe and her so flat on her back she couldna shift it for all her writhing and . . .'

'Thank you,' said Mhairi hastily, picking up the packet and hurrying from the room.

When Mrs Bain had gone, Mhairi stood a long time at her sister's bedside, looking down at the small, white-clad figure who lay helplessly moaning and burning on the pillows, her hair a dark cloud around her face and her dark-fringed eyes closed — except when they stared wildly around her in delirium, the soft grey-blue gaze unrecognizable. Should she give Annys the pills? She had no faith that they would work, but at the same time, they might, and nothing she had tried so far had been of any help. She tipped them into her hand and stared at the pathetic gobbets of man-made hope, at best a palliative, at worst a fraudulent and cynical betrayal. The shapes blurred and merged under her unseeing eyes to become merely a shadowy blemish on the palm of her hand. Suddenly she saw with absolute clarity: whatever pill or potion Annys took it would make no difference. Nothing and no one on earth could cure her: her fate lay in God's hands alone.

'Got you!' Fergus Adam's hand closed on the boy's shoulder. With a strangled yelp of terror the lad kicked and swore and squirmed with all his strength, but Fergus had a firm grip on him with both hands now and would not be dislodged. He had waited too many evenings in the chill damp of the rhododendrons which fringed the drive, smoked too many cigars, breathed too much evening air, to let his prey, once caught, escape.

'And now,' said Fergus with grim satisfaction, 'you are going to tell me what you are doing, skulking and lurking in the bushes of Silvercairns, where neither you nor anyone else has any right to set foot, let alone skulk and lurk, without permission. It is not the first time, is it? And before you waste breath on a lie, I saw you myself. And unless I am very much mistaken,' he went on thoughtfully, pulling the lad out of the shadow of the bushes and into the clearer light of evening, 'I have seen you before, in less than honest circumstances. Thieving, I believe, in the market on the Green? Well, well, and you actually had the nerve to show your face here. Not that you meant to show it, but how very fortunate that I happened to be passing.'

It had not been fortune at all, of course: merely watchfulness and a great deal of patience. For ever since his father's outburst in which Adam had vowed to put a spoke in the Wyness wheel as he had done before, Fergus had kept every sense alert for the smallest hint of what his father might be planning. Another explosion such as the last must be prevented at all costs; even if he planned a different method this time, his father had shown he had no scruples where other men's lives were concerned and the new plan might be just as lethal. Fergus had remembered the shadow in the bushes of

Silvercairns, remembered the boy caught spying in the Wyness yard and drawn his own conclusions. Now he looked down at the squirming urchin in his hands and all doubt fled.

'Let go of me!' yelped the boy. 'You've no right to touch me, you haven't, and me with a message for Mr Adam.'

'I am Mr Adam. I suggest you give the message to me.'

'I'm nay allowed. It's for old Mr Adam and if he doesna get it, he'll kill me.'

'I think he will anyway,' said Fergus, 'when I tell him just what sort of thieving rascal he's dealing with. Who is to say the message isn't merely a piece of paper you pinched, just as you pinched the wallet from my own pocket?'

'I never! It wasna me, it was Willy. Willy Bruce and . . .'

Fergus lifted him bodily from the ground and shook him and did not stop till his arms ached and the feeling of disgust had passed enough for him to speak with some semblance of control.

'So, you will betray anyone to save your own skin? At least we know where we stand. Now, are you going to tell me what message you were bringing, or must I frog-march you to the house, send for my riding crop and dust your trousers with it till you remember?'

Dod Henderson was no stranger to discretion. 'Twenty-three. I'm to say twenty-three, by water.'

'And why should I believe you, you lying little worm? Come now, tell me the real message or it's the riding whip for you.'

'Please, sir, that's all, sir, honest, sir. Here, look. I wrote it on my hand so's I wouldna forget,' and he spread out his grubby hand, palm upwards, to show two crude numbers inked on the cleaner skin of his inside wrist. 'See the two and the three? Now can I have my money, sir?'

Fergus looked at him for a long moment through narrowed eyes debating what best to do: if his messenger did not arrive his father would be suspicious, send after the boy and eventually extract every detail of Fergus's interference. If Fergus carried the message himself, or a new, amended message, Old Man Adam would still know he had been discovered and make different, more devious plans. Had Fergus held any illusions about his father's parental love and

[300]

loyalty they had shrivelled long ago: since Hugo's death and more particularly since the arrival of Hugo's son, Old Man Adam's attitude to Fergus had changed from dislike to outright hatred: a sly and devious hatred that chilled Fergus's blood. Increasingly he suspected that his father was plotting not only the downfall of his arch enemy George Wyness, but also that of his own son. It had become a game of cat and mouse between them. Thoughtfully he considered the last, the wisest and the most distasteful course.

'You must ask my father for that. But I am prepared to pay you something myself, on certain conditions.' With a shudder of revulsion he saw the cupidinous gleam in the boy's eye: this one could be bought, certainly, but, remembering the rapidity with which the boy had given away his friend's name, the buyer must accept that he was buying shoddy goods. It was a risk Fergus must take. 'If I let you go instead of beating you as you deserve, *if* I let you carry your message to my father, you will not tell him I have caught you, or he will beat you himself, for a bungling, incompetent fool, and certainly will not pay you. Do you understand?'

The gleam vanished from the boy's eyes to be replaced by a look of sullen defeat.

'Yes, sir.'

'If, as I say, you hold your tongue, I might just reward you myself for this evening's information. Might, mind. When I have checked that you have kept your word. If you continue to keep it, I will reward you in the future, for any further information you bring me *before* you give it to my father. Do you understand me?'

The gleam was back and strengthening. 'Aye, sir. I tell you first, and you pay me, then I tell him, and he pays me, but I dinna tell him that I've tellt you. Is that it?'

'In a nutshell,' sighed Fergus, who was already feeling tainted by the encounter. But if the integrity of Silvercairns was to be preserved, it was undoubtedly necessary. Suddenly, unable to bear the contact a moment longer, he let go of the boy's arm. The boy leapt back out of reach, but more from natural caution than from any intent to flee.

'Can I have my money now?' He added a belated 'Sir'.

Fergus felt in his pocket, produced a coin, held it between

[301]

finger and thumb and flicked it into the air. Deftly the lad caught and pocketed it in almost the same movement and a moment later was dodging and scuttling up the shadowed verge of the drive. Fergus watched until the small figure disappeared into the shadow of the stable block, then deliberately turned his steps in the opposite direction. There was at least another hour before dinner and suddenly he felt the need for clean air and the freedom of his beloved quarry.

The quarry lay in dappled darkness, the long shadows cast by the dying sun throwing their mournful veil over the deeper shadow of the quarry floor. The men had gone home long ago, in accordance with his father's extraordinary edict, 'for the wage bill is enough to ruin me as it is without them thinking they can line their pockets with evening work at my expense.'

When, in the sensible light of morning, Fergus had pointed out that an extra hour worked would more than pay for itself in productivity, Old Man Adam had merely countered with, 'The longer you give them, the longer they'll take to do the same work,' and Fergus had abandoned argument. Besides, he enjoyed the summer evenings and the opportunity to read, or stroll about the gardens at Silvercairns and gather strength before the daily ordeal of the dinner table. So that now, as he crossed the yard beside the quarry office and walked towards the path that spiralled down to the quarry floor, he was surprised to hear the sound of a hammer, muffled, but undoubtedly a hammer, and hammer against steel, not stone.

He stopped, listened, and the sound came again. Frowning, Fergus quickened his step until he was on the path itself and descending. Then as the path spiralled downwards, following the contours of the quarry basin, he rounded a bluff of jutting rock to have an unbroken view of the entire quarry side from brim to basin and saw, on the side nearest Silvercairns House, a cluster of dark shapes, lit here and there by the dull glow of a lantern, carefully dimmed. His first instinct was to shout out, his second to keep silent and to watch: to continue soundlessly down the track to the quarry floor, to mark the men's faces and see what they were at. They were so busy muffling sound themselves that they would not hear the small scuttle of a dislodged pebble, or if they did, would attribute it to their own activity. Moreover, eyes accustomed to the light of their own dim lantern would not see one more shadow in the many which cluttered the quarry floor. Fergus would find concealment behind the first suitable boulder, and watch . . .

'Tough as shoe leather,' frowned Mungo Adam, pushing away his plate. 'I don't know what's got into you these days, Lettice, letting them send up such rubbish from the kitchen.'

'I assure you, Papa, I . . .'

'Rubbish,' he interrupted. 'Fit for nothing but dogs or carrion crows.'

'Leo appeared to enjoy it,' said Lettice and could not resist adding, 'Perhaps that was why?'

'And what do you mean by that, girl?'

Lettice noted the belligerent look in his eye and decided on prudence as the safer path. The child Leo had been with them for almost a year now and though in clean clothes and properly scrubbed, she found him less distasteful than at first, and at times even quaintly appealing, he was still far from her idea of what a nephew should be. That would not have mattered if she had been allowed to discipline and train him into some semblance of civilized behaviour, but she was not. The edict had gone out to the entire household from the lowest scullery maid to Miss Lettice herself that Master Leo was not to be gainsaid, chastised, rebuked or even mildly corrected. Old Man Adam liked his new grandson exactly as he was and meant to keep him that way, oaths and all. Only Dr David had managed to disobey that edict with impunity when he had attempted to vaccinate young Leo and been kicked for his pains. Dr David had promptly put the boy across his knee and smacked him, only once but enough to make the child regard him with new respect and submit in silence to the vaccination. Though Old Man Adam was in the room at the time, he had not spoken out, except to say, 'Good lad,' when the operation was over. He knew the dangers of smallpox as well as anyone and did not intend Hugo's precious son to run the risk. Lettice had been in the room too, for Old Man Adam had insisted that the doctor call in person at Silvercairns. Surprisingly, he had agreed, and when, behind her father's back, Lettice had risked a smile of approval of his treatment of Leo, Dr David had grinned and winked at her, like one conspirator to another.

But in the unexplained absence of her brother from the dinner table, Lettice had no ally now and prudently set about mollifying her father.

'I merely meant, Papa, that as it is beef from our own estate, Leo found it particularly acceptable. You know how interested Leo is in everything to do with Silvercairns and you did order the beef to be slaughtered specially.'

'Humph,' growled her father, regarding her suspiciously from under frowning brows. 'But I did not order a beast so old it breaks the teeth to chew it. Get rid of it and give me some of that chicken pie instead. And fill my glass, dammit,' he called to the servant who was hovering nervously at the sideboard. 'Do I have to tell you myself when it's empty? You've a pair of eyes in your head, haven't you?'

At that moment the door to the dining-room opened and Fergus came in. He stood holding the door wide, waited till his father's glass was filled, then nodded dismissal to the servant and closed the door again. He filled his own glass with wine, took a plate and began helping himself from one of the many dishes on the table.

'You're late, sir,' snapped his father. 'Damned late. And now you have the effrontery to walk in as if the house was your own, order my servants about and help yourself to this and that without so much as a by-your-leave. What have you got to say for yourself?' he finished, glaring. 'Where have you been?'

Fergus looked his father in the eye and said deliberately, 'To the quarry.' There was a long pause in which father and son regarded each other, unblinking, but Old Man Adam was the first to look away. Fergus began to eat, paused, drank, then said lightly, 'This chicken pie is very good tonight, Lettice. Is Cook using a new recipe?'

'Why?' said Old Man Adam suddenly.

Fergus looked up in innocent surprise. 'Because I detect a hint of nutmeg which I do not remember being in . . .'

'Why did you go to the quarry, dammit? I ordered the quarry to be closed at six.'

'I know you did, Father, and it was with your interests at heart that I decided to check. I regret to tell you that there are those in the work-force who take no notice of your orders. In

[304]

fact, they had the nerve to tell me to my face that they were working there at your request.'

'Did they indeed?' growled Old Man Adam. 'Then I will deal with them in the morning.'

'There will be no need, Father. Naturally, I dismissed them on the spot.'

'You . . . did . . . what?' Old Man Adam opened and shut his mouth in a paroxysm of strangled rage, before recollecting caution. 'You should have left it for me to deal with.'

'I thought it best to settle the matter at once, Father. Would you believe it, they were actually driving a bore hole into the part of the quarry that you agreed should not be touched? I cannot imagine why, unless they planned to steal what they quarried and sell it.'

His father's face had already turned a deeper shade of purple, and now, all caution forgotten, he exploded. 'You interfering nincompoop! Can you leave nothing alone? You poke your nose here, there and everywhere, tut-tutting and wringing your hands like a reincarnation of that wretched Blackwell woman. I've put up with your mean-spirited ways too long already and I'll not do so much longer, do you hear me? And I'll tell you why. Because otherwise, come Christmas, we'll not have a roof over our heads – thanks to you.' Adam pushed back his chair and slammed out of the room, setting every glass on the table dancing and shaking the dust in a hundred tiny cascades from the worm-eaten panelling.

'Phew,' said Lettice, fanning herself with her table napkin. 'What, may I ask, was that about?'

For a moment, Fergus did not answer. Then he said slowly, 'I am not quite sure . . . but as to a roof over our heads, I am very much afraid it is he who is the threat, not I.' Briefly he told her what he had seen. 'So you see, the old devil is planning to blow the house down, though he does not know it.'

Lettice bit her lip in alarm. Her eyes sped to the crack above the window, the newer crack in the ceiling. 'You mean . . . ?' Then, seeing Fergus's face, she said quietly, 'We must stop him.' When Fergus made no answer, but continued to stare morosely into his glass, she said, 'I will tell him how much Leo adores the house and wants it for his own. You know how he

[305]

feels about the little horror.'

'And if that doesn't work?'

'Then you must watch him like a hawk and see he doesn't get the chance.'

'Oh, yes, I'll watch him,' but it was not of Silvercairns that Fergus was thinking. He was picturing a dark-haired woman with grief-stricken eyes, at her little sister's sick-bed. The eyes were bruised with fear and only bravery kept the unshed tears from spilling over, while somewhere in the background her family watched and waited with her, in shared fear and dependency and love. There had been a time when the fate of Mhairi Diack's family had rested with the Adams: had it still done so, he could have alleviated their suffering somehow. Visited the cottage with suitable gifts, paid for doctors. Thinking of her face as she would have looked up at him, with overflowing gratitude, Fergus's heart twisted with the old pain.

Impatiently he shook away dreams: he was a romantic fool, growing worse with age. He had forfeited all rights where the Diacks were concerned long ago. Now their fate was bound up with the Wyness quarry and the Wyness yard.

And Wyness had become his father's deadliest enemy.

Suddenly Fergus glimpsed as he had never done before the utter dependency of people such as the Diacks: honest, hard-working people whose lives could be devastated, ruined overnight, through no fault of their own, by people such as his father, or himself. Into his mind came a memory he had fought successfully for years to suppress: himself, short-tempered with a claret-caused hangover, dismissing Mhairi Diack's father merely because he had had the misfortune to cross Fergus's path, and refusing to reinstate him, in spite of old Mackinnon's urging, purely out of pride. It was a memory nothing could ever erase . . . except, possibly, restitution? Suddenly, he saw his way clear.

If, as he suspected, his father had a plan to ruin Wyness, then Fergus would prevent it: not to save George Wyness, who was rich enough and powerful enough to fight back, but to save those who depended on him. If Silvercairns suffered in the process, so be it: it was a risk he was prepared to take, for Mhairi's sake, and to wipe out the past.

[306]

With new determination he pushed back his chair, made his excuses and removed to his room. There he went over and over in his mind everything he could remember of his father's words, threats, behaviour since the occasion of the railway opening when Wyness had spoken those unknown words. He knew, as all Aberdeen knew, that there was an Australian contract, that George Wyness had a hand in an Australian property investment company, that Mhairi Diack's brother Tom was out there, drumming up custom. He had heard a rumour, as everyone else had, that the big contract was something special, and that the crowning glory of that contract was locked in a shed at the Wyness yard. Remembering, he cursed himself for not making that wretched Henderson boy tell him what he had seen. For the boy had seen something, had reported to Mungo Adam, and tonight had brought another, presumably important message.

He was turning over the significance of the number twenty-three and trying to fathom what it might mean when he had a different thought. Suppose he was on the wrong track? That fatal word had been spoken at a railway occasion and both men, he knew, had shares in the GNSR. Work on the line north should have started months ago, but still hung fire, though the contractors had been appointed, the plans made. Could there be any connection there? Perhaps his father was planning a boardroom take-over? Hoping to blacklist Wyness for ever where the lucrative railway work was concerned? Fergus began to look through the pages of the *Aberdeen Journal*, combing the columns for any reference to railways.

It was some hours later, his fire out and the household long asleep, before an answer came, but when it did it came with blinding clarity. He had taken up the *Journal* for one last, weary search and, the railways having proved a futile hope, was running his eye idly down the columns of advertisements for anything of the smallest interest that he might have missed when he saw, beside the ink-sketch of a ship in full sail, *To sail for Port Phillip and Adelaide, the fine ship 'Lucy'* . . . The date given for sailing was the 23rd, less than a week away.

*

It had been a full two weeks now and still no sign of change. In the first light of morning some three days after Mrs Bain's kindly visit, when breakfast was over and the boys had left for work, Mhairi sponged Annys's face and hands as usual, brushed the hair gently from her burning brow, tried to persuade her to swallow a little warm milk with sugar in it, and made her as comfortable as she could. Then she moved her chair to the window, where the light was better, and took up her sewing. She had been sewing for half an hour or so, one eye constantly on Annys lest there should be any sign of movement or change, saying the usual prayers over and over in her mind, when she heard the sound of horse's hoofs approaching up the track. No rattle of wheels, so it was not Fanny's carriage, and only one horseman, not two. Dr Marshall? She half rose from her chair to peer through the window glass, only to fall back again, trembling with shock. It was *Fergus Adam*.

Then alarm was replaced by frenzied activity. *Quick . . . my comb . . . no time to change my dress . . . but my shoes . . . where are my Sunday shoes?* Flustered and trembling, Mhairi did her best with her appearance. She was wearing her everyday dress, crumpled from sitting too long in the chair and spotted with cotton threads. These she endeavoured to brush off while shaking out the worst of the creases and at the same time trying to comb her dishevelled hair and twist it up again into some semblance of decency. Why had he called? Why today, at this hour? Perhaps it was something to do with Lizzie's child, Leo? Perhaps Leo was ill and Mr Adam wanted her to write to Lizzie? What other reason could there possibly be for an Adam to call at Rainbow Hill? So Mhairi snatched at and discarded a dozen reasons for his visit while the knowledge that Mr Adam himself was even now dismounting, tethering his horse, opening her garden gate, made her hands tremble the more. Then she heard his steps on the path and his firm knock at her door. She raised her chin, straightened her back and went to meet her foe.

She was startled, as always, by his handsome looks, his slim elegance and gentlemanly bearing. When she opened the door and he removed his hat, his high-necked cravat flashed white against the dark cut of his jacket over pale knee breeches and gleaming leather riding boots. Beyond his shoulder, down the short garden path, she glimpsed a horse, its bridle hitched over the gatepost and its soft mouth searching the grass of the pathway. She felt a moment's panic before manners came to her rescue.

'Good morning, Mr Adam,' she said with calm politeness and waited for him to explain himself.

'I must apologize, Mrs Grant, for the earliness of my visit, but perhaps when you have heard the reason you will understand. Firstly, how is your sister?'

'Ill.' Then, regretting her brusqueness, she added, 'She is no better than she was.'

'I am truly sorry to hear it.'

Mhairi could detect no sarcasm behind the words: in fact, the look on his face seemed one of genuine concern and his eyes, when she found the courage to meet them, were surprisingly gentle. She ought not to have done so, she told herself afterwards, over and over, but when he said, 'There will be a draught with the door open. Perhaps I could . . .?' she stepped back and invited him inside. Leaving the door to Annys's room ajar, she led him into the family kitchen and indicated a chair.

'Please sit down, Mr Adam. May I offer you tea?'

'No, thank you,' he said quietly, still standing. Then to her astonishment, she heard him say, with a kind of wonderment, 'It is refreshment enough for me to look at you, Mrs Grant.' In the moment's shock which followed he said quickly, 'But you must forgive me. I let my thoughts dictate my words and I apologize. I meant to say only that I have newly breakfasted and would not dream of putting you to any unnecessary trouble. You must have work enough as it is, with a family to care for and a sick child to nurse.'

Mhairi could find no words. The astonishing compliment, if compliment it was, had taken her breath away, but she could detect no lascivious purpose in his face. His eyes were compassionate and kind, his expression grave, and she felt herself drawn towards him by the bond she had always known existed but which she had hitherto rigorously denied. Now she had the strength to deny nothing.

'Believe me, Mrs Grant, I was truly sorry to hear of your

[309]

sister's accident and of her subsequent illness. If there is any way in which I can be of assistance, to you or to your sister, you have only to ask. I know that our families have been at odds for too long, and that you have every reason to shun my company, but when you hear the reason for my visit, perhaps you will forgive past wrongs and consent to regard me if not as a friend, then as someone who has your interests at heart?'

Mhairi dug her nails hard into the palms of her hands to keep back the tears which weakness, anxiety and too many watchful nights brought all too easily to her eyes, and fought against the deeper treachery which urged her to cross the small space between them, to lean gratefully against his chest and draw new strength from him, to allow him to hold her quietly and to soothe and comfort her. To take the burden from her shoulders for just a little while and give her peace. Abruptly, she looked away.

'Thank you. It was good of you to call.' Even to her own ears the words sounded harsh and she added, 'Perhaps if you do not care for tea you would like coffee before you go? Or a dram? I am afraid we cannot offer . . .'

'No, thank you,' he interrupted and took a step towards her. Before she realized what he was going to do he had taken her hands in his, and held them firmly so that she could not escape. His hands were at the same time firm and gentle, the skin warm and smooth against hers. She felt her heart beat fast with panic and tried to pull away, but he held her tight. 'Listen to me. This is urgent and I will not say it twice. I did not come only to ask after your sister. I came to warn you.'

Mhairi felt her mouth go dry and her heart pounded hard and high in her throat. Her eyes widened, but she no longer tried to pull away. His eyes held hers and for a moment she was powerless to move or speak. Then her pale lips parted on a whisper. 'Why? Dear God in heaven, *why*?'

'I do not know myself. But I do know that if you plan to ship anything by water on the 23rd, your plans are known to others, who wish you harm.'

She stared at him in mingled disbelief and horror, her eyes wide and achingly vulnerable.

'Believe me, Mrs Grant, for my part I wish you only . . .' He stopped, his eyes dark with sadness, and she knew that he, like

[310]

she, was remembering old encounters, old barriers between his family and hers.

'Friendship?' she supplied, her voice no more than a whisper.

For answer, Fergus drew her towards him, and before she realized what he meant to do he had kissed her, gently, on the lips. After the first shock, she felt an extraordinary sensation of contentment flow through her, as if at last she and her destiny had found each other, and her true place was here, in the comforting protection of his arms. Then there was a faint sound from the bedroom across the hall and Mhairi started out of her trance.

'I must go. Annys needs me.' The fear which leapt to her eyes was like a lance through Fergus's heart and abruptly he loosed her hands.

'If there is anything I can do . . .?'

But she was already on her knees at her sister's bedside, her hand against the child's forehead and her voice murmuring reassurance. Fergus, watching her from the doorway, felt his heart swell with love and sadness. He knew, as he had always known, that however many women his father produced for him to look over, he would take none of them. There would only ever be one wife for him: this young widow with the sweet face who was bending over her sister with such loving solicitude. Now she turned her head to look up at him with eagerness and a sort of fearful hope.

'I hardly dare speak the words, but I think the fever is less. Would you perhaps feel her forehead and tell me whether I am imagining it?'

He joined her at the bedside and hesitantly laid his cool palm against the child's forehead. 'No. I think you are right. The skin is cool.'

The smile which lit up her face was to stay with him for days. 'Thank you, Mr Adam.'

'One day, I hope you will call me Fergus. And now I must leave you. Remember the message I brought.'

Before Mhairi could answer, he strode out of the room, opened the front door and closed it behind him. When she pulled it open again to call after him, 'Goodbye. And thank you,' he was already unhitching the bridle.

[311]

He put his foot in the stirrup, swung up into the saddle, raised a hand in acknowledgement and was gone.

She was standing in the doorway, looking after him in wonderment, when she heard a faint voice from the room behind her and in a moment was once more on her knees at the bedside. She smoothed the hair from Annys's forehead with her hand while the child moaned and murmured and finally said in a voice that was faint, but distinct, 'Mhairi?'

'What is it, Annys, love? I am here.'

Annys turned her head in puzzlement. 'Why . . .? What . . .?' She half raised herself on one elbow, then fell back on the pillow and closed her eyes. 'I am sorry, Mhairi. I should be up and helping instead of . . . instead . . . of . . .' Her voice died away and for one heart-stopping moment Mhairi thought she would never speak again. Then, eyes still closed, the child said, 'Who was that?'

'It is only me, my love. The others are away to work.'

'No. No.' She turned her head this way and that as if to shake her thoughts into order. 'A man. There was a man.'

'From the quarry,' soothed Mhairi. She wanted to keep Fergus Adam's visit secret, even from Annys. As to the message, she would deal with that later, when she had thought what best to do. 'The men sent to ask how you are, Annys, as they send every day.' This at least was true. 'Today you are a little better, I told them, and will be better still when you have eaten a little of the meat jelly Fanny made for you, specially.'

'I . . . The children? How . . .?'

'Hush, my love, and stop your worrying or you will make yourself ill again.'

'But I dreamt . . . I dreamt that Dod Henderson . . .'

'You are to forget all about it, Annys, and get well. The children are missing you and Fanny asks for you every day. Mr Wyness looks in regularly to see how you are and is always sending little presents for you . . .' Mhairi talked quietly on, telling her of the kindness of the neighbours, of her brothers and how hard they were working, of Fanny and the little ones, until the child's eyes closed again and she slept. Mhairi hardly dared feel her forehead lest hope be dashed, but when at last she found the courage the skin under her hand was still warm, but not burning. The fever was certainly less: with a sigh of relief Mhairi settled back into her chair, to mull over once more the implications of Fergus Adam's visit. Not his compliments and his embrace: those memories were private, to be treasured and relived later when anxiety for Annys was stilled. It was the message itself which disturbed her. 'Your plans are known to others, who wish you harm,' he had told her. And in a mere two days they planned to ship the precious merchandise.

The 'others' he mentioned could only be Mungo Adam. Which meant that there were spies in the Wyness camp, and more dangerous ones than Dod Henderson: to know the shipping date, the spy must be one of the chosen few.

Oh God, what was she to do? She could not leave Annys alone and the message was not one she could entrust to others. Never had she wanted a visit from Jessie Bain more than she did at that moment, but it was afternoon before the woman came.

'Annys is better,' Mhairi greeted her at the door, her plaid already round her shoulders. 'If you will stay with her for me, I will take a quick trip into town to deliver the sewing I promised,' and she indicated a covered basket, 'and to collect more. I need all the work I can get these days and I will be as quick as I can.'

'Aye, lass, away you go,' said Mrs Bain after the first surprise. 'You could be doing with a bit of fresh air after weeks inside the house and your face as white as whey. Well, well. So wee Annys is better, is she? I am glad. Didn't I tell you yon Holloway's pills worked wonders? The mannie said . . .'

'Thank you, Mrs Bain,' interrupted Mhairi. 'But I must hurry if I am to be home again before she wakes. I don't like to leave her as it is.'

'Dinna worry, lass, your Annys will be fine with me and I'll have a cup of tea waiting for ye when ye get back, so we can have a wee news together. There's things that Holloway's mannie said . . .' But Mhairi, her plaid wrapped tight around her shoulders and her basket over her arm, was already hurrying fast down the path towards Woodside and Aberdeen.

*

[313]

'But who told you, woman?' cried George Wyness for the umpteenth time, thumping the desk in exasperation.

'I am afraid I cannot say,' said Mhairi, white-faced but resolute. 'But my informant is absolutely reliable.'

'A spy, eh? We all know how much you can trust a spy,' growled Wyness, glowering. 'But if you won't tell, you won't.' Suddenly he laid both hands flat on the desk, scanned the faces around him and said, 'Well, lads. I won't insult you by suggesting it's one of you, but someone we've trusted has tipped Adam the wink. So, what do we do?'

There was a moment's silence. Lorn was scribbling busily on a piece of paper which at intervals he pushed towards Donal for him to add his comments, while Willy sat frowning in thought.

'Suppose it's true what this informant of Mhairi's says, we can't change the ship,' said Wyness at last. 'It's the only one left that's guaranteed to get there in time.'

'We could maybe ship it by the Leith packet?' said Willy. 'There's ships going to Australia from Leith. Or from London.'

'Right enough,' said Wyness. 'But we don't know their captains nor their records. They'd maybe dawdle round the Cape or take time off for a bit of spice trading and turn up in Port Phillip whenever it suited them. Remember we've a deadline to meet and only the Christie ship can be relied on. Already they've delayed sailing specially for us.'

'Aye, right enough,' agreed Lorn. 'It'll have to be the . . .'

'What did you say, Mr Wyness?' interrupted Mhairi. 'About the Christies and the sailing date?'

'Only that they agreed to wait another day on account of us running that wee bit behind schedule.'

'When?' said Mhairi, her face pale. 'I mean, when did they agree?'

'Let me see,' said Wyness slowly. 'It would be Saturday when I saw them. Aye, late on Saturday because it was first thing Monday morning when we changed our plans.'

'Could I ask you, Mr Wyness, what you changed them to? I know it is secret, but it is important. You see, my message was, "if you plan to ship anything by water on the 23rd". By *water*, Mr Wyness, not by sea.'

[314]

'By golly, lass! You may be right.' He looked swiftly round him, noted the closed door, the closed window and beyond it the bustle of the granite yard. But caution won. 'Walls have ears, lass, as we know to our cost. You tell her, Donal.'

Donal did a series of lightning sketches on a scrap of paper, scribbled a date, and pushed it towards her. There was silence as she studied it and a different silence as realization dawned. They looked from one to another without speaking until finally Wyness said, 'We've a spy right enough. The question is, who?' There was another silence, before Wyness said briskly, 'No matter. It's too late now. So, what do we do about it, lads?'

It was Donal who answered him. He tore off a scrap of paper, wrote one short word, and pushed it across the desk. *Bluff.*

'I think I will take a ride up to Inverurie,' announced Old Man Adam at breakfast. 'I shall take young Leo with me and introduce him to the railway.'

'But I thought it was not built, Papa?' said Lettice in surprise.

'It isn't. Which is why it's time someone took the trouble to find out why not. If the Board in their wisdom choose to ignore the problem, then they can hardly complain if ordinary shareholders take matters into their own hands and do it for them.'

'What is it that you propose to do, Father?' asked Fergus lightly. 'Cut the first turf yourself?'

'If I was, I'd not tell you,' said his father, but without the usual undercurrent of venom.

Fergus felt his skin prickle: could this be it? The plot he had been waiting for? But *Inverurie* and the railway? Inverurie was sixteen miles north and in the wrong direction. As to the railway, as Lettice said, it was not yet built. Gradually alarm subsided. He was getting paranoid, seeing plots where none existed. Besides, today was the 22nd, not the 23rd. Tomorrow would be the time to worry. Nevertheless . . .

'Would you like me to come with you?' he offered. 'To keep an eye on Leo. I have not been out Inverurie way for years and

[315]

we could make a day of it.'

'Aye, we could,' sneered his father, 'if you didn't have a job to do and a quarry to see to. You should have been there two hours back. Away with you to your work and leave me to mine. Tell the kitchen to pack up a picnic,' he went on, turning to Lettice. 'Something the lad likes. We'll be gone all day.'

On the evening of the day Fergus Adam visited the cottage, Donal and the others had not returned for supper, nor to sleep. Mhairi, following instructions, lit lamps, upstairs and down, in the usual pattern, dowsed them at the usual times, and though she could not simulate their bundled figures striding out to work at dawn next morning, she had done everything else in her power to indicate normality to any watcher, while Annys blessedly slept, waking only briefly to ask for water, then slipping back once more into healing sleep. In the afternoon, Dr David called, nodded his satisfaction and urged Mhairi to rest now she had the chance. 'I will pass on the good news to Fanny,' he said and left smiling. That smile told Mhairi more clearly than anything else could have done that there was now real hope.

So the long day dragged on into evening, with still no sign of Donal or the others. Surely the work must be finished by now? Mhairi swung the broth pot over the flame at the usual hour, set the usual places at the table, and waited. No one came. Mhairi ate a hurried supper, washed dishes, waited again. Mr Wyness must have taken them home to Skene Square to sleep. He had told her it was a possibility, if time was short. Besides, the crate was to be shipped at first light and someone must stay on guard. Mhairi sponged Annys's face and hands, and prepared a dish of brose should she wake, but still she slept. Later, Jessie Bain called, to see how Annys did, looked around inquisitively for signs of the others, noted the table and the untouched broth pot and said she 'hadna noticed them passing, right enough. Working late, are they?'

Mhairi told her in all truth that they were indeed still at their work, a special order that was running late, and diverted her curiosity with a hefty dram and the good news that Annys continued to improve. *If all had gone to plan, they would be packing up the crate now.*

The woman stayed an hour. Mhairi went with her to the gate, holding the lantern high, for though it was summer and the night pale, there was no moon. Back inside the cottage she prepared to keep watch, as usual, at her sister's bedside. Annys might be 'on the mend' but she was taking no risks. *The crate would be roped and ready now, locked safely away in the shed. She wondered whose turn it was tonight to keep watch.*

Somewhere in the night an owl called. Across the tiny hall the fire stirred and settled, and still Annys slept. Overhead the loft lay empty, its occupants gone. Sleeping safely in Skene Square by now, or on duty in the yard. Mhairi thought of her brother Tom, as she often did in the quiet hours, knew he was homesick and lonely though he never said so, wondered what he was doing at this hour, on the other side of the world? But on the other side of the world it would be morning, wouldn't it? Perhaps even afternoon? Tom had written that they had summer at Christmas and winter in June. Everything upside down and inside out. Emusses, and kangaroos with pockets . . . parrot pies . . . Gradually her eyelids drooped lower until her eyes closed.

Annys stirred and Mhairi's eyes jerked open, every sense alert. Beyond the unshuttered window she saw the sky was pale, streaked with the quiet pink and gold that heralded dawn. Somewhere close at hand a robin sang. With a thud of excitement she remembered. *Today they would load the crate on to the barge.* Then Annys moved her head, asked for water, and for Mhairi.

'I am here, my love,' she soothed, raising the child's head on her arm and holding the cup to her lips. 'Drink this. Later I will bring you a little brose. Or would you rather have bread and milk?'

Annys shook her head, made an impatient movement with her hand, then said, in a voice faint and dry with illness, 'I had a dream . . .'

'Tell me later, when you are better, Annys. Just lie quiet now, and . . .'

'No! I want to tell you now, Mhairi. It was such a horrid dream. About Red Henderson. He spies and is bad.'

[317]

'Hush, my love, hush,' soothed Mhairi. 'It is not morning yet. You must go back to sleep.' Soon the child grew calm again and slept, but Mhairi's thoughts were in turmoil.

Just now, Annys had said 'Red'. She had meant 'Dod', of course. Sleep and lingering fever had confused her, that was all. But however much she tried to reassure herself, Mhairi could not shake off the feeling of unease which Annys's words had caused. Henderson was a common enough name in Aberdeen. She could think of a dozen Hendersons and none of them related. But suppose Red and Dod were? Suppose they were cousins, in league together? And hadn't Red come from Silvercairns? Sacked, he had told them, like her own father had been, after twenty years' service to the Adams. But suppose he had not been sacked at all?

As the awful suspicion took hold and grew, she remembered something else. Red had been one of the fatal blasting team. She had heard the story over and over in the days after the accident: the powder, the bore hole, the fuses, the tamping. Suddenly she remembered a story Mrs Bain had told, though Mhairi was not supposed to hear it, of a ramrod through a man's forehead. 'Something wrong with the tamping,' she had said. And now Red was one of the men chosen to help transport the precious crate, this morning, at first light. Fergus Adam had warned her of treachery afoot and now, with absolute clarity, she saw that he was right. Mungo Adam meant to ruin the Wyness yard and the quarry too and as he could not do so by fair means, had resorted to foul. At the thought of what they would lose if the Australian contract was not met, Mhairi's heart raced with dread.

It was already morning, the sunlight strengthening beyond the little window till the trees which had been mere black shapes against the dawn began to take on colour and detail. Then through the thudding silence of her fear came the trudge of feet on the path as the first of the quarry workers made their way up Rainbow Hill, and she knew that it was too late. By the time a message reached the Wyness yard, even by the fastest runner, the crate would be loaded and on its way. Whether to triumph or disaster lay in the hands of Fate.

*

The doors of the shed that had housed Donal's 'secret' were thrown open at last, to reveal a huge packing-case, nailed and reinforced with cross-struts, the whole bound round with rope and firmly secured. The destination had been printed in black paint on all four sides, with, in larger letters of warning red, *Handle with care*.

George Wyness beamed. 'Well done, lads, well done. All finished and exactly to schedule. That's what I like to see.' He clapped Donal on the shoulders, ruffled Lorn's hair and would have done the same for Willy had he not dodged neatly out of range, grinning. 'Well, Fanny, are we ready for the final ceremony?'

In spite of the earliness of the hour, for it was not yet eight o'clock, Fanny Wyness was of the company, holding Mhairi's son Hamish firmly by the hand. The child was freshly scrubbed and eager and the moment Wyness spoke, cried, 'Yes, Mr Wyness, I'm ready.'

At that moment a shadow darkened the door and Red appeared. 'The wagon's here, Mr Wyness. And they've sent to say the barge is waiting.'

'Good lad. All going to schedule.' Wyness looked up briefly, then turned back to Hamish. 'I'll not be a minute. There's one more ceremony to perform, then we'll load up. Give him the hammer, Donal.'

Donal produced a miniature hammer which he handed solemnly to Hamish, then a square of card and four nails.

'One for every year of your age,' explained Fanny, smiling, as Donal held the card in place against the side of the packing-case and put the first nail in position. 'Now, take great care not to hit your fingers – or Donal's', she added as she saw Donal wince. Solemnly, with Donal's hand to guide him, the child knocked in the four nails.

'There,' he said, stepping back and regarding the pasteboard card with pride. 'I launched Donal's stone mannie, didn't I?'

'You did indeed,' said Wyness and read aloud, '*To The John Murray College, Melbourne, from George Wyness and Partners, Aberdeen.* Now, when we've loaded this crate on to the wagon and sent it on its way, how about taking a trip to the harbour to see it arrive?'

[319]

'Can I ride on the barge, Mr Wyness? Please?' cried the child. 'I've done it before. I was captain!'

'Aye, well, Red here is captain today, aren't you, Red?'

'Am I?' The man looked startled. 'I thought . . .'

'You're the best man for it,' said Wyness and, taking him a little aside, he added, 'I must have someone trustworthy, and Willy's needed here. Lorn will go with you, to lead the horse.'

'Can I go too?' cried Hamish, over and over, until Mr Wyness said, 'Aye, lad, if you nip home and ask your mother first, but you'll need to run fast for the barge won't wait. She sails at eight o'clock on the dot.' That quietened him and he walked obediently, holding Fanny's hand, to watch the careful transport of the crate from the wagon, via a wooden slipway, to the barge. The crate was secured with binding ropes and Red stepped aboard.

'You know how to work the locks, lad?' called Wyness as Lorn untied the ropes that held the barge against the bank and tossed them aboard.

'Aye.'

'Then away you go. And see you in the harbour.' He, Donal and Willy together heaved against the barge till it slipped out into mid-channel. Lorn attached the tow-rope which looped low over the water to the collar of one of the Clydesdales and set off along the towpath southwards towards the harbour. Somewhere, a clock struck the hour.

Lorn had gone perhaps a hundred yards when there was a shout from the barge.

'The water! It's disappearing!'

Sure enough, the water level on the banks of the canal was lowering before their eyes until, with a lurch and a shudder, the barge hit bottom, settled into the mud and stuck fast.

There was a long moment's silence, before Wyness said quietly, 'The devious, scheming, four-eyed villain!'

At that moment there was the sound of hoofs approaching from the towpath north and a horseman came in sight, an old but upright gentleman, immaculately dressed, his clothes as black as his horse's gleaming flanks. He drew in the reins and sat looking down at the little group with a genial smile 'like the grin of a man-eating tiger', Lorn reported later to Mhairi, 'about to strike'.

[320]

'Well, well. Having a little transport trouble, Wyness, old boy? Glad to see you're using my railway – a little prematurely perhaps as the rails are not yet laid, but they will be, very soon. The contractors started today. By the way, if you need any help to lift that crate out of the mud, just let me know and I'll lend you a man or two. Can't have it getting in the way of my line.' He would have moved on, but Wyness blocked his path.

'That's a very kind offer, Mungo, and I'm grateful. But as the crate is only paving stones, I reckon I'll leave it there. To be collected. With that fellow you pay to blow up honest folk and carry tales. Unless, of course, you'd care to buy them from me, for yon railway of yours? The usual rates, delivery included? But I won't keep you, old chap. You must have work to do.'

There was a moment's thunderous pause, then with a roar of fury Mungo dug heels into flanks and drove his horse at a gallop down the towpath towards the town.

'Coming, lads?' said Wyness.

'Might as well,' said Lorn, with a grin. 'And I reckon we'll not be needing this.' He untied the rope from the horse's collar, coiled the slack neatly and tossed it on to the deck of the barge. 'Fancy a ride, young Hamish?' He scooped the boy up on to the Clydesdale's back and, with Fanny Wyness holding him on one side and Lorn on the other, they led the slow procession back to the yard.

'I want you, sir!' The door to the office crashed open and Mungo Adam stood framed in the doorway. His chest was heaving, his face was purple, and flecks of spittle frothed the corners of his mouth. 'You snake in the grass. You evil, sneaking toad.'

'What is it now, Father?' said Fergus quietly. 'Have you been found out again?'

'I've found you out, you traitor. Bribing my employees, carrying tales to the enemy. And don't tell me it wasn't you because the boy told me and there's no one else would have done it. But I'll pay you back, I warn you. I'll wipe that supercilious smile from your face.'

'As you did with Mackinnon?' Fergus hated himself for

[321]

saying it, but it was his only weapon.

Suddenly the shifty look was back, the wariness. 'Someone's drained the canal, dammit,' he blustered. 'Cut the banks, opened the locks, and drained it into the River Don. Needed it to start the railway work, they said. But it has left the barges high and dry. They're queuing up to sue already and goodbye to any dividends if they succeed. It's enough to drive anyone wild.' He stopped, a look of cunning replacing the wariness. 'You'd best get over there and see if any of the barges are ours.'

'Very well. I'll ride in this afternoon, Father.' Fergus turned back to his desk to be stopped in his tracks by a roar of fury.

'You will go now, do you hear me, sir? Now!'

Fergus regarded his father for a long moment, noting the mottled cheeks, the frowning brows, and still, behind it all, the gleam of anticipation. He shrugged. The man was obviously mad. 'Very well, Father. As you wish.'

Lettice was in the dining-room, checking the silver of the place settings for dinner, when her father flung open the door.

'Where is Leo?'

'In the kitchen, with Cook. He likes to scrape out her mixing bowls and lick the spoons.'

'Send for him. Tell him his grandpa has a surprise for him.'

When the boy arrived at the run, traces of chocolate pudding still smeared around his mouth, Old Man Adam said, 'Well, Leo, how would you like to see an explosion? A real one?'

'Can I light the fuse, Grandpa? I've got a tinder box, look!' and he produced a silver one which Lettice recognized as one of her father's own which the light-fingered little wretch must have purloined. But Adam did not even notice.

'Maybe, one day,' he said with that air of suppressed excitement which had worried Fergus and which now made Lettice look at him with growing apprehension. 'Today you can give the signal, and if you do it right, then we'll see.'

'Where is Fergus?' said Lettice in alarm. 'He mentioned no blasting.'

[322]

'Your brother is a cowardly, niggardly, carping miser where that quarry is concerned and needs a lesson he'll not forget. But young Leo is made of braver stuff, eh, Leo? He'll be a quarryman after my own heart one day, and not afraid to blast the bedrock to the heavens when the time is right. And that time is now. The men are ready, waiting only for me to give the signal.'

'But, Papa,' cried Lettice, 'shouldn't you wait for Fergus? You know he does not like . . .'

'Quiet, girl. From today Leo is master of that quarry, and your snivelling worm of a brother can go cap in hand to whoever he pleases, for he'll find neither house-room nor employment here.'

'But, Papa, you cannot do that! He is your son and . . .'

'He is no son of mine!' roared Adam in a voice that set her heart thudding with real fear. 'Your brother has thwarted me once too often. After this morning's fiasco, I swear he will not set foot in my house again, if I have to pitch him down the steps myself.' Then his voice softened, again with that undercurrent of glee. 'Now, you see this flag, Leo? The big red one? You and I are going to go out on to the terrace and when you wave that flag, carefully, to and fro, the man will light the fuse. Then you and I will listen for the bang and watch the dust cloud rise. After that, we'll ride over there and see what's what, and it will be something splendid, I promise you. Are you ready?'

They went out of the room hand in hand, her father carrying the furled flag under one arm and Leo skipping and jumping with excitement at his side. Lettice stood beside the table, appalled. In the grate beneath the ornate marble fireplace, under the huge, gilt-framed mirror, the fire still burned with quiet contentment. Flowers in a crystal vase added their scent to that of beeswax and clean table-linen. Floorboards gleamed around the rich pattern of Indian rugs and the newest parlourmaid had brought a sheen to the table-top as bright as any mirror-glass. The silver candelabra had never been brighter, the crystal glasses never more sparkling. Even the damp patch in the ceiling had vanished under the latest brush of whitewash. In the quivering silence, Lettice knew with dread that she would never see this perfection

[323]

again.

She heard steps on the terrace outside and moved to the window, waiting for the inevitable and helpless to prevent it. Where Fergus was she did not know, but there was no time to look for or send after him. No time to do anything but wait and when the time came, endure. She saw the flag wave slowly to and fro, to and fro, the old man's hand over the child's, bearing the weight of it and guiding. Then a pause of expectation, a quiver and shudder and rumble that crescendoed to a crashing roar which shook the floor under her feet, tipped the pictures from the walls, smashed ornaments, shattered glasses, rattled windows in their frames until, with a crack which seemed to burst her very eardrums, the house wall split, plaster showered down around her and the chimney stack crashed down on to the terrace outside in a shower of flying boulders, builder's rubble, birds' nests and caked soot.

Fergus was riding home along the road to Hirpletillam after a fruitless sojourn with the canal authorities, whose offices were already besieged by numerous irate and vocal bargees, when suddenly the ground shuddered, a distant rumble spread and grew to a thunderous crack, and ahead of him, beyond the trees, a slow cloud of white dust rose and hung in a quivering arc above the misted roofs of Silvercairns.

'Oh God! The quarry!'

He spurred his horse to a gallop, crouched low in the saddle, and raced towards Silvercairns and whatever destruction his father had wrought. To his precious quarry first, where he found predictable devastation, but mercifully no one killed. George Bruce had seen to that, emptying the quarry well ahead of time. The main casualty was the granite itself: a jagged wound had been gouged out of the north wall, showering blocks and boulders piecemeal and ruining in one stroke Fergus's careful programme of harvest from his beloved quarry. Seeing his face, George Bruce said over and over, in apology, 'It was the master's orders. Nothing I could do.'

'Where is he?' said Fergus, knowing he had been sent deliberately on a fool's errand, knowing this would be the

[324]

showdown.

'At the house with the boy, Mr Fergus. They gave the signal from the terrace.'

For the first time Fergus remembered Silvercairns, the cracking wall, the subsidence, and the warnings his father had refused to heed, and knew with cold certainty what he would find.

'Round up your best men,' he ordered, his face white, but resolute. 'Fast as you can. Bring picks and shovels and follow me to the house.'

They found the terrace buried under a heap of fallen masonry, a space on the skyline where the chimney should have been, and a crack in the house wall a foot wide.

Inside, on the dining-room floor, Lettice lay inert under a layer of plaster and as white as the Wyness statue. Mrs Gregor the cook was bending over her, surrounded by a clutch of terrified servants, slapping first her hand, then her cheek, while the bruise on her forehead rose like a phoenix's egg through the layer of dust and darkened before their eyes. Overhead, in the corner where the damp patch should have been, daylight shone down in dusty rays through a jagged fissure in the wall.

'Oh Mr Fergus, thank God you've come, sir!' cried Mrs Gregor. 'There's the master missing and that wee laddie who's a holy terror right enough, but a nice wee laddie for all that, and the house falling about our ears and Miss Lettice like the dead and dust everywhere and the pans likely burning in the kitchen and my heart thumping fit to bust my chest open and . . .'

Fergus took charge. Ordered everyone to the safer regions of the house, set Bruce and his men to work, saw Lettice carried on a makeshift litter to the drawing-room sofa with instructions to tell him the moment she came round, despatched a servant at the run for a doctor and told Bruce and his men to use the utmost care as they tackled the devastation of the terrace.

'My father might be underneath,' he said, white-faced, 'and the boy.'

Half an hour later they found Leo, miraculously unhurt, crouching terrified in a cavity under a fallen lintel, his mouth still ringed with chocolate and his red hair white with dust, but Mungo Adam, though close beside him, was buried under several layers of his own chimney stack and when at last they brought him out, he was undoubtedly dead.

'Retribution,' pronounced George Wyness, though without triumph. He had been angry enough to learn the full extent of his rival's plots against him, but Old Man Adam had been a worthy rival: villainous, dishonest, but a Colossus worth the toppling. Now he was gone, competition in the granite trade would lose its savour. Young Fergus Adam was fanatical where his quarry was concerned and more so since his father's death, or so folks said, but he was straightforward and above board. There would not be the same relish in worsting him. Besides, one could not help feeling sorry for the man, with his house half ruined and a weight of debt round his neck enough to cripple him. Then there was the lad. The same age as Hamish Grant, seemingly, but a wild little varmint.

'Yes, dear,' said his wife. 'He brought it upon himself. Everyone says so. Died by his own hand, though of course no one thinks he meant to. Not with the little boy standing beside him. It was a miracle the lad escaped unhurt.'

'That reminds me,' said Wyness, beaming. 'Annys Diack is out of her bed at last, and that's a miracle we never thought to see. Sitting in a chair by the fire, Mhairi says, and reading her school-books all hours of the day, till her legs are strong enough to hold her up again. She's a good little lass, that one.'

'Does that mean the children will go home again soon?' asked his wife, careful to speak without expression. They were good children and no trouble, but it irritated her to see Fanny fussing over them when she should be fussing over children of her own.

'In a day or two, maybe. When Mhairi can manage. And if Fanny can spare them.'

'It is high time she was married, with children of her own,' said his wife, refilling her husband's breakfast cup for the second time. 'I have told her so repeatedly, but of course she will not listen. I never thought she would grow up to be so obstinate. She used to be such a docile, obedient child.'

[326]

'Yes, dear,' said Wyness solemnly, but there was a strange look in his eye. He had had a letter only yesterday, delayed for some reason in the post, but welcome for all that. 'But don't worry. I expect it is only a phase.'

The Christie ship had sailed on schedule, the precious crate safely stowed away in the hold, and in the days following its departure the Diack family went over and over every detail of what had happened: the suspicion, the change of plans, the packing up of a duplicate crate in the secrecy of night and the locked shed, the despatch of the real one, openly and by road the previous day, labelled paving stones for Liverpool, the bluff when Red's treachery was suspected – for once George Wyness had known there was a spy in their midst he had distrusted everyone except Donal, Willy and Lorn. Red Henderson had been marooned on the barge for hours, to everyone's intense enjoyment, and their only regret was that his wretched cousin Doddy was not with him. Naturally, neither would ever work for Wyness and Partners again.

One detail only Mhairi kept resolutely to herself: the source of her information. There were other, sweeter aspects of that meeting which she blushed to remember and which filled her with secret guilt. She ought not to have let him kiss her, ought not to have found pleasure in his company. He was an Adam and therefore her dear husband's enemy. But Alex was dead, nothing could ever bring him back and deep in her heart she treasured the memory of what Fergus Adam had done for her, like a knight in a childhood fairy-tale, riding to her rescue. The thought brought a warmth to her heart and lifted the loneliness.

'Has Donal's statue really sailed?' asked Annys, looking large-eyed over the rim of her brose bowl. She was rapidly regaining her strength and soon, Mhairi had promised, she would be allowed to go for a ride in Fanny Wyness's carriage, to take the air and bring the colour back to her cheeks.

'You know it has,' said Mhairi patiently. 'Donal himself saw the ship put out to sea. It should reach Australia in plenty of time for the opening ceremony of the college. February 2nd, Tom wrote. Fifty years to the day after John Murray himself first claimed the land for Melbourne. Of course, it was only a little settlement then and some people say that it was not John Murray who founded it, but that does not matter. His descendant is wealthy enough to build a college in his name, for the good of the community, so who are they to argue?'

'Do you think Tom will stay for the opening ceremony?' said Annys. 'I wrote a letter to him a long time ago, asking when he would come home, but he did not answer. I hope he will not stay there for ever, Mhairi, with the emusses and the kangaroos.'

Mhairi did not immediately reply. It was a fear that had grown in her mind as the months passed and still he did not come home. Now there might be a greater lure than kangaroos to keep him, for rumours were beginning to filter through of the discovery of gold. If they were true, then Tom might seek his precious fortune that way and who knew how long that particular search might take? It would soon be three whole years since he had sailed. Too long to wait, she thought, thinking of Fanny Wyness. Too long to be lonely.

'He will come back one day,' she said quietly, then to banish sadness added, 'But you have been up for long enough. If you go to bed now and rest while I prepare the boiling fowl for tonight, I will let you get up again later. Then in no time at all you will be strong and well again and Hamish and Catriona can come home, where they belong.'

Tom Diack swung the canvas kitbag from his shoulder, dumped it on the quayside at his feet and looked around him, drinking in the familiar sight of granite buildings, spray-wet and glistening in the sunlight, the white-capped waves in the harbour mouth, the sea-wind snatching at the rigging and overhead the familiar herring gulls, wheeling and swooping in greedy expectation over the newly arrived ship. The hatches were open, the derricks already busy unloading, shore porters were everywhere, trundling barrows, heaving trunks, while all around them alighting passengers merged in a milling, hugging, chattering mass with those who had come to welcome them. Tom heaved a long, slow sigh of pure pleasure. He was home, at last and for good. Grinning, he picked up his kitbag, waved farewell to his travelling companions, and set out for the town. His luggage could wait till tomorrow. Today was for his family, and for Fanny.

At the thought of Fanny his confidence wavered. It was three years since he had seen her: she might have changed, forgotten him, fallen in love with someone else. He remembered that artless letter from Annys which had finally tipped the wavering balance and decided him to leave others to welcome that blessed statue and put it into place. To let others take the credit and acclaim for the splendid college which the statue would embellish, standing in solitary glory on an incline outside the imposing Grecian entrance, its columns of polished Aberdeen granite echoing the polished beauty of the statue itself. It was a pity Mr Wyness could not see it: it would make him inordinately proud.

But Tom, too, was proud and the thought that Fanny might have chosen someone in his stead slowed his steps almost to a halt. Perhaps he should go first to Rainbow Cottage? Find out from Mhairi how the land lay? He felt a slight uneasiness when he thought of Mhairi: there had been something odd about her letters, something uncharacteristically reticent. He hoped she did not still bear him a grudge for leaving, and for staying away so long. But he had done what he set out to do and need not be ashamed. If Fanny was indeed waiting for him, to go first to the cottage would be wasting valuable time that could be spent more sweetly.

He quickened his steps as he reached the Castlegate and turned westward into Union Street. He remembered the day of the Queen's visit – a day like this, of September sunshine and brisk air – remembered their walk together up and down the flag-decked streets, her earnest anxiety that he should like the coffee she had made him and her simple joy when he did. He had taken her on his knee and kissed her . . . He strode faster with a new excitement, remembering their walk on the canal bank, her kisses and her tears. But he was almost at Skene Square. Suppose Mr Wyness was at home? It was too much to hope that Mrs Wyness would be out too, but . . . Then he turned the corner and saw the house whose simple, classical lines he had reproduced a dozen times for rich Australian pastoralists. There was a gentleman's horse at the door, with

[329]

old Mackie holding the reins. The door opened and an unknown young man came out on to the steps, stood a moment talking to someone unseen, raised his hat in farewell, then Mackie led forward the horse and the gentleman mounted. 'Goodbye, Fanny.' The words came clear across the space between them, then as the horseman moved away in the opposite direction from where Tom stood watching, Fanny herself appeared. She held a small child in her arms and another stood beside her, waving as she was.

Tom stopped in his tracks. All joy drained out of him and a feeling of such desolation took its place that he thought he would cry out with the pain of it. Then she turned her head and saw him. She was wearing the same red dress, her hair looped up into a chignon at the back as it had been the day wee Hamish stole her bonnet and loosed her hair in tumbling confusion. Wee Hamish . . . Perhaps the child at her side was not hers after all, but . . . Then she turned swiftly back into the house and hope died. Only to spring joyously alive again as she reappeared in the doorway without the children, leapt down the steps and came running towards him to fling her arms round his neck, sobbing and laughing and kissing him in a display of such reckless abandon that Mrs Wyness, who had emerged on to the step to see what had caused the commotion, turned swifty back again and told the inquisitive Ina to 'Take the children to the nursery at once. It is no fit sight for young eyes.' Ina did so, but by dint of pressing her nose to the nursery window, had a most gratifying bird's-eye view of the street.

'Well!' she said aloud. 'Who would have thought Miss Fanny had it in her? It's disgraceful, that's what it is, and in the public street!' But she kept her nose eagerly to the window in order to be able to describe every detail to her fellow servants when she returned to the kitchen.

'I have saved a little money,' he told Fanny later, when she had led him by the hand inside to meet her mother and that lady, after the briefest of welcomes in which she managed to combine encouragement with reproof in equal measure, had left them blessedly alone together in the drawing-room. Tom no longer found the room intimidating: in fact he hardly noticed it. All he was aware of was Fanny's sweet face brimming over with love for him and the soft pliancy of her body against his as they kissed and murmured and kissed again, filling the emptinesses of three lonely years. She had not changed, he thought with joy, except to grow a little older, a little more mature, as he had. 'Oh darling, I have missed you dreadfully, every hour of every day,' he murmured, his lips against the soft curve of her throat.

'Have you? I am glad,' and she twisted her head to find his mouth with hers. 'It serves you right for leaving me alone,' she said, a long time later.

'Alone? And who was the handsome gentleman suitor I saw at your door? Don't tell me he had called to see your mother?'

'That was Dr David.' She gave him a flirtatious look that would not have disgraced Lettice Adam herself. Had he not known Fanny to be guileless and open and incapable of deceit he might have been jealous. As it was, he took her by the shoulders, shook her a little and said, not altogether in jest, 'If I catch you making eyes at anyone but me, young lady, I will put you over my knee and spank you till you cry for mercy.'

'Oh dear, then I would certainly have to call the doctor, wouldn't I?'

Mrs Wyness heard the squeal and resultant scuffle from the hall where she was hovering in indecision, not wanting to interrupt too soon, but on the other hand . . . She turned the handle, opened the door a crack and pulled it quickly shut again.

'There,' gasped Fanny triumphantly. 'You will have to marry me now. Or she will tell Papa she saw you spanking me.'

'Then I hope it hurt,' he growled.

'Not at all, as you very well know. Oh Tom, I am so happy.'

'And I.' There was silence for a while as they sat, arms entwined, her head on his shoulder, his cheek against her hair, then he spoke, in a voice of sober responsibility. 'I meant what I said. I have saved some money. Not much by your father's standards, but a great deal by my own. And certainly enough to build us a house, where you and I can live together in comfort. A modest house, for we will not be rich, but our own, with a garden and a nursery for our children. I will speak to your father the moment he comes home.'

But the mention of children had reminded him. 'Was that

[331]

young Hamish standing with you on the steps? And Mhairi's Catriona in your arms?'

She nodded, grave-faced.

'Ah. Let me guess. They are staying with you because Mhairi has had another baby?' She shook her head. 'Because she is expecting one at any minute? No? Then it can only be because she and Alex are fed up with them and want a little time to themselves, as you and I do.' He attempted to kiss her but she pushed him away.

'Tom, there is something you should know. I had thought it would be best if Mhairi told you herself, but now that you have asked . . .' She took his hands in hers and said, 'Listen carefully and try to understand. First of all, the children are with me because Annys has been ill. There is no need to worry,' she said quickly as Tom started with alarm. 'She is better now and convalescing. The children will go home again in a day or two, for which Mamma will be glad though I will not. I have grown fond of them.'

'As I have of you,' interrupted Tom, trying once more to embrace her.

'No, Tom. You must listen. There is more, and this is the difficult bit. It will be a shock to you,' she warned, then slowly, choosing her words with care, she told him of Alex's death, of Mhairi's grief, of the quarry's eventual recovery and of the family decision not to call Tom home. 'It was Mhairi's own wish,' she finished quietly, 'and I agreed with her. She did not want you called home on her account. She wanted you to come home by your own choice, as you have done now. Mhairi has been very brave,' she finished quietly, as Tom said nothing, his face still tight with shock. 'Besides, it is almost three years now since Alex died.'

'Three years?' cried Tom, leaping to his feet and pacing the room in agitation. 'You should have told me! Three years and I did not know my friend was dead!'

'You are lucky,' said Fanny quietly. 'You have had three more years of Alex than we have had.'

Suddenly Tom's eyes were wet with tears. 'We grew up together, Fanny. He was my . . . friend.'

She put her arms around him, murmuring comfort, led him to the sofa, soothed and reassured him, and finally wiped his

[332]

eyes on her lace-edged scrap of a handkerchief. 'Soon, I shall send you away,' she said softly. 'You will go to Mhairi and console her, but without reproach. You will thank her for giving you your freedom, and make your peace with her. She will welcome you with love, I know. And eventually, when you have mulled over all the family news, perhaps you will come back again, to me?' She looked up at him with such tender understanding and such brimming love that Tom had no answer but to hold her close and kiss her, over and over till her steadfastness restored him.

'I used to think you were a frail and helpless little thing,' he confessed to her. 'I used to fear that you would not survive the smallest setback, but I see now that I was wrong. Like Mhairi, you have strength and courage and instinctive wisdom.'

'And?' prompted Fanny.

'And I want you to be my wife and the mother of my children.'

'Our children . . .' repeated Fanny in awe, then suddenly she giggled. 'I am sure Papa would let you marry me today, whether you can build me a house or not, if you could only promise him a grandson.'

'Oh, I think I can, darling, don't you? With your loving help?'

Fergus Adam sat at his desk in the library at Silvercairns and looked once more at that damning document. A mortgage for Silvercairns, taken out by his father with a grasping Glasgow firm of dubious repute. And that other wounding paper of scribbled amendments to his will, fortunately neither dated nor signed, but destined, Fergus knew with certainty, to have been formally added on his father's next visit to his lawyer in Aberdeen.

'Most unfortunate aberration,' that lawyer had murmured with professional sympathy when Fergus had shown him the paper, as conscience required. 'Advancing years . . . strange whims and fancies . . . wounding, but understandable . . . and unintentional, I am sure. He thought most highly of you, Mr Adam, as a man of sober responsibility and good sense.'

But all Fergus heard was his father's taunting words: 'You

[333]

snake in the grass. You evil, sneaking toad. But I'll pay you back . . .' And he fully meant to do it. *I leave my quarry and all interest therein to the boy known as Leo Lennox, son of Hugo Adam and . . .* Here he had left a space, obviously ignorant of the girl's name. *To my son Fergus I leave my undying loathing*, this crossed out, *the comfort of his own conscience*, this also crossed out and finally, in triumphant capitals, *NOTHING*. Unsigned and unwitnessed, it was invalid in law, his lawyer assured him, but the intention remained, to sour his enjoyment in Silvercairns and to place an obligation upon him which he could not deny.

Fergus raised tired eyes to the window and looked out across the faded garden. The leaves were turning now, the grasses withering. Here and there the vibrant blue of Michaelmas daisies studded the borders, with the blood-drops of rose-hips, brilliant in their filigree of spikes and burnished leaf. Already the first leaves had fallen from the silver birch, plucked by the wind and tossed on to the path. Soon it would be time to pack up and leave this wounded invalid of a house. But he would rebuild it somehow, shore up the wall, reinforce the terrace, and now that he was in undisputed charge, he would make sure no further blasting rocked the foundations of Silvercairns. As to that mortgage, he would pay it off somehow. The Guestrow house, for instance, was a needless luxury, as were those railway shares of his father's for which the old man had paid so dearly. The canal had been filled again, compensation promised, but it was only a matter of time before it would be emptied officially, to form the bed of the new railway north. Shares in the company would fetch good money.

And Lettice must be persuaded not to spend so much.

At that moment, Lettice herself came into view, with Dr David Marshall at her side. Her forehead was still bandaged, but with a diaphanous chiffon scarf which gave a touching air of vulnerability to her elegance. She and the doctor appeared to be talking earnestly together and Fergus saw to his surprise that they were holding hands. Perhaps he need not worry about his sister's dress bills after all: it looked as if they might soon be someone else's responsibility. But one responsibility remained that was his and his alone.

As if in answer to his thought, there was a knock at the door. 'Can I come in, Uncle Fergus?'

'You are in,' sighed Fergus, regarding the grubby-faced, red-headed urchin who was treading mud liberally across the patterned carpet. 'I told you to knock and then wait.'

'Sorry,' he grinned, unrepentant.

'Well? What do you want, Leo?'

'Aunty Lettice won't play with me. The doctor is making sure that her head is better and she told me to go-away-you-little-pest. So will you take me to the quarry instead, like you promised? I want to learn to blow the rock up properly, like you do, so I can help run the quarry when I'm big and I promise I'll be good.'

For the first time since his father's death Fergus felt his spirits lighten. Perhaps the Lennox child would turn out all right, after all. At least he was still young enough to learn.

'All right, you little horror. Run and tell Mrs Gregor where we're going – and tell her to put a coat on you. It can be cold in the quarry.'

He was bundling the papers away into a desk drawer when he noticed the envelope addressed in neat black ink, *Fergus Adam, Esquire*. He did not need to open it to see the signature, or to read the words, *in friendship*. He knew them too well to forget, as he knew with equal certainty that, whatever happened to either of them, their lives were bound inexorably together, till the end of time.

He closed the drawer and went out of the room, whistling.

WILLIAM SAROYAN